# Voluntary Chaos

*For my children,*

*Alyson and Tyler*

## ACKNOWLEDGEMENTS

I am exceedingly grateful to my dedicated writer's group, Ellen Ruderman, Kathy Checchi, Paty Kouba, and Valerie West, without whom this book would never have been completed. Also to Maureen Connell, professor and novelist, whose encouraging spirit and knowledge of novel-writing influenced me throughout the process. I want to thank my brother, David, for his many insights, and my good friends, Kathryn Hunter and Marsha Russell, who read every word, and pushed me to seek publication. And most of all, I thank my adoring husband who not only read each chapter and gave his honest appraisal, but celebrated my perseverance with love and admiration.

*"Love is a springtime plant that perfumes everything with its hope, even the ruins to which it clings." –Gustave Flaubert*

ISBN: 1--4392-1617-7
ISBN-13: 9781439216170

Visit www.booksurge.com to order additional copies.

# Voluntary Chaos

Joan Jackson

# CHAPTER 1

Spring 1979

Sylvia was finally alone. Her husband, Tom, and their kids, Alice and Trevor, had just left for the airport. She dialed Anthony's number. It rang once, and she hung up. She paced in her kitchen a few minutes. She leaned on the oak railing that overlooked the family room and noticed the toys scattered on the floor. She took the four steps down, got on her hands and knees, gathered up Trevor's Tonka trucks and Alice's fragrant felt-tip pens, and tossed them into the built-in cushioned window seats that lifted open for toy storage. Gathering, tossing, gathering, tossing. Then back to the kitchen, where she hovered by the phone and began pacing again. She figured at least fifteen minutes had passed. It shouldn't take him this long if he could get away.

She went out the sliding glass door off the kitchen nook and walked onto the cedar deck that spanned the back of the house. She lit a cigarette. The air was chilly but refreshing. The foggy, gray Oregon sky allowed a slim silver ray of light to break through the dense cloud cover, illuminating the pink and white clusters of rhododendron blooms that dotted the fence line of their backyard.

Another spring was here, and nothing had changed. She stared at the snow-capped peak of Mount Hood and wondered what had become of her. Her life was a yuppie cliché with all its suburban trappings: the new cedar-wrap house in an upscale lake community, a neighborhood school, a vintage Mercedes in the garage, two beautiful children, ladder-climbing friends, and a handsome husband. Now it was even more of a cliché. She was the thirty-two-year-old mother, the bored, dissatisfied housewife leading a double life with Anthony, her neighbor up the street. Like most obsessions, theirs thrived on the clandestine. They exchanged love letters and had lunch in secluded restaurants, meetings in parks, and sex in obscure motels. They devised a telephone code: One ring meant "home alone, safe to call"; two rings meant "not safe, will try to leave the house to call."

She heard the distinctive whine of the downshift of Anthony's chocolate-brown Targa as he drove down the hill past her house. After two years, she still felt as breathless as a lovesick adolescent at the sound of his car. She ran to the family room window. The pine trees her husband had planted almost blocked her view of the street, so she barely caught a glimpse of Anthony as he pulled to a brief stop at the intersection below her house. All she could see was his tan, muscled forearm poised on the open window of the car door and the chunky gold link bracelet below his casually rolled-up blue oxford-cloth shirt cuff. She watched as his car turned the corner. She lit another cigarette and waited by the phone. She closed her eyes and imagined the feel of his hand touching her face, slowly sculpting the outline of her brow, cheekbone, and jaw, his fingers gently brushing her lips. The familiar heat washed through her body, leaving a small pool of wetness in her panties.

Sylvia grabbed the phone on its first ring.

"Finally," he said out of breath. "I couldn't call back because Jane got on the phone. I told her I needed cigarettes, so I only have a few minutes. So they left?"

"Their flight should be taking off in half an hour." She swallowed. "Tom knows."

A beat of silence. Sylvia could feel his cool confidence wither ever so slightly.

"What'd he say?"

"He asked me if I was having an affair."

"And?"

"And I denied it." She wondered what he'd say if she said that she couldn't lie anymore, that she had told Tom everything. She wondered if her guilt for wanting to break up her family would be less if she got it out in the open. Probably not. This kind of guilt might last a lifetime. Besides, she and Anthony were making this a team effort, and her loyalty was now with him.

Sylvia rationalized the part Anthony's wife, Jane, played in the beginning. She had seemed desperate to belong, attaching herself to Sylvia soon after they'd met. Sylvia's best friend,

Jessica, had known Jane and Anthony in college in California. When they bought a house in the same neighborhood as Sylvia and Tom, Jessica had introduced the couples.

Jane had asked Sylvia, "Do you mind if I stop here with the kids after school until our house has completed construction, and wait for Anthony to come home from work? Living every day in a hotel room gets old."

"Sure." Sylvia had agreed but thought the request was quite bold. She didn't like Jane's forced cheer, incessant chatter, or her tendency toward melodrama over the insignificant.

"I swear I can't sleep at night trying to decide—do you think hardwood floors are better in the living room or plush carpeting?" she had asked Sylvia.

Sylvia had feigned interest. "I do like hardwood floors. Of course, you'd need area rugs …"

"Then plush it is. See how helpful you are? Come up to the house and help me with color swatches and tile samples. Please?" Jane had begged.

Sylvia had gone up the hill to their six-thousand-square-foot house. California money had arrived in Oregon.

"Anthony is so picky. I have to make the right decision, or he'll be upset with me. Is cobalt blue too strong for a kitchen counter?"

Sylvia couldn't imagine that he cared that much. Still, their daughters were in first grade together and inseparable, so she'd just put up with the situation until they moved into their new house.

Sylvia heard the inhale and exhale as Anthony lit a cigarette.

"What did he say exactly?" he asked.

"Well, he didn't really *ask*—he said he *thought* I was having an affair, like a statement of fact. And I denied it."

"Then he's just guessing."

"He *knows*." Sylvia hesitated. "I can't live like this anymore. Maybe we should go back to your original plan and tell all."

He let out a deep sigh. "We can pull this off without them finding out if we each ask for a divorce with six months in between, like we discussed."

"Then we'd better get started, or one of them *will* find out."

"Only if they want to. Let's talk about this tomorrow afternoon, when we're together. I'm counting the hours—two days feels like two weeks."

"I know."

"I need you, Jake. I can't live without you." He had nicknamed her Jake because he'd said, "When I'm with you, all is right with the world; everything's jake."

Sylvia believed him and found it unsettling. Not being able to live without her didn't sound as romantic anymore—rather, slightly desperate. But wanting to move forward faster, wasn't she getting a little desperate herself? And to think that when they met, she didn't find him attractive at all, and never saw it coming.

*****

Anthony had started dropping by unannounced in the middle of the day when he checked on his house construction. He often asked to use the phone. At first, Sylvia was standoffish and felt his unannounced visits were an intrusion. She already had enough interruptions with his wife and kids. She'd say she was just leaving for the grocery store, or putting one-year-old Trevor down for a nap, or taking their dog, Red, for a walk. When she did let him use the phone, she'd go upstairs and wouldn't reappear until he'd hung up and was ready to go.

Then she and Anthony began to talk—about their childhoods, foreign travel, his work, her French study. He'd just taken a job as the financial officer for an apartment developer in Portland. A number cruncher. Unlike Tom, he must excel at balancing a checkbook. She hadn't engaged in a substantive one-on-one conversation with a man in years. She liked his worldly charm. He was effortless and self-assured—the easy confidence of a man who had never struggled. His sultry eyes and swarthy attractiveness added to his allure. And more than that, he was fascinated by her.

She couldn't help but compare him to Tom, who was Anthony's polar opposite. Tom had a youthful handsome face with sandy-colored hair and a blue-eyed twinkle. He was six foot one, solid with broad shoulders, and looked like he'd just run in from a football field. He was entertaining at parties. He warmed a room with his dimpled smile and gift of jovial banter, moving swiftly from one small audience to the next, cracking off-color jokes. What Sylvia used to find appealing, she now found tiresome and lacking in substance. Underneath she sensed he was unsure of himself, trying too hard to be the center of attention. He had restlessness in his demeanor and appeared uncomfortable standing in one place with little interest in engaging in deep conversation. While Tom was motivated and well suited to sales, where he worked to provide the extras he never had, it seemed he was always struggling—ever since college when he barely graduated. Sylvia was attracted to his struggle then, admiring his strong work ethic even if his delivery fell short. But she'd begun to wonder if he'd ever find his way. Having grown accustomed to a harder way of life, perhaps he was more comfortable with relentless struggle, somewhat like a martyr, and doomed to learn no other way.

Sylvia was drawn to watching Anthony at neighborhood gatherings. He laughed easily and talked expressively with his hands. He absorbed the object of his attention (usually a woman) as he listened intently and exuded a polished sophistication with Italian flair. He was one of those men who could throw a woman off balance by casually placing his hand on her shoulder or touching her arm. The unexpected attention might cause her to giggle nervously or laugh too loud or even blush. She might wonder about him—is he trying to come on to me? Does he fool around? But he seemed unaware of his effect on women, which made him even more attractive.

She couldn't deny to herself that she began to think about him: when she woke up, when she carpooled Alice to gymnastics, when she was in the produce department, when

Tom was away on business and she went to bed alone.

Jane and the kids, Alexia and six-year-old Ricky, came by almost daily; sometimes the late afternoon rendezvous would turn into dinner. Since Tom was often out of town, Jane would insist that they all eat dinner together. Anthony would bring pizza, spaghetti, or fried chicken on his way home, and they'd eat in Sylvia and Tom's house without Tom.

When their move-in date finally came, Sylvia and Tom invited them for a special candlelight dinner to celebrate. They were all seated at their round, antique oak table in the dining room. Tom sat across from her. Anthony was on Sylvia's right.

Anthony was speaking off-handedly, but unpretentiously, of family trips to Europe to visit his parents. "We try to go every summer. My dad took an international assignment with an American company for a year in Milan. My mom loved it so much they've stretched it to ten years."

Jane rolled her eyes. "Anthony's mother insists that we call her *Franca* now. She is such a phony." With a nervous laugh, she quickly added, "Don't worry, Anthony can't stand her either."

Not knowing a *d'accord* from a *prego,* Tom jumped in, "Sylvia's a Frenchie. She studied there and can speak like a native."

Sylvia yearned for the glamour of international travel and envied their lifestyle. The last time she was in Europe was her first, eleven years ago. Having harbored a dream since college of pursuing her master's in French, this conversation brought back her longing for *la culture française.* Jane expressed surprise that Sylvia never told her. But Sylvia had told Anthony and now felt ill at ease that he sat quietly without acknowledging it. Jane asked her how long she had lived there, if she had lived with a French family, if she'd been to Italy.

"I was there four months between my junior and senior year, finishing my studies at *l'Université de Grenoble.* Yes, I lived with a French family. And no, I only traveled within France since it was purely for French study. I used to teach it."

"Go ahead, say something in French," Tom said.

Sylvia felt like a trained seal. Her mother used to do the same thing at dinner parties.

"Speak to me," Anthony said.

Sylvia turned to him. "Well, I haven't used it in ten years—" His arm accidentally brushed hers. She looked into his penetrating, amber eyes and suddenly felt off balance. A warmth flowed through her body. She felt her face redden, her hands tremble, and almost forgot what she was going to say. *"Pendant mon séjour en France, j'ai fêté mon anniversaire de vingt et un ans."* Sylvia had a good accent. When playing the nationality guessing game, a pastime in France, the French paid her the utmost compliment—they never fathomed she was American.

Jane clapped and said she sounded so real, then asked what she said. Sylvia translated: "While in France, I celebrated my twenty-first birthday."

Sylvia had never suffered from lack of appetite before, but now she pushed her fork around the plate, spreading the mushrooms and chicken to the edges. She excused herself from the table to get her bearings.

The two families had been socializing on weekends. Sometimes Jane suggested they share babysitters, so Alice and Alexia could be together. Sylvia and Tom had never been this involved this fast with other friends before. Sylvia now felt trapped. With her strong attraction for Anthony, she felt like she was straddling a runaway horse. Her sense of obligation to be neighborly and maintain the friendship required that she stay the course, but her inability to tighten the reins on her feelings allowed them to lunge headlong at full speed.

Sylvia planned to keep her feelings a secret. One afternoon after a dental appointment finished earlier than expected, she decided to stop by Jessica's house. When Jessica shared, for the first time, how she'd never cared for Anthony's wife, it was like a dam in Sylvia burst under pressure. She gushed about her feelings for Anthony.

"I *thought* you were shedding pounds," Jessica said.

"What do you mean?"

"Love'll do it every time. That's what happened to me when I had my affair, and *he* was Italian. My doctor."

"I'm not having an affair."

"Yet," Jessica said.

Not wanting to appear naïve, Sylvia didn't express her surprise at Jessica's candor about having an affair. She did feel relieved to finally express her pent-up feelings. Verbalizing them, however, felt like a way to sanction the inevitable.

A week later, after the kids were in bed, Anthony

dropped by with a bottle of Bordeaux. Tom was out of town. Now that Anthony and his family had moved into their new house, he wanted to thank Sylvia for her generosity. He poured each of them a glass of wine. They sat in separate wicker chairs facing the fireplace, not looking at each other. The silence was heavy with only the sound of the crackling fire as they sipped their wine.

"Maybe honesty isn't always the best policy," he said.

Sylvia could almost hear her heart pounding. "Maybe. It takes courage to be honest."

He turned and gazed at her longingly. "I'm afraid to be honest with you."

"Don't be," she whispered.

She closed her eyes as he reached for her hand and kissed the inside of her palm. "I can't deny my feelings for you any longer," he said.

Six months into their affair, Anthony's original plan was "to sit down with our spouses, tell all, and ask for a divorce." The good Catholic altar boy wanted to confess—but to his wife and Sylvia's husband, not his priest. At the time, Sylvia had been appalled by his suggestion. She loved him madly, but divorce seemed too drastic. Could being in love with someone else justify a divorce? Did couples in affairs necessarily leave their spouses? Break up families? Neither of them had done this before. Maybe Anthony was having a Catholic guilt trip in reverse—*thou shall not commit adultery*—and if thou has, break up the family and marry the adulteress to prove the sin was meaningful. Maybe he was being noble. Or maybe he knew he loved her that much. She was ashamed that Anthony's wanting her enough to leave his family had given her a quiet thrill.

Back then, when her affair had just started, Sylvia recommended marriage counseling to Tom. In her heart she knew her attempt was false, but she wanted him to think she was sincere. Her guilt was also a motive—to give them one last chance to see if there was any hope for saving their marriage. Maybe he'd surprise her. They had three or four sessions. "I can't change," he had said. "I don't know how to talk about my feelings. I can't do this." She hoped he'd want to try. He just rolled over and played dead. She felt rejected, like she didn't matter and wasn't worth the effort. But she hadn't played fair—she hadn't confessed her affair.

Six months turned into two years. During that time, Anthony changed his mind. "Honesty isn't a good idea—too painful for everyone."

*****

After she and Anthony hung up, Sylvia found herself pacing again. She called Jessica. "Can you come over?"

"Sure, in about an hour. You sound upset," Jessica said.

"I am. I think Tom knows."

"Oh, my God, see you in a few."

Sylvia went to the refrigerator to see if there was any beer. Jessica, like Tom, was a beer drinker. Sylvia learned to love red wine while a student in France and preferred Bordeaux, but couldn't justify spending that much on something only she enjoyed. Oregon Merlot was fine. Their seven-year-old Irish setter, Red, who'd been asleep on the kitchen floor, sauntered over and joined her. Sylvia opened the door, and they stood together staring into its contents.

Sylvia stroked her head. "Do you want your dinner, Roo Roo?" Red barked. Sylvia knelt down and wrapped her arms around Red's back, her long, softly permed, auburn mane blending with Red's matching fur coat. "I'm not really alone, am I?" she cooed.

Because of Tom's heavy travel, Sylvia spent two weeks out of almost every month without a husband, and it was lonely. Sometimes she felt that life was passing her by.

When Tom was home, he lost himself in their children. He sat on the floor and played Barbies with Alice or raced cars with Trevor. When they were infants, he would change their diapers and sometimes bring them to Sylvia to breast-feed, if he heard them cry before she did. Tom openly displayed his affection for them, marching up the hill from their house, holding Alice's hand with Trevor on his shoulders, running and bouncing like a horse in canter. Neighbors in their yards would stop and speak to them. Sylvia might receive a neighborly call. "I just saw your darling husband—how lucky you are that he takes such an interest in the kids." Sylvia had to stifle what she wanted to say. Like a kid, Tom loved to play and show off, but he rarely showed that same open affection to her.

She began to recognize that she felt taken for granted and betrayed. After ten years of marriage, they still couldn't afford vacations. She juggled the bills and balanced the checkbook. Tom would call the bank for an accurate balance in his business account; it never occurred to him that he'd written checks that hadn't yet cleared, so he was often overdrawn. When she confronted him with it, he'd tell her it was no big deal. He was the one who traveled, stayed in hotels, ate dinners out, and had fun socializing. When he called home, she could hear either music in the background or the boisterous voices of people joking and laughing. Sometimes she felt like hanging up.

Sylvia looked at the kitchen clock. Jessica was due to arrive soon.

The phone rang.

"Hi, Mom," Sylvia said.

"Are you all by your lonesome? I can't wait to see those kids. I just wish they were here longer than four days."

"They're on their way. They *will* be with you longer than with Tom's parents. You know they'd rather be with you the whole time, but—"

"Of course, they have to go to their house—they're his *parents*, and they're wonderful people, country people, so down to earth. And Alice will get to ride a horse."

Her father got on the phone, and they talked until Jessica arrived. Sylvia missed her parents. When she and Tom lived in Ohio, her parents were a three-hour drive away, and she saw them a lot. Then Tom changed jobs again. They'd moved six times in seven years—and Sylvia never protested. She didn't want to pressure him because she thought he was doing the best he could. Maybe she should have. She was melancholy when she hung up the phone.

Jessica called out to Sylvia as she came in the front door. “I brought some beer in case you didn't have any.”

Sylvia stuck her head out from the kitchen. “Good, I don't.”

Jessica looked stunning as always. Even without makeup and in sweats. Sylvia loved that they were often mistaken for sisters. Jessica was movie-star beautiful, a perfect size four, and tanned from tropical trips with her husband. Sylvia noticed when they were out together that every head turned to look at her—man or woman. Sylvia was definitely not the “ugly” sister, just less noticed. Jessica had done Pepsi commercials when she lived in her native Los Angeles. And she was fun.

Jessica popped open a beer and drank from the bottle—she was no snob. Sylvia loved her down-to-earth quality, raucous laugh, and up-for-anything style. They met on the tennis court six years before when Sylvia and Tom first lived in Lakeside, Oregon. Jessica had talked her into joining the Ladies Day Ski Club, and they had become fast friends. Then Tom was transferred to Ohio. Two years later, Tom's division in the company was dissolved. Tom took another sales job that brought them back to Oregon, and Jessica and Sylvia had picked up where they left off. Sylvia poured herself a glass of red wine.

“That was smart that you didn't admit anything to Tom,” Jessica said. “Say nothing until Anthony has filed for divorce. Make him go first.” Jessica was the strategist.

They went out to the deck and lit cigarettes.

"I'm afraid to go first, but I don't know how long I can live the lie. Tom and I haven't had sex in two months either," Sylvia said.

"You have to hold out *and* you have to have sex with him."

"The thought disgusts me. Amazing, isn't it?"

"Not when you're in love with somebody else," Jessica said. "Do you guys still go out, as couples?"

"No. We've managed to avoid it. Our girls aren't friends anymore, so Jane has stopped calling me."

"She really chased him in college—had no pride. She might threaten to kill herself over this."

"You've had too much beer."

Jessica laughed at herself. "She might *say* it, but she'd never do it—she's just a needy drama queen."

Red strolled out to join them and flopped onto the deck floor at Sylvia's feet. Sylvia slipped off her shoes and snuggled her feet under Red's furry chest. "Anthony is always saying he needs me."

"That bothers me. Needy people are control freaks who never let you have your own space. The void inside *needs* to be filled, and they look to somebody else to fill it, which never works." Jessica, the therapist.

"You don't think I should divorce Tom."

"Tom does give you lots of space," she said.

"Obviously, too much."

"I just think you should take your time."

That night Sylvia went upstairs, Red following. Red had been the family mascot since Alice was two years old. As Alice's first friend, she was named Red not only because of her fur color, but because Alice could pronounce her name easily. Alice and Red were inseparable. They slept together, ate together, chased ducks together, romped in the snow together, roamed the woods together, and got lost together. And they both got carsick, but not necessarily together.

Sylvia crawled into bed and patted the mattress to coax Red, who dutifully leaped up and snuggled beside her. Sylvia only did this when Tom wasn't home. Tom didn't believe dogs should be in bed; for that matter, he didn't believe dogs should even be inside the house, but Sylvia wouldn't hear of putting Red outside. When Tom was little, his dog, Lucky, wasn't allowed in the house. His mother, Eleanor, was always a stickler for cleanliness. Even the sheets were labeled in the linen closet: "H" for head and "F" for feet. "You wouldn't want your head where your feet have been, right?" she'd say, waiting for reassurance that you agreed.

Sylvia never took issue with her quirky "rules for living." She just nodded her head in agreement and tried to please her when she stayed in her home. She helped with dinner and washed dishes by hand. Eleanor didn't believe a dishwasher could clean them thoroughly enough, so she didn't own one. She washed her hands ten times a day, calling to everyone to do the same. A devout, converted Catholic, she believed that "cleanliness is next to godliness," so she truly worried about dirt, and more specifically, animal dirt. "They'd come in from that barn smelling like you-know-what—I wouldn't let them set foot in the door—all the clothes had to come off and go right in the machine. No telling where they'd been." No telling where dogs' noses had been either, she used to say, and then add that she knew where they'd been but didn't want to think about it.

Sylvia chuckled to herself, picturing Eleanor's reaction to Red in her bed. When Tom was out of town, Sylvia, Red, and the kids would often climb in and snuggle together, hiding under the sheets, teasing Red. Then they'd fall asleep, legs and arms collapsed over each other, Sylvia sandwiched in between, and Red sprawled over their feet.

Sylvia called her parents the next morning to talk to Alice and Trevor. Tom had gone on to New Jersey for a business meeting; afterward, he'd take the kids to his parents, who lived an hour and a half away. Sylvia was glad the children would spend some needed time with their dad. Alice particularly missed him when he was away on business. She frequently asked when he'd be home, so Sylvia suggested they mark the days on a calendar. When Tom finally walked through the door, Alice's face glowed, her eyes sparkled, and her whole body relaxed as she melted into his arms. She had a crush on her father like many eight-year-old girls, but there was a deeper bond between them—ever since he put her on the back of a horse at the age of two—which he continued to nurture through his love of horses. Alice now shared the same passion.

The phone rang a long time before Alice picked up. "It's Mommy," she called out. "Granddad's taking us to a model train place today, then hamburgers."

Sylvia recalled the elaborate train exhibit in Akron, which displayed rooms of new and vintage model trains winding through tunnels and over mountain passes and towns.

"Sounds great, honey. How was the plane ride?"

"Daddy and I played Crazy Eights. Trevor threw up. It was yucky," Alice said.

"Is he sick?"

"Not anymore. I think he ate too much candy."

*Figures,* Sylvia thought. Tom probably gave three-year-old Trevor Pepsi and red licorice, Tom's favorites.

Sylvia heard her mother's prompts in the background. "Grammy and I are going to make oatmeal cookies later," Alice said. "And we made a tent in the living room."

"Already? I bet Grammy was in there with you," Sylvia said.

Alice laughed. "She tried to crawl in, but it fell down and she pretended she was hiding from Trevor under the blanket. He laughed so hard. He wants to talk to you."

Trevor immediately told Sylvia he was sick on the plane. Once he got her sympathy, he talked trains and tents. Sylvia glanced at the clock and saw it was time for her to switch gears. She was meeting Anthony in two hours.

She took Red for a walk. She showered and stood naked in front of the expanse of mirror that spanned the double sinks in their master bath while she blew her hair dry. She stared at her body and liked what she saw. She was her high school weight again. Like Jessica had said, you shed pounds when you're in love. She had all the right proportions: broad shoulders; full breasts (well, they drooped from breast-feeding, but to her, a proud badge of devoted nurturing); flat tummy wrapped tightly to her hips; smooth, muscular legs with concave inner thighs and trim calves and ankles. She shut off the blow dryer and set it on the counter, then slowly grazed her fingertips back and forth over her nipples, which stood erect to her touch. She felt a twinge pulsate between her legs. She put on Anthony's favorite bra and panties—white lace bikinis with matching sheer bra that showed her nipples. She dabbed Joy behind her ears, at her throat, and on her wrists. Brown eyeliner, brown mascara, no eye shadow, no blush. She smiled at herself—aglow in natural beauty, oozing sensuality.

She finished dressing and went downstairs through the kitchen and family room to the garage. She hit the garage door button, jumped in her car, and turned the key. The engine churned but wouldn't turn over. Again. Clicking. Again. Nothing.

"Damn old car. Shit. Not now," she moaned. She wished she'd driven them to the airport so she had Tom's car. "Stupid!" she yelled. She ran back into the house and grabbed the phone, flailing through her purse for the hotel number. Then she realized he wouldn't be there yet. She called his office. Gone. She called the hotel.

"I'm sorry, no one by that name has checked in," the clerk said.

She ran back to the garage and tried again. Nothing. She had to think. *Call AAA. There'll never be enough time,* she thought. She called AAA, then the hotel four more times. When the clerk could connect her, she worried that Anthony wouldn't answer.

"Hello," Anthony said.

"My car won't start," she choked. "I called AAA. How much time do you have?"

"It's okay, Jake. Deep breath. We *will* see each other even if I have to wait all day," he said soothingly. "Call me when you're ready to leave."

An hour later she was on her way. She felt drained by the roller coaster of her emotions and frustrated with their control over her. She was possessed. Who was she kidding? She was just as needy as he was. He was good for her. His composed demeanor calmed and comforted her. She felt secure in his steadiness and that she could rely on him to be there for her. The more she thought about him, the more she began to relax and unwind.

Sylvia saw the familiar Greenwood Inn set back from the freeway ahead on the right. The white frame and brick two-story hotel nestled in a grove of towering Douglas fir trees had a quaint and charming quality. She pulled into the parking lot, spotted his Porsche, and pulled in beside it. She glanced up to the second story and saw him standing against the white railing, a red rose in his hand. She felt a flutter in her stomach as she looked at her handsome, five-foot-ten, Italian lover with black wavy hair, who wanted only her. He wore gray slacks and a fine-knit burgundy long-sleeved sweater with collar that fit loosely over his trim, muscular frame—the casual look of a European gentleman. Their eyes locked, and they smiled. As she approached him, he extended his hand. He took her hand and led her into the room.

He handed her the rose, cupped her face in his hands, and said, "I'm so sorry to continue to put you through all this because of how we have to see each other. You deserve better than having to rush to motel rooms. I'll make it up to you."

She stared into his eyes. "It's worth it to be with you."

He kissed her gently on her forehead, temples, cheeks, ears, drawing his tongue over her neck and chin, tracing her lips. "I think of you every minute I'm away from you," he whispered.

Dropping the rose, she drew a breath sharply as her mouth hungrily sought his, and their bodies melded together in passionate longing.

"I miss you so much, I ache," she said.

She felt his hardness press against her as he rubbed his hands over her buttocks, pulling her to him. He reached under her skirt, stroking her bare legs from behind and moving to the inside of her thighs. Then delicately under her bikinis, he softly glided his fingers over her wet lips, parting them slightly. At his touch, she threw back her head and let out a faint cry. He lifted her deftly and placed her on her back on the bed. She stared deeply into his amber eyes, searching, praying that he'd be with her always, that he'd always want her this much.

"I have to look at you," he said, sitting beside her. He slowly began unbuttoning her blouse. He unzipped her skirt and tossed it on the adjacent bed. She watched his somber expression as he scanned her body with his eyes. He seemed mesmerized. "My favorite underwear," he said quietly, almost to himself. His open hand grazed over her breasts and nipples, across and down her abdomen. She reached up and touched his face as his hand brushed over her panties, her dark mound, and between her legs. "You're almost too beautiful to make love to," he said.

"I'd better not be," she teased as she put her hands under his sweater and stroked his firm, hairless chest.

He laughed softly. "You *are* amazingly beautiful. I'm under your spell."

"Then we're even." She sat up and pulled his sweater over his head, her face inches from his. He kissed her hard, his tongue deep in her mouth. While he unhooked her bra, she unbuckled his belt and unzipped his pants. He pushed off his slacks which dropped off the bed onto the floor. He pulled her onto his lap and began kissing and sucking her nipples. He stood her up on the floor, quickly pulled off her panties, and parted her lips with his tongue. Rolling her back onto the bed, he slipped off his jockeys. She reached up for his shaft and then slid her hand up and down.

He groaned. "I need to be inside you."

Reeling with desire, she spread her legs and gasped.

"Now."

He inserted the head just inside, held it there a few seconds, thrust deep, and pulled out, teasing her. Her hand over his, she pushed him back inside her, reaching toward him with her hips, begging him for more. The room slowly began to circle around her. It was like a feeling of being devoured, deliciously consumed by him, yet completely freed like she'd never felt before. Feeling so safe and so loved, she surrendered to him completely, knowing she'd always need him and could never let him go. As her body released in waves, she felt him, too, let go in a full climax riding their final wave at the same time. Both breathing heavily, their glistening bodies slipped into relaxation. He lay resting on top of her a moment, before rolling onto his side. They dozed wrapped in each other's arms.

Sylvia stirred first and noticed the food boxes on the table and two unlit candles. She kissed him on the shoulder. "You brought lunch—how lovely. Shall we?"

He pulled her to him and stared into her eyes. "I just want to stay like this and not ever get up." He glanced at the table. "Except to pour our wine." He got up, opened a bottle of Chianti, and poured two glasses. He lit the candles and crawled back into bed with their wine. He kissed her lips and handed her a glass. "Just a few more minutes to savor this."

They finally got up, wrapped in towels, and sat across from each other at the table. They hungrily dove into salad with vinaigrette, ravioli with marinara sauce, and a rustic hard-crusted round loaf of bread.

Sylvia didn't want to break the mood, but they needed to talk. "You're not worried that Tom knows?"

"He suspects something, but he accepted your denial, right?"

"It's hard to say. Tom doesn't like to confront. For him, saying he thought I was having an affair is very direct."

"True. I'd rather risk getting caught though than telling them. My concerns are financial and emotional. Jane might shoot us if she found out."

Along with Jessica's remark, this was the second comment about Jane's hysteria. But he wasn't laughing. Sylvia figured it only happened in movies and tabloids.

"I think we should stick to the plan," he said. "Anyway, I'm still waiting for that deal to come through at work."

"The glass wall that you can see through to the other side but can't break yet?"

He took her hand from across the table. "In six months all should be in place and I'll ask her for a divorce."

Sylvia didn't know the details of his financial wall but trusted implicitly that as an accountant, he was the expert and knew what he had to do to make this work. Still, her "other life" was getting old, and she drove home wondering what would become of her.

# CHAPTER 2

Fall 1979

Sylvia was descending the stairs when she heard the garage door open and the phone begin to ring. If it was Anthony calling, his timing wasn't good. She stood by the phone in the kitchen and let it ring a third time to be sure. Alice's and Trevor's muffled voices rose and fell from the playroom upstairs. As she picked up the phone, Tom came in from his tennis match looking sweaty and flushed.

"Hi, Jessica," she said as she gave Tom a nod and a closed smile.

"Tell her hi for me," Tom said.

The clamor of feet running down the hall, then down the stairs, resounded through the kitchen. Alice and Trevor's playroom was directly above the garage. They could feel Tom's arrival before he walked in the door.

"Daddy, you're home," Alice called out. The kids burst into the room and wrapped themselves around their dad, Trevor hugging his bare legs.

"Jessica, I'll have to call you back; it's a little hectic here. Oh—Just a sec. I'll ask him."

"What a greeting," Tom said cheerfully. He knelt down to hug them both.

"Tom, Jessica wants to know if I can play tennis with her tomorrow, around noon. Will you be here to watch the kids?"

"Should be, yeah, no problem," he said.

"Sounds okay, but let me call you later." Sylvia hung up. She didn't want to commit to playing. Anthony had been out of town for five days and was waiting to hear what she could arrange. With Tom home, tennis could be her excuse. Jessica would understand.

"We should get a fourth and play doubles," Tom offered.

"I haven't played for so long, I need the singles workout. Maybe another time. Anyway, the kids need to spend time with you." Sylvia had become good on her feet.

"Come see what I drew for you," Alice said, pulling him by the hand.

Trevor thrust out his hand clutching a Matchbox car. "See my race car."

"Is that the one I brought you from my trip?" Tom asked.

Trevor nodded then turned to Sylvia. "Can I have a cracker?"

Sylvia smiled at him and went to the pantry. "Dinner won't be ready for an hour. How about cheese and apple slices *with* your crackers?"

"Yes, yes, Mommy," Alice said. "I'm hungry."

"Cheeeez." Trevor grinned.

"And apples," Alice said as she hugged Trevor and wouldn't let go. Trevor struggled to free himself, and Alice pulled him onto the floor where they rolled around in giggles.

Alice began chanting, "Cheese and apples and bears, oh my." Trevor joined in.

"Do you want something to drink?" Sylvia asked Tom. She finished placing the Red Delicious apple slices in a neat row next to the fan of crackers and cheese. "Cheese and apples and bears, oh my," continued from the floor.

"Grab me a beer, would you?"

Sylvia set the snack plate on the table and handed Tom his Bud. Alice and Trevor scrambled up and stood side by side at the table. Alice sandwiched a piece of cheese between two Wheat Thins, then ate the whole thing at once. Trevor looked at his sister, then the plate. Sylvia noticed that he meticulously took one cracker and ate it, then one piece of cheese and ate that. They breast-fed the same way—Alice hungrily, Trevor cautiously, oftentimes finished after nursing from only one side, which left Sylvia uncomfortably lopsided.

Beer in hand, Tom turned to go upstairs.

"Daddy, wait, you have to see my picture first," Alice said with her mouth full, Wheat Thin bits spewing.

"Jeez, slow down, I'll wait," Tom said. "What are we having for dinner?"

"Pork chops and rice," Sylvia said.

"I hope we have applesauce."

"We do," Sylvia said, knowing applesauce was a must. He couldn't eat pork chops without it.

Alice grabbed an apple slice and pulled Tom toward the doorway. As they headed upstairs, Trevor began to put a second cracker into his mouth while running to catch up, but Sylvia stopped him.

"Wait 'til you're standing still, honey. You might choke if you run with it in your mouth," she said. Trevor did as he was told and carefully folded his fingers over the snack in his hand. He ran, and Sylvia watched him swiftly scale the stairs. When he reached the top, he instinctively turned and held the snack out to show her.

"Good boy," she said. "Eat it in the playroom where your dad and Alice are."

She returned to the kitchen and sighed. She and Tom hadn't spoken to each other all day. She had managed to avoid him after last night.

Tom was gone for ten days and returned home around midnight the night before. Sylvia didn't awaken until she felt his body press against her and his hand stroke her breasts. A sneak attack.

"I love your boobs—they're still big, just longer," he said.

Sylvia winced in the dark at the familiar joke he often made to their closer friends when the conversation might turn to pregnancies and breast-feeding. "Sylvia went from a thirty-four C to a thirty-four long."

He reached for her hand and placed it on his erection. "Rub me."

She began stroking him.

"Harder."

She felt her body stiffen as he rolled on top of her. His stale breath smelled like beer. He kissed her hard, and she kissed him back. She feigned heavy breathing to get it over with. When he entered her, she was dry. Three minutes felt like thirty. When he finished, he immediately went to the bathroom to wipe himself off, like he always did. She lay still in the silence feeling used and unclean. It was hard to believe there was a time she didn't think she'd ever get enough of him, when she could barely keep her hands off of him. That was in college. It wasn't until their honeymoon that she discovered she was left wanting, when he'd satisfy himself and practically jump out of bed to play tennis or water ski or meet other resort guests for cocktails before dinner. She was too shy to talk about sex—she thought if you're in love, sexual satisfaction just came naturally. Their lovemaking had never really satisfied her. Tom wasn't comfortable with oral sex, and when she later got up the courage to ask him to massage her clitoris, he lost patience. It took too long. She always thought she must be frigid. So she faked it. The only orgasms she ever had were the ones she gave herself, until Anthony.

Sylvia heard the shower running upstairs and slipped outside to have a cigarette. She didn't smoke in front of Tom because he hated it. She realized she'd better try Anthony at the office *now.* She set the cigarette on the deck railing, ran back in, grabbed the phone, dialed the number, and rushed back out, stretching the cord across the kitchen table. "It's me. I only have a minute while Tom's in the shower. I have a two-hour window tomorrow at noon."

"Saturdays are tough, but I'll think of something," Anthony said.

Sylvia called Jessica and filled her in. Jessica said she'd cover for her.

Ten minutes later, Tom strolled into the kitchen, grabbed another Budweiser, and sat at the kitchen table.

"How are your classes going?" he asked.

Standing at the sink, Sylvia looked up but not at him. "The education classes are boring, but the French class is great."

"I'm still not sure why you're doing this, but if it makes you feel better—" he said.

"It does," she said. She turned on the oven to preheat and began slicing onions.

She loved being back in school. The classes brought a needed diversion and structure to the emotional upheaval of her two lives. She only needed nine credits in education to obtain her Oregon teaching certificate. This was her contingency plan in case of divorce. With Trevor still at home, she doubted she'd go back to teaching otherwise. Sylvia hadn't worked since Alice was born, which was the same year Gloria Steinem gave mothers permission to pursue career fulfillment outside the home. She and Tom had grown up with stay-at-home moms and never considered any other way, although Sylvia admitted only to herself that while she loved raising her children, being at home often left her feeling cut off from the world and lonely, especially after all their moves. She sometimes wondered if it was just her or if many mothers felt this way—a longing for personal fulfillment in careers waiting on the sidelines with no chance of getting on the playing field before the game was over. Maybe she had children too soon. Maybe the feminists had a point.

To brush up on her French, Sylvia enrolled in an advanced conversation class. Although it was below her abilities, the class was perfect after her ten-year hiatus. Claudine, her professor, was Sylvia's age and from Bordeaux. She was a striking, curvy brunette who held her students captive with her intelligence and spontaneous humor. Sylvia dreamed of being a college professor and could imagine herself in Claudine's shoes. Sylvia's fluency came back *rapidement.*

"Do you really want to go back to teaching?" Tom asked.

Trevor was now in preschool three mornings a week; next year he would graduate to four mornings. Sylvia had arranged her current class schedule around his.

"I'm not sure. I have until next spring to decide—when I'll have my teaching certificate. Maybe part-time, or I could sub. Even then, I wouldn't feel right about leaving Trevor."

"I agree, but it *might* make you feel better—anyway, we may need it."

Sylvia stopped abruptly and turned toward him. "What do you mean?"

"George and I have a plan," he said. "We want to start our own business."

George, Tom's sales manager, lived in Fresno and hired Tom as a sales rep a year ago for a company based in Beverly Hills that made stitchery kits and sold them through women's magazines. He and Tom used to work together as sales reps, each covering his own territory, George the West Coast, Tom the East. They succeeded in building female sales teams to sell plastic food storage products for Rubbermaid through "parties" in homes, like Tupperware. The term used was *direct sales*. Sylvia likened it to pyramid sales and Mary Kay cosmetics, without the pink Cadillac. The owner of the stitchery kit business, Larry Kramer, hired George as the sales manager to convert the sales approach from magazine ads to direct sales through catalogues. George, in turn, immediately hired Tom.

"But your job with Larry's company has been great," Sylvia said.

"We're tired of working for somebody else—Larry makes all the money while we do all the work. We figure it'll take six months to set up a processing plant in Fresno and get the stitchery kits ready for our own sales catalogue. In the meantime, we'll be recruiting the same women who work for us now to join our company."

"While you're still working for Larry?"

"It's the only way it'll fly," Tom said. "We'll need our salaries while we're setting up in Fresno. And I'll need to come up with my share of the investment."

"How?" Sylvia asked.

"A second mortgage on our house."

Anger welled up inside her. After all his job changes and their moves, she thought Larry's company might finally be the opportunity Tom needed. Not because of George, but because of Larry. She was relieved when they traveled to Beverly Hills, met Larry Kramer, and had dinner in his home. Him, she admired—here was finally an upstanding, intellectual, shrewd and successful businessman who owned several companies. He split his time between Beverly Hills and Manhattan. He was an amateur photographer with his own darkroom in his poolside cabana. His wife played the violin in the symphony, and they had four children.

"George must have been planning this for a long time, even *before* he hired you," Sylvia said. "You're the Pied Piper of women—he needs you to draw them in." Sylvia carried the chopping board covered with onions to the table, sat down across from him, and resumed with vigor. Tears streamed down her face.

"So?" Tom said.

"So you're his ticket, and he'll say anything to convince you."

"What's important is he knows this business."

"He doesn't sell; he preaches like an evangelist. He and his wife wear matching Hawaiian shirts to cocktail parties."

"You don't like him because he's not in Larry's class."

"I *never* liked him, and I don't trust him," she said, wiping the tears with the back of her wrist. "Will you get me a slice of bread?"

Tom handed her the slice, and she held it in her mouth to absorb the onion juice.

"I just want my own business."

Sylvia realized that he wasn't asking for her opinion or advice. He was telling her what he was going to do. He didn't know she no longer trusted his business acumen and found him lacking in follow-through. So why would he expect this to be any different than before? She'd always gone along with his job changes and moves, mostly because she felt sorry for him. And she felt sorry for him because she always believed he felt more at home in a stable wearing cowboy boots, saddling horses, and cleaning stalls than in suburbia, wearing a suit and climbing invisible ladders to material dreams. He even walked with a bow-legged swagger. He could build a split-rail fence and loved to chop wood. Sylvia often said he was born a century late.

She took the bread from her mouth. "How much is George putting up?"

"He has one hundred thousand from his military pension," Tom said. "We need to mortgage thirty thousand."

Sylvia's defenses were up. A second mortgage seemed impossible and too risky. She arranged the onions over the pork chops, covered them with foil, and put them in the oven. She sat back down and started biting her fingernails. She wanted another cigarette. "Would it be an equal partnership if he's putting up more?"

"Yes." He pulled her hand from her mouth. "Quit biting your fingernails."

"How can we afford another mortgage?"

"George can cover us if necessary. It's all worked out."

"I'm not moving to Fresno."

"Nobody's asking you to."

"What if I refuse to cosign the mortgage?"

"Because you don't like George?" He jumped up from the table. "What did I ever do to you except give you the lifestyle you demanded?"

"I sure never asked for *this* lifestyle," she said. "You dragged me all over the country, and I handled all the moves by myself—you were never there." Sylvia had packed and unpacked their household so many times she had nightmares of endless stacks of dishes, glasses, and crystal that needed to be carefully wrapped in brown packing paper and placed in cartons and labeled. Each time she finished a stack, another would appear.

Tom dismissed her with a wave of his hand. "I'm doing the best I can, which you don't seem to appreciate. You're spoiled and always have been."

Sylvia became aware that his increasing resentment of her must've always been there, simmering just below the surface. When they were engaged, Tom knew that her parents were worried that he wouldn't be able to provide her with the same comforts they'd given their daughter. In college, Sylvia learned that Tom's rural upbringing and his family's financial struggles were a source of embarrassment to him. He drove a new white convertible Mustang from his "dad's" car dealership. He trained and showed horses on the "family" horse farm with his twin brother, Jim, throughout his childhood. That's what he told everyone, but he twisted the facts. His dad was head of maintenance at a small college in nearby Wooster—the horse farm and car dealership belonged to the small town's mogul, who had taken Tom and Jim under his wing. But Sylvia was only twenty and in love with him. She overlooked his tendency to impress others by fabricating a story to hide his real background. Later, she wondered if he felt insufficient in comparison to his brothers—his twin, Jim, was a veterinarian and his older brother, Don, a dentist—and if he struggled to match their successes. She sensed that she'd become the target for his inadequacies that began long before she knew him.

"Don't you mean 'difficult'? That's what you say about me to our friends—and now I'm spoiled, too? Or am I difficult because I'm spoiled?"

"See what you do? You're *making* this difficult," he said.

Sylvia didn't understand what that meant except that it was derogatory and seemed like a male thing—blame her for something to avoid looking at himself. Was a woman difficult when she didn't agree with a man? Or when she wanted to examine all the details and a man looked at it as tiresome analysis? Maybe it was when a woman made herself unavailable to him, closed herself off, and he couldn't reach her, so he said she was "difficult" to avoid the truth.

"We're drifting further and further apart," she said, her voice breaking. "There isn't much point to a marriage with one partner *in absentia*."

"*In absentia*, you and your fancy words," he said, mocking her. "Look who's talking. When I *am* here, you're in another world."

Sylvia was sorry she started this. She didn't want to take the next step. She didn't know if she could lie again about Anthony, and she didn't want Tom to ask. "We should never have moved back here. I was happy in Ohio." And she had been. She found she liked the small-town atmosphere of Chillicothe. She gave birth to Trevor there. They were close to family and an hour from Columbus, where they had lots of old college friends. Their house was a vintage colonial on two acres with a creek. Tom made the decision to move and find another job because he'd heard the direct sales department was being eliminated.

Tom went to the refrigerator and got another beer. As she watched him drink, she realized that any attraction she might have had for him—his rugged, Redford-handsome good looks—dissipated when he opened his mouth. He was no more than a rough-hewn, beer-drinking, insensitive cowboy.

"So it's my fault you're not happy?" he asked. "Lots of people go through this after ten years of marriage—it's just a phase. We should ride it out for the kids' sake."

Sylvia heard him. He was just as miserable as she was. Maybe he was right. Maybe their discontent with their marriage was typical of most couples at this stage, a ten-year itch. But it was more than that; she had a yearning to be wanted and cherished again. And respected. She tried several times over the past few years to bring them closer. Once, when he had just gotten back from a trip, she dressed in a sexy nightgown and delivered drinks and hors d'oeuvres on a tray to him in front of a fire, but after a few minutes he was more interested in watching a basketball game on TV. After a few rebuffs, she didn't try anymore. Still, she questioned whether Anthony was her soul mate or an escape from her own emptiness. She wanted a crystal ball.

Trevor bounded into the kitchen, dragging his blankie behind him. Red followed. As if to humor Trevor, Red stepped on the trailing blankie in a playful pounce, causing Trevor to come to an abrupt halt, fall on his behind, and laugh hysterically. Trevor jumped up, ran to Sylvia, and clutched her leg, giggling as he nuzzled his face into her lap.

She leaned down to kiss the back of his head, to breathe in his smell, which always filled her with an indescribable longing for a time in the past when she felt comforted and safe.

She noticed his fingers were losing their dimpled joints—the knuckles were coming.

"Did Red get your blankie?" she teased.

Tom finished his beer. He grabbed Trevor, tossed him in the air, and ran out to the backyard, Red close behind.

Within a week, Tom presented the bank papers for Sylvia to cosign. They didn't discuss it any further, and she signed. Two weeks later, the bank approved the second mortgage. Sylvia was upstairs in the laundry room folding clothes and picked up Tom's faded, red college football jersey that he always slept in. Sadness swept over her as she recalled when she used to press it to her face to smell the essence of him and imagine him holding her. And then it was gone. The dryer was tumbling, and she was putting a load in the washer when Tom came in to find her.

"You scared me."

"I have bad news," he mumbled.

"I can't hear you," she said, shaking her head and pointing to her ear.

"We need to talk," he said more loudly.

Sylvia followed him down the hall and into the master bedroom, carrying a stack of folded clothes. Tom stood in the far corner where two large windows on each adjacent wall converged and almost joined, giving the impression of an all-glass corner. A towering Douglas fir tree stood so close to the windows it appeared to be within touching distance, like a natural escape ladder.

The late afternoon sun filtered through the Levolor blinds, throwing bars of shadow and light across his face. He squinted as he looked at her, then looked down again. "George and I were fired."

The clothes fell from her arms and silently tumbled to the floor. She slowly walked to the wingback chair next to where he was standing and plopped down. She raked her fingers through her auburn hair, pulling it back from her face. She waited.

"When our bank called Larry for employment verification on the second mortgage, he guessed what we were doing and confronted us."

Tom still wouldn't look at her, but then, they usually spoke to each other with heads turned, looking down or up, avoiding eye contact, with only occasional direct glances.

"How are we going to live? Pay *both* mortgages?"

"George can pay me a salary for a while with his pension."

"For how long?"

"Six to nine months."

If only she had refused to sign the mortgage papers.

*****

While Sylvia and Anthony continued to discuss their timeline, Tom and George pushed forward with their new company, The Creative Circle. It could work, but only if they could print a sales catalogue showing all the stitchery kits, in record time, for Christmas. Two hundred kits had to be designed and finished before they could be photographed for the catalogue—cross-stitch patterns of watering cans filled with daisies, needlepoint pillows with homespun phrases such as "Home is where the heart is," latch-hook rugs, and macramé wall-hangings or plant holders to hang from the ceiling. The Christmas catalogue photo shoot would take place in Tom and Sylvia's home in early November.

Four days before the shoot, fifty kits were still unfinished. Tom and George frantically began calling all the women on their sales teams for help. Women from Tualatin, Monmouth, Klamath Falls, all parts of small-town Oregon, poured into their home throughout the day and evening for two days. Some brought their children dressed in pajamas. Their husbands dropped them off and went bowling or to the nearest sports bar. Sylvia felt like the hostess of a modern-day quilting bee. Maybe Tom had found his pioneer roots after all.

The female task force spilled into Sylvia's kitchen. They filled her refrigerator with potato and macaroni salads, tuna fish casserole, and lime Jell-O molds. Tom prepared hot dogs and hamburgers on the grill. Dirty glasses and dishes stacked up on the kitchen counters and filled the sink. The dishwasher ran nonstop. They sat on chairs, couches, stairs, and floors in every room downstairs, except the bathrooms. They ate and chatted as they sewed. Their children slept in any empty bed. Sylvia sat at her kitchen table weaving a needle of green embroidery floss up and down through a painted pattern of "What are little girls made of?" wondering, *How did I end up here?*

She was the only woman here who didn't believe in Tom. She had believed once, and as she looked around her, she knew these women would follow him anywhere, just as she had. She'd outgrown his world, now that she accepted the truth of him. Her affair made her face what she had long denied, maybe what she'd always known. She didn't fit in here and was no longer willing to pretend.

Sylvia tried to respond politely to the woman seated next to her, who was talking about her quick-meal recipes with Campbell's Soup, but was distracted by the back of the Bentwood chair that strained to support the weight of her three-hundred-pound frame. Sylvia smiled and nodded. They stitched all night.

The morning of the shoot, the photographer arrived at eight o'clock. He promptly began dismantling every room of their house. Pictures came off the walls; chairs, couches, tables, and lamps were moved from room to room. A floral-patterned shower curtain found its way to the family room, and lighting cables ran throughout the lower floor to the outside. He said he needed a variety of "creative backdrops to enhance the finished products for the catalogue."

Sylvia, exasperated with the mayhem in her home, said to Tom, "I think I've done all I can here. I'm exhausted, and the kids need a break. I'll take them and Red to Mount Hood. I'll be back tonight."

"I think they like the mess. You're the one who can't take it," he said.

"You're probably right, but I can't leave them unsupervised, so they're going with me."

"Do what you want then."

On their drive to the mountain, Sylvia pulled into a gas station and called Anthony at his office. "I feel like I'm suffocating. I can't do this anymore."

"What do you mean?" he asked.

"I'm going to ask for a divorce after the holidays."

"I'll be waiting."

Sylvia let the comment slide. He wouldn't be waiting. He hadn't even brought it up yet with Jane. The "glass wall" was still unbreakable.

Alice came by the phone booth. "Who are you calling, Mommy? Let's go."

"I'll be right out, honey." She turned back to the phone. "I know it's not what we planned. Me first, I mean."

"Don't worry, Jake. Who goes first doesn't really matter. I'll follow in six months. It's still basically the same plan," he said. "Are we still good for Tuesday?"

"As far as I know."

"Seems so long. I need to see you. I love you, Jake."

"I love you, too. I've gotta go." She said good-bye to Anthony and joined her children. She veered onto a trail road that meandered deep into the forest canopy and parked the car in a clearing. She spotted a large field in the distance.

As Alice opened the door, Red bolted into the lush undergrowth and headed for the field. Alice laughed, took Trevor's hand, and with a teasing lilt in her voice, said, "Let's find Roo Roo." Sylvia and her children loved to play this hide-and-seek game with their dog. They would quietly watch Red point and focus into a field of tall, flowing grass, her silky auburn feathers of fur wisping in the breeze. With ears cocked and nose twitching, she'd suddenly disappear.

"There she is, Mom," Alice called out. Red leaped into the air at full speed, flushing out birds in all directions.

Sylvia worried more about the immediate impact of a divorce on Alice than on Trevor, who at three would most likely not recall their life together as a family unit. Alice needed her mom but wanted her dad. Sylvia counted on Tom's devotion to his children, which she trusted would never waver. Once divorced, he might spend even more time with them to mitigate any long-term damage that could often occur in split families. Besides, Alice and Trevor were used to a part-time father. How much worse could it be than what they already knew? Of course, money could be an even bigger problem now.

The Christmas catalogue barely printed in time for the holidays, which didn't leave enough room for the sales they needed to cover the costs. As planned, Sylvia and Tom were living off of George's pension, which paid the existing monthly bills. Sylvia contacted Claudine, who recommended several students for Sylvia to tutor; she decided to put the money toward her classes next term.

They agreed there would be no Christmas gifts other than for Alice and Trevor. Tom chopped down a Christmas tree in a nearby woods. Sylvia and Alice cut holly branches from the bush in the backyard and made wreaths to send to their relatives in Ohio. They wore bulky work gloves to protect their hands from the prickly holly leaves when they fastened the sprigs onto the round, wire frames.

On Christmas day, Tom made Alice close her eyes as he led her to the backyard. Red was barking madly. Sylvia ran out to see what the commotion was about and almost fainted. Standing in the middle of the yard was a chestnut-colored horse.

"Daddy, my dream come true," Alice squealed. She bolted down the deck stairs in her nightgown.

"How could you?" Sylvia asked him.

"Don't worry; I just borrowed it from the old judge up the street. He said she can ride it anytime she wants, and he'll keep it in his barn." The judge's property was the last vestige of rural living that predominated this area before the developer turned it into a sixty-home subdivision. He wouldn't sell out.

"But she thinks it's hers," Sylvia said.

"She'll never know."

# CHAPTER 3

Winter 1980

The resolve to ask for a divorce required more courage than Sylvia imagined. There was no ideal way or time, but if she approached it in a delicate, gentle manner, like whispering or walking on tiptoes, Tom somehow wouldn't feel it when it happened. By choosing the moment carefully, she hoped she could sidestep a dramatic reaction. January seemed too soon after the holidays, and since February was Tom's birthday month, she didn't want him to forever associate this month with her wanting to leave him. There was also Tom's business, which was only a few months old and struggling. A divorce discussion would only add to the dreariness of the winter months with the intermittent ice storms and lead-colored skies. The ceiling seemed so low and heavy, she almost felt the need to walk hunched over from the invisible weight, a weight she likened to her own, from the guilt, shame, and heartache that pressed on her, pushing her down, becoming more burdensome with each passing day. Now wasn't the time.

While she waited for spring to usher in the seasonal lift to her spirits, Sylvia decided to at least gather information on divorce from an attorney that Jessica recommended. Better to have the facts, she thought, *before* a conversation with Tom. Sylvia made an appointment to meet with Al Seidmann in his downtown Portland office. He told her there would be no fee for an initial consultation.

On her drive downtown, Sylvia's stomach developed a familiar hollowness that gripped her when she was either frightened or excited. She mentally rehearsed what Jessica had advised as she took turns biting her fingernails and smoking a cigarette, one hand on the steering wheel.

"Don't tell him you're having an affair. He's an attorney, not a therapist. Even though an affair doesn't matter in a court of law, men can't remain impartial when it's the woman who's fooling around. Their egos get in the way, and they'll take the guy's side every time. Of course, they'd never admit it." Jessica ought to know. Her husband was an attorney.

While Sylvia sat alone in the law office reception area, she took in her surroundings. Restored historical building. Mahogany trim. This might be like sleepwalking where you're moving without the awareness to grasp where you're headed. Worn overstuffed chair and sofa. Beige shag carpeting. Seidmann came out, introduced himself, and ushered her in.

Sylvia must have expected a short, slightly built, balding, middle-aged man with wire-rimmed glasses for her attorney, or she wouldn't have inwardly registered her surprise upon meeting him. As she followed his towering bulky frame down a dimly lit corridor past several open-door offices, she noticed his purposeful stride and thick black crop of straight, slightly mussed hair that grazed the tops of his ears and shirt collar. No gray yet, at least from her cursory observation, which meant he might not even be forty. They entered his spacious corner office with windows on two walls. Old-fashioned, two-inch-wide wood Venetian blinds covered the windows. So different from the modern narrow-slatted ones she had at home. He motioned for her to sit in one of the forest-green leather chairs facing his desk, while he took a seat in the brown high-backed leather swivel behind his desk.

He clasped his hands behind his head as he leaned back in his chair, smiled without showing his teeth, and casually asked her what he could do for her. He didn't wear glasses, and his bushy eyebrows almost joined above the bridge of his nose. She tried to recall what that was supposed to say about someone. Shifty? Gullible? Untrustworthy? Then she pushed it out of her mind.

His comfortable, relaxed approach did help put Sylvia at ease. She gave him a general explanation of her desire to divorce her husband due to "irreconcilable differences," to use only one attorney because there was no money, and to part amicably for the sake of their children. Seidmann talked about the legal aspects of divorce for almost twenty minutes, at times posing specific questions to clarify Sylvia's circumstances.

"I hesitate to represent both you and your husband as you request, Mrs. Beekman. May I call you Sylvia?"

Sylvia nodded.

"One of you will end up feeling cheated," Seidmann said.

If he only knew who was doing the cheating, Sylvia thought. She glanced down at her hands in her lap and, as was often her routine with strangers, folded them over each other to hide what was left of the nubs of her fingernails.

Looking up at him, Sylvia said, "With so little to divide, I don't see how that would happen to us."

"You don't see it now. I'm here as your adviser to tell you what I know based on my experience. I'm going to be direct with you. I think it will be you who will feel cheated."

"But I'm the one who wants the divorce," she said.

"Precisely."

"I don't understand."

"Your unwillingness to ask for all you're entitled to after eleven years of marriage with two children and no employment—"

"But I'll be—"

He put his hand up. "I know, I know, you'll be teaching. And that's good, but it won't be enough to give you and your children the lifestyle to which you're accustomed. In short, Sylvia, I smell guilt. Guilt interferes with what's best for you. That's why you listen to your attorney."

"I'm only trying to be fair," she said.

"Impossible in divorce."

He was way off in his assessment that she'd be the one to feel cheated. If he knew about her plans with Anthony, he'd see it differently—unless he did have the nose to detect it and inferred what was going on. She didn't want to get sidetracked. She would ask for child support only. Never alimony, as Seidmann proposed. He was probably like all attorneys—looking for a battle when there wasn't one. She was determined not to let him do that to her and Tom.

He reluctantly agreed to represent Sylvia and Tom but on the condition that he meet with Tom as well. She took his card and told him she'd get in touch when she was ready.

He would charge eight hundred dollars plus court costs. As long as there were no settlement disputes, the divorce would be final ninety days after the filing. Sylvia was surprised that dissolving a marriage took so little time, but then, getting married took even less. Even if she waited until June to ask Tom for a divorce, it would be over well before the end of the year—this information alone made the visit to the attorney worthwhile. She could wait a little longer in hopes that Tom's business would start to improve.

In early March, Anthony suggested that Sylvia come with him for a two-day business trip to Seattle. A needed getaway for both of them, he said. She decided it would be better if she went with Anthony when Tom was out of town and the kids could stay with friends. Anthony had flexibility in his schedule, so he could accommodate her there. This way she wouldn't have to supply Tom with details of where she was staying or even a phone number. Not that he was in the habit of giving *her* these details. Tom would maybe call every three or four days when he was away; in fact, he changed cities so frequently, Sylvia hardly knew where he was staying most of the time he was gone.

Sylvia did have to give Tom her reason for going and a phone number to give to the parents where Alice and Trevor would be staying. What could be her excuse? A seminar for one of her classes? A friend she hadn't seen in a long time? Not a hotel. She wouldn't be able to spend the money. How would she explain that? Something with Jessica? Nothing made enough sense. She thought of her youngest brother, Scott, who lived in San Diego and worked for a company that required him to go out of town occasionally. She could tell Tom that Scott was going to Seattle on business and wanted her to come and stay with him. That way she could justify the expense of the gas money for the drive to Seattle. And Scott knew about Anthony.

Last year Sylvia had told Scott about her affair. He'd been shocked at her behavior and told her so. She had expected no less. Tom had become a member of the family. Scott said that he'd always liked that Tom was uncomplicated, even if he did lack substance. He seemed loyal to Sylvia, devoted to the kids, and tried hard to provide for them, which he did well enough. At age twenty-four, Scott belied his lack of experience by expressing grave concern for Sylvia's leaving her marriage for someone else, particularly the effects on Alice and Trevor. Since Sylvia was the big sister that Scott looked up to and admired, he listened patiently to her explanations of marital discontent and the depth of her relationship with Anthony. He told her he still had doubts but better understood her decision to leave Tom. Scott had said, "I still don't like this, but I know you wouldn't do this without looking at everything."

After what Scott had endured while in high school when their brother, Steve, had his first psychotic break, Sylvia had misgivings about dragging him further into her double life. He had told Sylvia how his life had changed forever after Steve became ill and that he still avoided going home to Ohio if Steve were there. She needed to think it over before asking him to be her accomplice.

*****

It was daybreak when Scott angled his surfboard into the backseat of his 1964 black convertible Karmann Ghia. He carefully wedged its tip under the front passenger seat to keep it from sliding. He tossed his wetsuit in beside it, then opened the trunk and placed his briefcase and clothes for work inside. He jiggled the keys in the temperamental ignition, coaxing it to start, as he did every morning. The engine roared, and he backed out of his driveway, heading north on the coast road to La Jolla, only a ten-minute drive. The lush, exotic foliage of flowering oleander, hibiscus, and bird of paradise seemed to run past him. He was glad he had followed his girlfriend, Amanda, to San Diego.

As Scott recalled the harsh Boston winters he and Amanda had left behind after college two years ago, the fact that he was surfing in February brought a smile to his face. The winters *had* been conducive for studying though. He wondered if he would've had the discipline for the rigorous demands of chemical engineering had he been surrounded by San Diego's chart of elements. Its blend of sunny days, balmy nights, and jasmine-scented breezes was a formula he found intoxicating. Who was he kidding? Even surfing before work gave him guilt pangs, like he was cheating, or cutting class, or getting away with something that was against the rules. Fun was supposed to come after a hard day's work, not before.

Scott figured this was as rebellious as he'd ever get: moving to Southern California and surfing on a workday. He knew he was a lot like his dad: meticulous, responsible, tenacious, measured, soft-spoken, and now, just like him, a chemical engineer. Growing up they played trumpet duets and rounds of golf together. Although his dad had never said it out loud, Scott saw himself as the only surviving son and felt his dad was counting on him to follow in his footsteps. Scott took the baton without hesitation. He knew that his older brother, Steve, was never going to lead a normal life, even though his parents hadn't given up hope.

The marine layer hung heavy over the horizon. *Probably won't lift until early afternoon, if at all,* he thought. The cool wind whipped around him, and he shivered. Goose bumps peppered his arms and legs. Up ahead he saw several cars parked along the roadside. He looked beyond the curling swells and spotted the familiar bobbing cluster of black-suited torsos perched vertically on the ocean surface, their boards jutting skyward at a forty-five-degree angle.

He thought about his phone conversation with his parents the night before. They had asked him if he could come home for a visit this summer. Sylvia would be there, too, and the kids. He missed them all. But he couldn't imagine going back there. Steve was home again after another disappointing round in a mental hospital or halfway house. Scott couldn't remember which. The revolving door had become a blur.

Flashes of anger would still well up when Scott was reminded of what had become of his home life once he started high school. Steve's psychotic break ten years ago marked the end of Scott's idyllic childhood and the beginning of his desire to escape.

He could still hear his mother's frantic voice when he came home from school that day. She was on the phone. "You have to get home right away. Something's wrong with Steve. I can't make him stop."

Scott heard the repeated thud of heavy footsteps going from the stairway to Steve's room on the second floor. Scott approached cautiously and could hear that Steve was talking loudly to someone, repeating over and over, "Jesus will save me." Scott peeked around the corner to see who was with him.

Steve was furiously running up and down the stairs. He had on his Big 10 red track shorts and gray T-shirt. His long, lean legs glistened with sweat. He was breathing hard. His face was drenched and expressionless. He seemed to be in a trance. There was no one else there.

Scott ducked and ran to his mother, who was trembling. "Your father's on his way home. He said to call the village police."

In the background, the rhythmic pounding on the stairs reminded Scott of a bass drumbeat that provided accompaniment to Steve's loud, monotonic lyric.

"Maybe I should try to talk to him again," she said.

"What's wrong with him, Mom?"

"I don't know. Maybe a nervous breakdown." She wept. "All that track pressure."

She got up suddenly and walked to the stairs. Scott followed. She stood at the bottom and looked up at the back of her eldest son as he raced up the stairs. He turned at the top. They watched him as he came down. When he reached the bottom step, facing her, she reached out her hand and gently placed it on his shoulder, looking intently to meet his glassy stare. His eyes wild, he stopped. Scott was frightened.

"Steve," she said quietly. "It's okay. Let's walk in the backyard."

Steve hesitated. He looked at her as if he didn't recognize her and shook his head, then said quietly, "They won't let me."

"Who won't let you?" she asked.

"If I stop, Jesus won't save me. I'm bad."

He turned and began his climb again.

She had started to protest when she and Scott heard the crunch of tires on the gravel driveway. The car door slammed. They hurried toward the family room just as his father rushed in, his face ashen.

"Did you call the police?" he asked.

"I couldn't," she said.

Scott's dad disappeared for a few minutes. When he came back, he said, "He needs a hospital. We need to call a psychiatrist."

Scott was shocked. Had Steve flipped out? Was he crazy? He slowly backed away, then turned and ran to his room and shut the door. There was no home-cooked dinner that night. For many nights thereafter, his dad took him for curb service or brought home Kentucky Fried Chicken. Steve was in and out of hospitals and institutions over the next several years. His parents were distant and anxious. Scott spent more and more time at his friends' houses. His mother's mood depended on Steve's vacillating condition. When Steve was home, he either slept all day or stayed up all night. His mother said she couldn't sleep, so her doctor gave her some pills.

When Scott was at school, he could forget Steve's catatonic stare, his mother's frequent bouts of tears, and his father's absorption in finding a "chemical cure" for Steve's "imbalance." But he always dreaded going home. He never knew what to expect.

Scott felt helpless and often resentful when he reflected on the past ten years and what his parents were still going through. He was leading a life his parents had wanted for him and took some comfort in that. He called them every week and visited once a year; instead of going to Ohio this summer though, he decided to encourage them to visit him.

Scott made a U-turn and pulled in behind the last car. He jumped out, grabbing his full-body wetsuit. He stretched it over his washcloth-size Speedo, struggling to adjust each arm, then placed his car keys on top of the left front tire. His board under his arm, he sprinted down the embankment to the beach.

He stood at the shoreline and took several deep breaths. Relief spread through him as he inhaled the salty air. Scott found solace in the thunderous sound of the crashing waves. He waded in up to his waist, then flopped onto the board. His six-foot length extended just beyond the end so that his toes carved a continuous slice in the water as he paddled. His years on the swim team had conditioned his smooth, muscled arms to cut swiftly through the water. He appeared to glide effortlessly. Scott joined the silent cluster, all heads pointed toward the horizon, and waited. As a large swell rolled toward him, he paddled hard, caught the wave, and hopped into a crouched position until he gained his balance. He felt the exhilaration spill through his body as he stood on his board and rode the wave home to shore.

*****

Sylvia ultimately saw Scott as her only chance to go away with Anthony and decided to call him. He could always refuse. She waited until he'd be home from work, hoping he was alone. He and Amanda had separate apartments, but they spent many weeknights together and almost every weekend. This night she was lucky. Scott moaned when she explained what she wanted from him.

"I'm sorry to put you in this awkward position, but it's important to me," she said.

"Jeez, Syl. Tom won't try to call me, will he?" Scott asked.

"Not when he knows you won't be home." Even Sylvia couldn't imagine that Tom would check on her alibi.

"I guess I'll do it this once. What *are* your plans at this point? Still thinking about divorce?" Scott asked.

"I've talked to an attorney, but I haven't said anything to Tom yet," she said. "Before summer I will."

"I think I should meet Anthony," he said.

"I do, too, but I don't know how."

"Maybe I really will go to Seattle and make it legit."

"Very funny."

"He'd better appreciate what he's getting in you."

"Thanks for that. Actually, other than my family, I've never felt so appreciated and valued as I feel with Anthony."

"Speaking of, I just talked to Mom and Dad."

"I haven't talked to them for about two weeks. Anything going on?"

"The usual. Steve's home again. Sort of taking his meds. Mom's weepy dealing with him every day. Dad's looking for a 'cure.'"

"He shouldn't be living with them. He should be in a halfway house," Sylvia said.

"You know he won't stay. Last time he just walked home."

"They don't know what tough love is, not that I would either."

"C'mon. Even *you* would after ten years. With Dad's retiring, they should be enjoying themselves. It makes me so mad."

Sylvia was frustrated for her parents but felt compassion for Steve. She understood that Scott wouldn't feel the same way. Only three years apart, she and Steve spent their whole childhood together. Steve had been such a happy, normal child, except for his hair falling out in patches when he was eight years old. The doctor told her parents it was from nerves. Because Steve's illness seemed to have occurred without warning, Sylvia harbored a quiet fear that one or both of her children could end up with schizophrenia.

"I was planning to take the kids home this summer. Maybe I can help them somehow," she said.

"Mom told me. She's living for your visit."

"So am I. I hope Steve won't be a problem."

"He'll just burrow upstairs in his room and avoid all of you."

"Probably. But I don't think they tell us the whole story—what really goes on."

"You're right; they don't. At least I know they didn't tell you everything when I was living there and you were in Jersey. They didn't want to worry you."

"So they wouldn't tell you now either."

"True. I do know Steve pinned Dad against the wall once, but I think that's exceptional."

"Great. It's those exceptions I worry about."

"I'd better get back to work. Let me know the dates so I know where I'm supposed to pretend to be."

"You're the best to do this for me. I owe you one."

"What are baby brothers for?"

A week before she and Anthony were to drive to Seattle, Tom asked Sylvia if she had any cash on her because he didn't, and he wanted to run to the store. She told him to look in her wallet in her purse in their bedroom. She had about fifteen dollars.

A few minutes later, Tom walked into the family room, where she was watching TV. The kids were in bed.

"Did you find it?" she asked.

He stood in front of her holding a business card. "And this," he said, putting Al Seidmann's card in her face. "What's this all about?" He tossed it on the coffee table and stood there with his hands on his hips.

She slumped against the back of the couch and closed her eyes. This was it. The time for the conversation she wasn't ready to have was here. She sat up and looked at him. His pursed lips and the challenge in his eyes made her feel vulnerable and want to retreat. "Maybe I should've talked to you before talking to an attorney—except we don't talk and—"

"What do you want to talk about, Sylvia?"

"About our marriage that hasn't been working for a long time. I've gathered you feel the same way." She wasn't used to direct eye contact with him. She became so uncomfortable she had to blink and look over his head.

"I told you before. I think this is a normal phase in any marriage," he said.

The condescension in his tone pulled her back to the front lines. She jumped up and moved swiftly to the TV set. She'd been watching *The Love Boat,* unable to even imagine herself on a luxury cruise ship, just bobbing from one exotic island to another. She shut it off and stood there with her arms crossed.

"What's normal? To coexist? To not talk, ever? To not enjoy or value each other's company enough to want to spend any time together?" She was waving her arms and stomping around the room. Her emotions had taken over, which she didn't want to happen. She went behind the couch around the other side to avoid sliding in front of Tom and sat back down on the couch. It never failed. Just as she was feeling rotten about her selfish behavior and needs and ready to take pity on

Tom, he said or did something that brought her back to why she wanted out, even justified it.

The disdain in his voice with the "I told you before" statement, like she was a spoiled child who needed to be reminded, infuriated her. He talked at her. A flood of old hurts came rushing back. He flirted shamelessly with her friends like she wasn't even there. Jessica for one. Just the three of them were in Jessica's kitchen, when Tom had practically kissed her on the mouth with Sylvia standing beside them. He had gotten drunk at a football game the day she was due to deliver Trevor and come home and passed out on the floor. Her contractions had started in the middle of the night, and on the way to the hospital, he had to pull over to throw up. She didn't feel protected and cared for with Tom. The thought of growing old with this man chilled her.

"For Chrissakes, Sylvia, we're not newlyweds. And we have kids! You want too much," he yelled, pointing his finger at her.

"So our life as a couple is over? You call that normal?" she shrieked.

She was standing again and meeting his eyes. They looked intently at each other for several seconds.

Suddenly he pulled her close to him and kissed her hard. She recoiled as his tongue met hers, even pushed him away, but he persisted. Her stomach went hollow and not because she was frightened. Her shock at feeling even remotely turned on by Tom confused her. She stumbled backwards, and they fell onto the couch into each other's arms.

"Don't give up on us, Syl," he said. He started to kiss her again and move his hand under her sweater.

"Wait. Tom. I can't do this," she stammered. "Get off me."

He slowly pulled away from her and sat forward on the couch looking down at his feet, his elbows resting on his knees. "You're my wife. Whaddaya mean you can't?" He sounded wounded.

"It isn't just about sex," Sylvia mumbled. She shifted further away from him.

"I know, but it might help." He turned toward her, looking perplexed and scorned.

She leaned back and sighed. "Not at this stage."

He straightened and turned to face her. "You're looking for reasons to leave. What is it really?" Her rejection seemed to have taken the desperate bravado out of him. Without the phony posture, he sounded calmer and had a straightforward, even curious tone.

Not trusting his new stance, Sylvia thought he might be fishing, luring her to confess. "It's *really* that we've outgrown each other. We've gone in different directions."

Tom stood up. He trudged up the four steps to the kitchen. Sylvia saw the light from the open refrigerator reflect on the adjacent picture window. She stared at the deadened logs in the fireplace whose fire had gone out leaving smoldering chunks of blackened wood. Moments of silence hung in the air.

He came back carrying a Budweiser and sat down beside her. "It's all the travel, isn't it?"

"That's part of it. Being by myself so much."

"And the moves," he said.

"And we had a rough start. Two years of separation. Then Alice was born. The moves and the travel on top of that. As a couple we never had a chance. Maybe it all caught up with me."

Sylvia thought back to their marriage plans. In college Tom was in the ROTC program and had to serve two years of active duty after he graduated. After a six-month stint in Germany, he and Sylvia had become engaged. They had planned a June wedding but agreed to delay it if he received orders to go to Vietnam. He was stationed in Fort Lewis when he called her to tell her the bad news. But all he said about their wedding was, "We have to move the date up sooner." Neither of them had brought up the possibility of putting it off. She wondered if it nagged at him like it did at her.

"Lots of couples have rough beginnings. I don't buy it."

"I'm not trying to sell it," she said.

"Don't you think we owe it to the kids to wait?"

"For what?"

"For it to pass. For a bad patch to turn around."

She sat up and turned toward him. "I think we have waited. We tried therapy and that didn't help."

"I don't think therapy works, just time."

"And I think that was our chance. We don't see things the same way. I don't think it's good for kids to be in an environment where the parents are miserable."

"I'm not miserable."

"Well, are you happy?" Sylvia asked.

"I don't have time to think about it," he said. "The important thing is the kids need a father."

"With all your travel you'd be with them as much as you are now."

"It's not the same if we're divorced."

"So we hide behind them and stay together for the kids?"

"There are worse reasons."

"It would be easier on them if we divorce when they're young. They wouldn't remember us as a family."

"Such nonsense. You read too much."

"I try to stay on top of—"

"I don't care what the experts say. They'll just change their minds tomorrow. I still think we should wait."

"I think we should admit it's not working and end it for both our sakes."

"You've got great timing."

She looked into the fireplace again. "I know the business isn't doing well, but there's never a good time."

"Sounds like you've made up your mind."

"I'm just not willing to live this charade anymore," Sylvia said.

Tom went to the fireplace, grabbed a poker, and tried to stoke the smoldering logs without success.

With his back still turned, he said, "I guess I'm done trying to talk you out of it."

"Did you really want to?"

He let out a deep breath and looked at the ceiling. Moments passed. "I'm not sure what I want. It doesn't really matter anyway, does it, Syl?" He set the poker back in its stand and took the last slug of his beer.

"I would hope we could do this amicably." Her throat swelled on her words, and she had to gulp to squeeze them out.

"No other way but friendly," he said sarcastically as he raised his empty beer can in salute. "I'm going to the store."

Sylvia heard the garage door, then the car engine, and he was gone. The weight of what took place pressed down on her so that she didn't feel she could get up. All of a sudden she didn't want to be alone. The dreaded conversation had finally happened and without a major confrontation, yet she felt no relief, only questions. If there wasn't someone else in her life, would she have pushed him away? It seemed absurd, but she felt like she would've been cheating on her lover. She had wanted Tom to surrender without a fight, to give up peacefully, to concede defeat. Now that he had, she felt sorry for herself. Did she want him to find her out? He had confronted her with the business card but stopped short of accusing her of infidelity. If he thought she was having an affair, did he want to know or not? Sylvia decided he didn't want to know because after all this time he could have easily found out. Her behavior was wrong and dishonest, yes, but he chose to look the other way. He would pay a high price to stay in denial. It struck her that he had told her what he wanted after all.

Tom and Sylvia didn't discuss the divorce again before he left on a business trip the following week. Sylvia made her arrangements with Anthony. She drove her car to a long-term parking lot at the airport where they agreed to meet then drive together to Seattle.

Anthony was waiting for her when she pulled into the lot. He was leaning against his car holding a dozen red roses. When she got out of her car, he started singing, "You fill up my senses, like a night in a forest." He walked over to her and embraced her, nuzzling his face in her neck, the roses brushing against her back.

"Did you wait long?" she asked.

"I was so excited I came a half hour early."

"Thanks for the roses. They're gorgeous."

"So are you." He smiled.

Sylvia giggled.

"Everything work out okay when you left?" he asked.

"Not a hitch."

"Then let's get going," he said. "I can hardly wait to act like real people." He opened the car door to his chocolate-brown Targa, stepped back, bowed slightly, and swept his hand outward saying, "Your car awaits, my lovely."

They pulled out of the parking lot and headed north in the steady drizzle. They listened to Fleetwood Mac, Rod Stewart, and John Denver. They sang and laughed and made a pact not to talk about the current state of each other's marriages or their spouses.

The three hours flew by in spite of the increasingly inclement weather. They decided not to stop on the way up so they could maximize their time in the city. None of the usually distinctive mountain peaks, Mount Hood to the east, Mount Saint Helens or Mount Rainier to the north, were visible. The steady drizzle turned to rain. By late morning when they arrived, the blanket of fog still hugged the waterfront as they climbed the hill toward their hotel to drop off their bags.

"I do have a surprise that I haven't told you about," he said as they sipped their espressos inside the quaint coffee shop in Pike Place Market. "But I have to break our pact a little."

"I guess it's okay."

"Maybe I should wait to tell you," he teased.

"You *have* to tell me now," she said.

"I wrote to my parents about us a few weeks ago. I got the reply last week at work."

"Oh God," she said. "I suppose you wouldn't tell me if it was bad—would you?"

"Probably not." He laughed. "They loved you when they met you last year. My mom and Jane could never stand each other. Mom always thought Jane was too provincial for me, and a whiner. They're afraid of Jane's wrath, but as my dad put it, 'When you're lucky enough to find the love of your life, you must not let it slip by. Everything happens for a reason.' Then he went on to invite us to Italy and Greece for a month when we're finally settled."

"This is like a dream come true. They're really behind you, aren't they?"

"We're both fortunate that way," he said.

"Your mom seems so enterprising. Didn't she want Jane to sell those antique Greek copper pots and pans she brought over?"

"Jane didn't want anything to do with it."

"I bought them, remember?"

He nodded. "Now she wants to sell Italian packaged pasta here, like tortellini and gnocchi," he said.

"Clever idea. There might be a market for it," Sylvia said.

"You two will probably start a business. I can feel it."

"A French teacher in business? Sounds unlikely, but I'll have a good accountant to help me."

"Count on it. It could be fun. An import business—foreign travel every year. Maybe you'll even take students to France," he said. "I want you to do what you love, Jake."

"Now I *am* dreaming. You mean no more stitchery kits?"

"Tom's doing his best," he said as he placed his finger to her lips. "Let's go back to our pact and maybe our hotel?"

She answered him with a kiss on the lips that became more passionate than she intended. "We'd better go," she whispered, "before they kick us out."

They walked back through the market where Anthony spotted the bookstore that he had wanted to show her.

"One detour," he said. "You'll love this place."

They wandered hand in hand through nooks and crannies and narrow corridors lined with bookcases jammed with books from floor to ceiling. Anthony climbed on a wooden ladder with wheels to reach the higher shelves in a section marked "French" and selected a book at random to show her.

"Used French novels. Here, you look," he said as he backed down the ladder.

"This doesn't exist in Portland. Not even at Powell's," she said as she began to climb up.

She found a novel by Francoise Sagan, which he bought for her, plus a current issue of *Paris-Match* magazine that they found in another section.

"Now can we go back to the hotel?" she asked as she put her arms around him outside the store.

"I almost thought you'd forgotten," he said. "We're not too far. How about walking? Does the rain bother you?"

"What rain?"

# CHAPTER 4

Spring 1980

The rumblings of divorce in the Beekman household happened to coincide with the more dramatic geological rumblings occurring beneath Mount Saint Helens sixty-five miles away. After one hundred and twenty-three years of inactivity, the general public didn't believe that a major eruption would take place. That belief shifted slightly on March 27, when the first steam-explosion blasted a crater through the volcano's ice cap. By early April, dozens of explosions had expanded the crater. The rise of molten rock inside the volcano was pushing aside the older rocks to make room for itself, creating what became known as "the bulge," an area one mile long and a half mile wide pushing outward four hundred and fifty feet. And it kept growing.

While none of this affected Sylvia's daily routine, a string of sunny days in April brought the slowly steaming mountain into clear view from all the windows along the back of her house. On drives to the grocery store, to her classes in

Portland, or on errands with Alice and Trevor, the mountain seemed to peek around every corner. She couldn't escape its fuming presence and began to feel connected to it somehow.

She, too, had been dormant for a long time. She, too, was releasing a lot of pent-up energy. Whether the mountain would remain content in this quasi-active state indefinitely or would suddenly need to blow its top was unknown. For Sylvia, the lid was off. She filed for divorce and, since she would have her Oregon teaching credential in June, began looking for a teaching job.

Sylvia and Tom discussed separation, but Tom couldn't move out because there wasn't enough money to support two residences. They decided not to tell Alice and Trevor about the divorce yet. He'd have to move out when the divorce was final, which according to Seidmann's timetable would be in three or four months, but Sylvia wasn't sure how that would be possible. They decided to put their house on the market in early summer. They still slept in the same bed together, which seemed odd but so familiar it seemed silly not to continue. There were no angry scenes, no outward hostility between them, and no sex. Besides, they didn't want the children to ask any questions they weren't ready to answer. At least to the children it would look normal. It helped that Tom still traveled a lot, which catered to their strained avoidance of each other. It also gave Sylvia the bed to herself except when the kids and Red crawled in or when she snuck Anthony into the house.

Anthony had said, "After three years, the hotel stays are adding up. I don't think I can afford twice a week anymore."

While Sylvia was always aware of the excessiveness, Anthony had never brought it up before, so she had assumed he could handle it. After all, he was the numbers man. She also thought this would never have been a problem if they had stuck to their original plan and told their spouses six months into the affair.

"What should we do?" Sylvia had asked.

He had looked sheepish. "I hate to ask, but I was hoping we could rendezvous some afternoons at your house."

"Instead, maybe at this point we should 'tell all.'"

"I don't see why we should tell them now, when we're so close to pulling this off without either of them finding out."

"They're going to know eventually. And we're practically asking them to find out by sneaking into my house."

"We just have to be careful, like we always have been."

"Maybe we should abstain."

"Now I *know* how uncomfortable this idea is for you." He chuckled. "I am sorry to have to ask, but I don't see any other way."

Sylvia figured he was probably right. There wasn't much point in telling their spouses now. And she had been half joking when she suggested abstinence. So she had grudgingly relented.

When Alice and Trevor were at school and Tom was out of town, Sylvia and Anthony began meeting in a shopping mall parking lot, where he'd leave his car. Sylvia looked furtively in all directions the moment she entered the lot, barely acknowledging Anthony when he approached. He scrunched down on the floor of the backseat of her car with a blanket thrown over him until they were safely hidden in her garage. She missed the old days rollicking in hotel rooms.

After several weeks without incident, these home stays ended rather abruptly. Sylvia received a phone call from Alice's school while Anthony was there. (They previously agreed that Sylvia would always answer her phone.) Alice was sick, and Sylvia needed to pick her up at school. Of course, she had to take Anthony to his car first. For the first time, Sylvia felt that Anthony stood in her way.

On the drive over, Sylvia lit a cigarette and spoke to Anthony's blanketed frame curled up on the floor in the back. "You realize this means we can't rendezvous at my house anymore."

"I figured as much," he said, his voice muffled.

Alice's stomachaches became chronic. Several times a week either she had to stay home or the school had to send her home once she got there. Maybe Alice, not unlike a threatened animal, could instinctively sense imminent danger on the home front and wanted to be there to protect it. Sylvia took her to the doctor, who found nothing wrong. "Is there anything going on at home that might upset her emotionally?" he asked. Sylvia lied.

After that day, Sylvia watched Alice carefully for any other signs. She had fewer friends at school this year and seemed to withdraw more into her art and craft projects, although this had always been a primary interest for her. When she was only three years old, she would draw and paint for hours at a time. Sylvia, surprised by her total absorption and concentration at that age, encouraged her. When they lived for a brief five months in Southern California, Sylvia shortened the legs of an old kitchen table and set it on the patio outside so Alice could finger-paint, work with Fima clay, watercolor, and make as much mess as she wanted. Each year her various teachers remarked on her advanced art ability. When Alice was seven years old, Sylvia enrolled her in classes at the art museum and had several of her watercolors framed. Sylvia saw that Alice was drawing the same horses and Pegasus that had been her focus for two years, so nothing disturbing was revealed in her subjects. Yet she felt that not telling her about the divorce was unfair and was probably making her sick. Alice was most likely internalizing the secrets that spun around her at home.

Sylvia needed to discuss this with Tom, who had returned the night before after ten days on the road. Trevor didn't need to be picked up from preschool for another hour, and Alice wouldn't be home until after that. It was a good time to talk.

Tom was sprawled on a redwood lounge chair on the cedar deck. Red was stretched out next to him on the deck floor.

The air still carried a winter chill that gave Sylvia goose bumps as she stepped out the sliding glass door and onto the deck. Tom's face was thrust skyward toward the April sun's feeble rays, his eyes closed, his arms folded across his chest as if to trap the sun's warmth in his red flannel shirt. Sylvia noticed the cuffs were fraying, exposing a white rim at the edge of the sleeve where the red threads had worn away. One of his old favorites. Red sat up. Sylvia petted her then moved in front of Tom.

"You're blocking my sun," he said.

Sylvia moved to his left. "I'm worried about Alice."

"You should be."

Sylvia ignored the sarcasm. "So, you're worried, too."

"Divorce ruins kids."

"That's just it. We haven't told her yet."

"So?"

"You act like you have nothing to do with this."

He turned his head and looked at her; his blue eyes were steely and hard. "You're the one who's rushing out the door, and I think we both know why." He turned back toward the sun.

"Fine." Sylvia wasn't going to take the bait. "Can we just talk about Alice?"

"What about her?"

"Her stomachaches are happening more often."

"You said that was common in third grade."

"I'm convinced it's more than that now."

"Why? She's still doing well, isn't she?"

"She does well no matter what. You know that," Sylvia said.

Alice had never really liked school. Sylvia always felt Alice would've been happier in a more progressive environment, like Montessori. The traditional school structure seemed too rote and confining for Alice's exploring, creative mind. She was in their talented and gifted program, which helped a little.

"Then what's the problem?" he asked.

"I'm sure Alice senses that we're hiding something from her, and it's tearing her up inside. I think she needs to know."

"I don't want to tell her yet. I don't think I can."

"Maybe it's in her best interests, not yours." Sylvia immediately regretted the jab.

"How about telling her teacher?"

"I already have."

Tom sat up, swinging his legs to the side of the lounge chair. Red scrambled to get out of his way. "Who else knows that I don't know about?"

Sylvia couldn't tell him that his twin brother, Jim, and his wife, Cindy, knew about her affair two years ago. Jim and Cindy were not only family, but also two of Sylvia's dearest friends. Sylvia was closer to them than Tom was and needed to tell them in person when she had the chance. She, Tom, and the kids had stayed in their home in Boston for her brother Scott's college graduation.

"I don't remember. You know I told my parents and Jessica."

"Your web's just all tangled up, isn't it, Sylvia?"

"I learned from the master."

"I think you already had it down." Tom stood up and started to walk away.

It drove Sylvia crazy that they never seemed to finish a conversation. He always left the room in mid-sentence.

"We need to talk about this. When do you think we should tell her?" Sylvia asked.

"I don't know. I'm not ready yet. I'll take her riding this weekend on her horse and try to feel her out."

She spoke to Tom's back. "I'm not looking forward to this either, you know."

Tom shook his head and walked down the deck stairs to resume his yard work. Sylvia sat on the lounge chair stroking Red as she watched the continuous trail of steam leak out of what had become her favorite mountain. She took a moment each day to just sit and contemplate. She decided to call her mom. Sylvia wanted her opinion on telling Alice and to check on her more regularly now that Steve was back home.

When Sylvia told her mom two years ago that she wanted to divorce Tom, Sylvia was shocked that within five minutes her mother had guessed she was having an affair, and even more surprised when she had guessed it was Anthony. Her mom had said she wasn't born yesterday and had noticed how he couldn't take his eyes off of her when they visited Sylvia and Tom three years ago.

"Oh, Sylvia," she had said in her downcast, disappointed-in-her-daughter tone—the same one she'd used when Sylvia refused to go with her dad to the Country Club Cotillion to "come out." "How could she do this to her father?" was the point her mom had stressed. Sylvia's point had been, "Pretending there's a society in Stow, Ohio, because a new country club was built was a phony joke that I will be no part of." Anyway, her dad hadn't cared nearly as much as her mom.

"You're still coming with the kids this summer, aren't you?" her mom asked.

"I'm counting on it. I need to find a teaching job first." She stopped herself before telling her mother the house would go on the market this summer, too.

"We want to make the plane reservations, so we need to know the dates," she said.

"It's three months away, Mom. There's plenty of time."

"It's already May."

"Okay, it's two months away, because I'd like to come in July. So the kids can go to the festival," Sylvia said.

"They can enter the bike parade again," she said enthusiastically.

"They'd love that, Mom."

"Your dad and I think you should seriously consider moving here, where it's safe. We don't have active volcanoes in our backyard."

Sylvia laughed. “You have tornadoes.”

“One has never touched down here in the Village of Silver Lake,” she said with pride.

“And our volcano may fume for months or years,” Sylvia said. “Besides, it’s too far away from us to be a real threat.”

“Well, I’d feel better if you were closer, honey.”

“Me, too, Mom. I miss you guys a lot.”

Her mother let out a sigh. “Where are you looking for a job?”

“The Portland area, but if I could teach here in Lakeside, it would be perfect.”

“We’re so proud of you going back to your profession. If only you could wait until Trevor’s in first grade—”

“I wish that, too. At least I don’t think it would be full-time. Foreign language teachers are mostly part-time now,” Sylvia said.

“And how about Alice?” she asked. “Is she still having stomachaches?”

“More than ever. We’ve gone through lots of Pepto-Bismol. I was going to ask you—”

“Is all this turmoil really worth it? Why don’t you wait and see? Your father and I haven’t always had a bed of roses, you know. Why don’t you just go on like you have been? Lots of people have affairs and don’t leave their marriage because of it. The French do it all the time, don’t they? At least, that’s what I hear.”

Sylvia smiled sadly to herself at her mother's feeble attempt to change her mind. "Living a duplicitous life isn't something I'm proud of, even if it *is* like the French. Fortunately, you wouldn't understand that, Mom."

Sylvia knew her assumption was safe. Her gorgeous, somewhat glamorous mother had confided in Sylvia of the numerous advances various men at the country club dances had made toward her that she had rebuffed. During a difficult time with Sylvia's dad, she packed her bag once and almost succumbed. But the cheap, scuffed shoes of the potential object of her affection turned her off, and she bolted, never to almost stray again. Her mother's maxim that "you could always tell what kind of a man he is by the shoes he wears" had helped to keep her on the straight and narrow.

"Don't think I didn't have opportunities. I'm being practical. How are you going to make ends meet with his company barely getting by?"

"I really can't talk about this now, Mom. How's Steve doing?"

Silence. Then a stifled sob as she stammered, "Not so good. He barely talks to us. He's in his room a lot."

"Wouldn't it be better for him if he were back in the halfway house?"

"He has to be willing. It's the law."

"If he didn't think he could stay at home, maybe he'd be willing," Sylvia said, even though it was an unfair argument. Her parents could never turn him away, and Steve knew it. He never stayed for more than a few months in any facility that wasn't a lockdown unit. She also realized that without their love and steadfast support, Steve could be on the street like so many others with his illness who had no family.

"He said he didn't belong there. He never thinks he's as sick as the other mental patients," she said.

"He doesn't think he's sick, period," Sylvia said.

"Most of them *are* much worse than he is—alcoholics and drug addicts *and* mentally ill. If you saw them, you'd agree."

Sylvia's household wasn't the only one living in denial. "Is he taking his meds?"

"We have to tell him, but he takes them."

"That's good at least."

"It's better than it used to be, when he refused to take them at all."

"Listen, Mom, you have enough going on without worrying about me, too. I know I'm doing what I have to do and we'll be all right in time."

"I know that once you've made up your mind, there's nothing anyone can say. Just like your dad."

This was an old refrain, which implied she was as stubborn as her father was, "In your dad's eyes, you can never do any wrong," to imply Sylvia could get away with almost anything and her dad would defend her. Sylvia took her mother's remarks as reassurance that she could rely on both of them. Even if they didn't agree with her choices, they would never fail to stand by her.

"This isn't a snap decision, you know," Sylvia said.

"All I would ask is that you allow yourself room for a change of heart."

"That's fair."

"What did you want to ask me?"

"It can wait. I'll talk to you later, Mom. Thanks for taking care of our trip this summer." Sylvia decided she would call her mother every week. Even if her own news wasn't always uplifting, it wasn't as dire as dealing with Steve.

Sylvia went upstairs and lay on the bed, staring at the ceiling. Her mother's words had a ring of truth and reminded her of what she thought when she began her affair. A marriage *didn't* have to break up because of it. How bizarre that she found more virtue in choosing the chaos of divorce and financial ruin than staying married and continuing in an affair. To leave room for a change of heart sounded wise, but she didn't know how to envision a future without Anthony as her husband. She understood what her mom and Jessica were trying to say. Jessica still advised Sylvia to wait and let Anthony move out first, especially since Tom didn't want the divorce.

Sylvia checked the time. Alice would be home soon, and Tom would be leaving to pick up Trevor.

She decided to give Jessica a quick call and dialed her number. It rang and rang. Then she remembered. Jessica was in Hawaii with her husband and three other couples. Their lifestyles were so different; Sylvia wondered why she thought Jessica could give her advice at all. Jessica and her mother seemed to express the same approach—don't be foolish, put on a good face, the risk isn't worth it, keep the peace, slip it under the rug, play it smart. In other words, manipulate to your best advantage. Jessica played tennis the same way, and Sylvia didn't really enjoy her game. Jessica was a lobber and played to win. Sylvia liked a hard ball and preferred a good rally.

Sylvia sat bolt upright in bed at the sound of a crash from downstairs. She must have fallen asleep. The sun was low in the sky, and she figured it must be close to dinnertime. She heard loud music—Elton John's "Yellow Brick Road." She got up and went down to the kitchen. Red was eating, and Alice and Trevor were picking up LEGOs from the floor. Tom was draining spaghetti in the sink.

"I guess it woke you up," he said.

"What was it?"

"Trevor dropped the box of LEGOs."

"Thanks for letting me sleep," she said. She looked around. The table was set. The dog was fed, and dinner was ready. He would manage without her quite well. She suddenly felt like an outsider.

"Here, big guy," said Tom, as he put Trevor in the wooden high chair without the tray attached. He pushed him up to the table's edge and handed him a piece of Italian bread. Sylvia sat beside him and spooned some spaghetti with meat sauce into a bowl for Trevor. Alice took her place, and before

Tom sat down, he asked Sylvia if she wanted a glass of red wine, which she did. He poured two glasses.

"How was school today?" Tom asked Alice.

"We had a sub. We got to have a spelling bee, and I came in second."

"That's wonderful, honey," Sylvia said.

"Do you want to go riding tomorrow?" he asked.

"Can we, Daddy?"

"I'll call after dinner about a horse for me to ride."

"I wish I could ride all day and never go to school," Alice said.

"Me, too," Tom said.

"You already don't have to go to school," Alice said. "What about you, Mommy?"

"Umm, I wish I could lie on a beach and read and swim with you all day."

"And ride horses on the beach." Alice turned to her brother. "What do you want to do, Trevor?"

Trevor looked around at all of them and stretched his arms over his head. "I want to be big and drive a backhoe."

They all laughed.

The phone rang once and quit. Sylvia quickly offered more spaghetti to distract from the interruption, but Tom and Alice were busy feeding Red a strand of spaghetti from the table. No one seemed to notice the phone at all. Trevor said he was done and wanted to get down. She wondered how she could call Anthony back since he had given her the code that he was home alone and it was safe to call. She got up to let Trevor down and started to clear the table.

"Wait, Mommy, I want some more," Alice said.

"I'll have a little more," Tom said.

Sylvia left the spaghetti on the table and refilled her wine glass.

"I need to check with a student about tutoring tonight," she said. No one looked up, so she slipped upstairs. She took the bedroom phone with her into the bathroom and called Anthony.

"Can you get away? Jane left with the kids and her mom for the evening," he said.

She felt a rush pass through her at the possibility of seeing him. Since they hadn't seen each other in a week, her need to be with him overwhelmed her now. "I can't talk. I said I had to tutor. I'll call you from a phone booth."

She went back to the kitchen and started to clean the dinner dishes.

"I'm taking the kids for ice cream," Tom said. "Do you want to come?"

"I can't. I do have to tutor, so I need to leave pretty soon."

It was another ten minutes before they were out the door. Sylvia called Anthony back.

"I have to see you," she said.

"We should have a good two hours. They went to a play at school," he said. "Maybe you could come here."

This would be a first. Sylvia didn't care how risky it was either. "I'll park my car on Highland Circle and walk from there."

Sylvia left a note for Tom saying that she would be back in about two hours. She threw on her parka and jumped in the car. It took five minutes to drive up Eastridge and behind their subdivision to Highland, which was tucked almost behind Anthony's house. She could walk a short distance to the wooded area in back of his house without being seen.

Twigs cracked and leaves shushed under her feet as she made her way in the dark toward his back deck. She smelled cigarette smoke as she approached.

"Jake?" he whispered.

One flight up, she could see his silhouette on the deck off the living room and the glow of his burning cigarette. He smudged it out on the railing. He was barefooted and in his bathrobe.

"Come down here right now." She stood at the bottom of the deck stairs. "That's an order."

"I want you to make love to me in my bed. Anyway, I'm not dressed."

Looking up at him, she slowly climbed the open cedar steps. "Too risky," she said.

"I'll be the judge of that. Take off your coat."

She took off her coat as she climbed.

"Now your sweater."

She removed her sweater.

"Your bra."

He took her clothing from her hands and tossed them to the side. He brushed his hands over her nipples, staring at her breasts. He looked into her eyes and cupped her breasts in his hands. He bent down and lightly sucked each nipple. She grabbed his head in her hands and pulled his mouth to hers. He moaned as she hoisted herself onto his hips, over his robe, and rubbed against his hardened shaft, wrapping her legs around his waist.

He carried her inside and started up the stairs. Halfway up, she slid down his body, opened his robe, and caressed him with both hands. He stepped down two steps, unzipped her pants, and shoved them to her ankles. She sat down and pulled him into her mouth. Moaning, he gradually withdrew and opened her knees. Staring into her eyes, he slipped two fingers inside her. She yelled out. He kissed her on the mouth, then took her hand and guided her further up the stairs.

Almost at the top she said, "Here. I want you to do it here from behind."

She turned and placed her hands on the landing at the top and dropped her knees several steps down. He knelt behind her, spread her thighs with his knees, and pushed hard inside her. She didn't want him to stop. She thought of her dinner conversation at home, and instead of lying on the beach all day, she wished she could lie on top of him all night and never be without him again.

He heard it before she did.

She couldn't run with her pants at her ankles. He picked her up off the stairs and flung her over his shoulder, her bare ass in the air, and ran with her through the kitchen toward the door that opened on to the deck. She heard Jane's voice as he rushed outside.

"Anthony, where are you? I need your help," she screamed. "Ricky, don't you throw up here—get to the bathroom *now*."

Fortunately, their house was so big it took several minutes to get from the garage, through the family room, and up four steps to the kitchen. There also was a wall between the family room and the kitchen that blocked the view to their position on the deck, where she pulled up her pants and he grabbed her clothes. The deck stairs weren't visible from the inside either, so Sylvia could make it down without being seen.

She moved quickly and quietly. She caught the smell of Anthony's cigarette and his voice calling to his wife, "I'm out here," as she disappeared into the woods.

Sylvia sat in the car breathing heavily, her head against the steering wheel. Part of her wished she could just drive away and leave all of this. Another part felt ashamed for what she'd done. What scared her was that most of her shame came after the fact and that, in a few days, she'd feel the same need to do it all over again.

# CHAPTER 5

Spring 1980

"*Lundi, mardi, mercredi, jeudi, vendredi, samedi, et …*" the little boy recited without finishing. A worried look came over his face, and he glanced over to Sylvia for help.

Sylvia softly clapped her hands and said enthusiastically, "*Très bien*, Jean-Paul."

She turned to the girl sitting next to him who was waving her hand. "Natalie?"

"*Dimanche*," Natalie said confidently.

"*Tout le monde, répétez tous les jours de la semaine*," Sylvia instructed with a sweep of her hands.

Slowly, all five children including Alice repeated the days of the week. They were seated in a circle with Sylvia on the living room floor. Red wandered into the middle and plopped herself against Alice's knees. Trevor was dutifully watching *Sesame Street* in the family room during their class time.

A mother of one of Alice's classmates who lived in the neighborhood, learned that Sylvia had been a French teacher and asked if she would consider teaching a beginner's class after school. Sylvia agreed, and the woman had spread the word.

Sylvia was astounded at the extra money she was making with this, for so little time. Two half-hour classes a week at twenty dollars each brought in eighty dollars a week. She considered putting the money aside for herself for later but decided she needed it now. If she could pay off Sears, she wouldn't have to deal with their weekly harassment calls anymore.

She'd been looking for a regular teaching job, but most openings weren't announced until June at the earliest, when the school year was almost over. In the meantime, the in-home class was the perfect alternative. She wondered why she never thought of it herself, although she probably would have dismissed the idea.

When the neighbor first suggested it, Sylvia had been reluctant. With the pending divorce and her ongoing affair, she preferred to keep a low profile in her neighborhood. Since Anthony, Sylvia had gradually pulled back from neighborhood gatherings, with the exception of the occasional unavoidable weekend party when Tom was home. She had even begun to avoid certain mothers at Alice's school functions, especially Jane and her PTA clique. But the neighbor mother had been persistent and offered to organize the whole thing. So far, she was glad she'd accepted.

"*Quel jour est-ce aujourd'hui*?" Sylvia asked them.

Alice, smiling, raised her hand. Sylvia turned to her, winked, and said, "Martine?" Each child had chosen his own French name.

"*Aujourd'hui c'est vendredi,*" Alice said.

Sylvia had them all repeat Alice's answer, without translating into English, "Today is Friday." It was Sylvia's belief that a foreign language should be taught in that language. With beginners it was difficult and took a lot more energy. Sylvia would act out phrases, like charades, or use props, such as calendars. Somehow it worked. Sylvia's dream, though, was to teach advanced French where the students actually had conversations and discussed literature or current events.

The main reason she was enjoying this class was that Alice finally seemed interested in learning *français*. Sylvia was delighted. She had hoped that her children would be bilingual, but her attempts to introduce French to Alice when she was a toddler were rebuffed with a scowl and arms folded across her chest. Maybe she thought her mother was playing a trick on her. Alice had no problem when Sylvia spoke French on the phone or if one of her French girlfriends came over. Maybe Alice could detect when its use was real. Sylvia hadn't tried again, until now, when Alice had decided on her own.

Sylvia turned on the cassette tape to play "Alouette," a simple tune the children would recognize, as well as an ideal song to teach the parts of the body. They were in the middle of the rousing chorus, the only part they knew.

*Ohhhhhh ... Alouette, gentille alouette, Alouette, je t'en plumerai.*

The doorbell rang. Sylvia looked at her watch and saw that the half hour was over. She headed for the door, encouraging the children to keep singing, but before she got there, she saw Anthony's wife, Jane, peek her head in, grinning. Sylvia hadn't seen her in months even though her daughter, Alexia, had been in the French class for several weeks now. Since Alexia was in a carpool, she was dropped off at the beginning of class, and then walked home with two of the children.

"Sorry to just walk in, but I didn't want to disrupt their lesson, in case you were in the middle of something," she said.

Over the last three years, Jane and Sylvia had gone from daily visits (when Jane and Anthony's house was under construction) and every weekend together as couples to surface chitchat and rushed smiles at school. It had been Sylvia's doing in the beginning, rejecting invitations, saying she was busy with school or Tom was out of town, but it had really come to an abrupt halt when Alexia lost interest in Alice. Alice had been heartbroken over the rejection. She always had a tendency to latch on to one best friend, so Sylvia wondered if Alice had become too possessive. Or moody and intense. Sylvia noted that the stomachaches came later. Because Jane's circle of friends revolved around Alexia's, when Alexia no longer wanted to play with Alice, Jane called less and less and, eventually, not at all.

Even so, for Jane to apologize for opening the front door and interrupting was out of character. There was awkwardness in their brief eye contact. Jane looked away, and for a split second Sylvia wondered if Jane suspected something, then decided it was just paranoia after so many months. Jane looked thinner, which gave her a willowy appearance and added height. It accentuated the fact that she was taller than Anthony. Red trotted over, walked between Sylvia's legs, and promptly sat on Sylvia's foot. She looked up at Jane as if waiting to be greeted. Jane wasn't a dog person.

And she went on. "I hope I'm not too early. How are they doing? Alexia really loves it, although she really ought to be learning Italian. That's what Anthony's parents would want anyway. But you would know that after all the stories I told you about them."

Sylvia was already annoyed with Jane's nervous chatter. *As if she knows what Anthony's parents want, and to imply that I know she's right!* Sylvia leaned forward and began rubbing Red's ears.

"Listen to me, rambling on when you have a bunch of kids to look after," Jane said.

"That's okay. They're just singing, or they were," Sylvia said.

The song was still playing on the tape, but the children were fooling around, tapping each other's noses repeating "*le nez.*"

"I wanted to leave a check for you, too," Jane said. "I'm sorry I haven't paid you yet. I owe you for the whole three weeks, don't I? I totally forgot. I have so much going on."

Sylvia stood there looking up at Jane's face, which still carried a pinched expression that was either from worry or her sexless marriage. Her black-brown hair was bobbed just below the ears. Her straight-cut bangs were too short and easily exposed the deep furrow between her eyebrows. What *did* he see in her?

"We're leaving for Big Sur in two weeks to see our old friends the Nybergs. I think I might have mentioned them a long time ago. We're taking Ricky and Alexia out of school for the trip, which I hate to do, but it'll be worth it. How much do I owe you?"

The bow-shaped mouth was still moving, but Jane was talking too much, and after Big Sur, it became all jumbled. Sylvia wasn't sure she heard right. Too stunned to respond, Sylvia took one step down from the foyer into the living room and shut off the recorder. *Why hadn't he told me?* Her stomach caved as if someone had punched her.

Sylvia couldn't talk with Jane or even look at her any longer. She just wanted her to leave. Sylvia could hear the clamor of kitchen drawers opening and shutting and realized the children had disappeared into the kitchen. Standing on the opposite end of the living room with her back to Jane, she closed her eyes for one second. Smiling tightly, she turned and said off-handedly, "You don't owe me anything. I enjoy it too much."

"Now, don't go treating me any differently than anyone else," she said in a singsong tone. She dove into her purse and began rummaging around.

"Consider it a small favor for old friends," Sylvia said. "I need to see what the kids are up to." She circled through the dining room and into the kitchen. The children were now in the family room with Trevor. She grabbed the kitchen counter to steady herself and took a deep breath. Trevor bounded up the steps from the family room followed by Red, Alice, and the others.

"Mommy, Mommy, Mommy," he said gleefully.

Alice was offering them apple juice to drink.

Trevor jumped in, "Me, too, Alice."

Glad for the diversion, Sylvia reached into the cupboard for a stack of plastic drinking cups and said, "Here, honey, let me help you."

Jane said, "Nothing for you, Alexia. We have to go right now. Your dad's in the car. You know how he hates to wait."

*Anthony's in my driveway?*

"The check's on the table. You know I won't take handouts," she said teasingly. She nudged Alexia and gave her a disgruntled nod.

"Thank you, Mrs. Beekman," Alexia said.

Sylvia told her she was very welcome.

And then Jane was gone.

Sylvia took the cups to the table and noticed the check lying there. She stared at the upper left corner: Jane and Anthony Parmentiere. She wanted to tear it up.

The phone rang. Another mother saying she would be a little late. *How could he? A family trip?* Alice asked if they could have a snack. Too close to dinner. But what was for dinner? *How long has he known?* A snack's okay. The kids gathered at the kitchen table for their juice and pretzel sticks.

"Mrs. Beekman, how do you say 'apple juice' in French?" Sara (Natalie) asked.

"*Jus de pomme*," Sylvia said absentmindedly.

They started repeating *jus de pomme* over and over. Even Trevor was getting in the act. Any other time, she would have enjoyed this. They seemed so eager to learn. *Damn him. We're down to once a week in a hotel because he said he couldn't afford it. So how can he afford a luxury vacation?* Colors, numbers, days of the week, months of the year, every object in a room. Learning a language could be so tedious. "What's your name? My name is—" And teaching beginners could be laborious. Right now, anything would seem like drudgery.

Within half an hour the other children had been picked up. Sylvia grabbed a bag of potato chips and sat in front of the TV. Red crawled up beside her and laid her head in Sylvia's lap. Sylvia leaned down and kissed her head, stroking her body.

"Roo Roo, *mon chien*," she cooed.

Trevor and Alice joined her on the couch.

"What's for dinner, Mommy?" Alice asked.

"I don't know. What would you like?" Sylvia asked.

"Can we order a pizza?"

"Yeah, pizza," Trevor said. "I want Hawaan."

Alice and Sylvia laughed. "You mean Hawaiian," Alice said.

"Perfect for Friday night. Let's order pizza," Sylvia said.

The kids gave a cheer, then Alice started tickling Trevor, and in two seconds they were rolling around on the floor. Red made a beeline for the kitchen and was now letting out her soft intermittent bark for dinner. Sylvia got up to feed Red and to call Farucci's for the pizza. Her hands were shaking so badly she could hardly dial the number.

Tom was due home late tonight. Another long weekend without any plans. And another dull Sunday of clipping coupons from the newspaper fliers. She vowed there would come a day when she grocery shopped without them. She and Anthony were supposed to see each other on Monday. She didn't think she could see him. Alice and Trevor were watching TV now. She poured herself a glass of wine and went on the deck for a cigarette. Sylvia felt betrayed. She lit the wrong end, then she burned her finger. It took her three tries.

She went back down to the family room and asked the kids if they wanted to play Candyland until it was time to pick up the pizza. Alice went to the corner storage seat to get the game. The phone rang once. Sylvia didn't get up. They set up the game and began playing. Trevor was on Gumdrop

Mountain when it rang again. Once. Sylvia kept playing. She wouldn't talk to him tonight.

Tonight she needed to be with her kids playing games, eating pizza, reading stories, and watching TV. If she did something normal, she might feel normal, and then maybe she could make it last for the whole weekend.

Not forty hours later, on Sunday morning at eight thirty under a high cloud-covered sky, normal life stopped. The Beekman family was finishing a blueberry pancake breakfast in their kitchen when a distant, thunderous explosion sent the resounding message that the waiting was over.

"What was that?" Alice asked.

"Sounded like a sonic boom," Tom said.

Then it hit her. "Oh, my God!" Sylvia jumped up from the table and ran to the deck. "She erupted!"

Alice rushed outside. Tom grabbed Trevor and was right behind her. They stood in awed silence as the mushroom-shaped plume grew taller and taller. Tom and Sylvia spent most of the day holding their children and watching the dramatic chain of events unfold on their TV screen. May 18, 1980, was a date they would remember for a long time.

No longer content in her quasi-active state, Mount Saint Helens let go of all the pressure that had been building deep inside. Along with the release, the mountain's appearance was altered forever. She was tall and symmetrical until the north face collapsed under the blast. The resulting rock debris avalanche left her with a crater shaped like a horseshoe and thirteen hundred feet shorter. But the volcanic eruption spread much further than her own flanks.

Within three minutes, 230 square miles of old-growth forest flattened into a fan shape north of the mountain. Within fifteen minutes, a massive column of ash thrust fifteen miles into the sky and reached the East Coast three days later. Within two weeks, small particles entered the jet stream and circled the earth.

For Sylvia, the timing of the explosion made her feel even more connected to the mountain than before. The angry mountain took care of Sylvia's immediate problem. She couldn't possibly see Anthony tomorrow if she wanted to, and she still didn't.

The Portland sky soon turned a hazy, yellowish hue that day, and there was a faint odor of sulfur when the wind changed direction and blew southward. Sylvia and Tom learned how lucky they were that the wind had been blowing east at the time of the blast. Most of the ash blew away from them. Even so, the ash fragments that did hit their area became small spheres one-quarter inch in diameter, like tiny mud balls that rained down clogging gutters, windshield wipers, drain spouts, and car engines. Pewter-colored mud was three inches deep at the curb of their street. Everything green, from the towering Douglas fir trees to each single blade of grass, was blanketed in gray silt.

Sylvia was relieved that Tom was at home when it happened. He seemed to instinctively know what to do.

He talked to the neighbors to compare notes on general maintenance, such as unclogging spouts, furnace protection, and chimney hazards.

"Don't go outside until I get you a mask to wear," Tom told Alice. "And that goes for all of us. Not until they lift the warning."

When Alice worried about Red going outside, he reassured her that dogs could handle it better than humans, so she would be safe. It probably wasn't true, but they couldn't keep a mask over her nose anyway, and at least Alice was comforted.

By taking charge in a calm and confident manner, Tom kept everyone relaxed, which reminded Sylvia of Tom's Vietnam days. As a second lieutenant, he had been asked to be an aide to a general, which was a long shot for any new officer. The general was the head surgeon for the army, and Tom had traveled with him to all of the military hospitals. Sylvia had been astonished when Tom had shown her pictures of himself sewing up wounds on Vietnamese children. He basically had become a medic and was a natural. Maybe Tom should have stayed in the army or been a paramedic.

Sylvia was a natural as the news monitor for their household. Fascinated by the reports of the impact of the eruption, she continually tracked the latest details on television and in the newspaper. The TV announcer's voice echoed throughout the house: "Ash continued to spew for nine more hours after the initial blast. In the direct path of the landslide was Spirit Lake, whose temperature rose from forty-two to one hundred degrees, killing all of its wildlife." Sylvia either sat transfixed on the couch or turned up the volume so she could hear from the kitchen. "The Columbia River, which divides Washington and Oregon, was forced to close at the Port of Longview, seventy-five miles away, because the forty-foot-deep channel had been reduced to seventeen feet by ash sediment washed downstream."

Sylvia didn't want to drive to the store because she was worried about her car engine getting ruined, or that the windshield wipers would smear mud and cut off visibility. So she stayed home, and Tom braved the elements. The children loved to see what he brought back and rushed to the kitchen to help him put away the popcorn, TV dinners, chips, and popsicles. They smelled the Kentucky Fried Chicken before he got to the kitchen, so he put it right on the table with the corn on the cob, coleslaw, and biscuits. Sylvia spread out the napkins and paper plates, and they all dove into the bucket.

Trevor and Alice seemed happy that the family was held captive at home. School was closed. Their dad couldn't travel. And Sylvia spent all day in her sweats without makeup. She felt more normal than she'd felt in a long time. She was surprised that she didn't really want a cigarette either. Now that the world outside her doorstep had turned into a giant ashtray, the thought of dropping her own ashes was suddenly distasteful. They talked to their parents in Ohio, Tom's brothers, Sylvia's brother, and out-of-town friends in between who were worried about their safety.

"Can lava come this far?" Alice asked.

"And the big rocks?" Trevor added.

Unfortunately, Trevor caught a news segment where boulders twenty feet in diameter were flowing down the river closest to the mountain. Then he saw a twenty-five-foot wall of debris take out bridges. Sylvia watched Tom pull Trevor onto his lap and lovingly reassure him that this was happening far enough away that it couldn't come here. If only he had been able to comfort her like that. Still, Sylvia knew she was part of the problem. Little by little she had given away so many pieces of herself, it seemed that there was none left over. If he had pulled her in, she might have responded in kind. Years before, Tom said that she showed Red more affection than she did him. It was true. There was a time when she couldn't keep her hands off of him. His pointing it out to her felt more like an affront than an invitation, and she withdrew even more.

When Alice heard that the temperature inside the volcano was six hundred degrees, she fired questions, most of which Sylvia couldn't answer. "What causes a volcano? Why is it so hot inside? Did it melt all the snow on the mountain?" Sylvia could answer that it melted around 70 percent of the snow, which meant a lot of water rushed down. "Let's call Granddad, honey; he could explain it to you." And he did.

"Granddad said the Indians called Mount Saint Helens 'Fire Mountain,' which he said made more sense. Don't you think so, Mommy?" Alice asked.

"I do." Sylvia appreciated that her dad would side with ancient wisdom.

While Sylvia found comfort in her cocoon of captivity, she couldn't ignore the pit in her stomach when she heard the familiar whine of the Targa downshifting as it drove down the hill past their house. She wouldn't allow herself to run to the window for a glimpse of him, but she wanted to. After two days, her longing set in, and she had a difficult time not thinking about him. She thought about calling his office when the opportunity arose but knew a short phone call would leave her feeling worse.

On Thursday morning, Sylvia ventured out to the grocery store for the first time since the eruption. The roads were mostly cleared of muddy ash, and the traffic seemed lighter than it normally would be. Although she had it with her, she didn't bother wearing her mask. She pulled into the parking lot in a space toward the front of the store.

As she was about to get out of her car, the passenger door opened. Anthony quickly slid in the seat and said, "Just drive, Jake, anywhere."

She was too startled to speak. What was this, a heist? She pulled onto the main road and headed away from the shopping center. She felt him staring at her, but she kept her eyes on the road. "How did you know where to find me?" she finally asked.

"I've driven up and down your hill a hundred times, hoping for a chance to catch you. Tom was in the driveway just now. The garage door was open, and your car was gone. I stopped to ask him how everybody was doing, then played him. He bit. And here I am."

"How clever."

"Pull in this parking lot and drive behind the motel," Anthony said.

Sylvia didn't like his tone and was unnerved. She pulled in and turned off the ignition.

"Why won't you look at me?" he asked her.

She turned to look at him. "I am now."

"You're driving me crazy. You haven't returned my calls. How could you just shut me out like that?"

"Shut *you* out," she said. "I'm the one who needs to know why—"

Anthony acted like he didn't hear her. "That's not the way you treat the person you love. If you're upset, you talk about it. You didn't even give me a chance. And I needed to know how you were." He slumped back against the seat and stared at her. He looked like he hadn't slept.

"You're twisting it all around."

"It's real simple, Jake. When you love someone, you trust them. You give them the benefit of the doubt."

"And are you doing that now? Giving me the benefit of the doubt?"

"You could have reached me if you wanted to. We both know that."

"How dare you act like you're the victim here. Like I did you wrong. How do you think I felt when Jane—"

"The big family trip?" he asked sarcastically.

"It came as a shock when Jane—"

"Did you ever think that she might tell you that on purpose?"

"No, why would she do that?"

"Maybe to make you think all was well between us."

"You mean she made it up?"

"No."

"Then you *are* going to Big Sur."

"That's not the point."

Sylvia fell silent. Nothing made sense. He was talking rings around her, and she needed to get groceries. With all of her coupons.

"I just found out myself last Thursday," he said.

"What do you mean?"

"She organized the whole trip and then told me what was happening. I had no choice."

His rambling was beginning to remind her of Jane. She did feel calmer and wasn't sure why. The fact that he so desperately wanted to convince her that he was innocent was probably part of it. It didn't seem like a full betrayal now. More like a half-truth.

"You always have a choice," she said.

"Maybe on paper that's true, but you and I decided that we would do this six months apart, remember? So I can't start mine yet, and I still have to keep some semblance of peace at home."

"Why did she want to tell me?"

"I think she's suspicious. No sex will do that—" he began.

Sylvia gathered the courage and asked, "So, how long has it been?"

Anthony took a beat. He looked deeply into her eyes, then took her chin in his hand. "Is this what you've been worrying about?"

A rush of emotion welled up inside her. She gently pulled her head away and looked down at her lap without speaking.

"I've scarcely been able to put my arm around Jane without thinking that it should be you by my side. And to answer your question, it's been over a year."

Sylvia flopped her head against the headrest. "I really needed to know that."

"I'm sorry, Jake. I should've told you before, but I thought you'd assume—" he said quietly.

"I've been too afraid to assume and too afraid to ask. I've just tried not to think about it."

"I understand."

"In that case, I guess Jane might sense there's somebody else."

Anthony added, "Maybe she doesn't really want to find out the truth, so she's not asking me directly. Just poking around. I think she made a point to pick up Alexia with me in the car, because later she managed to tell me she told you about the trip. And arranging to see old friends without telling me fits, too. Now do you see?"

"Too many games for me."

"Come here. Let me hold you at least."

Sylvia leaned across the gearshift, but it was too uncomfortable. He coaxed her into the backseat for "five minutes." He held her and stroked her hair and gently kissed her all over her face. As Sylvia felt her anxiety leave, heated passion took its place.

"I want to make love to you, but not here," he said.

"I have to go anyway."

"I know. Will you call me at the office as soon as you can?"

"As soon as I can."

When they pulled into the grocery store parking lot, Anthony told her to drive around toward the opposite end where he had parked his car.

As he got out, he turned, smiled at her, and said, "I'm glad we're back to normal."

"Me, too," she said but didn't know the meaning of the word anymore.

She turned the car around and drove to the front of the store and parked. All of her coupons were paper-clipped together and sticking out of the top of her purse. She decided she had to change something, *anything*. Sylvia grabbed her purse, got out of the car, and headed for the store entrance. She paused by the trashcan, reached into her purse, and threw all the coupons away.

# CHAPTER 6

Early Summer 1980

Tom and Sylvia had first moved to Lakeside because of its lake. At least for Sylvia that was the main attraction. Having grown up in a small lake community in Ohio that was idyllic for raising children, she harbored a quiet desire to find a similar environment for her own children. It didn't appear to exist anywhere else, at least not in any of the places they had moved to, but Lakeside had come the closest. Lakefront homes, swimming and boating in the summer, and a school system that was considered the most academically challenging, therefore the most desirable, in the state of Oregon.

The local school board and administration was said to boast that it could pay its teachers less than any other district because teaching here was its own reward. To be a teacher in Lakeside was an honor. For Sylvia it would mean a regular paycheck with benefits and a job close to home. When she heard that one of the high school French teachers was pregnant and might not return, she couldn't believe the luck of her timing. She made a friendly nuisance of herself with frequent visits and phone calls to the administrative offices hoping to learn about the opening before it was in print for the public. Her efforts paid off.

The first week in June, she received the call for an interview with the hiring committee. Thanks to Claudine, her mentor at the university, she had good references. Her main problem, as she saw it, would be the ten-year gap from her last teaching experience, which had lasted only two years. She taught junior high and high school right after college but quit when Tom returned from Vietnam and she became pregnant with Alice. While she'd heard there was a teacher shortage and didn't think there would be an abundance of available French teachers to choose from, she still had to convince the hiring committee she was up to the task. The opening was for beginner's French at Winoga Junior High, which was a mile from her house. She had to have this job—and the right outfit to clinch the interview.

The day before the interview, Sylvia studied her closet and searched for competent with flair, demure yet fun, intellectual without bohemia. Most of the committee would be made up of men, and she had to be careful. To the average American male, a female French teacher had an air of the mystique, which often translated into the *oo la la* Cancan dancer, Brigitte Bardot and topless beaches, or unshaved armpits and unfiltered cigarettes. She had to use her attractiveness to her advantage with a certain *naiveté* and appear savvy enough to handle today's feisty, uninhibited junior high student, which she had been warned was a different animal from ten years ago. Sylvia chose her knee-length pleated, cotton plaid skirt and long-sleeved navy silk blouse and navy blue pumps. She'd have to wear hose, which she hated.

The next morning she got Alice off to school and dropped Trevor at day care for three hours. At least Tom was out of town so she could mentally prepare herself without any distraction. She pulled her hair back at the neck with a navy blue and burgundy striped grosgrain ribbon. Her stomach was in knots. She had a cigarette and gargled with mouthwash. She grabbed a steno pad in case she needed to take notes.

Anthony called to wish her good luck. Her parents had called the night before. Even though it ran through her mind, she didn't expect to hear from Tom. And she didn't.

The receptionist at the administration office welcomed her with a nod and a smile and directed her to the conference room where they were already waiting for her. Just as she thought. Four men and one woman: two junior high principals, one vice principal, the dean of students, and the head of the foreign language department at the high school.

"You're a Lakeside resident I see," said the principal of Winoga Junior High. "We like that."

He went on to explain that the program was changing slightly from last year, which meant that they planned to hire two French teachers, one for each junior high. Thanks to the last teacher, who made crepes in class and even staged a French wedding with her students, French had become so popular that one teacher wasn't enough to cover both junior highs anymore.

"How innovative," said Sylvia brightly.

Sylvia already heard from one of Jessica's friends that the former junior high teacher was well-liked but let the students run the classroom. Several students later complained that they were not prepared for the next level in high school. The teacher apparently taught the class in English and was more interested in making the class "fun" than teaching the language. To Sylvia, a teacher should be able to accomplish both.

"A growing program is our primary goal," the principal continued.

The vice principal added, "We encourage the better students to sign up for French or Spanish in junior high because it satisfies one year of the two-year foreign language requirement for college. Then in high school, with only one more year to go, their schedule is freed up for the wider range of electives offered."

To Sylvia, the foreign language program was sounding more like a popularity contest and a course requirement to get out of the way. Still, they were friendly and didn't seem to stand on ceremony or pretense, which made Sylvia feel comfortable and at ease. They seemed like people with whom she would enjoy working. They asked her how she felt about working with the "dreaded" junior high student and her approach to foreign language teaching and discipline.

"Contrary to what students this age might *say* they prefer, for instance a cool, fun teacher with a *laissez-faire* approach, I think they respond best to a teacher who is well-organized and fluent in the subject. A student will usually seek order over chaos. I also think the teacher establishes the boundaries from day one. The students will respect that environment if the teacher maintains a consistent approach and a sense of humor. I like the basics: raise your hand if you want to speak, no talking to your neighbor, no getting out of your seat without asking. I also would teach the class *in* French, which usually shocks them into silence the first week."

They all laughed at this. Sylvia went on, "After all, that's what they really want to learn to do. To *speak* French."

The dean of students glanced up from Sylvia's résumé. "I see you studied in France, so you must know the language."

Sylvia wondered if that meant no one would bother to find out. Many of her peers had studied in France and still couldn't speak a word of it. She decided to take the initiative.

"*C'est vrai. J'ai fait des études en français à l'Université de Grenoble.*"

Silence. They all looked at each other.

"Very impressive, Mrs. Beekman. None of us here speaks, but it sure sounded good," the other principal said.

The head of the department, a German teacher, cleared her throat. "Actually, I've already spoken to a Mrs. Claudine Menton, Mrs. Beekman's French professor at the university, who has the highest regard for Mrs. Beekman's fluency."

"Thank you, Diedre. I don't know about the rest of you, but I'll put my vote in right now for this young lady. I think the kids will just love her," said the vice principal, beaming at Sylvia.

"Will you excuse us a few minutes?" the principal said.

Sylvia went into the outer reception area. For a school district with a reputation for excellence, its hiring tactics seemed barely professional. She wondered if they took more time hiring a shop teacher. Shop was more hazardous and, in timber country, more practical. Knowing how to mill a two-by-four probably had more value here than learning how to order *escargot* and *foie gras*. After what seemed like no more than ten minutes, the committee called her back in.

Not only was the job hers, she could choose which junior high she wanted. And Winoga was it. The hours were longer than she expected. As a two-thirds-time teacher, she would teach every day from ten to three, which was two-thirds of an eight-hour day. Life would definitely be different, and she was glad.

Now that the job was set, Sylvia could put her heart into the Ohio trip. She called her parents to tell them the good news and that they could go ahead with the plane reservations for early July.

As the days passed and Sylvia thought more and more about being at home with her parents, she could feel the tension of the last few months slowly drain away. She closed her eyes for moments at a time and pictured swimming across Silver

Lake, rowing to the island, or playing with Alice and Trevor on the beach. She always looked forward to going home, but now she needed it. Sylvia was eager to put the divorce, Anthony and Jane, and even her new job aside.

Alice was noticeably more carefree, too. Sylvia believed that children acted like barometers for a family's weather patterns and that Alice was theirs. Before Mount Saint Helens erupted, Tom had told Sylvia that when he took Alice horseback riding and tried to find out if anything else was bothering her, she flat out said no. He didn't want to press her and had convinced Sylvia that they should wait until the divorce was actually final before saying anything to Alice. After watching him handle the children during the volcano drama, she trusted his judgment more than her own. When Alice's stomachaches lessened after the eruption, and then miraculously disappeared during the last week of school, Sylvia had doubted herself even more. Maybe being in the eye of the storm prevented her from seeing its effects.

Trevor kept pestering Alice. "How many days 'til the plane, 'til Ohio, 'til Grammy and Granddad's?"

Alice turned his relentless questions into a game. "Let's go to the calendar and find out!"

They raced down the hall to the playroom, where a large calendar hung on the door. Alice handed him a red felt-tip pen and let him put a red "X" on today. Then she counted with him the number of days left, just like Sylvia had done for Alice when she was little and Tom was out of town.

"Eight days," Trevor moaned.

Alice laughed. "It'll go fast, you'll see."

"We have lots to do to get ready. We *need* the eight days," Sylvia said. "Let's start packing some of your clothes and your favorite books."

"I bet you want *Goodnight Moon*," Alice said.

"And *The Lil Engine That Could*," Trevor said.

The three of them sat in his room to help him decide. Sylvia often marveled at Alice's patience, kindness, and sincere interest in her little brother. She had been this way with him since he was born. Sylvia surprised them with the news that she had decided to take Red with them, too. They were ecstatic.

"Can we take her to the lake and watch her swim?" Alice asked.

"Dogs aren't allowed in the lake, I'm sorry to say." But Sylvia had every intention of sneaking her in after dark when the boathouse was closed and no one was around. She'd surprise the kids with her idea later.

"What about at night?" Alice asked.

Sylvia grabbed Alice and hugged her. "I can't keep anything from you, can I?"

"You mean we can?"

"We're sure going to try."

"Will the water be dark?" Trevor asked.

"Yes, but we won't go in the water. Just Roo Roo," Sylvia said.

"I can't wait. Can we try the first night? With Grammy and Granddad, too?" Alice asked.

"I bet they wouldn't let us go without them," Sylvia said.

Tom arrived home later that evening. The children were already asleep. Sylvia was in the master bathroom when she heard him come in the bedroom and set his suitcase down. She came out with cream smeared all over her face and asked about his trip. He had his back to her and mumbled that it didn't go so well. Then he asked if the kids were excited about Ohio.

"Very. But they're wondering if you're coming later." If he came, this would be the last time they would be in Ohio as a family. At first, she thought that Tom should come for the children's sake. But then, the children wouldn't know it was the last time, and if they somehow overheard adults talking, or something slipped, it would be hysteria for everyone. It would be better if he didn't.

"I thought I might try so I could take them to see my parents, but I can't write it off for business. Besides, it might be awkward for everyone. You *will* see my parents, won't you?"

Sylvia went briefly back into the bathroom to wipe her face. "Yes, but probably not for more than a few days."

She came back out and sat on the opposite side of the bed and turned sideways to talk to him while he still unpacked. "Mom and Dad expect us to go visit them, but the length of time might be a little touchy. You know how my mom covets the time we're there. Probably even more this time since they paid for the tickets."

"A few days are fine."

As he turned around, Sylvia saw how haggard Tom looked. The pronounced bags under his eyes and the sullen expression around his mouth added to his withered appearance. His shoulders slouched either from genuine fatigue or from a load too heavy to carry alone.

"Mom did invite your parents over for a picnic, too," Sylvia added.

Red walked in and jumped on the bed. She looked up at Tom begging for a greeting. He patted her briefly, then shook his head and scowled. "She can't do that when she goes to my parents, you know."

Sylvia leaned over to give Red a bear hug. "She's not even allowed inside their house, so how is she going to get on the bed?"

"I told them about us," Tom blurted into the closet.

Sylvia didn't know what to say and wondered what exactly he had told them. *What reason did he give? Irreconcilable differences? My having an affair?* She still was certain that Tom knew even though he had never really confronted her. *Did he try to put the blame on me?*

"How were they?" she asked.

"Upset. Then Mom said she always worried about my traveling. That it couldn't have done us any good with me away all the time."

"She told me that a long time ago," Sylvia said.

"And they're worried about money—how we're going to make it."

"Did you tell them I have a job now?"

"Yes, so now they're worried about the kids with you working."

"Do they know *why* I have to work?" She stood up and faced him. "Do they know *why* you lost your job? Do they know that you mortgaged our house away?"

"Details they don't need to know. Including, they *don't* know that *you're* the one who wants out."

Tom always managed to shift the blame off of him and back to her. The problem was she always let him. But this time he had spared her the blame with his parents, which had to mean that he felt to blame, too, not that he'd admit it. She suddenly felt bad that her parents knew everything.

"What reason *did* you give them?" she asked.

"I didn't give them any reason. I just said we both wanted it," he said.

She got up to go to the bathroom and sat on the toilet. At least she wouldn't have to pretend everything was all right between them when she saw his parents. She heard Tom shoo Red off the bed and the old bedsprings squeak as he got in. In that instant, she momentarily grasped how wrenching it would be to divide everything. Their history together, in furniture. The antique brass bed that they found in Ohio was the first thing they bought as a married couple. Most of their antiques had sentimental value: the icebox, the mahogany kidney-shaped desk, the wicker chairs and table. The thought of their entire eleven-year-old household being cut in two made her ache.

Sylvia crawled in beside him. She reached over and turned off the bedside lamp.

"I told them we had to put the house on the market right away," Tom said to the ceiling.

They had agreed on this summer, but summer had barely begun. Now his parents knew something hers didn't. So they were even.

"You mean before we leave?" She fumbled for the light without success, swearing under her breath.

"We have no choice. Summer is the best time to sell."

"This is too fast for me," she said. *What if it sold before school started? Where would they go this fast?* She rolled onto her side to face Tom's direction. She could barely make out his profile in the dark.

"What difference does one month make?"

"A lot, to me. Something must have happened."

"Sort of. George is pushing it. He doesn't know how much longer he can pay the mortgage."

"*What?* He promised to take care of it for—"

"For as long as he could," Tom said.

"But when I start work I can pay part of it."

"I was expecting you to."

"So, maybe we don't have to do it yet."

"We don't know how long it'll take to sell. We don't want to foreclose, do we?" Tom asked.

The threat of losing the house hadn't crossed her mind. That she and Tom were dependent on George's benevolence alarmed her now. "Maybe we should have him sign an agreement or something."

"He'd never go for it. We just need to put it up for sale now. There's nothing I can do about it."

Tom had said the same thing about her. "You've made up your mind and want out of this marriage, and there's nothing I can do about it." Wanting him to do something about it was like dragging the horse to water. Tom would rather throw his hands in the air and go thirsty than risk making waves or appearing unreasonable.

Three days later the sign went up in the yard. Jessica still had her real estate license, so they asked her to handle it. Sylvia felt some relief to learn that the house had almost doubled in value in the four years they lived there. There would be enough from the proceeds to pay off all their debts and give Sylvia a small nest egg. She refused to let her mind wander to thoughts of where and how they would live, or if George would pull the plug. That, and facing the neighbors' questions. For now they told Alice that they had to move because Tom's business wasn't doing as well as they hoped, but she would still go to the same school.

Sylvia didn't know where she belonged. Anthony tried to reassure her with expressions of his love for her and their blissful future together, but the crashing reality of selling her home, finalizing the divorce in two to three months, and starting almost full-time work removed the tint from her romance-colored glasses. Words. What good were words to her now? She was still counting on him for the long term, but what Sylvia needed most was the unconditional comfort of home with her parents.

# CHAPTER 7

Mid-Summer 1980

The flight arrived on time at the Cleveland airport on a hot and humid July afternoon. Sylvia, Alice, and Trevor exited the plane in eager anticipation of the usual welcome at the gate: Grammy with tears of joy armed with flowers and a one-pound bag of M&M's, Sylvia's favorite; a stuffed animal for Alice and Tonka truck for Trevor, Granddad grinning at her side. They stood there looking around. No one greeted them.

The disappointment on her children's faces was obvious. "Maybe they decided to wait at baggage claim."

"They never do that," Alice said.

"Or they got stuck in traffic," Sylvia offered.

"Can we get Red now?" Trevor asked. "Is she barkin'?"

"She's probably so tired from all that barking that she's asleep in her kennel," said Sylvia.

They could hear Red's muffled barking throughout most of the flight. Sylvia wondered why the tranquilizer didn't work, then figured it might have worn off because of the one-hour delay out of Portland. She asked the stewardess if there was a way to check on their dog or, at least, change seats so they didn't have to listen to her and worry. The stewardess was sorry, but the flight was full. They just had to endure it, and Sylvia had to constantly reassure her children that Red was fine, just nervous on the plane.

Red's kennel was the first cargo item to be unloaded. Her toys and rumpled blanket were all strewn around inside, but she wagged her tail and let out a hoarse bark to greet them. Alice attached her leash and let her out. Grown-ups and children walking by stopped to admire Red, chatting with Alice and asking if they could pet her dog.

"Everybody loves Roo Roo and says how beautiful she is," Alice said like a proud parent.

Sylvia needed some help to collect their bags, manage the dog, and gather the kennel. She hoped her parents were okay. They had never been late before.

"Why don't you take her outside and wait for me?" Sylvia said to Alice. "Trevor, I need your help with the bags."

"I'm strong. Like 'Creble Hulk," Trevor said with a "grrr" as he took the monster's stance.

Sylvia laughed and found a porter. She told Trevor to help find their suitcases as they rolled by on the conveyor belt. Once everything was loaded, they joined Alice outside. Sylvia instructed them to stay with the bags while she walked Red across the street to a small patch of grass near the parking structure.

And they waited. A half hour passed. Sylvia called the house once, but there was no answer. Then she thought to inquire about a page. Her parents could've tried to page her, but because of the commotion with Red, the bags, and the kids, she didn't pay any attention to the loudspeakers. She hesitated to leave the kids and Red at the curb with the bags, but she needed to find out if her parents had tried to contact her. It would only take five or ten minutes. She bolted up the escalator and found the phone. Sure enough. They had tried. Something with Steve. She breathed a sigh of relief. She wasn't ready to hear that something might have happened to her mom or dad. Steve's ups and downs were so commonplace to her after ten years that she had come to accept that the Steve she once knew would never be back. She had closed off that part of her that missed him.

The message instructed her to get a shuttle and not to worry about the cost. Her dad would reimburse her, but she wished he didn't have to. At least when the house sold she could pay him back the five thousand dollars he had loaned to Tom three years ago.

"What's the matter, Mommy?" Trevor asked.

"Everything's okay. Grammy and Granddad had to take Steve to the hospital. He got sick again. We have to find a shuttle or cab."

"Where will Red go?" asked Alice.

"We'll need a van, I think," Sylvia said.

The shuttle service wouldn't take a large dog unless it was in a kennel, which wouldn't fit, so the cab service arranged a van for the hour ride to Silver Lake. It was expensive. Seventy-five dollars, which would almost wipe Sylvia out. Lucky thing her dad had already offered to pay, although she never needed much cash when she came home. Her parents would never let her pay for anything.

As they approached Silver Lake, Sylvia instructed the driver to take the back way, along the lake. Beautiful homes sat back from the water's edge with rolling lawns and private docks. The mile-long lake had an island in the middle. When they were kids, they took rowboats and picnic lunches there. Now she did it with her own kids. The bucolic neighborhood streets intertwined in a maze, some with sidewalks, some without. Even the names had intimacy: Maiden Lane, Hastings Road, and Lakeland Parkway. Giant maple, cherry, oak, and flowering dogwoods (although not in the summer) lined them all. Crocus, tulips, and daffodils flourished in the springtime, filling the small garden islands that separated street intersections. This lake community of two thousand hadn't increased in population in fifty years thanks to the efforts of the residents who managed to maintain their quality of life here. The same advantages that Sylvia had as a child still existed today: walk to school, home for lunch, freedom to bicycle anywhere, swimming and boating in the summer, catching turtles in the lily pads on the lake's rim, ice skating and sledding in the winter. Carpools didn't exist. She rolled down a window to breathe in the fresh lake smell.

Red stood on the backseat and immediately stuck her head out. Maybe someday Sylvia would be back for good.

She couldn't help but contrast her feelings for this place today from those she had in adolescence. It wasn't the place she disliked then; it was the way her mom used to embarrass her about it. "We're from Silver Lake," she'd say in a haughty tone in conversations with checkout girls, receptionists, or anyone she met for the first time. Sylvia had secretly harbored a similar feeling of pride, but would never have said it out loud to anyone. Too pretentious. She had simply pretended not to care and expressed minor rebellion in the form of Bob Dylan music, sneaking out to coffee houses, dating a college dropout who raced sports cars, and refusing to attend the phony cotillion.

They pulled in the driveway, the familiar white gravel crunching under the tires. The pin oak trees that her dad had planted forty years ago towered over the house. The half-acre lawn smelled of freshly cut grass. Stately roses stretched along the front walkway, and the Japanese maple spread its lacey leaves in profusion in the right corner of the yard. Red geraniums hung in baskets or filled ceramic pots on the front stoop and the brick-walled side patio.

They tumbled out of the van, grabbing luggage and letting Red roam the yard. Alice and Sylvia stopped and looked at each other when they heard shouting from somewhere. It seemed like it was coming from the backyard.

Sylvia paid the driver and told him to leave the bags in the driveway. She started to walk around the side of the garage to the back when Steve appeared. She almost ran into him. His thick medium brown hair was greasy and covered his ears; his unshaven stubble was filling in and would soon be a beard. He appeared bulkier and more unkempt than the last time she saw him.

"What are you doing here?" he asked. He weaved, trying to get around her. "Get out of my way."

Sylvia called to the kids to get in the house. Red was standing beside her now.

"Where are you going?" she asked.

"I'm *not* going back to the psych unit. And you can't make me." He pointed to Red. "Oh no, what's the *dog* doing here?" he moaned.

"We didn't want to leave her at home. Who's making you?"

"Making me *what*, Sylvia? You're not making any sense."

"Who's making you go back to the psych unit?"

"Dad. He tricked me, you know. He told me I was going in for tests, and he left me there for a month!"

"You mean ten years ago."

Her dad was standing ten feet behind Steve, listening to their conversation. He held his finger to his lips so she wouldn't acknowledge him.

"July 1970. We drove up together, and a psychiatrist, Dr. Herbert Rusk, told us I had a severe mental condition, that I was psychotic! I couldn't believe he was talking about me."

Steve began combing his hair with one hand. "And Dad left me."

"Maybe you can help me with my bags. We just got here." Sylvia pointed to the bags still in the driveway.

His face went blank. He blinked. "Sure." He glanced up and down and left and right, mumbling as he approached the luggage. Her dad had disappeared toward the back of the house. Steve reached for the heaviest bag, which was underneath a smaller one. As he struggled to lift it free, his arm began to shake. Beads of sweat sprung up at his hairline and slowly dripped down his temple. His brow furrowed in concentration and his face contorted in anger as frustration enveloped him. He let go of the bag. "I can't do this." Dejected, he steered around the overgrown hemlock bush at the edge of the patio and went into the family room through the sliding glass door.

Sylvia stood there a minute. He was eight years old all over again. When his new Lionel train engine jumped the track because he hadn't slowed it down in the curve, he had worn the same expression. Steve couldn't wait to be at the helm to run the train through the miniature town their dad had built, and then he had done something wrong. He had said he didn't know how to do it right. That he couldn't do it. He had just shuffled away, head down in disappointment. That defeated little boy, who was trapped in this six-foot, two-hundred-twenty-pound frame, would never let him leave home. It was too late now and too scary.

Alice came out and said that Grammy was crying. Sylvia's dad met her at the door and gave her a hug. "Nice welcome home for you."

Sylvia asked if she could do anything.

"You already calmed him down. That's more than we could do."

"What happened?"

"I was hoping he'd be in the clinic before you got here, but he wouldn't go. Maybe go in and see your mother. You're the tonic she needs. Speaking of, how about a snort?"

"Sure, I'll have a gin and tonic."

Her mom, all red-eyed and puffy, came in to greet her. She was already laughing with the kids and asking what they wanted to eat. Red was bowing on her front paws. Alice and Trevor became distracted with the dog and took off for the backyard to play. Sylvia hugged her mom and told her how happy she was to be home, how lovely the house looked, and particularly, how beautiful she was even after all she'd been through with Steve. At sixty-one she didn't look a day over fifty.

Her mom usually took two solid weeks to get the house ready before a visit from her out-of-town children. By the time they arrived, she was worn out. Sylvia's brother Scott had warned her never to surprise their mom with an unannounced visit. He said he did that once, and she seemed almost let down and disappointed; the house and garden weren't immaculate, and the refrigerator wasn't filled with his favorite foods. Always the hostess, even for her kids.

“I’m so glad you’re here, but I wanted everything to be perfect for you, and now it’s ruined.” Her mom flopped down in the swivel chair and reached inside her purse. She handed Sylvia a bag of M&M’s.

“Nothing’s perfect. We’re just glad to be here.” Sylvia ripped open the bag and dropped an ice-cream-scoop-size pile into her mouth. Through a mouthful Sylvia asked her mom if she wanted to talk about what happened.

“He wouldn’t get out of bed for his meds and was surly. When I insisted, he sat up and yelled at me to stop bothering him.”

It always sounded funny to hear her mom say “meds,” as if her acceptance of Steve’s condition depended on how readily she adapted to caseworker jargon. As if she could mother him out of it, as if Steve would someday outgrow his mental illness.

“That doesn’t sound that unusual. Why do you think he needs to go back to the hospital?”

Sylvia heard the familiar tinkling before her dad entered the room holding two drinks. He handed Sylvia hers and tapped the few ice cubes in his with his index finger.

“He was running around in the front yard in his underwear, saying we were all against him, and I was afraid when—” She started to cry.

“When he said he should just do away with himself,” her dad finished. He looked at his wife, Vivian. “Did you want something to drink?”

Her mom rarely drank alcohol. She said she didn't like the taste or how she felt after two sips. Occasionally she asked for a glass of sherry, but she did that just to be social. She shook her head no.

"Has he ever tried?" Sylvia took a sip of her drink.

"Once. We got home just in time," her dad said.

It dawned on Sylvia that there was a lot they hadn't told her and a lot more they had endured. She got up to get more ice cubes. "Have you talked to his psychiatrist?"

Her mom headed toward the kitchen with her. "That's who said we should bring him in, but Steve has to be willing."

"Where is Steve now?" Sylvia asked.

Her dad joined them in the kitchen, which barely fit three of them comfortably. "Upstairs in his room. I think I hear him coming down." The heavy tread on the stairs was unmistakable.

Steve started to enter the kitchen, but made an about-face and went to the living room. Sylvia peeked around the doorway and saw him sit in his favorite armchair, twirling his hair. His blue and black pinstriped T-shirt that looked like his pajama top had stains dribbled down the front and pulled across his protruding belly. He caught her glance and scowled, mumbled, then got up and returned to the kitchen. Holding his elbows close to his sides, he moved stiffly toward the refrigerator in what looked like an effort to avoid touching anyone. Sylvia had heard that schizophrenics were often physically uncomfortable with human touch, so she tried to remember not to touch him. Sometimes she forgot and had casually placed her hand on his shoulder or arm, which had caused him to pull back sharply and ask, "What are you touching me for?"

"Excuse me." Steve pulled a gallon jug of milk from the shelf and started guzzling it from the container.

"Is that the only milk you have?" Sylvia asked calmly.

"Steve, others want to drink from that," her mom said.

"Quit bugging me." He took another swig from the jug.

"This is our house, and you'll respect that others—" she began.

Her husband, Matt, waved his hand at her to "pipe down." He reached for Steve's pill tray on the counter. "Here's your pills, Steve. Looks like you missed this morning's dose," he said pleasantly.

Sylvia noticed that the tray's flaps were down in four or five sections. He'd missed several days.

Steve looked down at the tray and then at Matt. He slapped Matt's hand, knocking the tray to the floor, sending the pills skittering. "Forget it!" He yelled. "And I want everybody to leave, right now!" He stormed out of the kitchen down the three steps to the family room.

Sylvia followed him as far as the sliding glass door. Barefooted, he strode across the patio, then gingerly eased onto the gravel and stood in the middle of the driveway. He waved his arms up and down and shouted at whoever was in his head about how he couldn't stand the noise and everyone should leave him alone.

And she began to wonder. How violent could he get? The only incident she knew about happened a few years ago in a neighboring town. Steve had been questioned for "suspicious activity" because he was standing around a Dunkin' Donuts at midnight. When the police continued to press him for answers, he had become angry and belligerent. They had to hold him down to handcuff him, and he ended up in jail. Of course, Matt had bailed him out right away. Since he refused to take his meds, who knew how he might behave? And her kids. They might not be safe here. Somebody had to do something.

Her parents were now standing beside her. Sylvia felt helpless. She walked to the back patio door to look for Alice and Trevor. They were sitting cross-legged at the far end of the yard under a grove of pine trees with Red. She went back to her parents. Her mom was wringing her hands and looked up beseechingly at her husband. "Matt, try to talk to him." He went out and asked Steve to come inside. Steve wouldn't. He just yelled louder.

Since Steve always listened to his big sister, Vivian asked Sylvia to go out and try to calm him down. As she started out the door, Matt turned on his heel and ushered her back inside. "It's no use. No one can talk any sense into him. I have to call the Silver Lake Police."

Sylvia thought of the community police department as something akin to Mayberry but said nothing.

Vivian buried her face in her hands. “He can’t go back there.”

“We have no alternative.” Matt put his arms around her and spoke lovingly. “Chief DeCicca is good with him. He’ll get him to cooperate, like he has before.”

Sylvia rarely saw her dad initiate affection. Her mom said the “reserved Swede” in him made him uneasy with any outward display of feelings, but he never forgot a birthday or anniversary. And his cards were always mushy. Sylvia was glad to see him comfort her now when she needed it most. Then Vivian left the room.

“And then what?” Sylvia asked.

“And then they take him to Crestview,” Matt said.

# CHAPTER 8

Mid-Summer 1980

The policemen arrived within five minutes. Steve was still in the driveway when the two cars drove up. Sylvia knelt on the couch in front of the living room window to observe her brother. Shoeless, wearing his baggy, dirty blue jeans that were worn and frayed at the knees, he was like a stranger to her. She had less compassion for him here in Ohio than when she was at home in Oregon. Seeing him in their parent's house, perpetually agitated, with dark circles under his eyes and irritation in his voice, it was as if she had to choose between him and her parents. While she felt sorry for him, her compassion was for her parents.

She glanced up and down the street. No gawking neighbors. No flashing lights. No unnecessary drama. Good.

Vivian steered Alice and Trevor toward the kitchen to make chocolate milkshakes, but there was no way she could distract them from what was happening out front. They joined Sylvia at the window. Vivian bowed her head and said she was the one who needed to be distracted. She went downstairs to the basement rec room to play the piano.

"Do they have guns?" Trevor asked.

"Yes, but they don't need them now. Only if someone else has a gun, too," Sylvia said.

"Does Steve have a gun?" he asked.

"No, Trevor," Alice said, rolling her eyes.

"He's not yelling anymore," Trevor said. "What's Granddad doing?"

"Giving Steve his shoes and probably explaining to the policemen where to take him." Sylvia heard the theme song from the movie *The Sting* filtering from the basement.

Steve appeared remarkably calm now. He was probably afraid of the police because of experiences like the one at Dunkin' Donuts. If he never understood what he had been doing wrong in the first place, he might think they could take you down for anything.

The policemen ushered Steve, without handcuffs, into the backseat of one of the patrol cars. Matt walked along beside him until he was seated, then leaned into the car a moment. He shook hands with Chief DeCicca and walked toward the house, head down, as the cars drove away. She put her arms around her children and pulled them close to her.

When Matt came through the living room, Sylvia asked for the second time that afternoon if there was anything she could do.

"Actually, there is something," he answered. "I've gotta go to Crestview to sign Steve in and make sure a doctor sees him right away. I need to call first to let them know he's coming. While I'm doing that, maybe you can put some of his clothes together."

She said she'd take care of it. "How long do you think you'll be gone?"

"About an hour and a half." He tilted his head toward the ceiling as if to listen for something. He shook his head. "Is your mother playing what I think she's playing?"

Sylvia nodded. "I think she just likes the melody."

"I think you're right."

"Let's go out to eat when you get back," Sylvia said.

"Fine. I don't imagine anyone feels like cooking tonight."

Sylvia went upstairs to her old room—a converted attic that ran the length of the living room. The walls were the same robin's egg blue but were dull and grimy from neglect. All the curtains were pulled shut, and it was sweltering. The air was thick with cigarette smoke, and the large glass ashtray on the nightstand was teeming with butts three inches high. She opened the curtains and turned on the air-conditioning unit that sat in the window between the twin beds. It kicked on with a lurch and began to whir. One twin bed was made but piled high with Steve's clothes. Dirty socks and underwear were strewn helter-skelter on the floor. The bed Steve slept in was unmade. The mattress was rotated slightly off the box spring;

the sheets were twisted and pulled from the corners; and the pillows were bunched into balls. Her mom must have cleaned this mess a thousand times and probably couldn't bring herself to do it again.

The built-in bookcases had old textbooks from high school and pictures of Steve in his glory days as a track star. Numerous trophies lined the shelves. Also displayed was a scrapbook with all the newspaper clippings about him, touting him for the Olympics. So much hope then. She picked up a framed photo of the two of them in college, taken when he had accompanied her to a sorority dance. Her own loss took hold of her, and she could no longer look at what used to be or she might lose control. This room felt like a grave and the memorabilia an obituary.

She went to the dresser and grabbed shorts, polo shirts, and pajamas. The underwear drawer was empty, so she picked through the items on the floor and went back downstairs. Matt got his toothbrush, toothpaste, and deodorant. No razors allowed. He packed them into a small duffel and left.

It was almost eight o'clock by the time he returned. Vivian didn't feel like leaving the house, but the kids managed to talk her into going to Swenson's for hamburgers for "curb service." They told her she could go in her jammies if she wanted to because she only had to sit in the car. Besides, it had become a ritual for Sylvia to go to her favorite hamburger place her first night in town. Vivian finally agreed to go, but she wouldn't wear her pajamas. When they got home, it was almost nine thirty and getting dark.

Alice and Trevor, who were still on West Coast time, were full of energy. Alice hadn't forgotten their plan to sneak Red to the lake for a nighttime swim. She began working on Grammy and Granddad.

"To the lake? Now?" they asked.

Sylvia explained to her parents what the children had concocted before they left Oregon and how excited they were to try it.

"It's not dark enough yet," Granddad said.

Grammy flopped into an armchair saying she hadn't had a good night's sleep in days and couldn't keep her eyes open. "I should go to bed. Who knows what will happen with Steve tomorrow."

"You might sleep better if you go for a walk first," Sylvia said.

Granddad put his hands on his hips and looked at the children. "If we're gonna do this, we'd better get some bug spray. Those mosquitoes will eat you alive."

Alice threw her arms around his neck. "Oh, thank you, Granddad!"

"Well, we never did this before. It's worth a try." He looked over at Vivian and arched his eyebrows. "But only if we *all* go."

"I'm not going to be the party pooper," she said.

"You might want to throw on your swimsuits, kids," Granddad said.

"You mean we can swim in the dark, too?" Alice jumped around like a bean.

Trevor glanced at Sylvia, a concerned look on his face. "You said we wouldn't swim in the dark, just Roo Roo."

Sylvia knelt down to him. "You don't have to go in, honey, if you don't want to. Granddad thought it might be fun for you and surprised us with the idea. Okay?"

"Okay," Trevor said.

Sylvia wore her bathing suit so she could stay close to Alice, but also because she would love to swim at night. It had been years since she snuck down to the lake. The last time was with Steve, when they were teenagers. She wondered if he would remember and decided to ask him when she visited him. At least it would be something to talk about. She glanced at her parents. "You guys are amazing. How many grandparents would do this?"

"It's silly not to go along with their fun. How many chances do we get?" her mom said. "We need some fun right now anyway."

The kids wanted to give Grammy a special job, so they put her in charge of walking Red on the leash. Sylvia did warn them on the walk down that they had to be real quiet when they got there. They had to whisper. It was still illegal to swim after hours, and the police patrolled often. She could envision the same policeman who had escorted Steve to the local asylum finding them frolicking in the lake at night, thinking the whole family had lost its marbles.

The humid summer night air hugged them like a cozy thermal shawl. Everywhere they looked, lightning bugs dotted the darkness with their greenish-yellow glow. Alice showed Trevor how to move cautiously to try to catch one and cup it in the palm of his hand. When he couldn't do it, Granddad put his hands over Trevor's and trapped one for him. Then they let the lightning bug go.

They turned onto the lane that approached the lake. A faint mist hung eerily over the rippleless pitch-black water. Red began pulling on the leash so hard that Grammy had to hand her over to Sylvia. They walked in the direction away from the boathouse where a floodlight shined brightly at the entrance. Sylvia let Red off her leash as they reached the crest of the tree-covered, grassy hill that sloped toward the beach. On its right was the concrete walkway that led to the stationary dock and diving boards. The dog bolted, and Alice took off after her.

A wispy curtain of clouds that seemed to drape across the sky created a sheer-like film over the stars. The effect made it more difficult to see, and they hesitated before heading down to follow Alice.

Trevor brushed against Sylvia and took her hand. "Where did Alice go?"

Sylvia could make out her daughter's hazy contour at the shoreline and a few feet from her, Red's silhouette in the water. Sylvia bent down and lifted Trevor up briefly for him to see Alice before they began their descent. The ground was riddled with tree roots.

"Watch where you're going here," Matt warned Vivian as he grabbed her elbow.

They wound their way through the dangling swings that hung at least fifteen feet from the top of the giant swing set. It was the same set that used to stand in the shallow water next to a metal sliding board when Sylvia was a child. The sliding board was still in the water. As they approached the bottom of the hill, the lake opened up before them and the sliding board came into view toward the left end of the beach.

Trevor let go of Sylvia's hand. "Can I go down the slide?" he asked.

"Sure, but wait 'til I'm in the water to catch you."

"Look, Grammy." Trevor pointed. "Alice and Red are in the water."

Red was standing in the water up to her neck. Alice was lying on her stomach balancing herself on her elbows, her legs floating behind her.

"I see them, honey. Aren't you cold?" Grammy called out to Alice.

"Shhh, Mom. You have to whisper!" Sylvia said.

When they reached the stone wall that lined the beachfront, Trevor shook off his sandals, hopped off the two-foot wall down to the sand, and ran to Alice. He put his feet in the water, ran back to his mother and grandparents, and, cupping his hands around his mouth, whispered, "The water's warm!"

Sylvia and her parents chuckled as they watched him scurry off to rejoin Alice and Red. Within a minute, he was lying in the water next to them.

"What are we waiting for?" Vivian asked. She slipped off her Keds without untying them and, with a spring in her step, made a dash for the water. Sylvia was glad to see her mom feeling happy again, even if only for brief moments. They would all be better off if they lived closer to each other.

"Hell, I should've brought my suit, too!" Matt said as he and Sylvia sauntered over to wade in the water.

"It *is* warm." Vivian waded in up to her shins.

"I want to go down the slide," Trevor said. "Will you catch me, Granddad?"

"Me, too," said Alice.

"Your mom and Steve used to love going down the slide headfirst," Grammy said, kicking up small splashes with her feet.

"And Steve went off the high dive when he was only six!" Granddad added.

Alice and Trevor took turns on the slide while Matt stood at the end in two feet of water. Red trailed them and stationed herself behind the ladder. When she started to bark, Sylvia told them they had to stop.

"We'll get caught for sure," she said.

"Let's head home," Vivian suggested.

"Not yet; I want Red to swim," Alice complained. "She's not even trying."

"Maybe she's not used to the lake," Sylvia said.

"If I swim, maybe she'll follow me." Alice slowly started to breaststroke toward the floating dock fifty yards out, then turned over on her back and called to Red in a whisper. Red fixated on her then began pacing. Alice stayed in one place treading water, cooing softly to Red.

"You're too far. Come back in, Alice," Trevor whispered loudly.

Sylvia had total confidence in Alice's swimming skills, but she wasn't comfortable with her daughter being in ten feet of murky water by herself in the dark. The outline of the dock was fairly visible, but a shadowy area obscured the water in front of it.

"I can't see Alice very well," Vivian said. "Trevor's right. Make her come back, Sylvia."

"Aw, bunch of worrywarts. She's all right. Let her have some fun," Matt said. "I used to swim in the *river* when I was a kid."

"That's what you were used to doing, Dad. I'll go in with her," Sylvia said.

Vivian and Matt decided to put their shoes back on and wait on a bench in the grass above the stone wall.

"Come sit with us." Granddad extended his hand to Trevor.

"I want to go with Mommy and Alice, but I'm afraid," he said.

Sylvia didn't want him to do something that truly frightened him, but maybe swimming in the lake might help allay his fear. "Do you want to ride on my back to the dock?" Even though Trevor swam like a fish in deep water in a swimming pool, all confidence could disappear in unfamiliar waters, especially at night.

Trevor agreed. She backed her legs in to shore and asked him to climb on board. He wrapped his legs around her waist and held on tight to her shoulders. Red started to follow them, but stopped when the water was up to her neck.

Alice giggled when Sylvia and Trevor caught up with her. "Isn't this fun?" Then she pretended she was a sea serpent that was going to get them.

"Stop her, Mommy!" Trevor begged.

Alice arrived at the dock first and clambered on top. Sylvia guided Trevor to the ladder. Alice took his hand and helped him up. Sylvia stayed with them until she saw that Trevor was feeling safe, relaxed, and having fun with Alice. Now she could go back and try to get Red to swim out to them.

"I'll only be a few minutes. Stay here until I come back to get you," Sylvia instructed. "Maybe Red will finally swim because we're all here."

As she turned to go, Alice and Trevor were lying together on their stomachs looking in the direction of the island, which was not visible through the mist. "And be quiet!" she added.

She eased through the water on her back and noticed that a thicker cloud cover had settled over the night sky. She turned over on her stomach to move more quickly.

On her way to shore, Sylvia heard nothing but crickets and the riffle of water gliding smoothly over her body. Red was facing her direction. Her parents were sitting on the stone wall. She was halfway there when she heard panting. Startled, she whipped around. Alice was right behind her.

"I wanted to be with Red when she swims," Alice said.

"Trevor can't stay alone!" Sylvia gasped. She could see the dark shape of her son's body perched on the edge of the dock. "Go back to shore right now," she told Alice.

"Don't leave me here," Trevor wailed.

"Stay there, Trevor. I'm coming," Sylvia yelled, pulling hard through the water, never taking her eyes off of him.

"Hurry, Mommy," he cried out, bouncing up and down.

"I'm almost there," she said.

When she was about ten feet away, Sylvia watched in horror as Trevor suddenly plunged into the water. She scrambled frantically to reach him as his white-blond hair dipped under the surface. His arms were straight above his head, and the water was now to his elbows. *Kick, Trevor, kick!* She lunged herself forward with a strong thrust of her legs and reached for one of his arms. She caught his wrist and yanked him up on top of her as she flipped onto her back.

Her breath was ragged. His heart was pounding. Had she been two feet farther away she might not have been able to see him at all. With his arms straight up, he could've sunk like a stone. Why had he jumped? Had he slipped? Had he thought she was closer to him and would catch him?

The dock was so close she decided to rest there before swimming back to shore. She paddled backwards with one arm. Trevor wasn't coughing. *Must not've taken in any water. Must've held his breath.* He whimpered as he lay motionless on her heaving chest, while she repeated to him over and over that everything was okay.

She held on to Trevor with one arm and hoisted herself up the ladder with the other. She lay down on the dock with Trevor still on her chest, looking up at the sky. The clouds were gone. All she could see were stars shining, winking at her, letting her know all was right with the world, with her world, if only she could see it that way. *Do I want too much? Why must I always go for the moon when I have enough with the stars?* She blamed herself for being careless. How could she have left Alice in charge? Poor Alice. It wasn't her fault.

Trevor seemed calm, and his breathing was normal. He raised his head and rolled off of her. "Can we go back to Grammy's now?"

She put her arms around him and silently thanked God for his safe return to her. Then she went down the ladder into the water and turned around so Trevor could ease onto her back. They slowly started for the shore.

She could see Alice and her parents standing next to Red, who was rolling around on the sand. She could hear them distinctly. No one was whispering anymore.

"How're you going to clean Red off is what I want to know," Matt said.

Vivian looked up at Sylvia and Trevor approaching. "What were you guys doing out there so long?"

No one on shore saw what almost happened. Sylvia wasn't about to tell them. Her parents had had enough for one day.

"Oh, we were counting stars," Sylvia said.

She picked Trevor up, carried him to the bench, and bundled him in his towel. She couldn't let him go. She wanted to sleep with her kids flanked on either side of her tonight.

Granddad came up and put his hand on Trevor's back. "All tuckered out I bet. Want me to carry you?"

Trevor nodded.

"When your mom was about a year old and wanted us to pick her up, she would reach her arms up high and say 'carry you,'" Grammy said. "We loved that."

The image of arms reaching up sent a shiver through Sylvia. "I think we're ready for warm beds."

"Nobody caught us," Alice said as they headed home. "Let's do this again."

"Too scary," Trevor said.

"I'd be scared of that dark water, too," Grammy said. "Did you know that I just learned how to swim?"

"You didn't know how when you were little?" Alice asked.

Grammy shook her head. "No. I didn't have a place to swim where I grew up, so I never learned. We were poor; it was the Depression, and most people didn't have jobs. We were lucky because my papa had a job and worked in a factory to feed all five of us kids."

"What's the Depression?" Alice asked.

When they reached the house, Sylvia walked Red to the front sidewalk to hose her down. Matt went inside to get her some towels. She took Red into the mudroom to towel her off. As Vivian told her childhood stories to Alice and Trevor, who seemed to hang on every word, she helped Trevor out of his wet suit and into his pajamas. He seemed to have recovered from his ordeal. Sylvia wasn't so sure she had.

By the time they were all in bed, it was midnight. Sylvia leaned her head over to smell the tops of her children's heads as they slept on either side of her. Then she placed her palms on each one.

As tired as she was, she couldn't fall asleep. She kept thinking about the dark water closing over Trevor's stark blond hair and the patrol car pulling away with her brother in the backseat. She thought about her parents. For ten years they had tried halfway houses for Steve, different institutions, the latest drug theories, psychotherapy, and living at home, in hopes of alleviating their son's suffering. And over and over they'd endured heartbreak and disappointment each time. They must have felt like they'd lost a son. Trevor's close call in the lake lasted a few seconds, but from that, she felt she had touched the depth of her parents' sadness for the first time.

# CHAPTER 9

Mid-Summer 1980

Two days later Sylvia offered to accompany Matt to visit Steve. He suggested they have a late breakfast together first at Jack Horner's, his longtime favorite, where he used to meet his cronies every day before work. Now that he was retired, he still dropped in regularly, sometimes with Vivian.

Sylvia looked forward to these private times with her dad. Since her teens she had sensed a like-minded connection with him and decided she was more her father's daughter than her mother's. She related to his no-nonsense, unsentimental, intellectual approach. Sometimes she was more like a man than a woman on the inside and had said out loud that in her next life, if she had any say in it, she wanted to come back as a man. Men were less burdened with trivialities. Wouldn't life be simpler and more straightforward? Just getting dressed would be a lot less complicated: no jewelry, no makeup, and no heel heights to match pant and skirt lengths.

She sat across from him with her plate of French toast and link sausage and thought this might be a good time to bring up her divorce. She wanted to explain to him that this was not the emotional decision it appeared to be. To take this kind of financial risk for herself, but more important, for her children, seemed out of character and illogical to the extreme, but once he understood, she counted on the blanket approval he had always given her.

"Tom has made such poor business decisions that I no longer respect him," she said.

Matt cupped his coffee mug with both hands and looked into its contents as he spoke. "I don't think I know anybody who's gotten divorced for that. Things are different today though."

"I've wondered sometimes if I should've worked and Tom stayed home with the kids. He even said that once."

"Sounds like you won't be wonderin' much longer," Matt said with a wry smile. "When do you start teaching?"

"The end of August." She poured a hefty amount of maple syrup over her French toast and inhaled the fragrance. She took her first bite and sighed with pleasure.

"Maybe that's what you needed all along to offset boredom. Educated women might have a harder time staying home with the kids."

She suspected that Matt was disappointed that she hadn't pursued her career further before having children. "But it's better for the kids if the mother stays home, I think."

"Even if the mother is miserable?" He spooned a thick coating of brown sugar onto his oatmeal.

She knitted her brow. He was the eight-to-five, dinner-on-the-table, wife-stays-home-and-raises-the-kids, Nebraska cornhusker. He sounded almost enlightened.

"I don't know the answer to that," she said. "Mom was happy at home so I never questioned what to do when Alice was born. And I never thought of myself as miserable."

"Discontented, then. Your mother never had the career choices you had. You started a family right away, too," he said. "Plus, all those moves must have worn pretty thin. With your new job, you might have a different outlook on your marriage."

"Yeah, I might wonder why I waited *this* long for a divorce."

"Or be so absorbed in your work, you wouldn't need outside diversion." He raised his eyebrows.

She felt her face flush and looked down at her plate. Was that a reproach about her affair? She couldn't blame him—she just never heard one from him before. Her dad was always the safest place to be. When she sat down here today, she didn't really imagine that he might reprimand her for what she was doing.

She carefully wiped her mouth with her napkin and looked at him. "Whatever the reasons were three years ago, today I'm more certain than ever. It's too late for me to turn back now." She couldn't tell him that she and Anthony had waited long enough to be together.

"Why not stand still until you and Tom get yourselves back on your feet?" he asked. "Then go forward with your plans."

He sat tall in the blue Naugahyde booth and spoke in his usual calm, measured tone. Because of the deepened wrinkles across his forehead and around his eyes, he looked older than his years; but the contrast of his golf tan against his thick, wavy white hair gave him a distinguished, handsomely robust appearance. He even looked rested. Unlike Vivian, he slept through the night no matter what.

"It's pretty much done, Dad. The divorce will be final in September. And we had to put the house up for sale before I left." She set her fork down. Her appetite was gone. She suddenly felt bad talking about her problems with what he must be going through with Steve, but she thought he should know what was going on. Her timing was bad. She should've waited.

Matt took an amber plastic pill vial out of his pocket and set it on the table. He finished his last bite of oatmeal and removed the lid from the vial. He stuck his knife in and pulled out a tablespoon-size swirl of peanut butter. "Can't leave home without it."

It gave her solace to watch his endearing ritual. "Is there enough for me, too?"

He spread it on a triangle of whole-wheat toast and passed her the vial. "So, what's Anthony doing for your future?"

"Waiting six months to file for divorce after mine is over."

His eyes widened behind his tortoise horn-rimmed glasses. "Which means you volunteered to go first?"

Sylvia waited until the waitress finished refilling their coffee. "If I delayed the divorce, the money from the sale of the house would probably be absorbed in Tom's business venture or used to live on, and I'd end up with nothing."

"I'm afraid you're asking for more chaos than you bargained for is all," he said. "As long as you know we're always here for you if you need us. Hell, you and the kids could move back here if things got too tough."

She nodded and bowed her head. Her throat swelled with emotion. She mumbled a heartfelt thanks to him for always being there for her. "I'm not sure I deserve it this time."

"Nonsense. You deserve the best life has to offer."

She placed her hand over his and managed to give him a weak smile. "To hear you say that helps me believe it."

He put his other hand on top of hers. "That's what fathers are for. What do you say we go try to help Steve believe it, too?"

Once Sylvia saw the surroundings at Crestview, she understood why her mom refused to visit Steve. The one-story building was dilapidated and dingy. Patients with glassy, dazed stares shuffled the hallways, too drugged sometimes to hold their heads up straight. The county-run institution was nothing like the private one in Columbus where Steve had lived for two and a half years until the insurance ran out. The goal, to ease him gradually into independent living, had not been attained. Even if her parents could afford to spend the three thousand a month for him to stay longer, no one could predict how long that might take. He'd been home most of the six years since leaving there.

They were led down a dimly lit corridor to the smoke-filled visitor's lounge and told to wait there. There were no empty seats. A TV with a snowy picture droned in the background. Steve was soon led in. To see Steve in this dreary place was a shock for Sylvia, even though her dad had tried to prepare her on the way over.

They walked up to meet him. Matt tried to sound chipper. "You look pretty good, Steve. Feeling any better today?"

Steve nodded blankly, his eyes fixed on Sylvia. "When did you get here?" He spoke as if his tongue was too big for his mouth. His hands twitched at his sides.

Sylvia found it difficult to absorb that this drooling, mumbling, bearded, overweight person she hardly recognized as her brother blended in with the rest of the patients. She imagined that Steve didn't recognize himself either when he looked in a mirror, staring and wondering where the handsome, athletic, fun-loving guy went. Maybe that's why he avoided mirrors. And didn't want to shave. In his delusional state, he might think he transformed into someone else. Coping with this illness had changed everything about him. She reached up and kissed him on the cheek. "I got here a few days ago. The kids are with me, too."

Steve looked up at the ceiling. "Alice and Trevor." Then, as if startled, he turned to their dad. "Where's Mom?"

With a strained tightness in his voice, he answered, "She's home with Alice and Trevor." He motioned to several molded plastic chairs against the wall. "There's some empty chairs. Let's sit down."

Steve sat between the two of them. He jiggled his knees up and down. "When can I come home?"

Sylvia watched Matt intently then had to look away. With fingers spread apart, he looked down at his hands as he tapped them together several times before answering. "I'm not sure yet. I was hoping to talk to your doctor. Did you see him today yet?"

"I don't think so. Did you bring me some smokes?"

Sylvia reached into her purse and pulled out two packs of Newport 100's. She felt drained already and badly needed one herself. She handed him the cigarettes.

"Thanks, Syl." He struggled to remove the cellophane. "You smoke, don't you?"

"Yes. I'll have one with you."

Steve offered her one of his, but she said she had her own. He cracked a smile. "Good. More for me."

"Are you sleeping okay?"

"It's hard to sleep here. Everybody's crazy. Like that movie. Remember that movie? *Snake Pit*?"

Sylvia did remember. A 1940s black-and-white brutally depressing account of a mental institution for the criminally insane that she and Steve watched when they were young. They used to love to stay up late and watch old movies together.

Their visit lasted about a half an hour. Matt was able to flag Steve's doctor before they left, and they drove in silence most of the ride home. Sylvia went into the family room from the garage and found Alice and her mom lying facedown on the floor, their legs stretched out behind them, both intent on the pictures they were drawing. Red was sprawled on the cool tile by the sliding glass door but sat up and ambled over to greet Sylvia. Trevor was playing on the back patio in the dirt with the old Tonka cars and trucks Grammy had saved from Steve and Scott's childhood collection.

"You're back!" Alice said.

When Matt came in, Vivian sat up with her legs tucked underneath her. She had that look people have when they're afraid to hear what's going to come next—a guarded expression colored with foreboding.

"Mommy. Wanna draw with us?" Alice asked.

"In a little while." Sylvia sat on the couch opposite her mom and Alice. "Steve's stabilized, Mom. He knew me, and we sort of talked about my visit."

"Did he ask when he could come home?" Vivian asked.

"Yes. We told him we didn't know yet." Sylvia put her index finger in her mouth and started working on a nail.

"That place is a disgrace. I wonder if he's even safe in there." Vivian crossed her arms over her chest in weak defiance.

"He's safer in there for now. I don't think it'll be too long," Matt said. "We saw the doctor just as he was leaving Steve's room. He said he slept well the last two nights. They still have him on Haldol."

Sylvia wondered how the doctor would even know how he slept.

"After two days? Steve can't see straight on that stuff," Vivian said.

"That's the only thing that works well enough," he said. "He asked about you."

Sylvia detected a slight crack in his voice. Vivian's and Matt's eyes fastened on each other in mutual despair.

"When's he coming home?" Alice asked.

"We don't know for sure, maybe in a few days," Granddad said, then changed the subject. "Looks like we might get some rain this afternoon. Sky looks threatening."

Matt left the room, and Vivian excused herself for a minute and followed him.

"Having fun with Grammy?"

"Yes, but she seems so sad 'cause of Steve. I don't want him to come home yet. He scares me because he seems mad all the time," Alice said.

"I know how you feel, honey. When he does come home, he'll be better, maybe more like you remember him." Sylvia got up and turned on the TV.

"I hope so."

"I bet Grammy even feels like that, too, sometimes, but when he's not here, she worries if he's being taken care of. Your being here helps her a lot though."

"We made red Jell-O for dinner, and Grammy said maybe later we could go get ice cream cones at Stoddard's," Alice said. Stoddard's had been around for over thirty years. Their homemade custard drew crowds from a fifteen-mile radius.

"Sounds good, Alice. See? That helps Grammy take her mind off of Steve." Sylvia told Alice she was tired and wanted to take a short nap.

"Not yet, Mommy. Please draw with me now."

Grammy came back in the room and plopped herself down again beside Alice. "How about if I draw with you?"

"Oh, yes, Grammy."

Sylvia checked on Trevor, who was happily occupied on the patio, then went to the living room, stretched out on the couch, and closed her eyes. Just as she thought she could drop off to sleep, she overheard some of Alice and Vivian's conversation and snapped to attention. She went quietly to the doorway so she could hear better, craning her neck to watch them from behind.

"Did you know we have to sell our house?" Alice asked.

Vivian jerked her head up. "No. Your mom didn't tell me."

She peered briefly at her grandmother then went back to her drawing. "I don't want to move again, unless we can go to a farm with horses. Dad said maybe someday we can."

Vivian studied the pile of felt-tip pens and chose magenta. "Well, you have moved a lot, honey. How's your horse?"

"We had to give him back, but I can ride him if I want." Alice sounded dejected, but Vivian didn't seem to notice.

"Sounds like a pretty good deal to me." Vivian patted her on the back.

"It doesn't feel the same." She looked at Vivian's drawing. "Wow, you're so good, Grammy. And you made your cat pink!"

Vivian had taken art classes in oil painting and loved to sketch in charcoal. She definitely had talent but put her easel away soon after the onset of Steve's illness. From time to time, Sylvia tried to encourage her to go back to classes, but Vivian only said she'd think about it.

"That's what's fun about drawing. You can do whatever you want. I like your Pegasus best, though, flying through the rainbow sky. You have a wonderful imagination."

"My teachers think I'm good at art." Alice grinned. "Maybe I got it from you."

"I'd like to think you did."

"I wish you lived near us."

"Me, too. But I'm sure glad you're here for a whole month," Vivian said.

"Except I won't see my dad." Alice vigorously colored in the pot of gold at the end of her rainbow.

"I know you must be disappointed, but I bet he'll call you as much as he can."

Alice beamed at her Grammy. "That's exactly what he said! Maybe he'll call."

Sylvia backed away from the doorway and returned to the couch. Alice needed her Grammy, who was probably the only person she'd talk to so openly. She dozed off thinking she wished they lived closer to her parents, too.

A loud clap of thunder sent shivers through the house. Sylvia leaped up and ran to the family room, where Trevor stood bug-eyed by the sliding glass door looking out at the Tonka cars scattered all over the patio.

He twisted his hands. "I need to bring them in."

Alice offered to help him. "Let's hurry before the lightning!"

A ragged bolt of lightning jerked across the sky followed by another sharp clack of thunder. Trevor and Alice screamed, and they huddled together on the couch with Sylvia, burying their heads in her lap. Red barked and climbed up beside them. As Matt came in the room, the television went dead.

"Whew, that was a good one, wasn't it?" He grinned. "You guys don't get these in Oregon I bet."

"It's too loud," Trevor said, his face still buried in Sylvia's lap.

Matt scooped Trevor into his arms and held him against his shoulder. Pangs of regret came over Sylvia as she saw how much Trevor needed the comfort of a father's arms at these unexpected moments. He hadn't had it often enough in his short life with his dad gone so much, and she worried that the future held even less of a chance for him after the divorce.

"It's pretty exciting all right." Matt rubbed Trevor's back. "Let's go look at the sky and watch for the lightning and I can tell you all about how it works. C'mon, Alice."

Trevor slowly turned his head away from Matt's neck, lifting it up ever so slightly. "What about the trucks?" he murmured.

"Oh, they're okay for now. Let the rain clean 'em off, and then you can bring 'em inside."

Matt, Trevor, and Alice went to the living room to get a better view.

Sylvia and Vivian were sitting together on the couch looking at a blank TV screen. They looked at each other and laughed.

"Well? What'll we do for dinner without electricity?" Vivian asked.

"Peanut butter and jelly is always good," Sylvia said.

"These storms usually don't last longer than a few hours."

"Or broasted chicken from Stutzman's."

"Wonderful idea. Hope they're not shut down, too. We can call to find out."

Matt and the kids came into the family room. Trevor was exuberant about counting between the lightning and thunder to see how far away the storm was.

"We could play cards," Sylvia suggested.

"Let's play Oh Hell," Vivian said.

"Or Crazy Eights," Alice said.

"Matt, will you call Stutzman's and find out if we can get some of their chicken for dinner?" Vivian asked.

They gathered at the round pale avocado-painted table by the picture window that overlooked the large backyard. Vivian began shuffling the cards. Sylvia glanced up to gaze at the scene outdoors. *How different it looked in springtime*, she thought, when the only blooms were the forsythia bushes flowered with yellow bursts clustered along both sides of the property line. Now, orange daylilies and pink roses were staggered between the bushes' dense thick foliage and drooped from the weight of the rain. The huge trees in full leaf covered the yard under their canopies, as if in protection, and the green enclosure on all sides made her feel safer than anywhere else she'd ever been, like she was being embraced by the whole backyard. To the farthest end a low wooden fence separated their property from the Loomis family, who had lived there for fifty years. The storm was letting up, but thick pewter-colored clouds still hung in the late afternoon sky, casting a twilight hue that accentuated the varying greens of grass, tree leaves, and shrubs. Raindrops pattered on the roof.

Sylvia noticed a tall figure at the fence line approaching the house. She strained to make him out. He wore no raincoat, so his clothes clung to him, and his hair was plastered to his head.

Vivian looked up and followed Sylvia's gaze. She sucked in a breath. "Steve's home."

# CHAPTER 10

Mid-Summer 1980

Matt dropped his cards on the table as he jumped up and opened the sliding glass door. Steve, dripping with rain, ambled through the doorway. No one said a word. The lime shag carpeting was turning a deeper shade of green around his feet from the water soaking into the thick pile. Clumps of dirt around the soles of his tennis shoes crumbled onto the carpet in muddy bits.

He glanced furtively at his family. “The power was off. Everybody was freaked out. I couldn’t stay there.”

“Power’s out here, too, son. Let’s get you out of these wet clothes. Maybe a hot shower?”

“I hate showers.” Steve began to shiver. “That’s all they have there. Showers.”

Vivian moved toward her son and looked at him intently. “You’d rather have a bath, wouldn’t you?”

Steve looked into her eyes and nodded. “Why didn’t you come to see me, Mom?”

Vivian's fragile composure visibly cracked. Her hands dropped to her sides. Her lips quivered. In a low whisper she stammered, "I was going to—later. You're home now. I'll start your bath." She left the room.

Sylvia saw the helpless look on her father's face and followed her mother.

When she caught up with Vivian in the dimly lit living room, Sylvia put her arms around her and told her that it was okay she didn't visit. "He knows you're devoted to him, Mom. But he's like a little boy."

Vivian's shoulders shook. "I should've gone to see him, but I just couldn't do it again. And I was wrong."

"The doctor said *not* to visit him the first few days, remember? Anyway, you're allowed to take care of your own needs, too."

"I'm never sure how to treat him."

"You're treating him fine. He's a sick man who may think he needs his mommy, but who really needs his meds and a good shrink. You didn't make him sick, and you can't make him well." Sylvia handed her a Kleenex from the box sitting on the breakfront.

Vivian sighed. "I think you're right. But then the experts say over and over that without family support, people with schizophrenia rarely have any chance for an independent life."

Sylvia reassured her mother that Steve had never been without family support and never would be. "It's a balancing act for sure, and I'm not saying I'd know how to do it either, but his growth may also depend—"

"I'm so glad to hear you say that, honey, because one of the things we worry about is if anything happens to your father and me, who will look after—?" She broke off as they heard Matt and Steve approaching.

"I haven't started his bath yet!" Vivian scurried to the bathroom.

Sylvia was glad her mother hadn't finished her sentence. She knew what she was going to say and wasn't ready to hear it. Sylvia's futile attempt to explain the balancing act of family support had fallen on deaf ears. Maybe overprotecting him would only reinforce his low self-esteem and his feeling that he's unable to do anything for himself. Her mother would hear only what she needed to hear, which was understandable at a painful time like this. Still, to think that her parents might someday expect her to take care of her brother frightened her.

The phone rang. Sylvia presumed it would be Crestview alerting her parents about their missing son. This wasn't the first time Steve had run away from a mental institution.

Once, at a private facility in a small town in Massachusetts, he had walked out in the middle of the night. He found a trailer park in the surrounding woods about three miles away, knocked on a door and had asked an elderly couple if he could call home. They had said they'd drive him back to the institution, a turn-of-the-century brick mansion on the top of a hill on the outskirts of town, and he could call home from there. Without incident, Steve had complied.

Vivian had then flown up to Massachusetts and stayed for a week in a local motel. Every day she had taken a taxi back and forth to be near her son. She had been appalled to find out he couldn't keep his food down and that what they served was strictly vegetarian. The only vegetables Steve had ever eaten were corn and potatoes, and occasionally canned peas. His lanky frame had turned skeletal, so she had snuck food in for him. When she learned that one of their treatments was placing him in a warm bath with earphones to a tape recorder that repeated the mantra, "You have schizophrenia and will never recover," she had brought him home. "Bunch of quacks" was what Matt had called the doctors there and demanded their money back. It was surprising Steve still wanted to take baths at all.

Matt called out to her that Tom was on the phone.

She picked up the phone. "Hi, Tom. The kids'll be glad to hear from you."

"I would've called them sooner, but I had to go to Arizona at the last minute. I just got back," he said.

Sylvia wanted to ask him if the phone lines were down in Arizona but held her tongue.

He went on to tell her that several people had looked at the house, but there were no nibbles, that business was still slow, and that he and George had to start planning the next catalogue. The last catalogue photo shoot had taken over their entire house. She would've lost her mind if she hadn't escaped with the kids to Mount Hood. She envisioned a repeat. That by itself would be enough to make her wish for a quick sale.

When he asked about her parents and Steve, she downplayed the events prior to Crestview and accentuated the frightful conditions there to help bolster Steve's status as a runaway. Tom had always been especially sympathetic to her brother's plight. He knew and loved Steve before he became ill and afterwards never considered him to be dangerous. She counted on that attitude now because she didn't want Tom to insist that she take the kids to his parents. Even though he couldn't really make her, she didn't feel up to an argument with him about it.

"I'm sorry Steve's having trouble again." There was a pause. "So, how're the kids taking all this?"

"Alice mostly seems worried for her grammy but is having a good time. Trevor's only worried about his Tonka cars getting wet on the patio. We were about to play Crazy Eights when Steve showed up."

"Have you called my parents yet?" Tom asked.

"I haven't had a chance. When things settle down here, I will." Sylvia chewed on her index fingernail.

"Sounds like things might not settle down, Sylvia. Let me talk to Alice."

"Alice is fine, Tom. So don't try to talk her into something she doesn't want to do."

"I'll be the judge of that," he said.

Sylvia called to Alice, who squealed "Daddy" as she ran to the phone. Trevor echoed her. She reminded Alice to tell her dad about their late-night swim.

"*I* want to tell him about the swim in the dark." Trevor crossed his arms over his chest.

She figured that version of events would seal their fate for good. "You can tell him about the thunderstorm and how Granddad told you about counting." She led Trevor back to the family room to let Alice talk alone with Tom. Matt came in and said that Steve was finally in the tub. Suddenly the TV jumped back to life.

Matt turned on a few lamps and sat beside Sylvia on the sofa. "What did Tom have to say?"

"He asked how you were holding up and said to give you his best. And he asked why I hadn't called his parents yet."

Matt dismissed the comment with a wave of his hand. "You just got here. You can call tomorrow. They'll be here for dinner in two days anyway."

Sylvia had forgotten about the dinner and wondered if her in-laws should still come.

The sound of the washing machine starting up came from the basement, then Vivian's footsteps climbing the stairs. She came into the family room and sat in the recliner.

"Should I tell Alice to get off the phone in case Crestview's trying to call?"

Matt rubbed his forehead. "Hell, they don't know their ass from a hole in the ground, and if their power's been out, they probably don't even know he's missing yet."

"But aren't you going to let them know he's here?" Sylvia asked.

"I couldn't care less right now," Matt said.

"What about his own doctor?" Sylvia tried again.

"What for? There's no emergency." Matt got up and changed the TV channel.

Vivian managed to crack a smile. "I just feel better that he's home again. Maybe he'll take his meds now."

Sylvia looked up at Matt. "How do you know what to give him if you don't know what he's taken?"

Vivian sat up straighter in her chair. "You forget your father's a chemical engineer. He can figure out the formula. He's been doing it for years, you know."

"Under the psychiatrist's advice though," Sylvia said.

"We have all the meds that his doctor prescribed right here!" Vivian leaned back hard in the leather recliner and the footrest popped up.

Her mother's defensive posture, whenever she felt she was being challenged, was a test of Sylvia's patience. While trying to prove her point might only make matters worse, sometimes she couldn't hold back, especially when there was so much at stake. "And what if Steve refuses again to take them?"

"One step at a time. I just told him he has to take them or it's back to Crestview. He seemed to get the message," Matt said.

"But what if the voices tell him *not* to take them?" Sylvia asked.

Vivian leaned forward and spoke in a hushed tone. “We just tell him the voices are wrong.”

Matt said he was going to fix himself a drink and left the room.

Sylvia wanted a drink, too, and stood up. “Even if he thinks it’s God’s voice?”

Vivian scoffed. “Steve’s been saying for years that God tells him not to take his meds. Besides, the voices lessen when he’s on his meds, which he is now, so I think he’ll listen to us.”

The conversation seemed to have come full circle. How would they know what meds he’d taken at Crestview? And when he’d had the last dose?

The phone rang again. It was Tom’s mother, Eleanor. Tom’s conversation with the kids must’ve had something to do with his mother calling now. Nervously, Sylvia took the phone from her daughter. It would be their first conversation since Tom had broken the news of their divorce a few weeks ago. Eleanor was a simple, moral woman who prided herself on running a shipshape household and raising four boys to do the right thing. Because Eleanor had often worried that Tom traveled too much and was shirking his family responsibilities, Sylvia suspected that she stewed over whether her son’s frequent job changes and relocations led to the collapse of their marriage. Tom was the most adored by his mother, so she also might blame herself for somehow misguiding him along the way.

"Hi, Eleanor. It's good to hear your voice." She took five minutes to explain why she hadn't called them yet.

"I didn't want to bother you all, Sylvia," Eleanor said. "I just wanted to make sure we were still on for dinner Thursday and wanted to know what I could bring. Maybe my homemade coleslaw? What do you think? Or is this a bad time to talk? You can call me back if that would be better."

Eleanor was the kind of person who always worried about saying the wrong thing, or not doing enough to make you feel at home, or intruding. Because she needed constant reassurance, Sylvia often felt worn out after spending a day with her.

"This is fine now. But I will need to call you back about the dinner plans, since we haven't—"

Eleanor interrupted. "Of course you haven't. If you need to change the day, that's fine with us. Or if you think it's too much right now, you're all welcome to come to our house. Maybe that's the thing to do. Your parents could drive you down, and we could all have dinner here." She paused. "But maybe they don't want to leave Steve alone. Steve is welcome to come, if he feels up to it. Anyway, you and the kids could stay here for a few days, and then we could drive you back."

Only ten minutes on the phone and Sylvia was already worn out. "I know Mom and Dad would enjoy going to your place, Eleanor, but things are unsure with Steve, and I want to be here, so—"

"Of course you want to be there. How is Steve? Maybe a quieter house would be better for him, I mean without the kids. They could stay here while you help your parents. Just until things are a little more settled for you all. We would be glad to pick them up if you couldn't bring them."

Sylvia found herself rethinking her position. Eleanor's suggestion might be better for Steve *and* her kids. Steve's welfare was the first consideration, but her children might find welcome relief with their other grandparents right now. Eleanor and Frank were ten years older than her parents and seemed stodgy, old-fashioned, and were too careful to be silly, so Alice and Trevor usually had more fun with hers. Under the circumstances it wasn't much fun here, so Eleanor's generous offer was worth considering.

"Thank you so much for offering, Eleanor. You might be right. Let me think about it. Is it okay if I let you know about dinner tomorrow morning?"

"Tomorrow's fine, dear. We'll be right here, you know that."

They said their good-byes, and Sylvia hung up the phone.

She heard Matt's trumpet blasts from the basement rec room and went down to watch him play. Trevor was sitting on the piano bench next to him, and when he finished his piece, Trevor clapped. Matt wiped his moistened brow with his handkerchief and said he'd promised Trevor they'd go to the Dairy Queen for dessert. He thought they all should go but wasn't sure Steve should be left by himself. Sylvia said she didn't mind staying home. She asked him to bring her back a hot fudge sundae.

After they left, Sylvia decided to change into her nightgown. On her way to the bedroom she noticed the bathroom door was still shut. *Steve must still be in the tub.* She paused at the bedroom doorway, which was adjacent to the bathroom, to listen. Nothing. When he was asleep in his bed, he usually snored so loudly you could hear him from anywhere in the house. Maybe sitting almost upright would inhibit snoring. She wanted to call out to him but thought better of disturbing him and went to the small bedroom.

Their open suitcases overflowed with the kids' clothes spilling onto the floor. Sylvia closed the sill-length sheer curtains at both windows and changed out of her clothes in the semi-darkness. The chirp of the crickets was the only sound, and she realized how much she welcomed the quiet.

She lay down on the bed and closed her eyes. Her thoughts now turned to Anthony. So far, she hadn't allowed herself to miss him, but he was always there, residing in her thoughts, a lingering presence that was both comforting and unsettling. He'd given her life new meaning yet at the same time distracted her from living it. Throughout their three-year affair, a part of her was engaged with what was in front of her, but a larger part was preoccupied with him. She was tired of leading a fractured life, pulled in different directions. Since she'd been in Ohio, confronted with her parents' problem with

Steve, she hadn't been as distracted with Anthony as before. But it had been only four days, days filled with tension and anxiety.

Now, in the peace and solitude of the evening, she wanted to feel the comfort of his body next to hers, his strong arms pulling her to him. A familiar swell of heat stirred from within. She slid her hands over her nipples several times, pinching them gently, making them hard. She slowly moved her right hand over her stomach down through her mound of hair to find the moistened hollow between her legs. *I haven't spoken to Anthony since I called him from the airport in Portland.* She spread her legs slightly and began stroking herself methodically in circles. *If only I could make myself come before they get back.* She rubbed faster. *He would never call me at my parents' house.* She yearned to feel him inside her. *I have to call him. I should do it now while I have this time alone.* She gave up on her orgasm and pulled her nightie back down.

He might still be at the office. She suddenly felt so tired she only wanted to lie there and do nothing. She rolled onto her side and stared at the off-white princess phone on the nightstand. He would wonder why she hadn't tried to call him. She slowly reached for the phone and dialed his office number. Her heart seemed to beat faster while she waited.

"God, Jake. Finally." Anthony sighed. "I've been staying late every night waiting for you to call. I even thought about calling there and using our code."

When he asked her if everyone was okay, Sylvia broke down and wept. He listened patiently and consoled her as she told him all about Steve and her growing concern that her parents' care for him was either inadequate or misplaced or both.

"There must be some place he could go," he said.

"If there is, it's probably unaffordable."

"I wish I could help." He paused. "At the very least I wish I could be there with you."

She tried to picture him here with her family, and somehow the image didn't come together. "Me, too," she said routinely. She heard the car on the gravel driveway. "I think they're back. Trevor's calling me." She said she didn't know when she could call him again, but she'd try as soon as she could and hung up.

She left the bedroom and met Trevor in the kitchen, the sundae cupped carefully in his hands. Vivian stuck her head in and asked if all was well. Sylvia told her she assumed Steve had fallen asleep in the tub, so she didn't bother him. Vivian said that was nothing unusual. She added that she and the kids were going to take Red for her evening walk. Trevor handed Sylvia her ice cream and left with Vivian and Alice.

All was quiet again until Sylvia heard the muffled, plaintive melody of Matt playing *Trumpeter's Prayer*, one of his favorites.

She finished her ice cream and headed back toward the bedroom, pausing again to listen for any sound from the bathroom. Nothing. She decided to go closer and walked down the short hallway toward the bathroom. The carpet squished under her feet. She switched on the hall light and saw water seeping from under the bathroom door.

She turned the doorknob. It was locked.

"Steve! Wake up!" He was always difficult to wake, but she couldn't imagine that he'd sleep in a tub overflowing with water. She felt weak, thinking he might have drowned. "Steve!"

At the same moment she heard Matt thundering up the steps shouting, "Water's pouring into the basement!" He was panting by the time he reached the bathroom. He pulled on the knob. "Steve! Steve!" He pounded on the door so hard the walls shook. "Sylvia, get the screwdriver. Hurry!"

Sylvia rushed to the tool drawer in the dining room.

"The Phillips!" he shouted.

She found it and ran back to him.

He knelt on the soggy carpet and fumbled with the screwdriver. "I need a flashlight. I can't see a goddamn thing!"

Sylvia ran for the flashlight then held it for him. Her insides felt like they'd drained out of her. "I should call nine-one-one."

"Just hold the light. Then call." Matt's hands trembled as he tried to unscrew the tiny heads. The five minutes it took him to remove the doorknob felt like an hour.

"Got it!" he said.

# CHAPTER 11

He began to remove the knob. Sylvia ran to the phone and called 911.

On her way back to the bathroom, she could hear Matt's grunts and groans mingled with the sound of the water sloshing in slow waves onto the floor. The door opened inward, which made it impossible for her to enter and help. For a few seconds she watched in frustration as Matt, in a squat position, tried to hoist Steve's naked body over the side of the tub. But it was too heavy to maneuver. The room was so small he couldn't get any leverage and kept bumping against the sink. Sylvia finally managed to squeeze in and shut the door behind her to give them more room. She spotted the empty aspirin bottle on the floor.

Out of breath, Matt whispered, "He's still breathing."

She knelt down in the inch-deep water and tried to put her shoulder under Steve's armpit. She averted her eyes from his exposed crotch, focusing on his back, which she noticed was freckled with dark moles. His skin was pasty white, and his belly hung forward in a flabby lump. She was glad he was practically hairless. Seeing her brother naked like this was embarrassing for her. Almost disgusting. She felt ashamed that it would even enter her mind in such an emergency. She wrapped her arm around his back to help Matt lift him over, but the floor was too slippery and there still wasn't enough room.

"I've gotta give him mouth to mouth," Matt said.

"Or get him to throw up."

The water level in the tub had dropped enough that they could push Steve's head toward his knees.

"C'mon, son. Throw up!" Sweat poured from Matt's face and dribbled onto Steve's back and into the shallow tub water.

Water drooled from the corners of Steve's mouth. A memory of Steve as a baby flashed through Sylvia's mind. Big brown eyes that twinkled. Baby drool hanging over his lower lip as he laughed. She choked as she tried to swallow her sobs.

The siren blared from a distance then seemed to overtake the entire street. Just as suddenly, it went quiet. Sylvia ran to the family room to open the sliding glass door and directed the emergency medical team through the family room, the living room, and finally into the narrow hallway to the bathroom.

Matt turned to Sylvia. He looked like he'd been in a storm at sea. He was soaking wet from head to toe. His thick, wavy hair had fallen forward and was matted to his forehead. His face was gaunt and ashen, his expression dour. With his arms hanging limply at his sides, he appeared drained and defeated. Sylvia reached up, clasped her arms around his neck, and held on. His voice breaking, he said, "I think he'll make it."

Within minutes Steve was on a stretcher and put into the ambulance. Sylvia watched her dad cross the driveway and climb in behind him. This was as close as she had ever come to seeing him cry. He was sensitive and felt things deeply, but he didn't seem able to unlock the emotions stored inside. His torso was stiff when he hugged, and he was uncomfortable expressing his feelings in words. Sylvia had never heard him say, "I love you," and it didn't matter. She always felt loved by him.

She sat in the dark in the living room feeling numb and anxious. She wondered if Steve felt loved by him. They were so different. Matt told her once that he couldn't understand why Steve was never curious as a child, that he didn't seem the least bit interested in the how, why, or what of things. Matt was an impatient man who liked things done right. There'd been more than one project he had attempted with Steve, like the kayak kit, where he had given up trying to show Steve how and finished it himself. Steve was a talented athlete but struggled in school. Maybe he had a type of learning disability, which would have gone undetected in the fifties.

When Scott came along six years after Steve, he was the clone of their father. He was inquisitive, academic, and musically inclined. Sylvia sensed that Steve had always felt inferior to Matt, and probably to Scott, too. She got up and stared out the front window into the night and waited for Vivian and her children to return.

After a few minutes she went to the family room and pulled a family photo album from the bookcase. Their childhood was all here and in the home movies. On every visit, Alice and Trevor asked their granddad to show the movies, especially the ones of Christmas with the snow angels and snowman Sylvia and Steve made in the backyard when they were kids. Sylvia didn't think she could endure it this time. She flipped through the thick, black construction paper pages, each picture held in place with tiny corners glued onto the page. Trick-or-treating: Steve wore a red cowboy hat and a big grin and posed with his hands on the guns in the holster. Sylvia stood next to him wearing a feather headdress and a fringed vest. He was five. She was eight. Her hand rested on his shoulder. She had always looked out for him. She had stood up to the neighborhood boys who thought he was too little to play with them. She had let him play dolls with her and her friends. Taught him to play War and Go Fish. Swam with him every summer at the lake. Steve had bawled when she went to college and later at her wedding. They had spent a happy, idyllic childhood together, and in a few short years, his illness had turned him into a stranger.

She closed the album when she heard her mom's voice and looked up to see the grinning faces behind the sliding glass door. Red bounded in the room, and Sylvia knelt down and buried her face in Red's fur, not even trying to muffle the sobs that she could no longer contain.

# CHAPTER 12

The Following Day

"Why aren't they riding in a car?" Trevor asked.

"Because the Amish don't believe in cars," Alice said.

"What's Theeawmish?"

Alice pointed to the horse-drawn buggy that had pulled onto the shoulder of the paved two-lane highway to let them pass. "*They're* Amish."

Trevor stared in amazement. A child in a black bonnet peered out from a tiny square window at the back of the carriage. Trevor waved. She waved back.

Sylvia shivered to think how fast the cars were driving on this hilly roadway. Gruesome accidents had taken place in this area with slow-moving buggies approaching the crest of a hill or a blind curve. Local drivers knew to apply their brakes in such spots, but the out-of-town driver could be caught by surprise, especially at night. The only warning symbol the Amish religion permitted was an orange triangle-shaped reflector that sat below the back window of most buggies, which would hardly be enough to signal a car going fifty miles an hour at night.

"And they don't believe in TV either," Alice said. "And they only wear black. Mommy, do they go to school?"

The sun's glare on the windshield made it difficult to see. Sylvia reached in her purse for her sunglasses. "Most of them I think. There were Amish children in your dad's school. You can ask Nana and Bumpa."

"Are we there yet?" Trevor asked.

"Pretty soon, honey. Maybe fifteen minutes or so."

The scenery had changed to rolling hills and winding roads about an hour outside of Silver Lake. Ponds bordered with cattails dotted the landscape, and an occasional oriole with its distinctive yellow markings or, Sylvia's favorite, the red-winged blackbird flitted among the marshy reeds. Tom's hometown of Millersburg was called the "Little Switzerland of Ohio" for its alpine-like beauty of grassy slopes covered in wildflowers and its renowned baby Swiss cheese. The large Amish community brought a foreign quality to the small town, which Sylvia later learned was more appealing to visitors than to the town's residents. Their strange ways were sometimes more tolerated than admired.

Because of their belief in hard work over convenience, the Amish were hired by the townspeople for various odd jobs that required manual labor. Many Amish women cleaned homes. Even Eleanor, a hardworking woman in her own right, hired an Amish woman to do the "heavy housework" once a month.

Driving through this beautiful countryside made the previous day's trauma seem like a long time ago. Sylvia wasn't sure how long she'd stay. She thought her parents wanted her with them, but they acted relieved when she told them she might stay a night or two with her in-laws to get Alice and Trevor settled.

Steve had been moved from the emergency room into the psychiatric unit of the hospital that morning. According to Vivian, the facility was a hundred times better than Crestview. She said the care of the professional staff resembled that of a private facility. The only hitch was their medical insurance wouldn't pay for a stay longer than two weeks, but Steve could continue to see their psychiatrist as an outpatient. While all of this was encouraging news, it was still too early to tell where this might lead. Sylvia was frustrated that it took a suicide attempt for Steve to get access to the kind of help he needed. For now, the important thing was her parents had a reprieve.

They asked her not to tell Eleanor and Frank the details of what had happened, which made sense. It all fit perfectly anyway. Since taking the kids to their house was originally Eleanor's idea, she was elated when Sylvia called the night before to take her up on it.

The two-story four-bedroom brick house was situated off the main roadway and sat back on a steep hill. As they climbed the drive, Sylvia beeped her horn. Eleanor and Frank rushed out to greet them.

Eleanor, flush-faced and beaming, leaned down and squeezed each child to her ample breast. She was a solidly built German woman with a stout stomach and thick, strong legs. She wore a blue paisley housedress that fell just below the knee and low-heeled navy pumps. Her bright blue eyes contrasted with her naturally wavy, white hair that curled just below her ears.

Red jumped out of the car and ran up the hill behind the house and sniffed around the cement building that was the old chicken coop. When Tom met Sylvia in college, one of the first things he told her about his childhood was that he had kept a pony in a stall in the chicken coop. The ceiling was so low that one night the pony had managed to chew on a lightbulb. Tom found him the next morning collapsed in his stall. The vet hadn't been able to save him, and Tom had been so heartbroken he never wanted another one. Eleanor and Frank used the coop for storage now.

"We'll have to tie Red up, you know, so she doesn't wander too far," Eleanor said.

"Can she come inside?" Alice asked.

"Well, not in the house, but the basement is warm." Eleanor knitted her hands together then smoothed the front of her dress.

Frank, who was several inches shorter than Eleanor, stood off to one side behind her. Because of his slight build he appeared much smaller than his wife. He wore oversize horn-rimmed glasses. "How about she can be with us on the screened-in porch? Why don't you kids bring her on down?"

Alice and Trevor ran up the hill with Red's leash. Eleanor said she had lunch all ready and suggested they go in.

Frank put both hands on Sylvia's shoulders and peered at her through lenses that made his eyes look enlarged. She half expected a pronouncement of some magnitude such as "Divorce should be avoided at all costs," but heard him say instead, "I'm so glad you'll be spending some time with us."

Sylvia kissed him warmly on the cheek and said how wonderful it was to be here again. And it was. The change of scenery was literally a breath of fresh country air for her. The view across the valley was exhilarating, and she inhaled deeply. It was already beginning to get humid and sticky, and Frank suggested they have a cold beer and sit on the porch, which was adjacent to the kitchen and overlooked their grape arbor.

"Sounds great."

"Let me help you with your bags first." Frank walked around to the trunk of the car.

"Not now, Frank. Lunch is ready. You can get those later." Eleanor stood there with her hands on her hips.

Frank went to the refrigerator in the garage and grabbed two Rolling Rocks. He popped the caps with a bottle opener and started to hand one to Sylvia.

"Oh, Frank, get her a glass," Eleanor chided. She shook her head and ushered them all inside.

Once the kids got Red settled on the porch on her blanket, they all gathered at the round oak kitchen table with a big lazy Susan in the center that was loaded with deviled eggs, sliced ham, homemade coleslaw, fruit cocktail (the kids' favorite), scalloped potatoes, and sliced bread. It was a feast. Trevor soon discovered that he liked to turn the lazy Susan and repeatedly offered what sat in front of him to Nana and Alice sitting across the table.

Sylvia felt so comfortable with Tom's parents and her children that she almost forgot the heavy news of the divorce that hung over them. Surrounded by Alice and Trevor, it was impossible to broach the subject, but the opportunity would probably come later that evening.

"Are you looking forward to teaching again?" Frank asked. "I can't imagine how you can speak French. Wow. You're a smart one, Sylvia."

"I'm a little scared about walking into a class of thirteen-year-olds. It's been so long." Sylvia signaled Trevor to turn the wheel so she could have more coleslaw.

"Toot, toot. Here it comes," Frank said.

"Bumpa, can we run the train?" Alice asked.

"Sure we can, but later this evening. It's too hot in the attic right now."

"Can we make popcorn balls, too?" Alice's eyes widened.

Nana laughed and, nodding, suggested that they save something to do for tomorrow. Then Frank mentioned they could maybe go to Orrville to visit the Smucker's factory where the jams and jellies were made.

"What a good idea," Sylvia said, but the kids seemed less than enthusiastic.

"Will you have to teach every day?" Eleanor asked.

"Yes, but just mornings." Sylvia fudged a little, not wanting to alarm her mother-in-law, who was apparently already worried about Trevor.

"I guess lots of mothers work these days. It was unheard of when I was raising the boys. Maybe I'm old-fashioned, but we scrimped and did without so I could be with them. Children need their mothers at home. Even when Frank was laid off, the boys mowed lawns and—"

Frank gave his wife a look, and she stopped. "It'll all work out just fine, I'm sure," he said.

Sylvia felt uneasy and wondered if her mother-in-law was deliberately trying to make her feel bad for going back to work because of the divorce. Maybe she and Frank didn't know about the financial condition of Tom's business and that Sylvia had to work, divorce or not. The best thing to do was nod and say as little as possible.

Alice and Trevor asked to be excused and joined Red on the porch. Eleanor offered to give Red the ham bone, as long as she ate it outside. Sylvia said she'd take care of the dishes, but Eleanor insisted they do them together, saying it wasn't often she had a daughter-in-law around for girly talk. Frank joined the kids with his coffee.

Eleanor turned to Sylvia as soon as they were alone. "While we have a minute, I might as well tell you that Tom's news about you two was something I've worried about for years. He just travels too much. And he made you move too much. How can anyone be uprooted every other year and feel like they've got a home? It's plain bad for a marriage." Eleanor grabbed a dishtowel and said she'd rather have Sylvia wash, if she didn't mind. She was too upset to wash and might break a dish.

*Poor Eleanor*, thought Sylvia. She really could only imagine the divorce was Tom's fault, which made Sylvia feel worse. It was feminism in reverse. The wife and mother couldn't possibly be guilty because she had no voice in these matters. Oddly enough, Sylvia *had* been voiceless. She just let it all happen without saying a word in protest then turned around and had an affair. If only Eleanor knew.

Sylvia stared into the dishwater. "I can only imagine how hard this is for you, but it isn't all Tom's fault. He's tried hard to provide for us, and *I* could've refused to move at some point."

Alice rushed in and asked if they could have Nana's homemade grape juice. Eleanor canned the dark purple bulbous grapes from their arbor and made juice. The treat was the small cluster that sat at the bottom of the glass. She enthusiastically retrieved two juice glasses and the pitcher from the refrigerator and poured one for each of them. Alice slowly made her way back to the porch, carrying the juices.

Eleanor stared at Sylvia. "If only he'd taken the job offer here in town with Grayson after college, don't you think? Tom was always a homeboy, not the worldly type. I know he would've been selling cars, but he could've been a part owner. Grayson worshipped the twins but had a special feeling for Tom."

Sylvia remembered the job offer from Donald Grayson. Tom had seriously considered it, and inwardly Sylvia had panicked. To choose Millersburg, a town of two thousand, was synonymous with giving up. To Sylvia, it meant playing it safe in life, sitting back without taking risks, settling for mediocrity. The stars without the moon. Living here was never an option for her.

"Well, he did have to serve overseas first," Sylvia began.

"I worried sick over that. Worried I'd lose another son."

"I know you worried. And who could blame you?"

Eleanor and Frank had lost their firstborn, Johnny, when he was twenty-two. He had been killed in a car accident when a semi-truck crossed the center divider and slammed into his car. Sylvia hadn't known Tom at the time, but two years later, after they'd been dating several months, he had broken down sobbing as he told her about it. She'd never known anyone who had lost a brother or sister or someone in the immediate family. The emptiness she felt at the time for not being able to relate to the depth of such sorrow had left her at a loss for words.

"My faith has gotten me through all of it, although I still can't abide a phone call after ten at night." Eleanor's voice quivered. She began putting the leftovers in plastic Rubbermaid containers. She held one up. "Got these when Tom worked for Rubbermaid." The company's headquarters were located in nearby Wooster, where Frank had worked at the local college as head of maintenance until he retired. "You two never should've left Chillicothe."

She was right. Sylvia had been happiest in that small town in southern Ohio and hadn't wanted to leave. But Tom didn't see a future with Rubbermaid or Chillicothe, so he found another job, which had taken them back to the Pacific Northwest. "Funny you should say that. I said the same thing to Tom."

The warmth in Eleanor's blue eyes turned cool. "A man doesn't always know what's best. If the family's welfare is at stake, the woman has to speak her mind, right?"

It appeared that Eleanor believed a wife and mother had a voice after all.

"In hindsight, I wish I had said more," Sylvia said.

Standing there with Tom's mother in his childhood home, Sylvia really did wish things had turned out differently. She thought she'd found happiness in the more provincial setting of Chillicothe. After five out-of-state moves and a second child, she had fully appreciated living closer to their families and old friends. Her support system had been only a few hours away. Sylvia passed Eleanor the last dish to dry.

"Of course, sometimes it doesn't do any good anyhow." Eleanor sighed and hung the dishtowel back on the rack under the sink. She grabbed the thicker terry cloth towel next to it and handed it to Sylvia. "Here's the hand towel to dry your hands."

Even though Sylvia found Eleanor tiresome at times, for the most part, she liked her. She admired the way that Eleanor knew where she stood on most matters and never straddled the fence. Maybe she envied it. It still bothered Sylvia to think about the last move. She had abruptly stopped breast-feeding Trevor at four months of age to travel with Tom to house hunt in Oregon and ended up having physical and emotional withdrawals. The move also meant that Alice had to change schools because she had already started kindergarten in Chillicothe. The decision had obviously not been in the family's best interest, and Sylvia hadn't put her foot down.

Sylvia excused herself and went upstairs to unpack their bags. When she heard the phone ring, she stopped on the landing to make sure it wasn't for her. She heard Eleanor talking and then calling for Alice and Trevor. Probably Tom. She passed the linen closet and had to look inside. She smiled as she saw the stack of sheets and the familiar "H" and "F" for head and feet.

She vividly recalled standing in this same spot with Tom, his twin brother Jim, and Jim's girlfriend Cindy, before they were all married. They had snickered and, in whispers, made fun of Eleanor and her labeled sheets. Eleanor had come out of her bedroom at the end of the hall with her hands on her hips and her hair in curlers and chastised them for not recognizing the importance of one of her sanitary rules. Cindy had been the only one who challenged her. "What difference does it make once they're washed?" But Eleanor would have none of it, saying the head must rest as far from the feet as possible. Head high, she had marched back to her room.

Alice and Trevor ran upstairs to find Sylvia and asked if she would go into town with them and Bumpa. She agreed to go as soon as she was finished. The two kids knelt on the floor by the bookcase in their dad and uncle Jim's old room examining the heavy antique-looking iron cars and trucks that sat on a shelf in the bookcase. Trevor jumped up and flopped on one of the maple twin beds. The bedsprings squeaked, and the soft mattress sunk in the middle. They all started to laugh. Sylvia said she was ready, and they headed downstairs.

"Who's that lady, Mommy?" Trevor pointed to a woman standing by the back door who appeared to be in uniform. She wore a white starched cap, pale blue cotton dress, and black low-heeled work shoes.

Frank came out from the living room looking dapper in his white duck shoes for town. "That's Esther. She helps Nana with the house cleaning." He let Esther in and guided her toward the kitchen area.

Esther looked to be around Sylvia's age and had a clean, rosy complexion and sandy-colored hair pulled up in a bun. She nodded and smiled shyly as she passed them. Sylvia noticed her black car sitting in the driveway and realized she was Mennonite, the liberal offshoot of the Amish who were permitted to own cars but only in black.

Eleanor joined them in the back hall. "I think I'll go with you to town. Goodness knows after almost ten years, Esther ought to know what to do on her own."

Alice whispered, leaning sideways to get a better look, "She looks like a nurse. Why does she wear that white hat?"

"Her religion makes her wear it to show that she's married. Just like when I go to my church and cover my head, usually with a scarf," Eleanor answered.

Alice paused. "To show that you're married?"

"No, honey." Eleanor gave her a patronizing smile but gave Sylvia an admonishing glance that meant Alice obviously had not seen the inside of a Catholic church before. Eleanor never did like it that Tom was the only son who didn't marry a Catholic girl. "I only cover my head for church to be humble in God's house, while Esther has to wear hers all the time."

"Even to bed?" Alice asked.

Eleanor and Frank giggled.

"Or in the bathtub?" Trevor turned his hands faceup and scrunched his shoulders.

They laughed harder, and Frank said he didn't think so as they all walked toward the garage.

The center of town was a short drive, about a mile away. The limestone county courthouse building with a large clock at the top sat back from the grassy square that was lined with giant elm trees on three sides. A horse attached to an Amish buggy was tied to a hitching post situated along one side of the square. On the opposite side Frank pulled into an empty parking spot designated for cars.

A small group of Amish men in full beards stood talking by the hitching posts. They wore black felt hats with wide brims and black pants with suspenders over deep denim blue long-sleeved shirts. Young boys who looked like small replicas of their elders stood nearby. Trevor and Alice stared. Sylvia found herself doing the same, wanting to absorb every detail. She had forgotten how refreshingly charming the surroundings were and felt a pang of sadness that this might be her last time here.

Eleanor put her arms around the kids' shoulders and guided them across the street. "They are strange looking, but it's not polite to stare at the plain people." She explained that "we" call them the plain people, and they call "us" the English. "They're hard workers, you have to give 'em that."

Frank asked if the kids, on the way in to Millersburg, saw any horses in the fields pulling plows. "If you did, that was an Amish farm." He said he'd take them to visit the Yoder farm in Killbuck so they could get a closer look. "They do everything the old-fashioned way. Beats me why, but they don't even use telephones or electricity."

"How do they see at night?" Alice asked.

Frank beamed, tweaking Alice on the nose. "Yessiree, you're the smart one, Alice." He winked at Sylvia. "Just like your momma."

They walked past a dime store and stopped at a simple-looking storefront selling Amish quilts and handmade Mission oak chairs. Frank mentioned that carpentry was an Amish specialty and their furniture sold for big prices.

Frank turned to Alice. "They don't need to see at night 'cause they go to bed when the sun goes down." Frank talked with his hands. Down swooped one hand. "And get up when the sun comes up." And back up again.

"They also have gas lanterns in case they do need a light though," Sylvia added.

"It sounds kinda fun to live like that, like camping," Alice said.

Frank whistled through his teeth and shook his head. "You might get tired of it once you saw all the work you had to do. Washing the walls, the floors, the dishes, the clothes, doing all the cooking and sewing. The girls learn how to do the inside work and the boys the outside, like plowing fields, planting crops, caring for the animals."

Sylvia asked if they sewed everything by hand. Eleanor said she knew an Amish woman who used a car battery to run a sewing machine, but that might be out of the ordinary. Sylvia was also surprised to learn that they didn't wear zippers, only buttons and snaps. They really were a foreign culture; most of them still communicated in Dutch, their language of origin.

Alice said she felt sorry for the kids with parents so mean, making them do all that work. "Don't they have any fun?"

"Sure, they play, too. They always sing while they do their chores. They don't listen to a radio or a record player so they make their own music," Eleanor said. "The whole family works together and prays together and *stays* together, which isn't all bad."

Sylvia felt the sting. Frank said he was tired just talking about it and suggested they get an ice cream.

"Mint chocolate chip, no, tutti-frutti. Maybe rocky road. Chocolate with marshmallow, or vanilla with chocolate chips." The kids excitedly ran through their favorites.

"Whoa, Nelly. This isn't Baskin Robbins." Frank laughed. "You can have chocolate, vanilla, strawberry, or the flavor of the day, butter pecan."

When they got their cones, they crossed the street and sat on a bench in the square and watched the world go by. The hot, humid day made cones melt too fast and clothes stick to bodies. It seemed that all the friends Eleanor and Frank had were in town that afternoon. They stopped and chatted, mentioning how nice it was to see Sylvia and the kids again, and over and over they asked where Tom was until it seemed like an echo bouncing off of every surrounding mini-alpine slope. The kids began to complain of the mess and the heat and wanted to go back. Sylvia's mood was spiraling downward at the strain of faking it to all who asked. She didn't think she could keep the smile plastered on her face for another minute and was overcome with a feeling of not belonging here anymore. In one short hour, the charming scene had become quaint, kitsch, and unstimulating. This was definitely not her world.

Eleanor's comments were slowly piling up in Sylvia's mind, too. Eleanor might have a firm opinion on most matters but seemed uncomfortable until she found a way to tell you. In her backdoor fashion, Eleanor let Sylvia know what was really on her mind: that Sylvia shouldn't work, that Sylvia was the one who didn't want to live in Millersburg after college, that Sylvia could have prevented the move from Chillicothe, and underlying it all, the marriage fell apart because they didn't attend Catholic church. Eleanor never meant to be hurtful; she simply saw things a certain way, the right way.

On the way back to the house, Sylvia said she should call her parents. She said she'd drive back tomorrow and leave the kids at Eleanor and Frank's for four or five days, if that was all right. She'd take Red with her.

Being here had naturally brought back a lot of memories. Her momentary wallowing in the past wasn't going to change anything, so she'd better accept what's done and stop kidding herself that the outcome could've been different. The history they all shared would remain with her forever, but this chapter was closed. She felt a renewed strength to push forward and reach for the life she longed to have.

# CHAPTER 13

The letters from Anthony started coming during Sylvia's second week in Ohio. She began looking for the mailman not only hoping for another letter, but also because she wanted to intercept any before her parents got to them. Vivian didn't openly object to this clandestine communiqué coming to her home, but she did think it was in bad taste. Sylvia hid them like she hid her diary when she was thirteen years old.

*My dearest Jake,*

*My life is empty without you here. I pass your house every day on the way down the hill, and it looks like a tomb. With the For Sale sign in the yard, I worry that you're somehow gone from me forever.*

*Not being able to talk to you is the worst though. I hear your voice, and I see you everywhere. It's crazy, but I even look for you in a crowd or in the neighborhood. I saw the back of a woman wearing a dark blue straight corduroy skirt and a floppy felt hat like yours, and I almost ran and grabbed her. My Annie Hall girl. You are "la-dee-dah." My heart skips a beat when I see a burgundy Mercedes like yours, which luckily isn't often. (I've almost rear-ended a few cars!)*

*I'm so despondent I can hardly concentrate on my work, so you can imagine how I am at home. I snap at the kids constantly and just stare at the TV like a zombie. To make matters worse, your name seems to come up a lot with the neighbors. First, because you'll be teaching some of their kids. And second, there's a buzz about your house up for sale and the reason why. Divorce was tossed around but dropped. Most people think it's financial. What really makes my insides drop is when they ask me what's going on, since the four of us used to be such good friends. When I say we don't see you guys anymore, some busybodies ask me why. I can't wait to get this all over with and be with you forever.*

*I find myself wondering: What if she never comes back? What if she decides it's not worth it? If you did decide that, you know I'd come and get you. I'd just make an announcement for all to hear, and I'd find you. So … don't even think about it.*

*The bottom line, my beautiful Jake, is you consume me. Can you tell?*

*Sorry if this is depressing, but you have to know how much I need you near me, with me, around me, and on top of me. Just the thought of feeling you next to me makes me weak. Better change the subject.*

*Thanks for calling to tell me about Steve. I hope he gets the care he needs, which, for now, does sound encouraging. As difficult as it was for you, I'm glad you were there when your parents needed you. Even if they don't want to hear anything from me, please at least tell them I pray for Steve. I'm counting the days 'til we're together again … and, until then, watching the mail. All my love forever.*

Getting mail from her lover lifted Sylvia's spirits immensely. She read and reread the letters and felt like the lovesick adolescent again. Only now, she had direction and focus. The divorce would be final in September. She had a good job, a solid man who loved her more than she had ever been loved before, and two beautiful kids who would survive this divorce. She would make sure of that.

When Eleanor and Frank called about bringing the kids back to her parents, they all decided to have the dinner together they were supposed to have the week before. Vivian was upbeat and had insisted they go forward with the original plans. With Steve safe and doing well in the hospital, a feeling of buoyant eagerness spread throughout the household, like an unstated sense of gratitude for the enjoyable moments at hand.

Around two in the afternoon the beige Ford Fairlane rolled slowly into the gravel driveway. Alice and Trevor burst from the backseat and rushed to greet Red, whose whole body waggled with enthusiasm. Sylvia ran to her kids while the two sets of grandparents greeted each other. Alice whispered with a roll of the eyes that she sure was glad to be back. They hugged Vivian and Matt and ran off to play with Red. Sylvia joined the grandparents in the driveway.

"Wonderful spread you've got here, Matt. Even more beautiful than the last time I saw it. You still do all the yard work yourself?" Frank rocked back on his heels and surveyed the front yard.

"Helluva lot of work, but I got more time now that I'm retired," Matt said.

Vivian offered to help Eleanor with the covered dish she brought as the two made their way toward the house.

"I forgot my pocketbook in the car." Eleanor turned around to retrieve it.

"I'll just take these candied yams inside," Vivian said.

"Did I hear candied yams?" Matt asked.

"You made his favorite, Eleanor!" Vivian called out.

"I remember what he likes." Eleanor winked at Matt and held up a canning jar from the backseat. "*And* I brought you a jar of my pickled watermelon rind."

Matt broke into a wide grin. "You sure didn't forget what I like. Much appreciated."

Eleanor wiped her forehead with her handkerchief. "Boy, it feels good to get out of that sweltering car."

"How about a drink?" Matt looked at Frank.

"Don't mind if I do. Bourbon and Seven, if you have it. But in case you don't, I brought my own." Frank pointed to his car.

Eleanor tsked, shook her head, and followed Vivian and Sylvia through the front patio and the open sliding glass door into the family room.

Matt and Frank settled themselves with their drinks in the family room while the women busied themselves in the kitchen with the meal preparations. Alice and Trevor soon ran in and asked if Sylvia would take them to the lake to swim.

"Those two could talk of nothing else but swimming in the lake during the whole car ride," Eleanor said. "You'd better get going so you'll be back in time for dinner, don't you agree, Vivian?"

"No hurry. You and Frank don't need to rush back, do you?" Vivian stood over the sink snipping the ends of the green beans with her kitchen shears.

It was settled that they had two hours to spend at the lake. Sylvia was pleased she could spend some fun time alone with her kids and wondered if the grandparents would talk about the divorce while they were out of the house. At least her mother didn't drink since she was the one in the family with loose lips and could absentmindedly let something slip even without alcohol. Sylvia had made sure that her mother was briefed before Eleanor and Frank's arrival, saying that Tom had just told them about the divorce a few weeks before the Ohio trip and that they knew nothing else.

The lake was a bustle of activity. Paddleboats, sailboats, and rowboats were scattered across the water from one end of the lake to the other. There wasn't a breath of wind, so the sailboats sat on the dark, crystal-smooth surface without as much as a flutter in their sails. Optimism for the usual late afternoon breeze ruled the waters here.

Sylvia noticed that the beach and dock were full of teenagers, young children, and their stay-at-home moms who spent the summer days sunbathing and socializing on the lake's tree-lined shores. *At least I'll still have my summers to come visit.*

"I like it better in the day," Trevor said.

"I like it at night." Alice dropped her towel and took off for the water.

Sylvia took Trevor's hand, and they ran after her. Sylvia and Trevor played in the water at the shoreline and watched Alice dive off the diving board. When she swam to the floating dock, she called to Sylvia and Trevor to come, too. Trevor happily climbed onto Sylvia's back, and she swam out to Alice. This time Trevor jumped off the floating dock right into Sylvia's arms and then dog-paddled back to start all over again. The two hours passed too quickly, but nobody complained, knowing they could come back tomorrow and spend the whole day. Sylvia would pack lunches, and they'd row a boat out to the island.

When they got to the house, the picnic table was set in the backyard and dinner was ready. Matt and Frank were still in the family room and the TV was on. They were watching a golf tournament. Sylvia didn't have to worry about these two talking divorce.

Sylvia and the kids changed out of their suits and helped take things to the table. Frank and Matt came out, drinks in hand. Vivian climbed over the bench and sat across from Sylvia.

Eleanor needed an assist from Frank to maneuver the bench. She giggled. “You all catch me if I fall backwards!”

“You’re too big for me to catch you, Nana!” Trevor said wide-eyed.

They all chuckled.

Platters of corn on the cob, tomatoes from Nana’s garden, fried chicken, potato salad, coleslaw, and candied yams were spread across the table. The conversation stayed light and inconsequential, just as Sylvia had hoped.

“Is that the phone?” Vivian asked.

“Just let it ring, will ya?” Matt said.

Vivian jumped up and excused herself, saying she didn’t want to miss any calls from the hospital. When she left, Eleanor leaned forward over her plate toward Matt and said she didn’t mean to pry but asked how Steve was doing.

“He seems stable for now. Could you pass me those yams?” Matt asked.

“Will he come back here?” she asked.

“Most likely. We’ve exhausted the halfway houses in this area.” Matt dove into his yams.

“It sure is a crying shame. Such a lovely young man.” Eleanor laid her fork down and said she’d wait to eat until Vivian came back.

“Did you end up taking the kids to the Amish farm, Frank?” Sylvia asked.

Relief passed over Frank’s face at the change of subject. “Sure did. Alice and Trevor even got to meet some Amish kids.”

"I wish I was Amish," Alice said. "They don't have to go to school past eighth grade!"

"I practically grew up on my uncle Morris's farm in my hometown in Nebraska but got away from it as soon as I could," Matt said. "I think you'd get tired of it real fast, Alice."

"Exactly what I told her." Frank stuck his fork in the air to make his point.

"We made popcorn balls and catched frogs in the cow trough," Trevor said.

Everyone laughed.

"Not at the Amish farm, Trevor, at Nana and Bumpa's," Alice clarified.

Granddad gave Trevor an affectionate squeeze. "You did? How many did you get?"

"This many!" Trevor spread his arms.

Vivian returned and apologized for taking so long. She said it was Tom and that he'd call back in half an hour.

"Where is he?" Alice asked.

"He's at your home," Vivian answered.

"If he's not working, he should come here," Alice said.

There was an uncomfortable silence as the grandparents ate with their heads down. Sylvia jumped in explaining he probably had to leave on another trip for work anyway.

"Daddy says we might get a farm with horses when the house sells." Alice looked around at all the bowed heads. "What's the matter?"

Sylvia looked for some reaction from her mom, who didn't know that Sylvia knew that Alice had told her about the house up for sale. More tangled webs. She was puzzled when she didn't see one, because her mother could never hide anything. She forced a chipper tone. "Your dad may want that for you, honey, but it probably won't happen right away."

"Why not?" Alice asked.

Sylvia gently stroked her daughter's hair. "Remember about the business not doing very well?"

"It's not?" Eleanor's head snapped up.

Tom obviously hadn't said a word to his own parents. It griped Sylvia that he'd asked to borrow money from her father but didn't have the nerve to address it with his own parents.

"Why do you think Sylvia has to leave Trevor and go to work?" Vivian sounded exasperated. "*And* sell their house?"

Eleanor turned red and looked back down at her plate.

"Mom, I also want to work," Sylvia said.

Frank said they weren't aware of any problems.

"Not with the *business* anyway," Eleanor mumbled. "Maybe there're some other things we don't know about."

"What is that supposed to mean?" Vivian's tone turned haughty.

Frank looked at Matt. "New businesses take time to get going, isn't that right, Matt?"

"At least five years is what I hear." Matt picked up his plate and straddled the bench to get up. "Alice and Trevor, why don't you help me with the strawberry shortcake?" They went inside.

Sylvia looked over at her mother and Eleanor, who avoided eye contact with each other. She raised her eyebrows at Frank and sighed deeply. "I'm sorry you had to learn about Tom's business this way, but that's the main reason we have to sell the house. We both contributed to our marriage falling apart, but you might as well know that I'm the one who finally asked for the divorce. I'm sorry for the worry it brings on all of you. It's not just one person's fault, so I would only ask that you try not to assign blame, for the children's sake. We haven't told them yet, so let's not ruin a lovely dinner together." Sylvia got up and started to clear the table.

Vivian and Eleanor nodded stiffly and apologized to each other. Frank said he was ready for his shortcake but would like a cup of coffee if it wasn't too much trouble. As she approached the back door, Sylvia heard the phone ring. The kids tripped over each other calling, "Daddy!"

# CHAPTER 14

When they were children, Sylvia and Steve, and, later, Scott anxiously counted the days from the time that school let out in June until mid-July when the Silver Lake Festival took place. It lasted one weekend each year from Saturday morning through Sunday evening. The community garden club organized the event, which always opened with the bike parade that started at the grade school and ended at the lake, a distance of about a half-mile. Most of the children in the community participated and decorated their bicycles in accordance with the year's theme. Prizes were awarded for various categories.

Down at the boathouse, the usual homemade dishes of potato salad, coleslaw, baked beans, Jell-O molds, sloppy joes, hot dogs, fried chicken, spareribs, brownies, spice, chocolate, and carrot cakes covered the long tables from noon until nine each night. A card table was set up as a "ticket booth" where kids, many who had saved their allowance money, stood in line to purchase the strips of paper tickets needed for games and food. Cotton candy, snow cones, a dunking machine, and amusement park-type games were set up throughout the grounds. During the afternoons there were separate swimming races for boys and girls from ages six through fifteen years. Sylvia and Steve and most of their friends had entered them every year as kids. Steve had always won his event and brought home small trophies to put on his bookshelf. In the evenings the adults provided vaudeville-style entertainment of skits, singing acts, and musical performances.

This year's theme was Johnny Appleseed. Sylvia helped Alice decorate Scott's old Schwinn bike for the parade. Baskets of apples hung on each side of her handlebars and a crown of leaves adorned her head. Her limbs were made to look like branches and her body a trunk with brown cotton fabric that Vivian bought for the occasion. Alice was an apple tree. Her bicycle wheels had green and brown crepe paper streamers wound through the spokes. Trevor didn't have anything to ride, so Matt said he'd pull him in a wagon. He could be Johnny Appleseed and wear a saucepan on his head. Matt bought a small bag of grass seed and said he could toss it as he rode. Trevor couldn't wait.

Matt would play in the ragtime band that performed every year by the lake at suppertime, and Vivian, her singing days behind her, would sit with Sylvia and the kids and enjoy the show. Steve had been steadily improving and was due home any day. For now, he was still safely tucked in the hospital ward, so Vivian and Matt were relaxed and happy and counting the days with Alice and Trevor until the festival.

Sylvia had invited her closest friend in Ohio, Lindsey, and her family to come to the festival during the afternoon on Saturday and join them for dinner there in the evening. Lindsey didn't live in Silver Lake, which was private, so she could only come to the lake as an invited guest. Just she and her oldest daughter, Kate, who was Alice's age, would come, she said, because her younger girls were too little to enjoy it. Her husband, Nate, didn't mind staying home with them since she and Sylvia didn't get to spend much time together.

Lindsey and Sylvia had been close friends from the day they met when they taught high school together. Lindsey was still teaching there. Tom had been in Vietnam then, and Sylvia had been living at home with her parents. When Tom returned, they had moved to New Jersey, but Sylvia and Lindsey wrote to each other and saw each other every time Sylvia came back to Ohio. And each time Alice and Kate were together, they acted like they'd never been apart.

Sylvia had confided in Lindsey about her affair and the divorce the year before. Unlike Jessica, Lindsey had said Sylvia would never move on anything so drastic without analyzing all sides. And that after two years, it obviously wasn't a rash decision.

Lindsey and Kate met Sylvia and Alice at the lake after the bike parade. They ran and hugged each other.

"I tried to get here for the parade, but fifteen things happened at once and I couldn't get away," Lindsey said.

Sylvia shook her head. "So what else is new? I think you should slow down. At least you made it before dinner."

"You know me too well." Lindsey grinned. "Where's Trevor? And your parents?"

"Trevor was tired after the parade. They'll be back later."

They wandered through the crowds trailing behind their girls, who were deciding what games they wanted to play. They finally settled in front of a table covered with small goldfish bowls. You had three tries to win a goldfish by tossing a plastic ring over a bowl. They kept sliding off.

"That was close, Alice! If you win one, we'll keep it for you!" Lindsey jumped up and down. Her long black hair tied in ponytails bounced with her. She had more enthusiasm than anyone Sylvia knew.

Sylvia leaned toward her in a whisper. "And flush it down the toilet."

Lindsey burst out laughing. "You're right. That's where it would end up in our house, unless the cat ate it."

"Not to worry. The girls are heading toward the boathouse," Sylvia said.

"For the food. Just like their moms!" Lindsey grabbed Sylvia's hand. "Sloppy joes, c'mon."

"My favorite thing here," Sylvia said. "They've used the same recipe for over twenty years."

Sylvia knew many of the people here, and as it turned out, so did Lindsey. She was civic-minded, like her own mother, and gave of herself until she dropped. She was a champion for the disadvantaged and regularly brought troubled kids home from school. She was voted teacher of the year several times and was now receiving national attention for a musical she had produced to help stop the nuclear arms race. Sylvia wondered if Lindsey's husband was worn down with all her causes. He always backed her and stood right beside her, but in the last few years Sylvia sensed that Nate wanted to get off the carousel, if only to wait out one ride. *Maybe he feels like a politician's wife*, Sylvia thought.

They found a spot on the grass by the water and sat down.

"I think you know more people here than I do," Sylvia said.

Many friends of Sylvia's parents came up to them to say hello and commented that they didn't know Lindsey and Sylvia were friends. They congratulated Lindsey on her latest success and usually asked Sylvia about Tom's whereabouts. Sylvia realized that what bothered her in Millersburg seemed to have no effect on her here, on her own turf. A few asked about Steve, but as the years passed and his illness looked lifelong, Sylvia noticed that most people steered away from the subject.

"I work hard on getting attention. You know that." Lindsey grinned.

"Have you ever thought of running for office?"

"God, no. I'm best at helping the kids who need it, in my own little way." She took a big bite of her sandwich.

"Taking your protest play to D.C. is not little."

"I love inspiring the local politicians to help us. That doesn't mean I want to be one."

Sylvia looked at her. "And you love the kids."

"I do." Lindsey's eyes spoke from her soul. "Especially the ones who don't get any love."

Sylvia put her arm around her friend. "I'm proud of you and maybe a little jealous. I'm having an affair, and you're changing the world."

Lindsey giggled. "That's my illusion. At least you're grounded in reality."

"Oh, I get it. Earthly delights." Sylvia finished the last of her sloppy joe. "Mine could be a fantasy world, too, you know."

Alice and Kate ran up to ask if they could have more money for games and snow cones. They were like two peas in a pod, one blonde, the other brunette, jabbering nonstop, having the time of their lives. When they each got five dollars from their moms, their mouths dropped and their eyes bugged out, and they took off toward the card table ticket booth.

Lindsey's expression turned serious. "Remember when I had panic attacks?"

"Oh, my God, I forgot to ask you," Sylvia said. "Sorry if I can't recall the details. Earlier this year, wasn't it?"

"January. They started when Nate's company wanted him to take a management job in Boston. I lost sleep for weeks. Should we move to support his career? Should I uproot my kids? Should I leave my work? Should I stay to be near my parents?"

"Whatever happened with those? Did they just go away?"

"It was gradual. I stayed home from school for a week because I couldn't see—"

"You mean things were blurry?"

"I mean everything was black. My doctor said I needed a shrink."

"Jesus, Lindsey. That must have been terrifying. I didn't realize—"

"It was. The shrink gave me some pills. Tranquilizers. I don't take them anymore."

"And Nate refused the offer, and you think he really wanted to take it." Sylvia lay back on the grass and looked up through the giant elms swaying in the wind.

"Right. The point is, I look at you and—" Lindsey's tone turned chipper.

"Sometimes I wonder if we should've stayed in Ohio. Maybe that would've been 'grounded in reality.'"

"I'm trying to tell you something, and you keep changing the subject," Lindsey said in mock annoyance.

Sylvia sat up on her elbows and smiled. "With our famous tangents, it's amazing we ever finish a story, isn't it? Go ahead, I'm listening."

"My point is I couldn't move like you have. You're not afraid of risk. I admire your courage, the kind of courage I don't have. You're strong, Sylvia, and confident."

"I never thought of it that way."

"It's true." She cocked her head. "Even though for selfish reasons I wish you lived here. You're the only one I can talk to on a gut level." She stood up and took Sylvia's paper plate to throw away. "*And* I'm jealous you speak *français*." Lindsey pronounced it "fronsay" on purpose. She loved to needle Sylvia with her "American" accent. When they taught together, she used to drop in on Sylvia's classes and pretend she was one of the students. The students loved it, and so did Sylvia.

"You forgot to mention you're jealous because I'm having great sex."

Several heads turned, and Lindsey laughed out loud.

By five o'clock Sylvia started wondering where her parents were. She debated whether they should walk home when she spotted Matt descending the hill with his trumpet case in hand. They met him halfway up the hill and walked to where the band was setting up.

"Hi, Mr. Anderson. How are you?" Lindsey reached up and gave Matt a kiss on the cheek.

He patted her on the back. "Pretty good. Having a good time? Looks like the girls could go on all night." He nodded toward Alice and Kate, who were barefoot and riding the old merry-go-round that sat by the dock in shallow water.

The iron contraption with wood seats had been there since Sylvia was a child. Kids often climbed to the center of its cement base to perch in the middle while it revolved round and round. Although she'd never seen anyone get hurt, Sylvia always worried someone could get his legs caught if it was moving too fast or get dizzy and lose his balance. Their kids seemed to have mastered it though.

"We're all having a ball. Thanks for inviting us," Lindsey said.

"I thought you guys would get here before this. Where's Mom and Trevor?" Sylvia asked.

"They're coming." He set his trumpet case down and unhinged its latches. "With Steve."

"He's home?" Sylvia didn't expect this today. "Isn't it kind of sudden? I mean, why today?"

Lindsey gave Sylvia a look and said she'd go check on the girls.

"Sometimes they don't give us much warning. When they called and said either today or Monday, your mother thought he'd hate to miss the festival." He blew on his spit valve.

"How is he?"

"Seems happy to be home. Says he'll take his meds." Matt pulled out his sheet music.

"Good news." Sylvia sounded let down. They were having such a good time. So free and easy.

"He said he wanted to eat here. I wasn't sure all this hubbub was a good idea, but he says he'll be fine."

If Steve was coming, she wondered if he'd just eat and go back home or stay with them for the concert. She hoped he wouldn't be sullen or disruptive and ruin it for everyone.

Matt joined the arriving band members and helped set up chairs and music racks. Sylvia found Lindsey and the girls on the dock watching a clown make balloon animals. Moments later she heard her mom's voice call to her, and Sylvia turned around. Vivian was beaming. There was Steve, clean-shaven, head high, walking beside her. He nodded to people as they passed by. And he was holding Trevor's hand. Sylvia's heart stirred at the sight of her dear brother as the adoring uncle, if only for this moment in time. When Trevor saw her, he let go, and ran into her arms.

*****

The month Sylvia spent in Ohio seemed to pass too quickly once she got through the harrowing first week and a half. Sylvia found herself mentally repeating her mother's maxim, *This too shall pass*, which helped her deal with the distress of Trevor's close call and Steve's suicide attempt as well as the more minor discomforts, such as her unease with her in-laws.

To her surprise, this mantra planted a seed that helped her cultivate a more relaxed approach to an upsetting situation and enabled her to act with more self-assurance. Knowing that nothing lasts forever could be reassuring. The dilemma for Sylvia was applying this attitude to the good times. Leaving the comforting embrace of her parents and the hazy summer days by the lake with her children was more difficult than she'd expected. Maybe she had stayed too long and reverted to being the child again. What if she forgot how to be strong and self-sufficient? This time it was Sylvia who counted the days, but not with anticipation. By the end of the month's stay, while she longed to see Anthony, her new life appeared as a daunting undertaking.

# CHAPTER 15

## Back in Oregon

August and September were normally the hottest, driest months of the year in Oregon, but this year was exceptionally hot. In late August, for straight five days, the temperatures climbed into the low one hundreds and the Beekman house was stifling. Sylvia closed all the windows and blinds during the day and opened them after sunset to try to keep the temperature down inside. Because it was too hot to sleep upstairs, Tom and Sylvia made up beds of cushions and sheets for all of them in the living room. She'd heard the best place to get away from the heat was the Oregon coast, only an hour and a half away, but even that wasn't possible right now, so for several afternoons she escaped with Alice and Trevor to the shopping mall. It wasn't Sylvia's idea of a getaway, but it was cool. With school starting in the coming week, they could at least do some school shopping. She prayed the heat wave would be over by then.

Tom was home that week, which helped a lot. She had teacher meetings every morning at the junior high and didn't have to make arrangements for Alice and Trevor since they could be with their dad. With September just days away, Sylvia was not only preoccupied with lesson plans, but also the inevitable upheaval that would come when she and Tom broke the news of their divorce to Alice. Sylvia wished they hadn't waited this long. Although there was no good time to tell Alice, Sylvia thought it would be a terrible burden for her to carry at the start of the school year.

On Friday, the last day of the teacher meetings, Sylvia came home at lunchtime as she had all week. No one was there, not even Red. There was no note. She figured they had all gone to a nearby park along the Willamette River where Tom had taken them before. She and Tom no longer reported to each other of their whereabouts unless it affected the children. She wasn't pleased that he hadn't left a note, but she wanted to give Tom some latitude since he was trying so hard to establish a relationship with them independent of her. Twice that week Tom had made dinner plans with the kids that kept them well into the evening. By the time they had gotten home, Sylvia was already asleep. When she'd left for school early in the morning, they weren't awake yet. She felt out of sync without constant contact with them, especially after being together every day in Ohio. What she found even more disconcerting was her children's happy, carefree demeanor. They didn't seem to miss her at all.

As tight as her schedule was, she and Anthony had been able to see each other the two evenings Tom had taken the children, which helped soothe her wounds.

Sylvia climbed the stairs to change her clothes and took the opportunity to call Anthony at his office. She stood by the bedroom window to watch for Tom's car, which seemed like a silly game to be playing at this stage, but out of habit and maybe some lingering fear of being discovered, she watched anyway in case Tom and the kids returned while she was on the phone.

"Do you think we could squeeze in a lunch today?" Sylvia asked.

"What I'd really like to do is take you away for the weekend. To celebrate the beginning of your school year," Anthony said.

Sylvia tried to untwist the coiled phone cord. "That's a lovely fantasy, but I'll settle for lunch. I should warn you though, I could be dangerous."

"Oh? How so?"

"I might jump your bones from across the table."

"I like the way you think." Anthony paused. "Maybe I can steal away for more time. After all it *is* Friday." He took a deep breath. "Can you meet me in the parking lot of Grove Creek Park in twenty minutes, and we'll figure it out from there?"

Sylvia felt the rush of excitement with their spontaneous plan. She hurried into her pastel plaid halter-top and yellow cotton culottes and ran down the stairs two at a time. As she went through the family room toward the garage, she spotted an unfamiliar white plaster mold of a unicorn about four inches tall sitting on the shelf of the bookcase. She picked it up and saw the initials A.B. scratched on the bottom. Puzzled, she set it back down and left the house.

The small park was set far back from the road along the south end of the river and was empty at midday. Sylvia drove through several winding park roads that led to a densely shaded, secluded grove of full-grown rhododendrons with only one parking spot. Anthony's car was there, but he wasn't in it. Sylvia got out and wandered toward the sandy riverbank where he sat on a blanket with a bottle of red wine, a baguette of French bread, and one large white take-out carton.

"How did you find time to do all this?" Sylvia beamed in astonishment.

Anthony hopped up to embrace her. "It's not a weekend away, but it'll have to do."

"Maybe I should threaten jumping your bones more often." She put her arms around his neck and laughed. As he looked into her eyes, she could feel the depth of his desire take hold of her.

He hungrily kissed her neck and her bare shoulders, and lightly stroked her bare back with both hands. "Oh, Jake, I can never get enough of you."

Sylvia felt so weak she didn't think she could stand. She pulled him against her with her hands on the back of his thighs, moving them slowly up and around his buttocks. His breath caught in his throat. He devoured her mouth with his and thrust his tongue deep inside. In their passion, they stumbled and dropped entwined in each other's arms onto the blanket. He untied her halter-top with one pull at the neck and dropped his head to suck her nipples, cupping her breasts in both of his hands. He teased her by circling his tongue slowly over each nipple while one hand crept up her leg, brushing gently over her moistened bikinis, across the top of her mound and back down, pressing harder each time, until his finger found its way inside. She groaned with pleasure, unzipped his pants and feverishly pushed them below his knees.

They rolled over each other several times before she ended up on top of him, where she stayed, where she could feel his full length, his hardness pushing deeper and deeper inside as she spread her legs. Their bodies glistened with sweat. When he came before she did, he massaged her while he was still inside until she came, too. She thought her heart would leap out of her chest. Panting hard she flopped off of him and onto the sand-covered blanket. His pants were around his ankles, and she was completely naked.

Coming to her senses, she said, "I hope no one is hiding in the bushes, watching us."

Anthony covered her with the lightweight tablecloth-like blanket he brought for their picnic, and then pulled up his boxers. "I think we're safe. I checked the area before you got here."

"I'm dying to go in the river."

"Let's. In our underwear." He searched for hers.

"But I didn't wear a bra."

"Wear your bikinis and … here." He handed her the panties then draped the cloth around her shoulders. They slipped into the tepid, slow-moving current. Once under the water, Sylvia threw the cloth back on shore, and they lolled there in the river's flow until they decided it was time to eat. Once on shore he gave her his shirt to wear.

"This was just what I needed today. You knew, didn't you?" Sylvia tore off a piece of bread.

"I could hear it in your voice. You don't ask that often for what you need, so it doesn't take much to know when you do." He handed her a glass of wine and offered her the carton filled with fried calamari.

"And you were there for me. I've never had that feeling with Tom."

"I always want to be there for you."

"I need to know that now more than ever," she said. "Tom's gone with the kids more than I expected, but that's a good thing, I think." Sylvia took a large sip of wine. "We're supposed to tell Alice this weekend."

Anthony took the glass from her hand, set it down, and took both of her hands in his. He bowed his head for a second and then looked into her eyes. "It might get worse before it gets better, but I promise you, it will get better. Remember that promise when the pain brings on the doubt, which it will. We will make it, Jake." He drew her hands to his lips and kissed each one. "Now. Say it. It will get better." She repeated it slowly at first, until the two of them were saying it together.

When she left Anthony that afternoon, Sylvia definitely felt relaxed. By the time she pulled into her driveway, she wanted to be in the "get better" stage, which she knew was a long way off. Tom's VW convertible was in the garage. She wondered if she looked disheveled. Without warning, the door between the family room and the garage opened, and there stood Tom as she stepped out of her car.

He glanced at her wet hair. "I've been waiting for you. We need to talk."

"I thought we were going to talk tomorrow." She moved past him and said she needed a few minutes. She turned back. "Where are the kids?"

"That's part of what I want to talk about."

"Tell me now. I don't need a few minutes." She sat down carefully on the couch in the family room.

Tom paced in front of the TV and looked at the floor. His red T-shirt looked too small, and his muscular shoulders bulged underneath. He was well tanned. He wore gray athletic shorts and tennis shoes without socks. He put his hands on his hips and turned to look at her.

"I'll ask this one last time." He looked up at the ceiling then back at her. "Do you really want this divorce?"

Sylvia was nonplussed. "It's almost final. Why would you ask now?"

"One *final* try." He choked up and looked away. "I still think we could lead separate lives but not get the divorce."

"You're asking me to pretend we have a marriage? That's so wrong."

"Wrong?" Tom raised his arms to the heavens. "What's wrong is to put our kids through the hell of separate homes."

"Living separate lives would be the same thing. How good is it for them to see their parents living a lie?"

"They don't care how we live. They just want their parents to be together."

Although they'd been through this argument before, Sylvia realized this time was for keeps. "So, you still want to stay married? For the kids?"

"Seems like the right thing to do."

"To keep their house intact? Or is this just about finances?"

"Both. I still think we're going through a phase." Tom picked up the plaster unicorn on the bookshelf.

"And how do we move out of this phase?"

"Time will take care of that." He set the unicorn back down.

Sylvia watched him. She thought of the initials, A.B., Alice Beekman. "Where did that come from? Where are the kids?"

Tom didn't answer.

"Tom? What are you not telling me?"

He cleared his throat. "The kids are with my girlfriend, who showed Alice how to make plaster molds. Just say the word or I'm moving in with her this weekend."

# CHAPTER 16

Sylvia was dumbfounded. Her kids were with his girlfriend. She couldn't look at him. She couldn't even speak. She got up from the couch and headed toward the kitchen.

"Sylvia."

She continued up the stairs and into their bedroom. She could hear Tom's footsteps in the kitchen.

"Sylvia!" he called up the stairs.

A few minutes passed. Sylvia stood at the top looking down, her arms loaded with his clothes. With one big heave, she threw them at him. In seconds, he was covered in plaid and striped boxer shorts, T-shirts, and khakis. His balled-up socks bobbed across the floor. Tom's mouth dropped open. She turned around for the next load. This time she grabbed the hanger section of suits and sport coats.

"Are you nuts?" Tom called out.

She came out of the bedroom and looked down at him. She was so furious she thought she'd burst. "You move in *now*!" And she pitched the rest.

Tom began to gather some of his clothes. Still bent over, he turned his head and gave her a brazen stare. "I was going to anyway."

"And I want the kids home immediately!" Her voice was strident and rang in her ears.

Tom went into the kitchen. She bounded down the stairs after him. "Do you hear me?"

He got a black plastic trash bag. "They're staying with me tonight."

"Then I'll follow you and get them myself. Is that what you want?" Sylvia folded her arms over her chest to stop her hands from trembling.

"Do as you like. But they'll be spending weekends with me anyway. It might as well start now." He slung the bag over his shoulder and turned toward the family room.

What was she going to do? Make it even harder for Alice and Trevor with an emotional scene? Get a court order to stop him from taking them there? She wanted them to see their dad as much as possible, but not like this. He had her cornered.

She followed him. "We haven't even talked to Alice about the divorce! And you're parading your girlfriend in front of her?"

"It's more gradual like this. Maybe she won't go into a tailspin."

"What's gradual with you moving in 'this weekend'?"

"I took them there twice last week and told Alice that Betsy's a friend." He set the bag down on the carpet. "Betsy lives on one of the canals and there's ducks, and she's trying real hard to make it fun for them and—"

"I don't want to hear about her."

"Well, get used to it. I'm telling Alice that Betsy and I are friends and I'll be living there for a while," he said. "Like a separation."

"*Living* with your girlfriend? What's the matter with you? I hate to tell you, but the hippy lifestyle is over. You missed it." Sylvia's trembling stopped, but her stomach was in knots.

"I'm not living in a commune. I'm just moving in with my—"

"Well, living with another woman is not acceptable for my children while you're still married to me."

"What would you have me do? Get an apartment? With what?" Tom's eyes flashed with indignation. He leaned forward, his face in hers. "You'd better get off your high horse."

Sylvia took a step back. She didn't have an answer to this. "What about telling her the truth?"

"And just what is the truth, Sylvia?"

He had her now. She was sure he knew about Anthony. She faltered and looked away. "That we're getting a divorce."

"Sitting her down and having a heavy conversation about *the divorce* would be worse for her."

"She'll ask, you know."

"Maybe."

"And you'll lie to her, right?"

"It won't hurt if she doesn't know the divorce is almost over. Why should she know? We can play it by ear. Let her down easy."

Sylvia bent over the top of the couch, her forehead cradled in her hands. She'd be the one left to deal with Alice's questions. Her blood was still boiling at his avoidance of facing Alice to save himself pain. She needed time to think this through. "You'd better leave that bag here, I guess. For now."

She saw the bag drop by his feet and noticed his tennis shoes were bright, white leather. She talked into the couch. "Did you buy new shoes?"

"No," he said. "They were a gift."

She watched his shoes turn toward the door to the garage and then heard the click of the doorknob.

"I'll bring the kids and Red back tomorrow night. I already have their stuff." And he left.

*Why does everything have to be so complicated?* Sylvia felt drained. And hot and sticky. She needed a shower. She lay on the couch and closed her eyes. She daydreamed that she was swimming across Silver Lake, all by herself. She wanted to feel buoyant and float. She thought about that night on the floating dock with Trevor. Lying there with him on top of her, staring at the stars. She could almost feel the thumping rhythm of his heart beating. She wanted them home with her now. She wanted to sleep with them tonight.

Sylvia woke up to a loud knock on the front door. She didn't want to answer it, so she tiptoed across the foyer and peered through the peephole. Jessica. She flung the door open.

"Do I need to see you!" Sylvia said. "It's dark out."

"That happens every night." Jessica headed for the kitchen. "Where is everybody?" She grabbed a beer from the refrigerator.

"I'll have one, too," Sylvia said. "Tom just left—"

"I'm pissed again at Greg and stormed out the house. I took a chance that you'd be here. So what's going on?" Jessica suggested they sit on the deck and have a cigarette.

Sylvia told her all the details: from the moment she got home from school to her afternoon with Anthony to the finale of the bomb Tom dropped.

Even Jessica was taken aback. "I wonder how long Tom's been seeing her."

"If he's moving in with her, it's probably been a long time."

"Did you ever suspect it? Weren't there any hints?"

"Not a one. I've been so preoccupied with my own affair, and with him gone so much, I never saw it coming."

"But I'm sure it started after yours. Maybe when he figured you were involved with someone else."

"Maybe. It still came as a shock." Sylvia lit another cigarette. "Actually, that he has a girlfriend doesn't bother me. I half expected it by now. But exposing the kids to her?"

"Taking the kids there would bother me, too." Jessica took a sip of beer.

"And he's so casual about it! I don't know what I can do to stop it."

"I don't think there's anything you can do about this right now, unless you want to call off the divorce."

"You must be psychic. He suggested we stay together and live separate lives."

"I knew it! Tom still wants you back, girlfriend or no girlfriend."

Sylvia gave Jessica a flinty-eyed stare. "You know I'm way past going backwards."

"After today on the riverbank, that would be out of the question I'm sure," Jessica said. "Just had to throw it out there again."

"It also feels unfair, which I know I don't have any right to feel. He's out in the open with his woman, and I'm still stuck in hiding and will be for a long time."

"That would piss me off, too. Anthony had better get moving." Jessica jumped up and clasped her hands together. "If nobody's coming home tonight, let's you and I go out. Hungry?"

"Starving. But I need to shower first."

Jessica waited upstairs on the brass bed while Sylvia got ready. "You could call your attorney, but I don't think he'll care much that the kids are with her, too. Unless she's harmful to them, which sounds unlikely if she's teaching crafts to Alice.

Mostly he'd think you're lucky because the father *wants* the kids with him. The problem is usually the other way around you know, which is how my husband would be."

Sylvia stuck her head out from the bathroom. "I know how lucky you've always thought I am that Tom loves to be with the children. But how do you explain his behavior now?"

Jessica went on to explain that because he's always been a pretty devoted father, Sylvia could trust Tom's instinct to try to do the right thing for them and that Tom was also trapped without the money to move out and live on his own. "People don't think as clearly either, during the emotional chaos of splitting up."

What Jessica said made sense. Just because Sylvia didn't like the way he was going about it didn't mean he was insensitive. "It makes me sick to think she'll be looking after them."

Jessica stopped before going down the stairs. "If it makes you feel any better, Tom's turn is coming."

"At least Tom knows Anthony. I don't have any idea who Betsy is."

"Betsy? Who has a name in this day and age like Betsy? Ross? Crocker?"

"That's Betty Crocker." Sylvia was finally laughing. "Bake much?" Jessica was a godsend tonight.

"Let's take my car," Jessica said. "I've got the top down. You need the wind in your hair."

## CHAPTER 17

Sylvia woke up the next morning to a phone call from Jessica, who wanted to show the house before noon, preferably with no one at home. Sylvia agreed to leave the house and then wondered where she would go. Still in bed, she stared out the corner window at the familiar Douglas fir tree that was so close to the house it appeared magnified. She had been spellbound by the majesty of these trees when she saw them for the first time on a family trip to Oregon when she was eleven. This one seemed to serve as a beacon as it reached upward, stately and confident in its purpose, a guide to the halting course she'd chosen. Maybe she'd climb out the window and sit in the tree until the prospective buyers were through.

The tops of the pine trees Tom had planted four years ago barely reached the bottommost part of the window. They reminded her of how excited she'd been about moving into this friendly, stylish neighborhood and its schools within walking distance. Even though she hadn't wanted to leave Ohio, knowing this house was waiting for her helped to alleviate her dread.

What if these people wanted to buy it? The thought of looking for an apartment and moving made her wary. This time she would be on her own. The house felt too quiet. Not even Red was home. Sylvia was really alone. She remembered a time not so long ago when she longed for some solitude. But this had been thrust upon her, like an uninvited guest, and felt awkward. Now that solitude had taken residence in her home, its presence was unwelcome.

She couldn't talk to Anthony either. He would be at home with his family on a Saturday. She could go through their phone code system, but just the thought of it was insulting to her. But there was something else, too. She felt reluctant to tell Anthony that Tom was moving in with his girlfriend, but she wasn't sure why. Was it that Tom's behavior reflected on her, and she felt ashamed? Or was it that she'd lost a position of strength, now that he didn't want her anymore? She wasn't a strategic thinker in the game of love, but she did feel her position was weakened. Tom's move was checkmate while Anthony still pondered his move. She felt jilted.

What would she do with herself all afternoon? And what if the kids called and she wasn't home? Yesterday she didn't think to ask Tom for a phone number. *How could I let him leave without it?* She couldn't reach them if she had to, nor did she want to. The thought of calling *her* house made Sylvia feel nervous, like she would be an intrusion, which didn't make any sense. *They're my children.* Maybe Alice and Trevor felt the same way and were afraid to even ask to call their mom. She didn't even know the address. She wondered what they were doing. Probably making unicorns by the dozen. Tom said he'd have them home tonight. She would have to manage until then or drive herself crazy.

She dragged herself out of bed and went downstairs to make some coffee. Hanging around the house would obviously not help her get her mind off of her children, and it was good she'd be forced to leave for the afternoon. She still had some preparation to do for next week and decided to spend the day at the library, where she could work on her lesson plans.

By ten o'clock she was on her way. She took the back way around the lake to the main part of town, which would take her through the canal area. Tom said her house was on one of the canals. *She must have money.* She drove around on the off chance she'd spot his car. *She probably gave him a new tennis racket to go with the shoes.*

The canals were a series of waterways that fingered off the west end of the main lake. The house fronts faced the water, so from the street side you looked at the rear entrances; the only way to really see the homes was by boat. These properties commanded a high price even though they were stacked tightly alongside each other like houseboats. Because of that, Sylvia could never understand the appeal of living on the canals. Throughout the lakefront and canal areas, the modest, cottage-style dwellings mingled side by side with the more imposing, showcase-type homes, which, to Sylvia, added character to the neighborhoods. She slowly wound her way through several of the narrow streets without any luck. Just as well. She wouldn't know what to do if she did see his car.

Sylvia forgot that the small town library was crowded on Saturday mornings. She had trouble finding a parking space. When she entered the foyer, a group of about ten wide-eyed toddlers sat listening while a woman was reading and dramatizing *The Very Hungry Caterpillar*—the same book her mom had given to Trevor last year. It was one of his favorites. Alice loved to read the story to him about the caterpillar that literally eats his way through the book. There's a little hole on each page that pictures a piece of fruit to show where the hungry caterpillar ate as he crawled. When he's finally full, he makes a cocoon, and it ends when he becomes a butterfly, or "flutterby" as Alice would say. Alice made up her own "foreign language" by turning syllables of words around: elephant became "phela-ant," buffalo was "fubbalo," and magazine, "zagamine."

Sylvia had brought Alice to Saturday morning story hour when they first lived here and then started bringing Trevor two years ago. She had to face it. She thought of Alice and Trevor no matter where she went.

She found a quiet stall in the back of the main room. The desk was small, so she put some of her materials on the floor. She had completed two weeks' worth of lesson plans so far, and hoped to have four weeks' worth done before school started. Ideally she wanted to stay a month ahead throughout the school year. At the end of each week, she'd plan the following week and never get behind. The problem she was having was knowing how much material she could cover in each class period. If she overestimated what they could do, it would throw off her whole week. And what if one class was much slower than the other? How could she coordinate testing them?

The junior high program covered the equivalent of French I over a year and a half: one semester in seventh grade and two semesters in eighth. The concept was to encourage the students to pursue a foreign language in junior high with the advantage of an extra semester, which they wouldn't have in high school. Sylvia would have seventh graders who had never had French and returning eighth graders who'd had one semester.

One of Sylvia's priorities was that her students learn to say *something* in French that they could use right away. What good did it do to learn to ask a typical Parisian question, such as *Où est la gare?* (Where is the train station?), when you had no chance to use it? Practical usage was the key. She decided to come up with a simple "expression-a-day" that she would first teach orally then follow with a printed sign to hang on the bulletin board, like a giant flash card. She had already made two-foot-wide signs from colored poster board with the expressions written in black Magic Marker: *d'accord, formidable, c'est tout, super* (used in slang like *super bon*), *tout de suite*, and *à la prochaine*. She put the meaning in English on the back. She decided to begin each class with verbal "warm-ups" to include: colors, numbers, days of the week, basic conversation of "hello; what's your name; my name is; how are you?" Then they would go over the flash-card expressions they had learned each day. Keeping them interested would be the main challenge.

Sylvia pulled the textbook and lesson plan book out of her canvas bag and had no trouble becoming absorbed in her work once she began. She didn't check the time until her stomach growled and saw that it was one o'clock already.

"*Sylvie*? I thought that was you." Sylvia heard in French.

It was Charlotte, the new French teacher at the other junior high. Sylvia stood up to shake hands, and they greeted each other with *bonjour*, in the traditional French manner.

The two met the week before at the evening reception for faculty and staff and connected immediately. They spoke French to each other at the outset and decided they would continue that way, like an honor system, and *tant pis!* if it seemed obnoxious to the rest of the world.

"Looks like you're working hard to prepare for next week," Charlotte said.

"Hopefully for the next month," Sylvia answered.

Charlotte tossed her shoulder-length blond hair as she laughed. She was long-legged, lithe, and striking in an Eastern-intellectual-Bohemian way in her shin-length gauzy print skirt and matching leather flats. "I honestly think we'll be lucky if we're done reviewing in a month." Like Sylvia, Charlotte believed in total immersion in the French language for beginners.

"Why do you say that?" Sylvia sat back down.

"I found out that last year's teacher only got the seventh graders a quarter of the way through the book. The review guide in the book covers material they've never even seen!"

"That's a definite disadvantage." Sylvia leaned back and stretched her arms over her head. "Are you sure?"

"I called Madame Coleman directly to find out where she ended with them last year. She told me herself, and she wasn't even apologetic. She said the important thing was they had a good time and wanted to keep taking French. Can you imagine?"

"As I suspected at the interview. A popularity contest. What should we do?" Sylvia asked.

"Do you have time for lunch right now and discuss it?"

"I was just thinking about lunch. *Allons-y*."

Sylvia suggested they walk to a nearby deli she liked, as long as it was air-conditioned. The temperatures had dropped to the low nineties, but the heat was still unbearable. She also didn't want to lose her parking space.

"Do you work at the library often?" Charlotte asked.

"My first time. I needed to be out of the house today." Sylvia didn't want to tell the truth to her new coworker and hesitated to come up with something.

"Of course. If I remember right, don't you have two children?"

Sylvia nodded. "Nine and almost four."

"And they'd be home today, I imagine," Charlotte said.

"Right. Impossible to get any work done. Were you doing work there, too?" Sylvia asked in a rush.

"Sort of. I wanted to see if they had *anything* francophone for resource material, but mostly I'm just killing time. Paul's children have been visiting from Connecticut, and today's their last day to spend with him. I thought it would be better if they had alone time."

Charlotte and Paul, who was the new dean of admissions at a local private college, had just moved from the East Coast. Charlotte didn't wear a ring, so Sylvia assumed they weren't married. She'd never met a couple that weren't married but were living together. Now she knew two. She got the impression when they met at the reception that Charlotte and Paul hadn't been together long, but she couldn't remember why.

"How old are his kids?"

"Darwin is nine and precocious like his mother. Franny is seven and was adopted by Paul and his ex-wife, who likes to think of herself as the maven of culturally forward thinkers. You know, the hip Eastern attitude of 'Why add more children to the overpopulated world when there are too many without families and living in poverty as it is?' Franny is black."

Sylvia was blown over. "And the ex-wife is white?"

Charlotte almost choked on her herbal tea laughing. "Oh, very WASP. And quite beautiful. A Katherine Ross look-alike."

"I have to admire the courage to do that. Paul must have wanted it, too." Sylvia took a bite of her tuna-fish sandwich. At some point in the conversation they had broken their pact and were speaking half the time in English, but she didn't care.

"Apparently she talked him into it, but you're right; he thought it was a good idea at the time," Charlotte said.

"And now he doesn't?"

"Well, how good is it?" Charlotte picked up her fork and daintily poked at her vegetable salad. "The suburban white family who save the black child from an addict mother and end up divorced with the 'father' on the West Coast."

"Maybe it's better than what she came from, but I get your point."

Charlotte and Sylvia talked for over two hours and not about their French classes. When Sylvia learned that Charlotte and Paul had only known each other for eight months, and Charlotte's divorce wasn't final yet, Sylvia told her that she was also in the process of a divorce.

"I guess I won't ask if you and your husband want to come over for dinner then," Charlotte said.

Sylvia's first thought was Anthony and how much she wanted to finagle a way to make a dinner with them work. She hadn't told Charlotte about Anthony yet, but she would at some point. She also knew Charlotte and Paul wouldn't have any problem getting together under the circumstances. For them, there would be no moral dilemma.

"No, I don't think I'd invite Tom."

Charlotte touched her arm and smiled sincerely. "Take it as an open invitation then, and bring whoever you want."

Sylvia blushed at the unwitting transparency in her remark. She changed the subject to their French classes as they walked back to the library. They set a date to get together in a week, when they would have some idea of their students' abilities and could discuss ideas for coordinating a teaching plan.

Sylvia decided to quit for the day and got in her car and started home. She thought about how an evening with Charlotte and Paul would be with Tom. She could picture him pretending to be interested and trying to sit still. Paul was erudite in tweed and smoked a pipe and had taught English at Cornell. They were probably intellectual snobs. Charlotte graduated from Middlebury College, the foremost school in the country for foreign language study, according to Sylvia's high school guidance counselor.

He had wanted her to go there, but Sylvia heard that because of its small size and remote location in the mountains, the students often jetted to New York City on weekends. After three years in her small high school of five hundred, she had become bored and wanted a larger campus for college. She also thought she might be out of her league at Middlebury and wouldn't fit in with the jet-setters. She had played it safe and went to the state university two hours from home. She never regretted her decision but sometimes wondered how different her life could've been had she made that choice. Except for a black stepdaughter, maybe not so different. Charlotte ended up with the same job as Sylvia, in the same town.

After talking to Charlotte, it dawned on Sylvia that her problems weren't so unique or life-threatening. With each setback in her effort to move forward in her life, she had gained some insight or clarity and a renewed confidence to act according to what felt right. For months she had shoved aside her instincts to tell Alice the truth of their divorce because she thought she and Tom should sit down together and tell her. Tom was never ready or wanted to "feel Alice out" first or find the right moment. Or maybe her waiting for him was an excuse because she wasn't ready for the confrontation herself. When he wanted to hedge again, even after he'd moved in with his girlfriend, it became glaringly clear to Sylvia that it was up to her to face Alice. Tom would rather hide, walk away from what was happening, and let someone else handle the messy feelings. And this time she would.

## CHAPTER 18

When Sylvia got home, she spread her poster-board flash cards on the kitchen table and thought she'd make a few more before the kids got home. She turned on the TV in the family room and watched the news. The presidential campaign was in full swing, and from the latest polls it looked like the Hollywood actor-turned-governor was even with Carter. Sylvia found the peanut farmer insipid and didn't think he'd stand a chance against the charismatic Reagan, especially with Cronkite's daily broadcast of "counting the days" for the hostages in Iran. On the global front, it seemed that Carter had effectively made most Americans feel small and inconsequential, an unpopular mandate for any incumbent.

On the home front, Sylvia would try to insure that Alice didn't feel to blame for the collapse of the marriage. Beyond that, she could only hope that Alice wouldn't harbor a grudge toward her, secretly blaming Sylvia for her father's departure. Sylvia wasn't that confident as it was that she would win a popularity contest as her daughter's favorite parent. A lot could change by November.

The TV news announced that Reagan was giving a speech at a college in San Diego, which made Sylvia think of her brother Scott. Alice and Trevor adored their uncle, and Sylvia wished they could see him more often. She wished it for herself, too. She decided to call him.

She went back up to the kitchen and dialed his number. While she listened to his phone ring, she stacked her flash cards in a pile. *C'est la vie* on a sky blue background sat face up on the table.

"I just walked in from surfing. Perfect timing," Scott said.

"I thought you and Amanda might be away for the weekend." Sylvia grabbed a Coke from the refrigerator and stretched the phone cord to the deck outside and lit a cigarette. It occurred to her that since Tom didn't live here anymore she could smoke wherever she wanted. Because it was hot, she turned to go back inside but realized the kids would be home soon. She stayed on the deck.

"She's with her parents this weekend. I'm 'baching' it."

"How does that feel?"

"Maybe better than it should. We kinda needed a break from each other. Amanda wants to buy a condo together, and I'm balking." Scott excused himself and sneezed. "Salt water up the nose."

"You mean you'd live together?"

"Yeah. That's what bothers me."

Sylvia wondered if this was becoming epidemic. "Because you think you should be married first?"

"Because Amanda is thinking about marriage, and she knows I'm not even close."

"Do you feel like you're being talked into something?"

"Sort of. She came up with the idea as an investment, which might be good financially, but it feels like a roundabout way to get a commitment out of me," Scott said.

"It sounds like whether to buy a condo or not is what's deciding your living together, not the other way around."

Scott cleared his throat. "So you think we should decide first if we want to live together."

"It seems like the right order of things." Sylvia pondered why she was in any position to give advice. She decided it was a big sister's prerogative.

"We practically do anyway. I'm either at her place or she's at mine, but *buying* a place together feels like a major commitment."

"You're right. It is." Sylvia looked at the clock. She saw it was almost five o'clock and wondered if the kids would be home for dinner.

Scott changed the subject and asked what was going on in Sylvia's world. She filled him in on yesterday's happenings (aside from the river "picnic"). He was genuinely surprised about Tom but mostly concerned about the effect it might have on Alice and Trevor. Sylvia explained that she felt compelled to finally tell Alice they were divorcing.

"That will be rough, but you must have been planning how to tell her for some time," Scott said.

"I have. In a way his moving in with a girlfriend takes some of the guilt off of me and makes the dreaded talk seem a *little* less so. I just have to do it." Sylvia exhaled.

"Are you going to tell Mom and Dad about his girlfriend?"

"Not yet. I have to come to terms with the situation myself before I can tell them about it."

"I talked to them a few days ago. Steve's been on an even keel lately, so they sound better than ever. They might even come out west in February, without Steve."

"Things might be on an even keel with me by then, too." Sweat beads were forming on her face and neck. It was too hot to stand in the sun, and she ducked back inside.

"You should plan a trip down here for Christmas."

She put her cigarette out in the sink. "That would be swell, but it's hard to think about right now. I can't fly us all down without a credit card, which I won't have until I establish my own credit."

"You can drive down. You'll have enough time with two weeks off, and I'd help with the gas costs."

Sylvia sat down in the bentwood chair at the phone desk and closed her eyes. "I just couldn't let you do that, Scott."

"No big deal. Anyway, if we do buy the condo, the kids will have a swimming pool. We can go to the zoo and the beach in La Jolla and decorate the tree together." Scott sounded exuberant. "Of course, I'll have to work."

"You're getting me pumped," she said.

"Then it's settled. Tell the kids, and then you'll have to come. Or I'll tell them." Scott chuckled.

She hung up the phone in a happy frame of mind. Scott was right. If she told the kids, she'd have to make it work. Maybe Tom could keep Red.

The phone rang almost as soon as she put it down. But only once. The coast was clear. She could call Anthony at home. By now, the thought of discussing Tom's story felt tiresome. She had to tell him, though, and picked up the phone.

"I saw a realtor outside your place with a couple this afternoon, so I figured you went somewhere," Anthony said.

"The library."

"You don't sound good. What's wrong?"

"Tom moved in with his *girlfriend* last night."

There was a long pause. "I guess I'm not surprised that he has one," Anthony said. "Are you?"

"You know how we used to hope that they would find someone else? Tom threw me off track when he'd keep saying he didn't want the divorce, so it never entered my mind. But I should've guessed because he also said, 'We could stay married but *live our own lives.*'"

"Does it really matter now?"

Sylvia poured a glass of red wine. "It's just that he's living with her already. Things flip-flopped on me, and somehow *I* feel cheated."

"Because it should be you and me living together instead of him."

Sylvia recoiled at his suggestion that they'd live together. "Well, yes. We're not even close to being together, and he's probably been seeing her a shorter time than we have been."

"You're in shock and I don't blame you, but we knew it would take a long time for us."

Sylvia never thought it would take this long. "Especially since he took the kids there last night. One big happy family."

"I'm sorry, Jake. I wish I could've been there to—"

"But you aren't here. I think it's time you stopped talking and started doing something. I'm tired of words." She lit another cigarette and stood back outside.

"I understand you're upset right now. But I do have some very good news."

"What?"

"That glass wall? Gone. The financial barrier is down, so now I can move ahead."

"Which means?"

"After Alexia's birthday in October—"

Anthony paused so long that she wondered if it was for effect.

"—I'm going to ask Jane for a divorce." He sounded triumphant.

She would've felt better if he'd moved two years ago on this—so he could be waiting for her rather than the other way around. He was the one who was always saying, "I'll be waiting for you, Jake," or "You can count on me," or "I can't live without you." She could hear him move away from the phone to light a cigarette, which made her want to put hers out.

"I can't hear you," he said in a singsong voice.

"I don't think I could feel happy about anything right now." Sylvia realized that wasn't true. Talking to Scott about a visit with her kids made her happy.

"I wish I could take you away—a weekend, just the two of us. I bet that would make you happy."

"Right now it doesn't. I don't want to hear about wishful thinking. I have a lot in front of me." She stubbed her cigarette out under the deck railing, stepped back inside, and closed the sliding glass door. She needed mouthwash.

"What are you saying?"

She heard the garage door go up. "The kids are home. I gotta go." She hung up and ran down the steps through the family room.

"Mommy, Mommy." Trevor thrust himself into her arms, and she picked him up in a swoop. He wrapped his arm tenderly over her shoulder and nestled his face into the crook of her neck.

"We had so much fun. I painted my unicorns," Alice said, beaming. She wrapped her arms around Sylvia's waist and pressed hard. Sylvia kissed the top of her head and placed her free hand on her back.

"I missed you so much," Sylvia said.

"Me, too. Can I go with Daddy and Betsy horseback riding tomorrow? Daddy wants to know right now." Alice had a pleading look.

Tom unloaded the overnight bags from the backseat of his car and headed toward the family room. "We've been trying to call you for half an hour."

"I need to talk to Daddy first," Sylvia said. Red was running circles from the garage into the house and back again, then jumped up onto Sylvia as if to say "you forgot me." Sylvia lovingly stroked her Roo Roo and asked Alice to take Red inside while she talked to Tom. Trevor said he wanted to go with Alice and slid down her body and followed.

"We're going to Brayburn's Stable on Stafford Road in the afternoon. She wants to come." Tom moved past her and entered the family room.

"Of course she wants to," Sylvia said. "But we need to talk first."

"About what?" Tom sighed.

"I need your phone number and address. And we need to discuss how often you're going to see the kids."

"I figure I'll see them when I'm in town. They can stay with me as much as they want." He dropped the bags on the floor.

"Too open-ended. We need a regular schedule that they can count on and that I can count on. Otherwise, their lives are too chaotic."

He rolled his eyes. "One thing at a time. I don't have a schedule. You know that. About tomorrow?"

Alice joined them. "Please, Mommy, can I go? I don't have anything before school starts." She clutched her hands together and bounced up and down.

"And it's Labor Day weekend," Tom said. "I wanted to take them for a picnic on Monday, too."

"One thing at a time, Tom. I guess tomorrow is okay, but I don't know about Monday."

"I'll pick her up around one o'clock." He started for the door.

"Wait. I want the phone number and address." She went to get some paper and a pen. She handed it to him and told him that in the future she wanted to be asked *before* he asked the kids to do something.

Alice followed him to his car, and Sylvia watched as he pulled her up and embraced her. Sylvia's heart ached when she heard Alice whimper that she didn't want him to go. He whispered that he knew, but he'd see her tomorrow. Sylvia knew then that it was too soon for a visitation schedule and that as long as he was in town, she'd be willing to let Alice and Trevor spend as much time with him as they wanted.

Sylvia walked out to Alice while Tom was backing out of the driveway. She put her arm around her daughter and pulled her close. Sylvia asked her if she was hungry. Alice had a hangdog expression. Her mouth was turned down at the corners, and her eyes had lost their sparkle. She said she wasn't.

"Not even for pizza?"

"We had it last night," Alice said.

"I know this must be hard, honey—"

"You don't know." She twisted out from under Sylvia's arm. "When is Daddy coming back to live with us?" Alice stared accusingly at her mother. "He's *never* coming back, is he? You're getting a divorce, aren't you?" Alice's face contorted into a pinched, angry mask. Her eyes were sullen and hard.

Sylvia's insides went cold as ice. "Yes, we are," she answered.

"I knew it a long time ago!" Alice yelled.

Sylvia was bowled over by the declaration. "You did?" They were standing in the garage, but Sylvia didn't want Trevor to hear the commotion, so she stayed planted there.

"You were on the phone once—"

Alice began sobbing and could barely talk. Sylvia reached for her, but Alice backed away.

"—and I heard you say you liked it better when Daddy wasn't here."

To think that Alice had been carrying this inside for who knows how long was too much to bear. All those months she had worried that Alice sensed something was wrong at home because of her stomachaches. She didn't have to sense it—she overheard it, and from her own mother. *And why didn't Alice feel she could come to me?* But Sylvia had been so unavailable, so preoccupied with her petty needs, she probably wasn't very approachable. Had she ever been approachable?

Sylvia clinched Alice's convulsing body against her and held her there. She swallowed back her own need to cry. Her voice turned husky. "I'm so sorry you heard me say that. I was wrong to say that."

Alice's sobbing subsided. She looked up into Sylvia's eyes. "So you do want Daddy here?"

Sylvia knelt down to Alice's eye level. She stroked Alice's sandy-colored, shoulder-length hair and moved her hands to gently cup her face. "I wanted to tell you before we went to Ohio, but I was afraid to. Daddy and I have decided we shouldn't be married anymore. We want to be with you and Trevor, but we aren't happy with each other."

Alice began to cry all over again. Sylvia guided her into the house.

Trevor stood there staring at them when they came in. "What's wrong with Alice?"

"Daddy and Mommy are getting a divorce!" Alice blurted.

Trevor knitted his hands together. "What's a divorce?"

"It means Daddy will never live with us again." Alice jerked herself away from Sylvia and ran upstairs.

"Because Daddy lives with Betsy?" Trevor asked.

Sylvia picked up Trevor and sat with him on the couch. She just held him and told him that she and Daddy loved him and Alice more than anything. That Daddy would live with Betsy for now, and Sylvia would stay with him and Alice. That's all she could say. She asked him if he wanted to help her with dinner, and he said yes. They walked hand in hand to the kitchen.

"How about spaghetti?" Sylvia asked.

"Mmm, yes." Trevor stood on a chair to get the silverware. "I'm glad I'm home, Mommy."

"I'm glad you're home, too. I missed you so much." She leaned over his head and smelled him—a smell no longer of infancy and baby powder, yet one that carried a newborn freshness into toddlerhood and had become his own particular smell, one that only a mother would know, like the comforting smell a child might find in his favorite stuffed animal because it's become a part of him and smells only of him. "Let's go find Alice and see if we can make her feel better. What do you say?"

"I can give her my blankie."

Sylvia couldn't speak.

Trevor ran to his duffel bag sitting on the kitchen floor. "Here it is!"

They went upstairs and found Alice lying on her bed crying. Sylvia thought about calling Tom. Maybe he'd come back and talk to her, even if he didn't agree with Sylvia's truth-telling. But if he came over, maybe she'd feel worse or think that he would come back for good.

Trevor walked over and thrust his blankie in her face. "Here. Take my blankie. Now you'll be better."

Alice pushed it away. She choked. "Eww. I can't breathe. Get that away from me."

Trevor hugged it close to him then held it out to his sister once again. She rolled on her back and looked at her brother. "You're giving me your blankie?"

Trevor nodded.

Alice managed a weak closed-mouth smile. She took the blanket and held it close, then laid her cheek against it.

He grinned and raised his eyebrows. "You can keep it for now, Alice." Watching her intently, he said, "But do you think you'll need it when you go to sleep?"

Alice handed it to him. "That's okay. I feel better. You can have it back right now."

Trevor retrieved his dingy white, waffle-weave, thermal baby blanket and immediately curled up like a fiddler crab on top of it in the middle of the floor.

Sylvia reclined on the bed next to Alice and gently patted her tummy. "Ready for spaghetti?"

"I guess so. Do you want to see how I painted all my unicorns?" Alice's hopeful expression was tinged with a defeat that looked too heavy for a nine-year-old to carry.

Sylvia pulled her up from the bed and said she wanted to see every single one in all their flying colors. And that's when it hit her. Winning a popularity contest for her daughter's affections wasn't so important to her after all. She wanted more than that. Watching Alice's face light up whenever Tom appeared made Sylvia feel overlooked and underappreciated. She was the one who kept it all together, who handled the daily grind, and she'd acted like her daughter should reward her for it. But here it was, staring her in the face all along. Just being there for her curled-up fiddler crab and her brave unicorn, she finally realized that they knew she was the one they could always count on, and that was the only reward that mattered.

# CHAPTER 19

September 1980

On the first day of school, Sylvia stood in front of her rambunctious eighth-grade class and launched into an animated French monologue. She introduced herself, gave some personal background, explained they would all have French names, and rambled on about baguettes and croissants, French cafés, Paris, and Sainte Chapelle. Finally, with index finger raised for emphasis, she told them they would only speak French in this class. While she was talking, most of the students stared at her in stunned silence. Some exchanged worried looks. Some laughed. One made comments loud enough for everyone to hear on his way to the wastebasket. "Don't tell me she doesn't speak English! What's she saying?"

After thirty minutes Sylvia told them in English what she had just said. Big sighs of relief passed through the aisles, as they all laughed together. She realized, however, she might have their undivided attention for a week or two because she was a novelty, but novelties wore off. If she wanted to hold them, she had to establish a firm set of rules. A well-respected, veteran teacher had advised her to start out strict and ease up later. "It's a lot more difficult," he said, "to get them back in the box once they're out than it is to never let them out in the first place." Sylvia had a bizarre image of a cardboard box full of frogs that broke free and were leaping around the room, on top of chairs, under desks, or in the closet, and were too slippery to catch. Chaos in every corner. She heeded his advice and ended the first day with her three simple rules, which she printed in large white chalk across the blackboard.

1) You must raise your hand if you want to speak.

2) You may not get up without asking permission.

3) Only French spoken here.

The last rule served a dual purpose. It provided the learning atmosphere she wanted to create with total French immersion as well as built-in classroom control since they could barely speak the language. It would require an enormous amount of energy on her part, like verbal charades, but she had to stay with it if she wanted this to work. She had a fourth rule, but it was more a part of her curriculum than a rule. Homework every night and a quiz every Friday. Sylvia placed a high priority on daily homework because, like math, each day's lesson built on what was taught the day before. It was essential to memorize the equations in math, or in the case of foreign language, the grammatical structures, in order to plug in the variables, or vocabulary, to solve a problem, that is, construct a sentence. A weekly quiz would keep them on track.

Once they could speak a little French, maybe some of her students would feel encouraged enough to stick with it, to push through the drudgery of the first three years of study (verb conjugations, vocabulary memorization, and pronunciation). Sylvia believed that only then could they have a comfortable grasp of reading and speaking the language and begin to love it as much as she did. After that, the pleasure of the connection to a different culture would come, and with that discovery, a broader worldview, which would encourage respect for other cultures.

When Sylvia had lived with a French family, she had found it remarkable that all seven of them had come home at noon for three hours to have dinner together. They had then returned to school and work until six or seven in the evening. By contrast, in America, a leisurely family dinner in the middle of a workday might appear lazy, as though breaking up the day would break the concentration and lead to lower productivity. And to serve watered-down red wine to children under fourteen years, and full strength over that age, instead of milk at lunch and supper, would run counter to good health habits as well as the law.

During the first month of teaching, Sylvia relied on her nervous energy to propel her through the new demands of work and home and on her motherly perception to detect any significant mood changes in her children. It was paramount that she maintain a positive, composed demeanor for them during this period of upheaval. Her mornings were a whirlwind: She had to pack lunches for Alice and Trevor, *be cheerful*, dress herself, get Alice off to school, get Trevor ready for day care, *be calm*, feed Red and put her in the backyard for the day (where she thought Red would be happier), drop Trevor off at day care by nine thirty, and get to school by ten for her first class at ten forty. *Be energetic.* Her school day ended at two forty, but she stayed until three, *be patient*, to be available for any students who needed help. Then she had to pick up Trevor, *be happy*, hurry to meet Alice when she got home, *be fun*, fix dinner, eat, *be engaging*, clean up dinner, feed Red and take her for a walk, get Trevor ready for bed, *be loving*, and read him a story, do homework or read with Alice until she went to bed. Then grade homework for her classes.

Somewhere between getting dressed in the morning and eating dinner, she managed to talk on the phone to Anthony. The only time they could see each other was when the kids were with Tom. Now that she couldn't arrange her whole week around trying to see Anthony, she found the adjustment of less time together an odd relief rather than a frustration. She needed him in her life as much as ever and had no doubts that her future was with him, but since she was unable to continue the lifestyle they had led for so long, she was also less willing to try as hard as she used to. She figured it was time for him to act on his promises. Still, she did count on "being with him" once a week at least. To insure this, she had resorted to sneaking him into the house again. Sometimes she worried that her next-door neighbor would happen to be looking down from her two-story window and see him scrunched on the floor of the backseat of her car. She looked forward to daylight savings, when it would be dark an hour earlier and she wouldn't worry so much.

On weekends, Sylvia scrambled to clean the house for last-minute visits from prospective buyers or for an open house, which meant she and the kids had to leave for several hours. The library was becoming their hangout. Alice sometimes socialized with classmates she ran into there, while Trevor enjoyed the story hour for toddlers. All in all, the library had become a place to which they looked forward to going.

The days were long and full and didn't always flow as routinely as Sylvia would have liked. She moved Red back inside the house during the day, since the dog had managed several times to break through the screen on the dining room window trying to get back in. Every day after school when Tom was in town, Sylvia held her breath anticipating disappointment for Alice as she watched her run breathless to the phone to call him. During the week he sometimes picked up both of the kids, sometimes just Alice, but he never seemed to be able to bring them home by eight o'clock, which threw the evening schedule off and made them tired and cranky in the morning. Alice usually hadn't done her homework either. And when Anthony was at the house, Sylvia worried that Tom might finally do the helpful thing and bring them home earlier. Either way, she couldn't seem to relax.

Her mind would wander to projecting "what if," and she would find herself creating different scenarios in order to plan ahead in the event of their occurrence. *What if Anthony was upstairs as the kids came in the house?* He could hide in the closet until the kids were in bed. *But then, how would I get him to his car?* She had no idea what she'd do. *What if they were pulling in the driveway as we were pulling out?* She couldn't come up with a solution to that one either. *What if Red got sick? How would I pay for that?* She would hope the vet would be amenable to a payment schedule. *What if the kids got sick for a prolonged period?* A substitute teacher would fill in, but she didn't know for how long. If only she had a babysitter. If only Anthony were free. If only Tom made more money. She couldn't keep wishing for things that weren't going to happen or inventing problems that hadn't arisen or she'd make herself sick. And that *would* be a problem—she couldn't get sick.

Maybe she'd worry less if the house sold. She'd at least have a sizable nest egg since the divorce settlement gave her all the profit from the sale. Jessica was doing her best to promote the house, but there were no offers. With the winter rains approaching, she said the likelihood of it selling before spring was remote. Tom's occasional off-the-cuff remarks indicated that the stitchery business was hanging by a thread. She worried that George might cut the cord with Tom and no longer pay the first and second mortgages, a total of one thousand dollars.

As it was, Tom was usually late with the two-hundred-and-fifty-dollar monthly child support. Sylvia didn't allow herself to consider that she was living below the poverty level—she just had to survive from one month to the next.

And on September 30, 1980, the divorce became final. Sylvia rifled through the papers and stared at the signatures and the judge's stamp. She wondered if it would feel different now that she was legally a "divorcée." Alice and Trevor were with Tom for the weekend, but Red was home because Sylvia wanted Red to stay with her. She called Jessica, who complained that her husband, Greg, was out with the boys again. They decided to get together at Sylvia's. Jessica came right over with a six-pack of Budweiser.

Sylvia thought they should celebrate in the living room she rarely used, like fresh surroundings to introduce her new chapter. One step down to the left of the entryway, the room had a beautiful cedar-paneled section of the wall around the fireplace that rose to the height of the vaulted ceiling, giving it a dramatic effect. The large picture window that faced the front yard was lined with rhododendrons and azaleas along its bottom, which lent a feeling of nature indoors. The fall evenings had become chilly, so Sylvia got some logs and built a fire in the fireplace. Red sat in regal repose in front of the warm fire. They sat on the floor in front of the fire drinking wine and beer and smoking. Sometimes Sylvia thought she and Jessica acted like a couple of college kids, and she loved it. Tonight it felt cozy.

"You need a night on the town," Jessica said.

"I'm too tired. I'd rather stay here," Sylvia said.

Jessica laughed. "I don't mean tonight. I mean you need a night with someone who will wine you and dine you."

"A date?"

"Greg's got just the guy," Jessica said.

"Greg wants to fix me up?" Sylvia asked in disbelief.

"Why not? You're single. And you're working too hard and need a break." Jessica inhaled. The smoke escaped her mouth in small puffs as she spoke. "Even Christy noticed how thin you're getting. She loves French by the way."

Jessica's daughter, Christy, was in one of Sylvia's seventh-grade French classes. There were several children in her classes whose parents she knew. But it was true, Sylvia was exhausted. If she didn't learn to pace herself, by Thanksgiving she might be babbling in tongues that no one would understand. By Christmas vacation, she would need that trip to San Diego, whether or not she had a reliable car.

"I'm glad Christy likes it. She participates and is keeping up with her homework." Sylvia didn't want to mention that Christy was already struggling to understand basic grammar. She couldn't distinguish a noun from a verb.

"That's amazing. She never does homework, and when she does, it's usually all wrong. She's like me, poor thing—an artist, not a student," Jessica said.

"We need artists, too." Sylvia got up and went to the kitchen for some cheese and crackers. "So far she's trying, and that counts for a lot."

Jessica called out to her. "You're making quite an impression with these kids. Christy says they say French things to each other in the halls all the time."

Sylvia came back in the room and took a chunk of cheddar and a Triscuit as she set the plate on the coffee table. "I do like it, and they're conscientious kids. Maybe the hard work will pay off."

"Let's get back to what's important here," Jessica said. "How about tomorrow night? We'll have drinks at my house; go to dinner and a movie. Or are you seeing your Lothario?"

"Hopefully tomorrow afternoon, but I won't know until morning."

"So you'd be free at night no matter what." Jessica was persistent.

"Even so, I wouldn't feel like going out after—"

"Do you guys still meet at that hotel?"

"Sometimes, but tomorrow we'll probably be here since the kids are gone."

"That must feel weird as hell. I thought you weren't going to do that again."

"I don't like it, but he can't afford hotels as often as before."

"I don't get it." Jessica wrinkled her brow. "I thought the big financial deal came through."

"It did. I'm not sure I really understand it either." Anthony occasionally talked about the commercial apartment deals he arranged for the developer he worked for, but he never talked about his personal finances." At least he's an accountant and knows what he's doing."

"That usually means he can track his money, not necessarily make it."

"Tom can't do either one, so—"

"I bet they're in debt," Jessica interrupted. "Big mortgage. Trips to Europe. Fancy cars. And Jane went overboard with extras on that house." Jessica sprawled full-length on the couch, propping her head on the armrest. "I think you should keep your options open. Go on a date. Make him sweat a little."

Not that Sylvia would ever tell him even if she did go out. "Wouldn't that be the same as cheating?"

"On Anthony? If he's not available to take you out like you deserve, then you're a free agent as far as I'm concerned. He's not even separated." Jessica sat up and threw her hands in the air. "What *is* taking him so long?"

Sylvia gazed into the fire. "I told you a hundred times."

"I know. Six months apart."

Sylvia counted out on her fingers. "August to September, September to October, so he's actually right on schedule." Was she trying to convince herself or Jessica?

"He's a month late. Anyway, Greg wants this guy to meet you. He's an old friend, a doctor, and he's handsome, funny, and smart, like you. Maybe you'll have fun for a change."

The thought of going out didn't appeal to Sylvia. The energy it would take to be charming, interesting, witty, and clever might deplete any reserve she had left. She couldn't imagine sitting in a movie theater next to a total stranger as her date. Now that she thought about it, she and Anthony had never even been to a movie theater together. They'd never make it through a whole movie anyway. "I'll have to think about it. This is the only kind of evening I want to have right now. Tell Greg thanks, but—you didn't tell him about Anthony, did you?"

Jessica looked down at the ashtray on the coffee table. Instead of answering her question directly, she said, "He asked me if there was somebody else. I said there used to be but not anymore."

Sylvia saw the nervous tension around Jessica's eyes and knew she wasn't telling the whole truth. A half-truth maybe? A lie by omission? Her husband was an upstanding attorney in town but a blabbermouth when he drank too much, which was often. Sylvia had lived with the secret for so long, she couldn't imagine how she'd feel if it was out in the open. Did it really matter anymore? As long as she was still in the neighborhood it did, for her children, for Anthony's family, and for herself. But she didn't want to seem overly concerned about it. Her love life couldn't be that important to Greg to talk about.

"It's not that big of a deal. I'm a free woman, right?"

Jessica's expression softened. "That's the spirit. I'm going to keep bugging you though."

"If Anthony doesn't ask Jane for a divorce after his daughter's birthday, I'll definitely consider it," Sylvia said.

"So, when's her birthday?"

The fire crackled. "In two weeks."

# CHAPTER 20

October 1980

Daylight savings arrived on Halloween, the last day of the month, but darker days had descended the week before.

Tom called and said he needed to talk to Sylvia without the kids around. They decided it would be easiest for him to come to the house after ten when the kids would be asleep. Sylvia imagined the bad news had to do with the house.

She waited at the kitchen table while she made up the weekly quizzes, one for seventh grade and another for eighth. She jumped a little when she heard the key turn in the front door. Annoyed, she decided she had to remember to ask him for all of the house keys back tonight. And the garage door opener.

He could see her sitting at the kitchen table. “What’re you working on? Schoolwork?” he asked as he shut the front door behind him. His casual tone made it sound like he was returning home from a tennis match.

"Every night," she said. She looked up at him as he approached.

Sylvia hadn't seen Tom in a few weeks. He had resorted to dropping the kids off without getting out of the car and waiting in the car when he picked them up, and he'd been out of town. He'd gained some weight but was almost distinguished-looking in his gray flannel suit, blue oxford shirt, and loosened tie. His dimpled smile exuded his trademark boyish charm, but as he got closer, she noticed that a trace of sadness lingered at the corners.

He glanced over her shoulder. "Do you like teaching?"

Part of her felt like she should distance herself from him, that she should be stern, standoffish, or at least aloof, but then, there really was no reason not to be cordial. Besides, being cheerful and eager to please was in their Midwest upbringing. "I do," she said. "I think it suits me."

Tom pulled up a chair and sat down across from her. "But isn't that age tough to handle?"

"They can be full of energy, but once you set—"

His glance toward the kitchen area told her he was half listening. He was looking at her as he started to get up, then blinked, and eased back into the chair.

"Did you want something?" she asked.

"I'm really thirsty. Do you have any Pepsi?" Tom drank Pepsi by the quart.

"Sorry. I have Coke. Or water?" Sylvia got up.

"Coke is fine."

Sylvia went to the refrigerator and handed him a can of Coke. "So what did you want to talk to me about?"

"A schedule for the kids. What's it called?" Tom looked up and down. His bright blue eyes turned a dull blue-gray as he stumbled through what he obviously didn't want to say. "You know, for them to see me."

"You mean visitation?"

He looked disheartened. "Yeah, that's it."

Partly relieved that the house wasn't going into foreclosure, Sylvia's shoulders settled forward. But something was amiss. "Did you have anything in mind?"

He pulled out a folded piece of yellow lined paper. As he handed it to her, he told her this was what he and Betsy had come up with. Sylvia stared at the loopy, grade-school script with tiny circles for dots over the i's. *She wrote this.* Sylvia started to read what was there.

Dear Sylvia,

Tom wanted me to write this since he says his handwriting is terrable. [*But her spelling is worse than his.*] Since he's living in my house I decided it was time to figure out what would work best for us as regards your kids visiting. [*Best for 'us'? How about what works best for the kids? And they're his kids, too!*] Their here to often [*(They're … too) Too often for whom?*] so we need to set up a schedule when Tom is in town. [*A schedule is up to Tom and me; we're their parents!*] They can't be here every day that he is. [*Why not? That's what he wants.*] So here's what we suggest.

Weekends: 1 night only not 2 (probably Saturday and home Sunday after dinner) Tom will pick them up around noon. [*A weekend is two nights!*]

Every other weekend. [*You mean two Saturday nights a month when he's in town?*] (We need some time alone.) [*The nerve of that bitch!*]

Weekdays: No overnights. (unless it's a holiday)

Two nights for dinner (Tuesdays and Thursdays are good for us, but we can be flexable here) Tom will pick them up around 4 and bring them home around 8.

We think this will work better for everyone conserned. [*Does 'everyone' include me?*]

Betsy Marner and Tom Beekman

The blood drained from her face at the outrage. She could hear her heart pounding in her ears. She got up so fast her chair fell over backwards and crashed to the floor on its back. "How could you let her do this? They're your kids!"

"Do what? You wanted a schedule!" he yelled back.

"It's too soon."

"Well, make up your mind. I thought you'd want this." He shook his head.

"You've only been out of the house a month! And it should be a schedule that works best for the *kids*, not her."

"It has to work for everybody, Sylvia, not just for what you think is best."

Sylvia tried to tone it down, afraid she'd wake them up. "But I'm the only one looking out for what's best for them. And they need to be alone with you, too, without *her* there."

"They don't seem to mind. They *like* her!"

Sylvia needed to control the urge to smack him. It made her even more furious that his girlfriend was practically illiterate on top of everything else. She began ripping the letter into tiny pieces, letting them float to the floor like confetti. She clenched and unclenched her empty hands as she moved from one end of the kitchen to the other. With her back to him she stopped, took a beat, and turned around. "How would you know what they like? Alice'll do whatever it takes to be with you. She wouldn't dare risk that by telling you how she feels about *your girlfriend*."

Tom stared at his hands folded in front of him on the table. "What am I supposed to do?"

"Stand up for your children."

"How can I when it's not my house? Where am I supposed to take them?" He was practically whining.

"That's not the point. Don't you think they need to see you more than a week a month? Don't you want to see them?"

"Of course, I do." Tom slumped back into his chair. "It's killing me, Sylvia." He laid his forehead on his arms on the table and began to cry.

Sylvia hadn't seen him like this since college, when he had told her about Johnny, his older brother, who had been killed in the auto accident. She had held him close then and said nothing because she couldn't imagine the depth of his sorrow. She moved toward him now with an outstretched hand, wanting to stroke the back of his head, but then let it drop to her side. She wasn't going to feel sorry for him this time. It wasn't her fault that he considered himself powerless to ask for what he needed. In the end it would hurt the children more than it would hurt him, and that, she couldn't abide. She had to come up with something for the kids' sake. She grabbed the Kleenex box from the built-in phone desk, took one out, and placed it in his hand. He blew his nose and wiped his eyes.

"Maybe you could see them here. Until you get your own place," she said.

"What do you mean?" Tom leaned over and picked up the chair on the floor then set it back on its legs.

"I'm not sure exactly, but during the week I could leave the house while you're here with them," she said. "*Without* your girlfriend. I don't ever want her near this house." Sylvia cringed at her own duplicity. She brought her lover here more times than she could count.

He nodded solemnly. "I know. It belongs to you now."

It must have occurred to Tom that the women in his life not only ran the houses, they owned them. No wonder he felt helpless. "Which reminds me," she said. "I did want you to give me the keys and the garage door opener, but if you're going to see the kids here, maybe you should keep them."

"That's nice of you."

She detected the sarcasm. "Think it over and let me know if you want to try it this way."

"Right." He stood up. His eyes were downcast, and he seemed sheepish. "I don't know what I'm going to say about the letter. I mean, it's all torn up."

"Just tell her I want a schedule, too, that we're all new at this, and I have to think about it." Why was she trying to help him negotiate with his girlfriend? "I wouldn't say anything yet about coming here to be with the kids."

He shook his head. "I sure never thought it would come to this." He turned and with head bowed went out the front door.

Sylvia trailed him to the door and bolted it when he left. *Neither did I.*

*****

Two days later, on the day she and Anthony planned to see each other, he asked if she could arrange for the kids to stay a little longer at Tom's. "I know it's late notice, but I'd like to take you out to dinner," he said.

"You mean in public? In Portland?"

"Anywhere you'd like to go."

"Trader Vic's. I'd like to go there."

"Then you shall have it."

It happened that Alice didn't have school the next day (teacher in-service day in the elementary school) and the kids were staying overnight with Tom. On a weekday no less. Maybe Tom finally stood up for himself. He said he'd take Red, too.

When she told Anthony she was totally free for the evening, he reserved a room in "their" hotel and said he could stay the night, if she would have him. She felt there must be a reason behind this celebration of sorts. His daughter's birthday was over a week ago, but Sylvia had made up her mind that she wasn't going to ask him about his talk with Jane. To Sylvia, it was a matter of dignity, hers and his. Let him come to her with the good news, in his own time. It appeared that this was it. She met him at the hotel, and they drove downtown from there.

They were sitting in a booth in a smaller room away from the main dining area, but it was crowded and all the tables were filled.

"You're radiant tonight," he said. "How did I get so lucky?"

"Just move closer and kiss me, right here, in the restaurant."

He did as he was told. Looking into each other's eyes, their lips touched delicately at first. With a slight smile curling around his eyes, he teasingly slid his tongue slowly under her upper lip. She sat very still with a hint of a smile and heightened the tease by sliding her hand softly down his side and around his back, placing her fingers just inside the waistband of his pants, then kissed him passionately.

"The waiter's going to be afraid to come to our table," he whispered. He eased back and reached for the breathing bottle of red Bordeaux, a '70 Médoc, and poured for each of them.

"And we'll never get out of here." She laughed.

Anthony raised his glass to hers. "We have the whole night ahead. Let's savor it."

"You can count on that." She took a sip. "I can't believe how perfectly this worked out for us."

She pulled out a cigarette, and a waiter abruptly appeared to light it. He apologized for not being there to pour their wine and asked if they were ready to order.

"She'll have a filet mignon, medium rare, with peanut sauce and a side of Pake noodles. Make that two. And the Caesar salad for two."

"My favorite meal. My favorite wine. And most of all, my favorite man." Sylvia sighed with pleasure.

"You deserve this, Jake. I just want to make you happy, more than anything."

"You're doing pretty well so far."

Anthony lit his own cigarette then talked about next summer and how they would go to see his parents in Italy and travel Europe together. Maybe take a whole month. It all sounded thrilling to Sylvia, but that was eight months away. She wanted to know what was happening now.

The waiter returned with a giant wooden bowl on a cart and proceeded to prepare their salad. They watched him without speaking. They ate their salads, talking about his mother, Franca, and her love for Firenze, and then ate their dinners, talking about Sylvia's love for Annecy near the French Alps.

They ordered espresso and decided to split a chocolate mousse. While they waited, Anthony turned sideways to face her and took her hands in his. "I've been wanting to tell you for days what's been going on, but I needed to wait until we had an evening together."

Sylvia was suddenly feeling the half bottle of wine she'd had, plus the glass of Chablis at home. Things seemed a little out of focus, and she had to concentrate hard.

"Things aren't going as I'd planned, but they're going to work perfectly for us."

She hung on to the last part of what he said, "perfectly for us."

He squeezed her hands and tilted his head at her. "Are you okay? You look a little lost."

She nodded.

"Don't worry, Jake. It's a little complicated, but stay with me."

Their mousse arrived, and they turned back toward the table. Sylvia needed to ground herself in chocolate and took a heaping spoonful.

"Jane went home to Long Beach yesterday, for an indefinite period of time. She took the kids with her, for now."

Sylvia almost dropped her spoon. "You mean she's leaving you?"

Their coffees arrived. "Not exactly. Maybe I'm telling this backwards." His gold link bracelet glinted in the dim light as he took a sip of espresso. "We just learned that her mother is dying of cancer, and Jane wants to be with her until the end.

She's even thinking about moving down and putting the kids in school there. It does depend on how long her mother has, which is never an exact science."

"What a mess. Jane must be a wreck."

"She is. But that's not the only reason."

The fog in Sylvia's head seemed to lift. She felt guilty that her heart lifted as well. She dropped a lump of raw sugar into her coffee.

"The day after Alexia's birthday, I sat Jane down and told her our marriage was in trouble and that we had to do something about it."

"Do something?"

Anthony swallowed and pushed on. "After about an hour of crying and asking what was wrong, that she couldn't live without me, that she'd do anything to save it, she said that we should see a counselor right away."

"A counselor?" *I thought he was going to go right ahead and ask for a divorce.*

"Like you and Tom did," he said.

"It was so brief it hardly—" She lit her own cigarette. "So you agreed."

"Of course." He cleared his throat. "You know, to make it look like I'm trying and to help her come to her own conclusion that it's over. To make the divorce more amicable. I figured we'd go once a week for the next month or two, and then, after the holidays, I'd tell her I'm done."

"But if Jane's in Long Beach, you can't go to counseling, so—"

"Right. Then came the problems with her mother, so I don't see us ever going to counseling. I think once she's down there, away from me, and home with the situation with her mother, she'll end up wanting to move back there. So that's when I tell her I want a divorce."

Sylvia felt queasy and put her cigarette out. "So you wait until Jane wants to move."

"Because of her mother, I'd have to wait anyway." He lit a cigarette. "Don't you see how it worked out? If we learned about Jane's mother *before* Alexia's birthday, I could never have told her our marriage was in trouble. Too heartless."

Sylvia struggled to follow his thinking. *But you could've told her you wanted a divorce.* "Timing is everything."

"And while she's away, I'm all yours."

"I think I'm going to be sick." She scooted out of the booth and wound her way through the maze of rooms lined with waiters and tables full of people laughing. She shut herself in the stall and bent over the toilet. *Did I miss something? How is this "perfect for us"?* Her mouth filled with saliva, her eyes began to water, and she retched her dinner into the bowl.

When she stumbled into the parking lot, Anthony was there to guide her into his car.

The next thing she knew, she was lying in a hotel room and needing to go to the bathroom. The heavy, rubberized hotel curtains were pulled shut, and it was too dark to see well. She sat up slightly to read the digital clock: 4:15. Anthony's curly dark hair contrasted against the white pillowcase. Naked, she slipped quietly out of bed and felt her way to the bathroom. Her head was pounding. She shut the door and thought about turning on the light, but the fan would go on, and she didn't want to wake him up. As she sat on the toilet in the dark, she felt the stickiness of his come between her legs but couldn't wrap her mind around any memory of their lovemaking. Nothing came back to her after standing in the parking lot. She just wanted to go home. Right now.

When she was finished, she groped her way to the chair next to the window and found her small overnight bag. She took it into the bathroom and dug around for her warm-ups. She slipped them on. *No shoes, and I need my purse.* She had to go back out to search for them. She started out the door and saw the glow of his lighted cigarette.

# CHAPTER 21

The lamp clicked on, and Sylvia squinted under its sudden glare.

Anthony was sitting in a chair in the corner in his jockey briefs and T-shirt. He stared at her as he took another drag on his cigarette. "Going somewhere?"

"I was trying not to wake you up." She felt like a teenager who was trying to sneak out of the house.

"Well, I'm up," he said with forced cheer, "but you didn't answer my question."

"I don't feel well." She looked around for her shoes. "And I need to go home."

He stubbed out his unfinished cigarette, breaking it in half. "Now, Jake, that doesn't make any sense." It was a condescending tone she'd heard him use before, but with his seven-year-old son. He got up and stood between her and the small hallway to the door. "You're not going anywhere," he sneered.

She felt trapped. "But I told you, I feel sick."

He walked slowly over to her, took her overnight bag from her hand, and set it on the floor. He felt her forehead and steered her toward the bed. "If you don't feel well, you need to stay here with me, so I can take care of you."

She stopped at the side of the bed and looked down. "No, I really just want to go home."

With both hands on her shoulders, he turned her body to face him. He gently stroked her hair then lifted her chin with his hand to look into her eyes. "You were going to leave without telling me, weren't you?"

She saw something there, hiding just under the surface behind the soft gestures. "I was going to write you a note—"

"A note?" He shook his head and looked up at the ceiling. His voice rose as he pointed at her, punctuating the air with his finger. "I think I deserve more than a note."

The sudden flash of anger that darted from him like lightning made her increasingly nervous. He had never talked to her this way. And the deep shadows under his eyes gave him a crazed look. "Yes, you're right; you do. You've been through a lot lately and deserve a good night's sleep, which was why I didn't want to wake you."

"But you also need to get some sleep and are still in no condition to drive. See how well we look out for each other?"

"I can't sleep here. It's too hot, and I have to get up early for school."

"You just have too many clothes on." He started to unzip her top. "Why don't you call in sick today? We can sleep in, and later I'll get us some breakfast, and we can have it in bed."

Sylvia stepped back and zipped her top back up. "I can't do this."

He leaned toward her as if to understand her better. “You can’t do what, Sylvia?”

She spotted her heels from last night. She bent down on her hands and knees to get them from under the chair. As she reached for them, he kicked them against the wall.

“I’m trying to talk to you.” He nudged her rib cage hard with his knee. “Get up.”

Her insides turned hollow, and she slowly sat back on her heels. In a quivering voice, she said, “I mean I can’t stay here with you right now.”

“Because?”

“Because I’m sick.”

“We already went over that, but let’s try it again.” In a singsong voice, he said, “You can’t be alone when you’re sick. So you’ll stay here with me.”

Sylvia swallowed the urge to cry.

“Now sit with me on the bed so we can go back to the beginning.” He sat down on the bed and patted the space beside him.

Sylvia did as she was told.

He put his arm around her and pulled her to his chest. “You were leaving because you’re upset about something. Just tell me what it is.”

“I’m too upset to talk,” she whispered.

“But why are you upset?”

She tried to clear her throat.

He hugged her tighter. "C'mon, Jake. Why are you upset?"

"Because I feel afraid right now," she whimpered.

"Afraid? Because I'm angry?"

She nodded her head against his chest.

"But you're the one who made me angry. You were ignoring me. Anyway, I wasn't asking why you were upset right now. I want to know what made you so upset in the first place that you were sneaking out to go home."

"Please, I'd rather talk tomorrow."

"My dad always said 'never go to bed angry,' which applies to us right now. I can't let you go home upset with me, especially when I have no idea what it's about. Maybe I can help you get started. Let's see." He moved back from her and started unzipping her top again. She didn't resist. "Something about what I said last night I would imagine."

He removed her top, threw it on the floor, and suggested they lie down on the bed and talk, to be more comfortable. As she scooted back toward the pillows, she stole a glance at the clock: 5:15. *How will I get him to let me go?* He pulled off her sweatpants and moved up next to her, resting on his knees. He stared at her naked body then looked down at his giant erection pushing under his jockeys.

"All I have to do is look at you and see what happens?" He smiled. "Now it's your turn to take my clothes off."

She dreaded where this was going but figured this might be the only way she could leave with his blessing. As she reached up to remove his T-shirt, her chest bumped against his hard shaft. He let out a short gasp and pressed her hips against him, rubbing and rotating them together. His tongue stretched for her nipples, licking circles around each one. Her confusion mounted when she found herself getting turned on and felt humiliated. When his finger slid easily inside her, she pulled his underwear down to his knees.

"Suck me," he said.

She complied. After several minutes, he pushed her back on the bed and went down between her legs. Her own sense of power began to reverberate within her, slowly climbing, climbing toward its peak until finally she released the anger and fear she had stored inside. He lifted himself over her and, holding himself up with straight arms, looked into her eyes as he thrust hard and deep again and again and again. He let out a long, low guttural moan and eased down on top of her.

His face was buried in her neck, and he was still breathing heavily. "Wow, that was amazing. Maybe that's what you needed all along."

Sylvia was weak all over.

He went into the bathroom. She heard the water running. It was now 6:00. She was running out of time. He came back with a warm moistened towel and washed between her legs. Then he pulled the sheet over her and tucked her in before climbing under himself. What could've been a tender, loving gesture, to her, ended up feeling like a ritual he was performing, a confession or an act of contrition, to wipe away any scent of his carnal weakness. She wondered if he was trying to appease his own guilt for the way he'd been treating her.

"Do you feel like talking now?" he asked.

What she wanted was to click her heels and be home. He sounded conciliatory, but she no longer trusted it. Was he lying in wait until she said or did what he decided was the wrong thing? "You're right. I was upset last night but was too drunk to figure out how to even begin to tell you."

"Now we're getting somewhere."

"Actually, I don't think we are. You're not moving along as promised." Sylvia was surprised at how easily she blurted it out. She didn't feel afraid. She wasn't concerned about his reaction either. Her intense feelings for him had always prevented her from saying what was on her mind, held her back, perhaps in quiet fear that he'd reject her if he knew what she really thought, or leave her if she demanded too much. Now she asked herself, *If I don't care as much what he thinks, do I still love him as much?* She didn't feel the same, and it had nothing to do with sex. Maybe the feelings she had for him were no longer in the way of finally feeling free enough to express herself openly.

He sat up and looked incredulous. "I did exactly as I said I would."

"No, you didn't. You said you were going to ask for a divorce after Alexia's birthday."

"If you're going to take everything I say literally, then you're right."

"How else should I take it?"

"I don't think you would've liked it if I held your feet to the fire. You know Jane's tendency toward hysteria. You know the best way to handle her is to ease in slowly. You eased into it the same way with Tom even without that problem."

"If you're referring to counseling, that was over two years ago," she said.

"If only I'd known that you were expecting me to ask for the divorce. No wonder you were upset last night." He cuddled up closer to her.

"It came as a shock, that's all."

"I'd ask for a divorce tomorrow, now that I know how much you need that from me, but—"

"I'm sure you would, but it's water over the dam now with her mother and all." Sylvia saw no need to antagonize the situation by pointing out the flaws she found in his reasoning, which he always seemed to twist around to his advantage anyway. She was convinced that he truly believed what he was saying. She excused herself to go to the bathroom.

When she came back, she told him she didn't feel right about calling in sick because she'd only been teaching for two months. Besides, it was almost too late for them to get a sub for her. She asked him if he'd help her get her things together because it was time for her to leave. He accepted her decision willingly. He even retrieved her shoes and handed them to her.

"I hope you understand why I got so mad earlier. Just talk to me from now on. Okay, Jake?"

"Got it," she said.

With one arm around her shoulder and the other carrying her bag, Anthony sang "Annie's Theme" as he walked her to her car. She held her face up to the rain. When she opened the door, he kissed her tenderly on the forehead and lips and told her again he was all hers.

She drove out of the parking lot. The air smelled fresher. The rain cleansed her. Her old Mercedes hummed along brand new. Her worries about the house selling or having enough money each month or Tom's visitation schedule seemed minor. Sylvia had never known Anthony to behave like this. She didn't know what she was going to do about him in the days ahead, and at this moment she decided she didn't have to know. Right now, all she wanted was to drive home.

# CHAPTER 22

At school the following afternoon, Sylvia was just starting to feel better when she noticed a phone message sitting in her mailbox. She had never received one here before, and she felt ill all over again. She imagined it had to be important for someone to contact her at school. A feeling of heaviness seemed to weigh down her hand while she reached into the box. She haltingly opened the folded yellow form.

It was from Charlotte, the French teacher. With relief she chastised herself for the negative images her mind conjured lately. She and Charlotte had spoken on the phone a few times, but they still hadn't met to discuss their classes and coordinate a teaching plan. She would call her back later that night.

The rain was coming down hard, so she ran to her car in the parking lot. Tom had asked her to pick Trevor up at day care and said he'd bring Alice home around three. She switched the wipers to high speed as she drove to MaryAnn Harper's, only ten minutes from school, but she could barely see out the blurred windshield. *Need to get new blades.* A foggy mist hung over the road. She lowered her window and stuck her head out to better see what was in front of her until she pulled into the quiet, dead-end street of modest, neatly manicured, one-story frame bungalows.

MaryAnn Harper took up to eight children in her home on a drop-in basis. She was a soft-spoken, gentle-mannered, Christian woman around Sylvia's age and attractive in a simple, homespun way. Trevor came here two days a week and attended preschool the other three days. Sylvia had hoped to have Trevor in preschool four days, but it was too expensive for now. Maybe in January. He never complained about going to MaryAnn's house though. And according to her, he got along so well with Jeremy and Jason, the identical twins, that she would've thought they were all brothers. Today he was so involved in the playroom with them that Sylvia had to practically pry him loose. They said their good-byes and took off for the car. On the way, Trevor called out, "Can I ride in the backseat again?"

Sylvia opened the back door. He giggled with pleasure and climbed in. He got a kick out of the freedom to roam around in the back since he had outgrown his car seat a few weeks ago. He was animated on the drive home and begged Sylvia to ask the twins to come over to play the next day. At the moment, she was so tired she couldn't imagine a house with three four-year-old boys.

Two blocks from their house, Sylvia looked in the rearview mirror to answer Trevor and saw a sudden movement to the right in her peripheral vision. She whipped her head sideways just in time to see a car pull out from the side street heading directly at them.

*Slam on the brakes or gun it?* She heard the sound of screeching brakes as her car swerved on the wet road.

"Get down, Trevor!" she shouted.

Like a moving target, they were hit broadside in front of the passenger door. The Mercedes spun in a half circle and came to a halt in a perpendicular position in the two-lane road. Trevor was lying facedown on the backseat, his face in his hands. Sylvia was shaken but otherwise seemed unhurt.

"Trevor?" She lunged from her seat and put her trembling hand on his back, the other on his head. She felt woozy. "Are you all right, honey?"

He slowly peeked out and raised his head. "Mommy?"

"I'm coming back there. Don't move." She opened her door, thinking how foolish she'd been not to wear a seat belt and how lucky that Trevor had been in the back. She saw two teenagers get out of the other car and run toward her as she climbed in the backseat with Trevor. One of them began nervously chattering, asking how they were, then apologized and said she didn't see the car with the rain and all.

Sylvia held up a hand to quiet her. "Leave me alone for a minute." They silently backed away, and she turned to her son. "Trevor?"

Trevor rolled over on his side then held his arms out toward her. Sylvia lifted him carefully onto her lap and, worried that he might be hurt, rocked him as she gently examined him.

"I hear a siren!" Trevor twisted himself around in order to stare out the back window. "Look! A police car's coming, Mommy!" His eyes were like saucers.

"It's coming to us, honey."

"Wow. Jeremy and Jason should see this!" He climbed off of Sylvia's lap and propped himself on the back of the seat to get a better view.

He didn't act like he was hurt, so Sylvia got back behind the wheel to wait for the policeman. The teenagers were sitting in their car. Sylvia was too shaken to even look at the damage. Cars slowed down to weave around the two cars. She noticed a crack in her windshield that began near the passenger door and was slowly creeping across to her side. Reality was slowly creeping into her vision as well. *Can I drive this car home? Is it fixable? Alice must be home by now, alone.*

"Here comes the policeman, Mommy. He has a gun! And he's walking around our car!"

The officer approached her door. She rolled the window down. Rain spritzed inside the car as he leaned down to look at Trevor, who was now squeezing between Sylvia's shoulder and her open window. Trevor's face was a foot from the officer's.

"How are you doin', young fella?" he asked.

Sylvia turned her head to look at Trevor, whose eyes were still saucers.

"I'm okay," Trevor answered solemnly.

"He seems all right," the officer said to Sylvia.

"I think so. At least no one was moving very fast," she said, then pointed toward her house. "I live right over there. Can we do this at my house? My daughter might be home alone." Sylvia hoped that Tom would wait with Alice until she got home, especially since he lived so close by. But she wasn't confident.

"It would be better to take care of this here," he said. "We'll need a couple of tow trucks."

"I might be able to drive my car though," she said.

"Don't think so. You have a front right flat. Have you looked at your car?"

Sylvia shook her head and began to cry. She felt a small hand pat her neck. "It'll be okay, Mommy," Trevor whispered.

"Another patrol car will be here in a minute. He can take you home," the officer said.

Trevor jumped to attention. "Do we get to ride in a police car?"

The officer smiled. "You sure do." He roughed Trevor's blond head.

Sylvia managed a weak smile back. "She pulled out and just ran right into me. I hope she has insurance."

When they walked in the door at home, Alice was on the phone. "Why can't I come tonight, Daddy?" Red began to bark, and Alice gawked at the policeman. "What's wrong?"

Sylvia held up one finger. "One second, honey. Let me talk to your dad." Alice handed her the phone.

"We got in a accident and got to ride in a police car," Trevor said to Alice.

Sylvia spoke briefly and then hung up the phone. "Your dad will be here in a few minutes. You'll be staying with him tonight."

She looked at the officer and motioned to the kitchen table. "Sorry for all the confusion. Would you like to sit down?"

"Don't worry about me." He sat down.

"Is that a real gun?" Trevor asked. "Did you ever have to shoot anyone? Can I see it?"

Sylvia guided Alice to the living room and explained what had happened and that she didn't know yet what would happen with their car.

The phone rang. Alice joined Trevor and the inquisition in the kitchen, while Sylvia answered it. She couldn't imagine more things happening at once.

"Thank God, you're okay," Anthony said. "I saw your car being towed a few minutes ago."

Sylvia was surprised at how glad she was to hear from him. His voice sounded so comforting that she suddenly felt the need to see him. But how could she? She didn't have a car anymore. She started to cry again.

Tom walked in the front door and introduced himself to the officer.

"Daddy!" Alice and Trevor chimed. They bolted toward him, and he swept them into his arms.

Sylvia pulled the phone cord as far as it would go to the other end of the kitchen. Anthony offered her the use of one of their cars since Jane was gone. She thanked him but wondered aloud if that was a good idea or not. He seemed to think it didn't matter. She told him that Tom and a policeman were there and she'd have to call him later. After she hung up the phone, she realized that he was alone, too. They were free to see each other tonight now that his family was gone. It felt foreign to her. This morning's trauma seemed so long ago that it was more like a bad dream, and she wished it hadn't happened. She was already trying to justify his behavior. *He's had a lot to deal with at home with Jane's mother. He hasn't slept well. Jane's hysteria would make anyone go crazy. And I hadn't told him at dinner what was on my mind.* She didn't know what she wanted to do tonight.

After the officer took down the necessary information from Sylvia, he left.

Tom was kind toward her and concerned. He even offered the use of his car for a day or two; he said he could use Betsy's. When he left with the kids and Red, Sylvia sat in the quiet of her living room. She lit a cigarette and watched the smoke waft through the air. She would smoke in her bed tonight, too, she decided. The thought of it felt delicious. She would have to check on her car tomorrow and figure out whose offer she would take. She was leaning toward Tom's. Safer. Less complicated with the neighbors. She felt hungry and realized there wasn't much in the house to eat. And she was too tired to move. So she just sat and smoked and watched it get dark.

About an hour later there was a knock at her door. She looked through the peephole. All she could see was one red rose. She smiled as she opened the door.

"Thought you might be hungry." Anthony held up a take-out bag from Farucci's and a bottle of red wine. He handed her the rose.

She threw her arms around his neck. "You're just what the doctor ordered."

# CHAPTER 23

November 1980

According to the insurance company, Sylvia's car was considered totaled because the cost of repairs exceeded its value. Jessica recommended the local Ford dealership, whose owner was from Lakeside and had a reputation for being honest and fair. Since she and her husband knew the owner socially, she said she'd get Greg to give him a call on Sylvia's behalf. It couldn't hurt. So she sent the car there and hoped for a trade-in on anything that was reliable. Within two days she owned a brand-new Ford Fiesta with monthly payments in the one-hundred-twenty-dollar range. It was pale gray with red vinyl interior and had cute little racing stripes running along the sides. Alice nicknamed their new car Fifi. Even though the engine was so small it sounded like hamsters on a wheel, Sylvia counted on it being a dependable vehicle for the drive to San Diego. As soon as school let out for Christmas vacation, they would be off. Before that, Sylvia still had to get through a Thanksgiving with just the three of them.

*Le Jour du Merci Donnant*, as it was called in French, was a holiday Sylvia didn't look forward to this year. She found it humorous that her students didn't understand at first why Thanksgiving wasn't a holiday in France, too. To create a more fun atmosphere for them, she taught "holiday" vocabulary by way of seasonal pictures. For Halloween she'd even disguised herself as the Hunchback of Notre Dame.

At home she wondered how to put up a positive front for this year's Thanksgiving dinner without the traditional festive family gathering. Granted they weren't used to spending the day with her parents or Tom's since they had moved from Ohio, but they had celebrated with friends the last few years. Alice and Trevor might feel the emptiness even more than she would. Tom was going to Betsy's family's house in southern Oregon. At least he had asked Sylvia if she would rather have the kids with her, which she did, and didn't argue with her about it. Nevertheless, Sylvia was feeling like the pathetic divorcée with the approaching holiday.

What added to Sylvia's dismay was that Anthony traveled to Long Beach to celebrate a "last" family Thanksgiving with Jane's mother, who was failing fast. He saw it as a last family Thanksgiving with his own family as well. While she understood the situation and was no longer worried about Anthony's intentions to divorce, it made her feel even more alone.

She tried to minimize the day's importance and think of it as just a day that would pass as quickly as any other. For her children, she wanted to maintain a cheerful posture and engaged them the night before to help her set the table with the fine china and silver for their very own Turkey Day. They decorated the dining room with pictures Alice had drawn at school of Pilgrims and Indians and turkeys. Trevor placed the harvest corn and colorful gourds in a basket for the centerpiece.

On Thanksgiving morning, Sylvia woke up early to prepare the turkey and organize the rest of the dinner, which she had started two days earlier. To her utter amazement, when she looked out the window the world was white. Up to six inches of snow had fallen the night before and was still coming down. The unexpected blizzard saved her spirits. She ran to wake the kids.

Alice and Trevor excitedly dressed in full winter garb and plunged out the door with Red right behind. Once Sylvia finished in the kitchen, she joined them outside. Red became a center of entertainment: She hopped, scooted, rolled, and burrowed in the white stuff. They laughed at the sight of Red feverishly chewing on the ping-pong-ball-sized snowballs that clustered in the tufts of fur between her pads. They made angels and a snowman. A few neighbors gathered, and they all took turns sliding down their hilly street on saucers and sleds with Red chasing after them, barking wildly. When they came inside chilled to the bone, the aroma of roast turkey permeated the house, and within half an hour they clamored around the table for the midday feast.

It didn't matter to Sylvia that there weren't enough mouths to eat it all. She had prepared everything: a fifteen-pound turkey, oyster stuffing, candied yams with marshmallow topping, mashed potatoes with gravy, corn, green beans, crescent rolls, her mom's homemade cranberry relish and cranberry Jell-O mold, and pumpkin pie with fresh whipped cream. She lit the burnt-orange candles, and they held hands as they each gave thanks: Alice for Roo Roo and their vacation to San Diego; Trevor for the food and snow; and Sylvia for her exuberant, healthy children and their special day together. After dinner, they cozied up under blankets in the family room with a fire in the fireplace and watched *It's A Wonderful Life*. She and the kids decided that even though this Thanksgiving was different from the others, this one was more fun than any they could remember.

In early December, the French teacher, Charlotte, invited Sylvia and a guest of her choice for dinner. Sylvia wasn't sure she and Anthony were ready for this, behaving like "real people" as he would say, like a normal couple, but she decided to ask him anyway.

"I think we should go," he said.

"But what will we say about you or us?"

"I won't wear my wedding ring for starters."

His wedding ring had become a problem for Sylvia. She was noticing it more and more. The gold band seemed to shine more brightly than she remembered; it stood out on his hand, gleaming at her, flaunting the truth of their situation. "That would help."

"It bothers you, doesn't it?"

"A lot actually."

"Then I won't wear it anymore."

"You mean ever?"

"See how easy that was?" He chuckled. "Let's not worry about what we say about me or us. We're not going on a trip with them, just dinner."

Sylvia arranged with Charlotte to get together on a Saturday when Tom would have the kids. It would be in two weeks, just before school let out for Christmas. Anthony said Jane *might* come back to Oregon for the holidays, but she hadn't made up her mind. She was worried that her mother would pass away while she was gone. Anthony said he was brainstorming something, but he didn't want to tell Sylvia until he knew it was certain. He was pushing for Jane to stay at her mother's for the holidays and he'd join them down there. That's all he would say about it.

Sylvia was getting accustomed to the relative freedom they had, at least compared to what it used to be like, and was glad she and the kids would be out of town during that time and spending Christmas with her brother. When or if Jane did return to Oregon for good was something Sylvia didn't want to think about; it was something she had no control over anyway. She and Anthony had taken some risks by going out to dinner a few times and finally seeing a movie together. For all she knew, they'd been seen and it was only a matter of time before Jane found out. Sylvia wondered if Anthony secretly wanted that to happen. Still, getting caught seemed like a cowardly way out. Since Charlotte and Paul lived on the other side of town, Sylvia didn't think that going to dinner there was a danger zone where exposure could lead to discovery.

To her surprise, Anthony suggested that he pick Sylvia up at her house. She left the garage door open so he could just pull inside and not have to sit in the driveway. When they arrived at Charlotte and Paul's, Anthony parked on the street in front of their house. He took Sylvia's hand and kissed the inside of her palm. "This is like a celebration for us. Our first night out as 'real people.' Let's relax and just have fun."

"You're right. I don't know why I'm so nervous." She kissed him lightly on the mouth and took a deep breath before getting out of the car. They held hands as they walked up the cedar steps to the front door.

Charlotte snuck in a roll of the eyes and an "Oh, my God, is he ever gorgeous" when she and Sylvia trailed the men into the living room. Paul asked about drinks, and Anthony offered to lend a hand. When they returned to the living room, Paul was telling Anthony how refreshing it was to be around someone who worked in the real world as opposed to academia where he was surrounded by those who pretended to be experts on life outside the hallowed walls.

"You talk as if you work in a vacuum." Anthony asked if he could smoke and received resounding okays from both of them. He held out his Marlboros to everyone.

Paul and Sylvia each took one, and he lit hers. "Exactly. Someday I hope to break out of the overprotective, stifling bell jar and breathe." Paul shot Sylvia a playful glance. "No relation to Plath I presume."

"In *prénom* only," Sylvia fired back.

Paul chuckled a bit smugly. "Touché."

"My sister's name is Sylvia," Charlotte said. "And you two are the only Sylvias I know. It's a more common name in France, I think."

Paul mocked a heavy French accent. "*Oui. Eeet ees Seelvee.*"

Anthony opened his hands and shrugged French-Italian-style. "You guys lost me back in the vacuum."

They all laughed.

"See? That's what I'm talking about," Paul said.

"So you really don't like being the dean of Admissions?" Sylvia asked.

"Don't get me wrong. It's a worthy position, and I feel honored that they chose me. It's the political side, the favoritism toward legacies and wealthy contributors that sullies my view of our esteemed private colleges."

"What would you want to be doing otherwise?" Anthony asked.

"Fishing for steelhead. Now there's something that takes skill, finesse, and patience."

"Never tried it," Anthony said.

"Seriously. To answer your question. Writing. Maybe for a corporation. I don't really know yet," Paul said.

Charlotte sauntered over behind Paul, tossed her long blond hair, and teasingly put her hands on her hips. "For heaven's sake, listen to you. You've only been at this job a few months."

"You know I'm just ranting. That's what we academics do." Paul leaned his head back to smile up at her, and she rumpled his hair.

Charlotte passed the Brie and water crackers. "Maybe no matter what we're doing, we think it can be better somewhere else."

"Especially if you've been doing it for a decade," Anthony said. "Making the decision to leave California to come here was a major one for me."

"Charlotte tells me you were crunching numbers down there, right?" Paul asked.

"Sort of. More like a mortgage broker for a real estate developer who's a friend of mine. Then he got into some trouble, and it was time to leave. So, we decided the offer to head up the accounting department for Haywood, the apartment developer here in Portland, was a real opportunity. Plus our house in California had tripled in value."

Sylvia had never really asked him the details about why they came to Oregon. She couldn't remember what Jane had said when they first met. She wondered what kind of trouble and why he would mention that here.

"Oregonians just love you guys coming up here with all your money. Did anyone burn the California state flag in your lawn?" Paul seemed to be enjoying himself.

Anthony looked to his right and to his left and whispered, "Quiet. That's just between us."

"Where were you two in California?" Paul asked.

Charlotte turned to Paul. "Sweetie, I told you they weren't together in California."

Sylvia smiled nervously and took a sip of wine.

Anthony grabbed Sylvia's hand. "That was B.S." He smiled at Charlotte and Paul. "Before Sylvia. Before *real* life began."

They all laughed.

Paul held up his glass and looked lovingly into Charlotte's eyes. "My sentiments exactly."

For the rest of the evening, the conversation flowed as freely as the wine. Sylvia felt relaxed and comfortable with Charlotte and Paul. And with Anthony by her side, she felt more pleasure than she would've imagined. Instead of watching him from afar in a social situation, she was sharing with him from the inside: as his partner, love interest, future wife, or whatever she was to him right now. The four of them did get along well, and she knew they felt the same way. Paul offered to take Anthony fishing sometime, and he and Charlotte suggested several times that they get together again.

Sylvia had never considered that difficulty before accepting the invitation; she found that it cast a pall over their wonderful first social evening as a couple. After a taste of living like a legitimate couple, it left her wanting more than ever for Anthony to move on with his divorce. At some point she'd have to tell Charlotte why they couldn't easily arrange more evenings together and why she couldn't reciprocate in the near future. The thought of explaining this to her new friend made Sylvia uncomfortable and frustrated. They weren't a real couple at all. They had been pretending, and she felt like a fool. Now that she was available, how could she allow herself to continually lower her standards, to be the "other woman" and demean herself by accepting less than she deserved? She was angry for letting Anthony reel her in again. Fortunately, with the Christmas holiday around the corner, it would be weeks before Sylvia would have to talk to Charlotte. She had to let Anthony know how she felt but didn't want to tell him over the phone, and she didn't think she could confront him in person, so she sent him a letter.

*Dear Anthony,*

*We haven't written letters to each other in a long time. I still have all of yours in my closet in an overnight bag. Our whole history is in there. Imagine. Three year's worth of letters. I'm writing to you here because I don't think I could express it as well in person.*

*After our lovely evening with Charlotte and Paul, I found it glaringly obvious how far we really are from reality. I'm unmarried. A divorcée. And completely free. You're completely married.*

*Now that I'm single, I'm more uncomfortable with this than I've ever been. To make believe that we're both free, like we're "real people," is a sham. You're dragging your feet, and it's humiliating to me. It degrades my sense of personal dignity.*

*As you know, I will be gone for almost two weeks. I need this space to reflect on our future behavior and decide what role I'm willing to play. At this moment, my feeling is that as much as I love and adore you and want to spend my life with you by my side, I can no longer see you under these circumstances. Until you've filed for divorce or moved out of the house, I don't think we should see each other.*

*As you've said so often, I'll be waiting for you.*

*All my love,*

*Your Jake*

# CHAPTER 24

December 1980

"Stop it, Alice." Trevor tried to push his sister to the other side of the backseat. "Mom, tell her!"

"Both of you. I can't drive with all that racket and commotion. Trevor, you come up here with me."

Trevor flopped over the front seat next to Sylvia. Alice stuck her head between the bucket seats. Sylvia saw her hand slowly creep around Trevor's seat and suddenly wiggle into his side. Trevor shrieked and buckled up with laughter.

"That's it. I'm stopping the car." Sylvia pulled off of the interstate onto the berm and sat patiently.

They were quiet. Several minutes passed.

Sylvia scowled at them. "We have a two-day drive ahead of us. Your fooling around makes it hard for me to concentrate on the road. If you can't behave any better than this, I'll turn around and go back home." Sylvia knew she was making an idle threat as soon as the words came out of her mouth, but she had their attention.

"I'm sorry, Mommy," Alice said. "Don't go back home. Let's draw, Trevor, or I'll read you a story."

"That's better." Sylvia turned to Alice. "Maybe you should sit in front, honey, in case you get carsick."

Arms and legs overlapped every which way along with bursts of giggles as the children exchanged seats. Sylvia stepped on the accelerator, and they pulled back onto the wet road.

"Go, Fifi!" Alice called out.

"Say it again." Trevor looked at Alice to time it together. They both chimed in.

Sylvia laughed. This little putt-putt car was no Mercedes, but it buzzed along like a worker bee. Basic maintenance costs were so much less that Sylvia found nothing but relief in owning this car over her Mercedes. She never wanted to be car poor or house poor again. Keeping up appearances had fallen to the bottom of her list of priorities.

Snow dusted the Douglas fir trees that lined the highway on both sides. She watched for icy patches in the shaded areas; otherwise, the road was clear and the sky a brilliant blue. In two hours they'd be leaving the state of Oregon. And in eight hours the weather would be a lot warmer.

Tonight they would stay with old friends of Sylvia's parents, the Crawfords, who lived in Folsom, home of the California state prison. Her mom had made all the arrangements. Sylvia was very relieved not to have to spend money on a motel room. The last time Sylvia had seen the Crawfords was at her wedding, but she always remembered when she and Steve stayed with them another time. At the time, she was about ten years old. Her dad had a business trip to Los Angeles and had taken her and Steve with him. Since Scott was only a few months old, her mom had stayed home. Two things stood out in her mind about that trip: Disneyland, which had just opened; and Mrs. Crawford's anger at her and Steve. They'd been throwing a baseball to each other from the pool to an open upstairs window, which happened to be right next to a huge picture window. Too close for comfort. When Mrs. Crawford saw what they were doing, she rushed out and screamed at them both. Sylvia never heard either of her parents yell like that. She remembered being afraid the rest of the day and just wanting her dad to come get them.

By the time Sylvia and the kids arrived, Sylvia was so tired she could barely lift her eyelids. Alice and Trevor hadn't slept in the car the whole day. She was friendly and appreciative toward her parents' friends, but it was taxing for her to make even light conversation. Before Sylvia could ask, Jean Crawford told her to go ahead and call her parents to let them know they had arrived safely. At dinner, Jean told Alice and Trevor the story about the "close call" with the picture window and how she had yelled at their mommy, which Alice and Trevor found very funny.

"Did Mommy cry when you got mad at her?" Trevor asked.

"I don't think so, honey. Did you?" Jean looked over at Sylvia.

"No, but I didn't come out of our room all day."

Alice asked if anyone ever escaped from the local prison.

"Funny you should ask," Bud Crawford said. "I just heard on the news that there's someone on the loose right now."

Alice's and Trevor's eyes bugged out. Jean looked down at her plate and giggled.

"So we'd better lock the doors and windows tonight," he said.

Jean nudged his arm and told him to stop scaring them. Bud snickered and said "April fools'," which only the Crawfords found very funny. Sylvia thought it would be difficult enough getting two children to sleep in strange beds without frightening them unnecessarily. Then they wanted to show Sylvia photo albums of them and her parents when they were double-dating. The extended evening made Sylvia wonder if she might've been better off paying for a Motel 6.

By nine o'clock, Sylvia graciously excused herself and the children and went straight to bed. Once in bed she took a moment before turning out the light to read again Anthony's response letter. Although it was difficult, she remained steadfast in her resolve and hadn't allowed herself to talk to him before she left.

*My dearest Jake,*

*I'm shocked and disappointed that you would do this to us at this critical point. And I have to ask myself why now? Why right before I'm about to leave Jane? Don't you want to be there for me like I was for you? It seems grossly unfair that you would treat us this way. Of course we're not "real people" yet. We both knew that. That's why I coined the phrase.*

*It makes me think you don't believe in me. After all this time and our well-thought-out plan to be together, which you totally agreed to by the way, I find your unwillingness to go through this last rough patch together as selfish and shortsighted. This is a side of you I've never seen. After all I've sacrificed financially and emotionally, you're willing to reject us for appearances' sake, for what other people think. How could you do that to us?*

*In case you're interested, Jane's mom passed away yesterday. She'll be coming back to Oregon with the kids in early January in time for school. I'm staying down there until then.*

*Remember I told you I had a surprise for you? While in Long Beach I was going to escape to see you in San Diego and meet your brother like you wanted me to. Now that won't happen.*

*Don't worry. I won't beg you to talk to me or see me when you get home. I wouldn't want to humiliate you further.*

*I've loved you the best I could. If what I've given the last three years is not enough, then I don't know what would be enough for you.*

*If you change your mind, I <u>will</u> be waiting. Remember that no matter what you do, or where you go, I'll love you forever.*

*A*

Each time she read his letter, she felt queasy, and afraid and all alone, and she wished she knew what he was thinking.

Maybe she had been too hasty. She wondered why he reacted like he was planning on leaving Jane next week instead of next month or even next year. Based on their last conversation, he was counting on Jane's desire to remain with the kids in Long Beach permanently. Now that she was in Oregon again, they would probably even go to counseling. But it was the last part of the letter that bothered her the most. If she *didn't* change her mind, did that mean he wouldn't be waiting? That unless she changed her mind about seeing him, he wouldn't move on his divorce? When he wrote that he'd love her forever no matter where she went or what she did, it sounded like he was resigning himself to a life without her, playing the suffering romantic. The true love could never be, which was her fault, because she didn't have the patience to wait *with* him. Each of them seemed to feel abandoned by the other but for different reasons. She wanted to call him.

She set the alarm for five thirty so they could get an early start. She woke up the next morning with the letter still in her hand.

By the time they reached Los Angeles, the traffic was bumper to bumper and it was hot. They rolled the windows down to cool off, but now that they were at crawling speed, the exhaust smells bothered Alice, so they had to roll them back up again. Sylvia had expected to avoid heavy traffic this early in the afternoon. Even though they'd lost time with the frequent bathroom stops, refueling needs, and fresh air breaks, they still managed to reach L.A. well before the commuter rush. Then she saw the flashing lights and realized there'd been an accident. She quietly thanked God that they were safe and her urge to "make good time" didn't seem as important anymore. Instead, she thought about their plans for the days ahead.

She'd promised the kids they would go to Disneyland with Uncle Scott. She hadn't said anything about SeaWorld because they'd already been to the new one in Ohio with her parents last summer. No need to spend the money for something they'd just seen. She figured they would be happy just to go to the beach, swim in the condo swimming pool, and explore San Diego with their uncle.

Sylvia's mind returned to Anthony and his letter. His idea to come to San Diego surprised her, especially after the news of Jane's mom. How could he leave her and the kids at such a time? It made Sylvia feel guilty for even wishing he'd go ahead with the divorce. Like her needs mattered now. Of course she wanted Scott to meet him, but not like this. She wondered how receptive Scott would've been, knowing Anthony was "escaping" from his family while he was with them during the entire holiday. Sylvia might've felt uneasy and awkward, too. But what about Anthony? Wouldn't he have been uncomfortable to introduce himself to her brother while she was divorced and he was still married? And what did he expect her to do with her kids?

In the end, she decided that she only had herself to blame. By continuing with their affair for three years, she had sent Anthony the message that as long as his intentions were good, she would continue indefinitely or at least remain beside him as long as it took to get through both divorces. She'd been open about it with her parents, her brother, even her brother- and sister-in-law. And she'd even used Scott as a cover for her to meet Anthony in Seattle. Why wouldn't Anthony think he could present himself without reservation?

"Are we there yet?" Trevor asked for the hundredth time.

Alice rolled her eyes. "Quit asking that. Why don't you go to sleep, and I'll wake you up when we get there?"

"I'm not tired. Can we swim in the pool when we get there?" Trevor pressed his feet against the back of Sylvia's seat.

"Sure we can," Sylvia said.

"Is it too deep for me?" he asked.

"Just at one end," Alice said. "Right, Mommy?"

"Probably. But you can swim well enough, Trevor."

"I'll help you if you need it," Alice said.

"How much longer?" Trevor glanced quickly at Alice. "I mean 'til Christmas."

Alice cracked a smile. "You *better* not ask that again!"

Trevor made a cheese grin at her.

"Christmas is six days away," Sylvia said.

"It'll be weird to have Christmas when it's hot outside." Alice looked pensive.

Sylvia wondered if Alice was really thinking that she'd miss her dad.

"How will Santa know where we are?" Trevor asked.

Alice turned to her brother. "He just knows." Alice suddenly bolted upright and pointed out the window. "Look! Orange trees!"

They marveled at the fields and fields of orange groves. Sylvia told them to roll down their windows. If they were lucky, maybe they could get a whiff of their lovely fragrance. Within an hour Sylvia smelled the salty sea breeze and heard the cry of seagulls and the dull pounding of the waves as the ocean's magnificence came into view. The children were awed into silence as they stared at the rolling waves crashing onto the continuous stretch of sandy beach.

"Can we stop, Mommy? Please?" Alice asked.

Sylvia thought a moment. She wanted to get there before dusk, so she didn't want to delay their arrival any further or worry her brother, but her right leg was stiff and sore from pushing the gas pedal, and they *were* on vacation.

Alice and Trevor seemed mesmerized and just continued to stare out the window, their faces aglow in the light of the sun sitting low in the western sky.

"If I can find an easy place to stop, I will," Sylvia said.

"Right there," Alice called out. "See the cars?"

She was right. As they descended a slope on the freeway, there was a designated park where the road wound under the highway. It looked pretty far to walk to the water's edge, but Sylvia pulled onto the exit ramp amid cries of glee from the kids. She was excited, too. As soon as they parked the car, they took off their shoes and made a dash toward the crashing waves.

Sylvia suddenly noticed that she and Alice were getting close to shore, but Trevor wasn't beside her anymore. She turned around and spotted his wee frame standing stock-still halfway back. She could tell he was knitting his hands and crying. She ran back to him and hugged him close. "What's the matter, honey?"

"The waves are coming," he sobbed.

"No, they're not coming any closer." Sylvia picked him up and slowly began to walk toward the shore. "They land on the beach and then go back out again. I'll show you."

He covered his ears. "And they're too loud."

Alice ran up out of breath. "What's wrong?"

Sylvia explained why Trevor was afraid. Alice suppressed a laugh and repeated to Trevor what her mother had just said. Then Alice told him that the waves couldn't stay on the beach because that wasn't their home, that they lived in the ocean and had to go back. Trevor asked what would happen if the waves decided to move somewhere else. Sylvia was touched and reassured him that waves could never move away. They were not like people.

By the time they reached the water's edge, he'd calmed down, but he didn't want to put his feet in the water, and he kept his ears covered. When they headed back to the car, instead of rejuvenating her as she'd hoped, the beach walk wore Sylvia out. She was tired of driving and anxious to get to her brother's home. With any luck, they'd arrive in about an hour.

They approached the outskirts of town, and Sylvia took the directions out of her purse. It was the second exit and only three turns to their condo. That was easy. They pulled into the stucco-building parking lot and found the number to Scott and Amanda's unit. They jumped out of the car in their bare feet when they heard a voice calling to them.

"Hey, you guys!" Scott threw a trash bag into the garbage Dumpster and broke into a run.

The kids rushed their uncle and tackled him head-on. He swooped them up and spun them around. Sylvia saw her brother maybe once a year, and each time Scott seemed to get handsomer. His tall, lean body was more filled out and less gangling, which was probably from surfing and training for triathlon competitions, and from simply becoming more mature as he moved into his mid-twenties. His features appeared more Italian than Scandinavian: deep-set hazel eyes; thick, rich, brown, slightly wavy hair, just falling over a widow's peak onto his forehead; a Roman nose; and a glorious smile. And he was tan. She would never have guessed that the chubby, almost homely, little boy with the wandering eye who wore opaque pink glasses could have become such a swan. Sylvia started toward them and hesitated as she felt slightly off balance.

Scott came to her, and she embraced her baby brother with welcome relief.

"Do you feel all right?" he asked.

"It just feels like I'm still moving," she said.

"That's a long drive." He put his arm around her and guided her inside. The kids followed. "Let's get you settled and relaxed. And there was a phone call for you."

Sylvia sucked in a breath. She hoped it was Anthony.

"Jessica said to call her as soon as you get in." Scott opened the door and showed them around the condo. "How about we get a Christmas tree tomorrow?" Scott asked the kids.

They enthusiastically said yes then asked if they could go swimming.

"Let's get your suitcases so you can change. Last one in the pool is a rotten egg." And they ran out the door.

Sylvia reached Jessica on the first try. "It must be important."

"It is. Your house sold," Jessica said.

Sylvia needed to sit down. She dragged the phone cord over to the living room and sank into the sofa.

"Full asking price. All cash deal. No contingencies. It's a rare offer, and we need to respond," Jessica said.

Sylvia was feeling off balance again. "I guess there's nothing to say but yes."

"There's one slight hitch." Jessica cleared her throat. "They want to move in next month."

# CHAPTER 25

Sylvia threw her head back in disbelief. "How can I possibly do that?"

"I know it's a lot to take in," Jessica said. "I bet Tom would help you with the move."

"But I don't have any idea where we're going! I don't get back to Oregon until New Year's, then school starts, and I'll have to pack everything."

"Look. I know it's a shock right now. I'll check with an apartment complex in the Mountain View area of Lakeside. My sister-in-law lived there after her divorce. They're large units and reasonable."

Sylvia stood up and began to pace the room. "Oh, my God. This is too much."

"C'mon, the good news is your house sold! You won't have to worry anymore about Tom coming up with the mortgage payment. And you'll have some money for once."

Jessica's forced cheer only made Sylvia feel worse. It was easy for her to say when she sat comfortably in her gorgeous house on the hill with no money problems. So what if her husband didn't come home for dinner every night? If that was the most she had to complain about, she was a lucky woman.

After Sylvia hung up the phone, she dug in her purse for her cigarettes and walked out to the small iron-railed balcony off the living room. She closed the sliding glass door behind her and feverishly lit her cigarette. *I just need more time.* It was dark outside, but from the lighted pathways she could make out the dwarf palms that hugged the edges of the neatly mowed green area behind the condo units, along with exotic-type flower bushes she didn't recognize. She could hear the exuberance in her children's voices coming from the swimming pool in the distance. *Wouldn't Mountain View mean a change in schools for Alice? And would they take large dogs?* It didn't occur to her to ask Jessica if she had talked to Tom. At the muffled sound of the front door slamming shut, she turned slightly to see who had come in, flicking the ash from her cigarette.

The top of Amanda's head was just visible behind the two bags of groceries she was carrying. Sylvia watched her set them down on the kitchen counter. Even though she was outside, she felt rude for smoking when they didn't allow it, and selfish for wanting to finish her cigarette and be alone for a few more minutes instead of going in to greet Amanda right away. She took a few more drags then stubbed it out on the concrete and carried the butt in her loosely closed fist as she slid the door open and went inside.

"You made it!" Amanda grinned.

Sylvia smiled, and they hugged each other warmly.

"Sorry." Sylvia held out her hand. "Where should I throw this?"

Amanda looked up at her sideways. "C'mon. You don't have to apologize. I have an ashtray here somewhere." She rooted around in the kitchen cupboards. "You can keep it on the balcony, and when it's full, empty it in the Dumpster."

"Sure, thanks." Sylvia took the clear glass ashtray and walked back to the balcony to set it outside. "I was just wondering where you were."

"I thought you guys might like some alone time so I stopped at the store." Amanda laughed. "But it looks like they left you."

"The kids are getting their alone time with Scott in the pool, which is perfect."

"For Scott, too. He's been counting the days until you guys got here. But you must be exhausted. How about a glass of wine? And if you want to go back outside and smoke, go ahead."

"That would be great. I just might do that," Sylvia said.

Sylvia hadn't been around Amanda a lot but found her so easy to be with it felt like she was a part of the family, like a sister she never had. She was tenderhearted and laughed easily; although soft-spoken, she had definite opinions and seemed comfortable expressing them. She was petite but athletic. While not classically pretty, her engaging warmth and vibrancy were accentuated by her aquamarine eyes, which made her strikingly attractive. She and Scott seemed well-suited for each other.

Amanda searched in the china cabinet for a wine glass and ended up opening the dishwasher. "Red or white?"

"Red for me." Sylvia glanced around and realized there was a lot of clutter. At the end of the hallway was a pile of clothes and an ironing board, and there were cereal bowls in the sink. She seemed to recall that Vivian had mentioned that Amanda wasn't going to win any awards for housekeeping. Sylvia, like Vivian, wouldn't be able to fathom not preparing for houseguests a week in advance so that everything was immaculate. To her, it was not only about keeping up appearances, but also a matter of personal pride. As tiresome as it was to keep up, a well-kept, orderly home had become a reflection of self-respect, like wearing makeup or choosing the right outfit. And she found she could think more clearly: Clutter on the floor brought clutter to her mind. Still, Sylvia sometimes wished she cared less about such things and could just let them fall where they may. A part of her had to appreciate Amanda's laid-back style.

The kids would certainly be comfortable here, which was the most important thing. Sylvia recalled how nervous she'd been when she lived for a month with Tom's brother, Jim, and his wife, Cindy, while her and Tom's first home purchase, a condo, was still under construction. Alice was only eighteen months old, and Cindy wouldn't let Sylvia "childproof" her apartment: Steuben glass animal figurines sat on an all-glass coffee table just beckoning to Alice. During the day when

Cindy was working, Sylvia put them away out of Alice's reach, then brought them back down before Cindy got home.

"I love your condo, by the way," Sylvia said.

Amanda handed her the glass of wine. "I'm *so* glad we bought this."

"How ironic. I just got off the phone with my realtor. My house sold."

Amanda rolled her eyes. "Oh no. Great timing."

"I still can't believe it." She explained what Jessica had told her about the move-in date and the apartment complex.

"A month hardly seems reasonable," Amanda said. "Did she tell you why?"

"Something about the buyers being from out of state." Sylvia took a healthy sip. "I'm thinking we might not be able to stay the whole ten days. But then, I'd have to tell the kids, and I don't want to ruin their vacation."

"Of course not," Amanda said. "Are you sure you have to accept these terms? I mean, how critical to the sale is it?"

"I didn't even think to argue that point, but Jessica didn't act like there was any wiggle room," she said.

"Do you want to call her back?" Amanda asked.

"Maybe I should call Tom."

Amanda handed her the phone. She told her not to worry about the charges and went to change her clothes. She had never called Tom at Betsy's before and hoped he'd answer. She took the princess phone out to the balcony and bit on a fingernail while it rang.

Betsy answered. When Sylvia asked to speak to Tom, Betsy hesitated. "Is there anything wrong?" she asked.

Sylvia wasn't about to talk to her. "The children are fine. Is he there?"

"Well, he is, but we're eating dinner."

Sylvia flushed with anger. "We just arrived in San Diego. It's very important that I speak to Tom."

The phone became muffled. Sylvia heard her voice but couldn't tell what she was saying. Then a chair screeched, and she heard Tom reprimand Betsy for the delay.

"Sylvia? What is it?" He sounded exasperated.

"Right now I'm pissed as hell at your girlfriend's attitude. Who does she think she is anyway?"

"Just tell me what's going on."

"I wanted to talk to you while the kids are in the pool. About the house."

"What about it?"

"Then you didn't talk to Jessica?"

"No."

Sylvia explained everything.

"This is really great news," he said. "What a Christmas gift."

"I understand your relief, but I'm not there yet."

"You'll find a place. Besides, you can't look way in advance for apartments anyway. When one becomes available, you have to take it right away."

When had he become such an expert? "I suppose that's true, but I'm not there to even begin looking."

"Maybe I could check the ads." Sylvia heard Betsy saying something in the background, and Tom told her he couldn't listen to two people at once. "Anyway, Jessica's idea about Mountain View sounds good."

"But I think it's in a different school district. And what about Red? This is just too fast. I can't—how is Roo Roo?"

"She's fine. I'll call Jessica and find out the details. *And* if it's possible to extend the move-in date," Tom said.

Sylvia detected a familiar impatience in his voice, like he was in a hurry to get off. He probably didn't want to be on the phone anymore with Betsy sitting there listening. "That would be a big help."

Tom said he'd call her back in a few days when he knew something specific. He also told her not to come home early and ruin the kids' vacation and that he'd definitely help her move. When she hung up the phone, Sylvia felt somewhat relieved. Tom did have a way of taking potentially frantic situations, such as volcanoes and moves, in stride; this was when he was at his best. Too bad his best was confined to such a limited area.

Amanda joined her outside. She was in her bathing suit. "Everything okay?"

"A little better. I'm glad I called him."

Amanda suggested that Sylvia try to put this out of her mind since there was nothing she could do about it now anyway. She was on vacation and needed to unwind. "Maybe you're even getting a little hungry. Do the kids like Chinese? Scott can pick it up."

"It'll be a treat for Alice and Trevor. I took them to Hunan's once in Portland, and they loved it."

They both went back inside. Amanda rummaged through a drawer in the kitchen and pulled out a menu.

Sylvia sat on a bar stool and leaned on the counter facing into the small, only-room-for-two kitchen. Behind her was a dining room table. The kitchen, dining, and living room areas were one big room, but each space felt separate from the other. "I think I'm actually beginning to relax."

"The next thing you need is a Jacuzzi."

"Now you're talking." Sylvia got up to change into her suit.

When they arrived at poolside, Scott was pushing Trevor and Alice around on his surfboard. Then they both flopped off, and Scott grabbed Trevor and tossed him toward the shallow end. Then he tossed Alice.

Trevor bobbed up like a cork. "Do it again!"

Sylvia and Amanda jumped in the pool with them. The water wasn't warm enough for them, so they went right back out and into the Jacuzzi. Soon Scott and the children joined them.

"We've been going back and forth, Mommy," Alice said.

Trevor eased in up to his neck. "I *love* the Jacoozi!"

"We all do," Scott said. "Especially in the winter."

"This isn't winter!" Alice said.

"How quickly you've forgotten real winter," Sylvia said to Scott.

"No, I haven't. It really *is* winter here, you guys. It's Christmas, isn't it?"

"Let's go get the tree," Trevor said.

"Not now," Alice said. "*Tomorrow.*"

"We don't have many decorations. Did you bring any?" Scott asked.

Alice and Trevor looked at him blankly. "Do you have lights?" Alice asked.

Scott broke into a grin.

"Scott, stop it. We have lights and some decorations," Amanda said. "But it might be fun to string popcorn and cranberries."

"And make paper chains!" Alice cried. "I can draw snowmen, reindeer, and stars and make hanging ornaments!"

"And we can buy some glitter to sprinkle on them. And we'll make Christmas cookies and frost them," Sylvia said.

"This'll be great," Scott said. "And since it's the weekend, we don't have to go to work."

"Anyone getting hungry?" Sylvia asked.

There was a resounding "yes." They all scrambled out and, shivering, wrapped up in towels. With the shore breeze the air was brisk, so they broke into a run. When they got back, Scott started a fire in the fireplace while they got into their pajamas. Then they ordered their food: egg rolls, fried wontons, mu shu pork, broccoli beef, sweet and sour shrimp, lemon chicken, chicken fried rice, and mixed vegetables.

"We'll have enough food for the whole weekend!" Amanda said.

Sylvia sat next to the fire, and Trevor crawled into her lap. "I always love the white take-out cartons. They remind me of romantic scenes in movies."

Amanda laughed. "And always in New York."

"And it's raining," Scott said. "And cozy."

Amanda curled up next to him on the sofa. Looking up at him, she said, "It feels romantic and cozy right here, even without the rain."

Sylvia watched them wistfully. She missed Anthony. She wanted the romance, the intimacy, the sharing of a life with the man she truly loved. She was troubled again about his letter; it was as if he didn't understand what she'd been trying to explain about her feelings now that she was a free woman. Her resolve was weakening. Maybe she should've spoken to him in person. She suspected she might try to call him before this vacation was over then realized he wouldn't be in Portland anyway. He was with his family and his wife in Long Beach.

"Who wants to go with me to pick up the food?" Scott asked.

Alice and Trevor chorused, "I do!"

"Can we wear our pajamas?" Alice asked.

"You can wear anything you want in California," Scott said.

"Even your underwear?" Trevor asked.

"If you're not too cold," Scott teased.

"Wow," Alice said. "That's unbelievable."

"I'm gonna look for people just wearing underwear," Trevor said.

Amanda and Sylvia were doubled over with laughter. Scott and the children left.

"Your kids are the greatest," Amanda said.

"Thanks. Of course, I think so. I just hope this divorce doesn't break down their spirit over time." Sylvia moved onto the sofa next to Amanda.

"Does Tom see them a lot?" Amanda asked.

"He used to see them every day when he was in town. But Betsy didn't like it. We're sort of on a schedule now, but Alice doesn't understand why she can't see him whenever she wants."

"Do you think Betsy's pretty good with them?"

Sylvia got up to get a glass of water. "I thought she was at first, but Trevor doesn't want to spend the night. Of course, he's young and wants me more than anyone. But he said Betsy told him he was too old to have a blankie."

"Who is she to tell him that? Did you talk to Tom about it?" Amanda asked.

"Yes, but he said Betsy was just teasing. Not very reassuring." Sylvia sat beside Amanda on the sofa.

"It sounds like Betsy's sort of in control."

"I'm getting that impression, too. Since he's living in her house, he thinks he has to defer to her wishes regarding the kids. I wish he'd get his own place."

"And so what's happening, if I may ask, with Anthony?"

"Oh God. I'm not feeling very good about him right now." Sylvia choked back tears.

Amanda put her arm around Sylvia. "I'm sorry. Are you still seeing him?"

Sylvia stumbled through their latest scenario. As she spoke, she gradually regained her composure and, oddly enough, her determination that she was doing the right thing for herself by not seeing him.

Amanda confirmed this as well, pointing out that he hadn't made any real attempt to separate from his wife. "Have you thought about dating?"

"My friend Jessica wants me to, but I told her a month ago I wasn't ready."

"They'd be standing in line if you ask me," Amanda said. "I say, go for it."

Sylvia smiled weakly. "I probably will, but not until we've moved."

It was ten o'clock by the time they finished dinner and Sylvia got the kids in bed. Amanda said she was tired, too, and called it a night. Even though she was sleepy, Sylvia wanted to spend some time alone with her brother. He seemed to want the same thing, and the two of them settled quietly in the living room with the last of the bottle of wine.

"It's so great you're here," he said.

"Thanks to you. It was your idea, remember?" Sylvia said. "The kids really needed to be away—it seems like a lot of upheaval with all the changes. Tom moving out is big enough; then add living with another woman and me working. Being here with you might help them get grounded and cope better with what's coming."

"Uh-oh. Something with that phone call from Jessica?" Scott asked.

"The drama never ends." After she went through the house sale, the Tom conversation, and the latest with Anthony, she finally asked about Scott's life.

He shook his head. "I thought I had concerns until I heard yours. The big news is that my company wants me to spend a few months in Jidda, Saudi Arabia, as a part of a team installing a desalinating water plant, the first of its kind in the world."

Sylvia's mouth dropped open. His understated tone reminded her of their father. "That's fantastic! What an opportunity. Aren't you excited?"

"Actually, yes. I think I'm still wondering if it's for real."

Here was Scott having graduated from an esteemed Ivy League college, pursuing a career in his chosen field of chemical engineering like their dad, and now looking at exotic international travel. He even lived in an exotic climate and surfed every other day. He was living life, and she was just surviving. Sylvia felt like the older sibling who makes all the mistakes, paving the way for the others to follow, even the parents. During Alice's colicky infancy, Sylvia's mom laughingly told her that she'd heard a pediatrician say that the first child was like an experiment, a test run, and should be thrown out with the bath water. Her mom was only trying to lightly point out that no parent knows what he or she is doing with the first one, but Sylvia felt hurt and never forgot it. Looking at Scott now, she was living proof of the pediatrician's theory: marriage too soon, kids too soon, an affair, divorce, and financially destitute. Well, almost. "When are you supposed to go?"

"After the first of the year," he said.

"And you guys just bought this place. How's Amanda taking it?" Sylvia asked.

"Pretty well. She sees it as a good career move, but neither of us can imagine being away from each other that long."

"At least her parents are in L.A.," Sylvia said.

"Normally that would help, but her mom and dad aren't getting along right now. They're even talking divorce."

"How awful. Aren't they about the same age as Mom and Dad?"

"Yep, early sixties. Anyway, her brothers are close by, so that's a huge help to her."

"Do Mom and Dad know about Saudi Arabia?" she asked.

"I told them yesterday. They're really excited but disappointed that they won't be able to come out here in February like they'd planned," he said.

"And I won't even have a house for them to stay in anymore." Sylvia began to cry. "I'm moving backwards. To apartment living."

Scott handed her some Kleenex. "One step back, two forward, you know."

"How could I have screwed up my life so badly? And for my kids."

He let her cry and after a few moments took her by the shoulders and looked into her eyes. "Your kids are terrific. And you didn't cause the financial problems, so don't blame yourself for all that's gone wrong."

"But I had the affair and asked for the divorce," Sylvia said.

"Who's living with another woman, for God's sakes?"

"But only because I rejected him for so long. At least, I'm pretty sure that's why."

"Why do you want to defend him, Syl? Tom has to carry *some* of the blame for what's happened."

Scott got up to poke the fire, and Sylvia recalled the last time Tom did that—after he found the lawyer's business card in her purse. It seemed so long ago. A lot had happened in only nine months.

"I've always felt like he's the underdog, trying to catch up to everyone else or climbing out from under, and needs help. So I end up giving him the benefit of the doubt." Sylvia told Scott about the time in Chillicothe, Ohio, when Tom had to meet with his boss for his annual review. He had asked Sylvia what he should say, how he should ask for less travel, and was so uncomfortable that he had said he wished she could go instead of him, that she'd do a better job.

"So did he get what he asked for?" Scott asked.

"No."

"Well, you're the one who has to climb out from under now. He's the reason you had to sell the house, isn't he?"

Sylvia nodded. "I guess."

"You'd have to sell it even if you weren't getting a divorce, right?"

Sylvia nodded again. "Mom and Dad were right to worry about Tom not having a profession."

"Parents always worry about their children's future, especially their daughter's. Amanda's parents are concerned that I'm not a doctor like the rest of her family."

Sylvia couldn't believe it. "They are?"

"I can tell her parents like me a lot but, according to Amanda, hope I'll be able to provide for her 'in the manner to which she is accustomed.' How much can an engineer make?"

Amanda's family led a fairly lucrative Los Angeles lifestyle: fancy Beverly Hills address; second home in Palm Springs; father, a renowned, highly respected shrink to the stars; brother following suit *and* a successful musician. When Sylvia and Tom became serious, her own parents said the exact same thing. Scott must be right. No matter what the circumstances, this was just what parents did.

"Is that why you're not getting married yet?" Sylvia asked.

"No. Even though we bought this condo together, I'm not ready for marriage. I'm too young."

"Hopefully you've taken a lesson from my mistakes."

"Maybe in part, but our age difference may have something to do with it. None of my college friends is even talking marriage yet."

"That's hard to believe. Most of my friends were married right after graduation."

"But I wanted to get back to Tom. Everybody makes mistakes. He made a bad business decision. Lots of people do, and they come back. And you'll come back. Even if it *is* without Anthony."

She buried her head in her hands. "How is that possible?"

"Because you're my big sister, and you're smart and capable, and maybe this is your chance to really prove it to yourself."

"But what if I don't want to do this by myself?"

"Maybe that wasn't your original plan, but plans change, and we have to adjust to what's in front of us, even if it wasn't what we expected. Looking at what's real instead of living in denial because it's not what we wanted it to be."

"Like Mom and Dad with Steve?"

"That's a good example. Mom's suffered, I think, because she's been unable to accept Steve's illness. She's taking it too personally, like it's her fault. If she doesn't move past that, she'll be stuck in her own guilt and Steve will never be able to move forward."

"You're awfully wise beyond your years."

"I don't know about that, but adversity at an early age has probably taught me something. I got the rug pulled out from under me when Steve got sick, remember?"

Sylvia never realized how much Scott's life had been impacted by Steve's illness. She was married and out of state, but poor Scott was just starting high school. It must've been hell. He hadn't talked with her about it until recently, and used to occasionally crack a joke, such as, "Overnight we went from being the Cleaver family to the Addams family." Maybe being the firstborn had some advantages.

"You sure didn't show it. Your grades never dropped, you had a girlfriend, you were in athletics," Sylvia said.

"Like I told you, I spent a lot of time at my friends' houses to avoid the scene at home. And my girlfriend helped me feel almost like a normal teenager. Her family's front door was always open to kids, so a lot of us hung out there after school, but me most of all."

"Maybe it also helped that you knew you didn't have anything to do with causing Steve's problem."

"Maybe, but Mom did, so she was depressed a lot." Scott twisted around to look down the hall. "We have a night visitor, and it's not Amahl."

He got up and came back with Trevor in his arms.

Trevor rubbed his eyes. "Mommy, I had a dream, and I got scared."

She held out her arms and took him into her lap. "What about, honey?"

"The waves were coming into our house," he whimpered.

# CHAPTER 26

Trevor's dream left Sylvia uneasy. She tossed and turned fitfully, unable to stop thinking about what it might mean. His fear of the waves was explainable, but not that they flowed into their house. It was uncanny that his dream fell on the same day that she found out their house had sold, which he didn't even know yet. Could he have sensed her fears? Maybe he overheard her talking. She tried to retrace the hours, but she couldn't imagine when he would have. She wondered if it was a sign of something foreboding. Did it mean they were being pushed from their home before they were ready? Maybe they were finally going under financially and their home was the last vestige of a bygone lifestyle. It made her want to consult a psychic, something she'd never considered before. By the next morning she decided she'd been wallowing in foggy thinking from the fatigue of the long drive and three glasses of wine. The combination made her too emotional. She needed some time to distance herself from the situation in order to see it more clearly.

With each passing day Sylvia's house dilemma receded further from her mind like an outgoing tide as she let the balmy breezes and sea air soothe her soul. With her children she basked in the sun's warm rays either poolside at the condo or at one of Scott's favorite beach spots, the Cove in La Jolla. The lagoon-type bay was surrounded by cliffs that provided protection from the large waves that buffeted its outlying rocky point. While Alice relished climbing the rocks as far out to the point as possible, Trevor, with Scott's help and a watchful eye for any stray wave that might make its way to shore, eventually found the courage to wade up to his waist into the gently lapping water. Most of the time he played in the sand, saying, "I'm not afraid anymore. I just don't feel like going in right now."

Sylvia saw herself in both of her children. Alice, adventurous and almost fearless, reached for what she wanted without looking back. Alice deftly made her way over the uneven terrain, her braids bouncing with each movement of an outstretched arm or leg, the waves crashing thunderously at a distance in front of her, which reminded Sylvia of herself as a child, practically a tomboy. Alice wasn't afraid because she trusted her own instincts, her sure-footedness, even though she had never been here before. The similarities with Alice, however, ended there. Somehow she seemed to thrive in uncharted surroundings, as if she was happier mapping out her own road rather than following the one someone told her to take. Her approach wasn't out of rebellion or defiance, but rather a pursuit of the twists and turns that lay hidden behind the obvious. Sylvia hoped her daughter wouldn't change as she grew older.

As for Sylvia, she wanted a map and seemed to flounder when the course wasn't laid out for her. Even though she'd had the survival skills to move her family many times, she ultimately didn't think she was happier for the experiences. Although she gained courage by learning to adapt to new surroundings, her overall feeling was of being unsettled and not really belonging each time she had to start over. The main reason she was happiest in Chillicothe, Ohio, was because her and Tom's families were nearby.

Sylvia also identified with Trevor's cautious approach. It wasn't fear necessarily; he just seemed to want to make sure the path was straight and solid before walking on it. If he sensed any shifting sand, he pulled back, and might not attempt it again. Once he felt safe, he jumped in with both feet, took off on a run, and beckoned others to join him. Sylvia felt this way in social situations. From the time she was a little girl, she hated to enter a room full of people she didn't know. One of the main reasons she was so attracted to Tom, besides his looks, was his social ease in groups. He took control of a room when he walked in the door, while she was comfortable one on one and would spend most of an evening talking with the same person.

Trevor consistently drew within the lines. Alice drew her own. Sylvia liked to think of herself as doing both, but since childhood she'd been so accustomed to walking the line of conformity she realized how uncomfortable she really was now that she was standing in full view outside the circle. She felt more alone, more directionless, and more afraid of starting over than ever before. Wary of trusting her own instincts, she wanted to feel protected even if, as Scott said, she was so capable and strong. While she was willing to work and provide for herself and the children for the time being, she didn't go through a divorce to be alone and on her own. She did it to be with Anthony, and she wasn't ready to switch gears now. Whether that meant she'd see him again or call him before he was separated from his wife was becoming murkier to her. Her inclination was to hold on, to not give in, at least until she got back to Oregon, but no communication with him was much harder than she thought it would be. He was never far from her thoughts. At times she felt like she was carrying him around in her pocket.

It had been four days since she spoke to Jessica and Tom, and neither had contacted her. The timing to reach anyone was bad during Christmas week, and now it was two days away. Even though Tom had said he'd call her back, she didn't rely on his intentions anymore. At least she'd learned that much. Not wanting to call him again, she decided to call Jessica. Surely the buyers would consider delaying their requested move-in date. Just because they wanted to move into the house in a month didn't mean Sylvia had to go along with it. Jessica should've handled that issue from the outset. *How could she call me with that upsetting news the day we arrived? She should never have told me that part at all.* Maybe their friendship made Jessica feel she had license to be less professional and, therefore, less demanding. Another thing occurred to Sylvia. Because of their friendship and Sylvia's financial straits, why wouldn't Jessica have offered to take a reduction in her commission? She certainly didn't need the money. And why didn't Sylvia even think to ask? It made her mad at herself for trusting others to look after her interests. She was too easygoing for her own good, couldn't think fast enough under pressure, and didn't seem to expect enough for herself.

She shared her thoughts about Jessica with Scott and Amanda, who were seated in the living room reading. The six-foot fir Christmas tree sat on display in the corner with their homemade decorations and old-fashioned colored lights like the ones Sylvia and Scott remembered from childhood. Being Jewish, Amanda never had a tree growing up, but said she loved the warmth and charm it added to the holidays.

"I can't believe Jessica hasn't called you back yet," Scott said. "Why don't you call her right now?"

"Should I ask about the commission, too?"

"I think that's usually settled up front, when you sign the agreement to list the house," Amanda said. "But it can't hurt to ask her."

Scott joined Alice, who was working on a puzzle of a German castle on the dining room table. Trevor was working beside her on one of Captain Hook and Smee. Sylvia went into the spare bedroom and closed the door. She dialed the number and tried to gather her thoughts while the phone rang. Jessica's husband, Greg, answered and chatted with her briefly about

San Diego, where he used to live when he played pro football. Then he teased her about his friend who wanted to go out with her. He said if she didn't go out with him, he'd think she was seeing someone. He loved to needle. She just wanted him to get off the phone. She didn't say yes, but she didn't refuse him either.

"What's up?" Jessica asked.

"Did Tom ever call you?"

"Yes, right after I talked to you," Jessica said. "He said he was going to call you back; that's why I didn't."

"Figures."

"I also thought you needed some R and R to calm the nerves." Jessica chuckled. "You were pretty wound up last time we talked."

"And with good reason, I'd say." Sylvia asked if Tom had explained her need to change the move-in date.

"As I told him, I can't blame you for wanting another month or so, but these people are moving in from out of state. I already told their agent we could work with them on this."

"Well, it's a real hardship for me, which you knew. Why can't *they* stay in an apartment for a month? Did you even ask before you called me about the offer?"

"I don't remember now. I guess you and I should've talked about this more," Jessica said. "I can't really counter the offer after I already agreed."

"Aren't Tom and I supposed to sign it though?"

"Yes."

"Well, obviously I haven't signed it."

"No, but Tom signed two days after he and I talked, which was right after I got your okay."

"What does that mean?"

"It's not totally cricket, but in a divorce situation and with you out of town, one owner *can* sign and make it binding. It's pretty much a done deal I'm afraid."

"I can't believe this! Why didn't you call me right after you talked to Tom? He told you I wanted to extend the move-in date, and it wouldn't have been too late then."

"Tom didn't make it sound like it was a deal buster. He only asked if it was possible, and when I explained to him about the buyers, he didn't argue," Jessica said. "*And* he said he'd call you."

Sylvia was livid. "But when he came in to sign, didn't you ask him then if he'd called me?" It felt like Tom and Jessica were working together behind her back. They just wanted the sale to go through.

"I didn't think to. He was in a hurry, on his way to the airport, you know, the usual with him." Jessica sounded a little defensive.

"Why don't you ask Greg if this is legally binding?"

"I did."

Sylvia didn't believe her. And there was nothing she could say. The wind had been knocked out of her sails. She fumed in silence. Once again, she trusted Tom, and now Jessica, to look out for her and she'd been let down. If she didn't believe she could rely on Tom, why did she wait this long to follow up? Partly because she needed time to think about it. But she also didn't want to make a pest of herself or seem like a worrywart. Was she so concerned about what others thought of her that she'd disregard her own well-being?

"I only wanted to get your house sold for the best price, which was what I thought you wanted most of all." Jessica sounded testy.

"Of course I want that, but don't I have some rights, too?" Sylvia asked. "Which reminds me, but I keep forgetting to ask. Since we're such good friends, would you consider taking a reduction in commission?"

There was a beat of silence. "I have to talk to my manager, but I'd be willing to go to, say, five and a half percent."

"What are you getting now?"

"Six and a half."

"Does that change have to be in writing before I get back?"

"No. I'll ask him today. I promise. You won't hear from me unless there's a problem."

"I'd like you to call me either way. Okay?"

"Sure. Syl, I know moving is overwhelming, but it's really only intense for a few weeks. And Tom will help you. Maybe I can even get Greg to pitch in, or Charlie and some of his friends." Jessica's son, Charlie, was in high school.

"That would be helpful." Sylvia sighed. "But I still don't know where we're going."

"Well, at least I have good news on that front. Mountain View has a three-bedroom, two-and-a-half-bath available in mid-January. No lease. A month-to-month rental for four hundred and eighty dollars. That's a steal these days. Most places are over six hundred. How does that sound?"

"Scary," Sylvia said weakly. She didn't have any idea what she could afford.

"I'm sure it is. At least for this move you're in the same town. And keep thinking of the nest egg you'll have. That might make you feel better." Jessica exhaled. "Greg and I were almost out the door when you called, so I should go. Let's talk in the morning about the details and the commission deal. I'll call you first thing. Okay?"

"Do they take dogs?"

"I think so, but I'll find out for sure. Try to enjoy yourself. And that weather! It's been pouring since you left, and I can't stand it." Jessica grew up in Southern California and after living fifteen years in Greg's home state of Oregon still acted like the weather was a personal offense.

Sylvia thanked her and hung up, then realized she forgot to ask about the schools. She felt good that she found the courage to ask about the commission, but the overall conversation left her with the unsettling impression that Jessica and Tom were more alike than not. Their way of handling this situation struck her as evasive. She could no longer look the other way or continue to let unresolved details hang in the air. That night, after she tucked her children into bed and crawled into hers, she lay awake hoping she wouldn't have her old nightmare about endless moving cartons.

The next morning Scott and Amanda went to work, and Sylvia waited for the phone to ring. She promised the kids she'd take them to the park later. The more she thought about Red, the more worried she became. *Large dogs are rarely permitted in rentals.* Sylvia concluded that she'd sneak her in no matter what the rules were. Within an hour Jessica called. The first thing she asked was what Red weighed. Dogs under forty pounds were okay. Red's weight was almost double that. Jessica pointed out that even if Sylvia could sneak her in, what would happen if she got caught and they said the dog had to go? *It would never work.* To add to Sylvia's dismay, Alice would have to change schools. Jessica reminded her that there was a redistricting process going on, which Sylvia had forgotten about, and Alice would have to change schools in the fall anyway. *It would still be a huge change. How will I tell my kids all this? And when?* She didn't want to tell them about the move until she knew where they were going, which meant she'd wait until they got back to Oregon and she'd found an apartment. Trying to forget all this and enjoy Christmas seemed impossible when all she could think about was getting home to look for other apartment options. On a happier note, Jessica got the commission reduction approved.

By Christmas Eve, with Scott and Amanda's calm, steady reminders of the positive things that were happening such as Sylvia's good job, the house selling (which would put about twenty thousand dollars in her pocket minus the bills), Tom's willingness to help her move, and that Alice and Trevor were resilient and healthy, happy kids, Sylvia was able to once again set aside her fears of what was coming, or what she didn't know was coming, and be grateful for the blessings that were right in front of her.

And as a ball gains speed rolling down a hill, so the remaining days with Scott and Amanda seemed to gain momentum. Before Sylvia knew it, their vacation wound down to a close. Two days before they were to leave, Scott and Amanda insisted on taking the children to SeaWorld, their treat, they said, without Sylvia.

"I think you need a day alone before the long trip," Scott said. "Kick back and do what you want to do, but don't pack. Just relax. Maybe even drive to the Cove and read. Watch out for the sharks though. And I don't mean the ones in the water."

"Very funny." Sylvia laughed. "I'm not sure I feel like getting into my car today anyway since I'll be practically living in it for the next few days. But what a swell gift—to have a day of my own—and the kids get to spend time with you two." She gave them each a big hug.

Scott, Amanda, and the kids left the condo around eight thirty the following morning. They figured they'd have lunch there and come back around three so they could all go to the beach one last time.

As she stood in the parking lot and waved good-bye, Sylvia had mixed feelings about spending the last day alone, especially since Scott was leaving the country for several months. Being with him again felt like being at home, where she was wholly accepted for who she was, where friends knew her and loved her. This made her miss her parents and home more than ever. She even missed Steve. Her mind wandered to the Mountain View apartment. *There'd be enough room for Mom and Dad and Steve to stay. But what about my Roo Roo? I'll have to figure out a way.* She was ready to get back to Oregon and start the process. A weight was lifting. With the money she'd have, maybe she'd fly them all out for a visit in March. During spring break.

She poured a cup of coffee and added a healthy dose of cream and sugar, the way she and her brothers drank it growing up. Many mornings before school they had "coffee and toast," a favorite breakfast treat: toast coated with chunky peanut butter to dunk in their coffee. She stood on the small balcony, sipping her coffee and gazing at the beautiful morning. It would be a perfect time to walk on the beach, but she really didn't want to drive anywhere. She'd go with them when they got back. She decided to have a Jacuzzi and read by the pool. She put on her suit and grabbed a towel, her cigarettes, her book, and the key to the condo.

The pool was deserted, which was to be expected on a weekday. She found a lounge chair and an ashtray and made herself comfortable. The sun was bright but the air still chilly, and she had goose bumps. She lit a cigarette and eased into the hot water and closed her eyes. She would miss all this but wondered how people who lived here got anything done; she'd probably feel pressured to be outside all the time and not waste the gorgeous weather. She went back to her lounge chair and opened her book, *The French Lieutenant's Woman*, and soon became absorbed. She had just reached the part of the long-anticipated love scene, which only brought back thoughts of Anthony and their initial attraction when they had sat in her family room in front of the fire, and he had taken her hand in his and kissed her palm. Before he had left that evening, they, too, had kissed with a hunger and passion so intense it was "wildly violent".

"Their hands acted first. By some mysterious communion, the fingers interlaced. Then Charles fell on one knee and strained her passionately to him. Their mouths met with a wild violence that shocked both; made her avert her lips. He covered her cheeks, her eyes, with kisses. His hand at last touched her hair, caressed it, felt the small head through its softness, as the thin-clad body was felt against his arms and breast. Suddenly he buried his face in her neck."

Sylvia felt restless and could no longer concentrate. The longing she felt for him now was sexual, but her deep love for him sought the fulfillment of a lifelong commitment to each other. She wondered if he'd be back in Oregon by now. If she called him, what harm would it cause her? Just to hear his voice would be enough. To tell him that she loved him more than ever, that she didn't know what calling him would mean at this moment. Then, acting deliberately, she rose from her lounge chair, leaving her belongings behind, followed the winding concrete path back to the condo, and dialed his office number. His secretary put her through.

Sylvia was suddenly overcome with emotion when she heard him answer. Her voice cracked as she said, "I couldn't go on any longer without speaking to you. I'm sorry if I—"

"Thank God," he gasped. "No apologies. My darling Sylvia, I've been lost without you. We must never do this to each other again."

His words were music to her ears. She couldn't wait to get home.

# CHAPTER 27

Winter 1981

At first Sylvia thought she'd been robbed, then realized it must've been Tom. *I never asked for his set of keys back.* When Tom said he'd help her move, it never occurred to her that he'd start the process without her. Since she hadn't explained the move yet to Alice and Trevor, all she could think to tell them was that Daddy must've decided to take what belonged to him, that in a divorce the parents divided their household belongings in half. His half was the family room, the kitchen table and chairs, which were still there, but she didn't remember what else. She was afraid to go upstairs in case other things were missing.

Sometimes when something starts to unravel it can come apart so fast that it's impossible to stop it before it's too late. So it seemed to Sylvia. Another way she thought of it was that troubles come in threes, but by now, she'd lost count, or wasn't sure what counted as trouble and what didn't. Was it when Tom announced he had a girlfriend? Or that Anthony didn't ask Jane for a divorce? Did her car accident count?

That added up to three right there, so maybe she should start counting all over again. Number one: Only one month to move out of the house. Number two: When she returned home, the family room furniture was gone.

The shock of seeing the empty room was one thing, but what left Sylvia with a feeling of being violated was that Tom, and most likely Betsy, had been traipsing through her home as if her privacy didn't matter. They could've taken whatever they decided they wanted, things that Tom and Sylvia hadn't even thought to discuss yet. And it might take Sylvia a while to determine if anything was missing. She was furious.

It was almost ten, so she put the kids to bed without unpacking. On their way upstairs she found herself looking around, searching for any missing pictures on the walls. Walking down the hallway, she glanced into her bedroom, which looked intact, then wondered as they passed the laundry room if he would've taken any sheets and towels.

As soon as the kids were asleep, she dialed Tom. Betsy answered.

"I need to talk to Tom," Sylvia said.

"Do you have any idea what time it is? I have a mind to hang up right now." Sylvia began to speak, but Betsy was unstoppable. "After what you've done to him, he should take you to court and get those kids from you. You're unfit to be their mother. Tom never did anything to you, and all those years you were cheating on him, sneaking around all over town, planning and conniving to dump your husband. You're nothing but a tramp."

Sylvia was caught completely off guard and couldn't imagine how she would know about Anthony—then it hit her. *Oh, my God! The letters!* "Who are *you* calling a tramp? How dare you set foot in my house! And go through my closet! You had no right." Sylvia panicked and was trembling with anger. "I'm calling my lawyer."

"Call whoever you want!"

Sylvia wished Betsy wasn't in the picture, meddling with her kids, keeping them from seeing their dad, and now having the gall to judge her. Betsy's strident tone still rang in her ears, and she shivered. What would Sylvia say to Tom now that he knew everything? She wished she hadn't called.

Suddenly Tom was on the phone. He was telling Betsy to go in the other room so he could talk to Sylvia alone. Sylvia couldn't make it out exactly, but it sounded as if Betsy was yelling at him until she finally must've left the room.

"I don't want to talk about this now," he said firmly.

"Why did you take the furniture when I wasn't home?" Sylvia demanded.

"To get a jump on the move."

Sylvia choked back sobs. "To take what you wanted you mean, and go through *my personal things*! It's outrageous what you've done."

"You're not the one to be pointing a finger at 'outrageous' behavior," he said.

"You had no right to just waltz in and go through everything." Sylvia could barely get the words out. "And with that bitch!"

"I didn't do it on purpose," he said. "Betsy and I were looking for a duffel bag on that shelf and the plastic bag fell—"

"You try to weasel your way out of everything. It's never your fault. I'm sick of your weak excuses! You *chose* to read what wasn't yours to read. Now your low-life, bartender girlfriend will spread it to whoever will listen."

"You have some nerve trying to make me out to be the bad guy here!" Tom yelled.

"At least you could think about the kids, who don't even know about the move, and come home to find the room empty! How could you do that to them?"

"Cut the drama, Sylvia. They'll only be upset because you are! You made your own mess, so get over it." Tom hung up on her.

With the phone still in her hand, Sylvia sat dazed at the kitchen table. She pictured the two of them sitting in the same spot reading her letters from Anthony. The thought made her sick to her stomach. Trouble number three had come. She jumped up and ran to her bedroom closet. She'd hidden the letters in a plastic bag on the top shelf under her purses. It looked like they were all still there, but how would she know if any were missing? There must have been a hundred of them.

She took the bulging bag downstairs, sat back down at the kitchen table, and rifled through the bag. Several letters were strewn on top out of their envelopes. Her hands shaking, she unfolded one—it was dated three years ago. Fluttering wings slowly began to beat within her until her insides were churning. She blushed with the shame of being exposed as she read the declarations of love and commitment to "being together forever" and the six-month plan to make that happen. She struggled to remember and couldn't, but decided that there weren't any sexual references. *At least we were more timid on paper than we were in the bedroom.* As she read, sadness enveloped her, too, because of their naïve, lovesick blindness that now looked sordid on paper. She wasn't feeling regret about their affair as much as she wished she'd handled it differently. She figured Anthony's original plan, openly divulging everything to their spouses, would've been too devastating.

Jessica had told her a long time ago about a couple in the same circumstances who decided to give themselves a year to divorce their respective spouses but to not see or talk to each other during that year. Neither would know if the other was going through with it. That way the reason to divorce was more about leaving an unfulfilling marriage and could stand on its own merit. Less messy and less guilt. The relationship could then develop more freely and in its own time. Jessica had said the couple did end up together and were very happy. Sylvia wished now that she'd had that kind of courage and integrity. All those wasted years in hiding and for what? To be found out after the divorce? *Why did I ever hold on to the damn letters? Sentimental reasons?* That was a laugh. She felt like burning every one.

She picked up the bag and walked across the dark, empty family room. She lit the gas fireplace and turned up the flame. She sat sideways on the brick hearth and placed the first envelope onto the grate, then lit a cigarette. It might take her all night, but she wanted to watch each one go up in flames, to burn away the shame and disappointment. What began in an act of frustration slowly became a more hopeful exercise to move toward the next phase of her life with a renewed sense of purpose. Halfway through the pile, fatigue overcame her determination, and she decided to finish another night. She climbed the stairs, tossed the bag onto the floor of the closet, and crawled into bed.

When she told Anthony the next day about Tom and Betsy, he was quiet at first. Then calmly he said that she had every right to be angry and mortified, but Tom finding out about them now was really water over the dam. He wasn't worried at this stage that Tom or Betsy would tell anyone, and least of all, Jane. Since Tom didn't live in the neighborhood anymore and Sylvia would be gone soon, there was little chance that they would run into Jane or him.

Sylvia never did call her attorney, but she was still angry with Tom. When she did have to talk to him or see him, she struggled to remain civil. She was really too humiliated to look him in the face and simply avoided making eye contact.

This was easy since that's what they'd always done. She was still puzzled by Betsy's anger toward her and decided to talk to Jessica about it.

"We've got to find out when Betsy and Tom started seeing each other," Jessica said.

"Who cares now?" Sylvia asked.

"You'll see. I played tennis with someone who knows her. I think they're old friends. Leave this to me."

When Sylvia took the apartment in Mountain View, she didn't ask Tom to help her move, but only to watch the kids and keep Red until she could assess the strictness of the dog rule. According to the kids, Betsy was a dog lover. Still, she was concerned that Betsy's anger with her might transfer to Red. This was the only apartment complex she found that even allowed dogs and was still affordable. In January there were only a few apartments available at all. She was feeling more divorced from her dog than her husband, and it broke her heart. The empty dog dish served as a constant reminder of the void left by her beloved pet and her worry that Red must feel abandoned by her. They decided that Tom would keep Red during the week and try to smuggle her in with Sylvia and the kids on weekends. She hoped to gradually move Red in permanently, but it wasn't to be.

After two months of juggling her back and forth, Red ran away from Tom and Betsy. She'd gotten out several times before and made her way to the old house, where each time the new owners would contact them and Tom and Betsy would retrieve her. Sylvia's first thought was Tom's negligence. *He must've left the gate open.* Or suspicions that Betsy did it on purpose. But Sylvia also knew how often Red escaped the confines of her old backyard and took any opportunity to slip out and roam the neighborhood. Sylvia felt certain that Red was brokenhearted, too, and needed her "real" family. Irish setters were known to be extremely loyal and one-family dogs.

But this time the new owners hadn't seen her. Tom and Sylvia spent whole afternoons, in separate cars, driving around with Alice and Trevor, looking for her. They posted signs with a picture of Red on telephone poles and in all the local stores and schools, but to no avail. The evenings were the hardest. Alice and Trevor would crawl in bed with Sylvia, and they'd cry themselves to sleep. Sylvia physically ached inside wondering where Red had gone, picturing her desperately wandering trying to find the family that deserted her.

Jessica, too, who'd known Red for years, mourned along with Sylvia. And in her usual style said there must be some way to find her. Jessica even called the police and fire departments to find out the best approach. "They think somebody could've taken her. A beautiful dog like that? She's most likely not wandering around hungry. Maybe if you think about her that way, it won't hurt so much." Maybe she was right. Sylvia found some comfort in Jessica's realistic support.

Even Anthony's good news didn't give her much solace. By the end of February, he had legally separated from his wife and was apartment hunting. Sylvia had stood her ground upon her return from San Diego. They talked on the telephone, but that was all. She wouldn't see him until he'd made an effort to follow through on his word. As she'd said to him, "At this point in our relationship, I'm more interested in what you do rather than what you say."

It wasn't long before Jessica had some real information on a different subject. "I found out when Betsy met Tom *and* when they became an item. And I was right."

Sylvia just listened, still unsure how it could possibly matter now.

"It was about two years ago. He came into the Rusty Duck, where she tended bar, and after a few drinks began pouring his heart out about how he thought his wife was having an affair. And he didn't know what to do."

"Maybe that was around the time he said that to me. Remember?"

"I do, because I came right over. According to Betsy's friend, it was love at first sight for her."

Sylvia had to process this, to take in what impact this had on her. Betsy wanted him a long time ago. Betsy hung on his every word, was there for him. "So, Betsy now knows from Anthony's letters that Tom's instincts were right."

"Yes. But it also means that from the very beginning she knew Tom didn't want you to leave him." Jessica sounded energized.

"When did they start having an affair?"

"She took him home with her *that night*!"

"What? So it started then? That's way longer than I thought." Sylvia couldn't finish. This was news she didn't need to know. Or maybe she did. It would explain why he never really tried to find out about her affair. And why he suggested they "lead separate lives" and stay married, which meant he wasn't really planning on marrying Betsy.

"He started seeing her on the rebound, out of rejection. And she knows it. Don't you see?"

"Is this supposed to make me feel better?"

"Knowing what he was really doing should. You don't have to feel so guilty for having an affair when he was doing the same thing."

"I suppose. So why do you think she got so mad at me?"

"She's madly in love with him, but she's his second choice. Tom always hoped you'd come around in time. That's why he didn't want the divorce."

"But she might not know that part."

"Woman's intuition. She knows. When she read those letters, it probably took her back to that night in the bar. And how he felt about you."

"Do you know how old she is?"

"Same age as you, maybe even a year older. Mid to late thirties, but not a looker."

"Hopefully, she'll get past the anger. He probably loves her now anyway."

"Don't count on it. She'll be jealous of you as long as you're around."

"Oh, great. And when Jane finds out, that'll be two women that want me dead."

Jessica laughed. "That's not what I meant, but you might want to watch your back."

"You should be a private eye. I think you'd like it, too."

If Jessica was right, Sylvia was worried for her children. Not that Betsy would ever intentionally harm them, but she could hold a grudge or belittle them or be short-tempered. Sylvia's concern was mostly for Alice because she so adored her dad. Betsy might not want to share him if she's the jealous type. And Alice was a spitting image of her mother. That couldn't help.

With Anthony's separation, Sylvia opened her door, but only partway. They spent time alone only when the kids were with Tom, every other weekend, and she permitted him to stop by their apartment two to three times a week. Usually it was after work, "just to see how things were going" and to say "hi" to the kids. Trevor was slower to respond to Anthony's presence, staying a little more closely by Sylvia's side, but Alice seemed genuinely happy to see him. It was hard to adjust to new surroundings at home and at school, and perhaps his neighborly, familiar face gave her some comfort and encouragement. Her dad was becoming less and less available, and perhaps Anthony's presence added a fatherly balance even if it was just on the surface. After several weeks of these short, habitual visits, Anthony surprised the kids one night by bringing Chinese food for dinner.

"We had the same thing in San Diego," Trevor said.

"You did?" Anthony asked.

"And my favorite is right here! Broccoli beef, 'cept I don't like the broccoli part that much," Trevor said.

"Me either. My favorite is chicken chow mein," Anthony said. "How'd you like San Diego?"

"We went in the pool every day. And the Jacoozi!" Trevor's eyes widened. "I used to be afraid of the waves." He stood on top of the coffee table and raised both arms above his head. "They were bigger than this! And really loud."

Anthony pulled him off of the table and into his lap and asked him to tell him more. Trevor giggled and went on to say how he wasn't afraid of them anymore. Alice surprised Sylvia when she squeezed in next to them on the couch and told Anthony all about SeaWorld, Disneyland, and the Cove in La Jolla. Later Anthony sat at the dining room table with Alice and helped her with her homework, something Sylvia couldn't ever remember Tom doing. She was overjoyed with his attentiveness to Alice and how gracefully he connected with her. Alice openly asked about Alexia and Ricky. Anthony hedged a little at first but told her they lived with their mom now and he only saw them some weekends. Alice's mouth turned down. She looked away as she said she only saw her dad twice a month and she didn't know why.

Anthony told Sylvia about his own nightmare in trying to see his kids. Apparently Jane was so upset about the separation that she'd been holding their children hostage, rarely honoring the visitation schedule. Sometimes they weren't home when he went to pick them up. He had little success in reaching them on the phone, and when he had tried to see them unannounced at school, the worried looks on their faces made him feel he would only add to their sense of betraying their mother. He didn't want to force the issue yet and hoped Jane would calm down in time.

Sylvia tried to talk to Tom about his lack of effort to see Alice and Trevor, especially since he was home more. She learned from him that his business was failing, and there wasn't as much money for travel expenses. Still, he only saw Alice and Trevor every other weekend and rarely during the week. The kids continued to call whenever they felt like it, but it wasn't long before Tom told Sylvia that it was too disruptive and they shouldn't call every day. Was this Betsy's doing, she wondered. The Tom that Sylvia knew would never find his children's attention disruptive. Based on the past few months, she wondered if she knew him at all anymore. Something definitely wasn't right.

# CHAPTER 28

Spring 1981

With teaching taking up more and more of her time, Sylvia found that Charlotte, the other French teacher, was becoming more and more of a confidante to her. And Charlotte lived nearby. She and Paul were just a short walk through the woods behind Sylvia's apartment complex. A familiar, narrow path between the fir trees slowly took form as their visits to each other's homes became more and more frequent. On weekend mornings they might have coffee together or take a walk, and occasionally, during the week, a late afternoon glass of wine before dinnertime. They not only practiced their French with each other, but were now comfortably sharing details of their personal lives.

Sylvia was finally able to reciprocate the invitation to Charlotte and Paul for dinner with her and Anthony, explaining why it hadn't been possible before, adding how immensely relieved she felt to be honest about what was really going on in her life. Charlotte said she felt the same way because Paul had left his wife when he and Charlotte moved from the East Coast only having known each other six months, and she didn't know anyone here. She was really starting over.

Sylvia told her that just moving across town made her feel like a newcomer. Going from a big house in a suburban neighborhood to apartment living with two kids was an adjustment in itself; on top of that, Alice left all of her friends with the change in schools. "But," she added, "there may be advantages to leaving the old neighborhood and any gossip behind. It might've been worse for Alice had we been able to stay." Sylvia went on to tell Charlotte that they hadn't given up on Red either. They lit a candle every night with a prayer for her return.

As it turned out, there were quite a few children in the complex who went to the same school, and Alice and Trevor made friends immediately. Kids on bicycles were a common sight. Just learning to ride a two-wheeler, Trevor soon joined in on their caravan rides throughout the complex and the quiet neighboring streets, something he never could have mastered on the steep, hilly streets of their old neighborhood.

Alice's new friend, Brittany, was in the same grade and lived two doors down. The two were constant companions. Her younger brother was a year older than Trevor, and they often played together or watched TV in the afternoons. Their parents had a carefree attitude and an open-door policy, and friends and neighbors flowed in and out on a daily basis, especially on weekends. Dinner was oftentimes a potluck affair, during which their father, who happened to be French, might prepare a bouillabaisse or ratatouille or just a big bowl of spaghetti with neighbors bringing bread, salad, wine or beer, and an appetizer.

And Sylvia realized that Jessica was right. It seemed that many of the residents were single parents or in the process of a divorce, so she didn't feel like such an outcast here. Sylvia couldn't remember living anywhere when she'd had this much fun or felt so relaxed. They'd landed in a genuine, down-to-earth neighborhood.

Even their apartment was open and spacious. Built into a hillside, the half bath, kitchen, and dining room were on the first level; the living room with vaulted ceilings was four steps down, and its back wall had floor-to-ceiling picture windows that overlooked the lush woods behind. A door opened onto a large covered deck that spanned the length of the wall. A full flight of stairs led down to three bedrooms and two bathrooms. Alice's room had a door opening outside onto ground level with a small concrete patio.

Sylvia's concerns about Tom were building, and she needed a friend's opinion. Her first thought was to call Jessica. But maybe she was too close. She'd always taken a more supportive position of Tom's actions with his children since Jessica always wished her own husband would pay half as much attention to their children as Tom did—Greg wouldn't think of getting down on the floor and playing with them. In the end, Sylvia didn't think Jessica could give an impartial point of view. So after school one afternoon she called Charlotte, who happened to be free for an hour or so until Paul got home.

Sylvia arranged for the kids to play at their friends' apartment, then strode down the hill to Charlotte's. It was one of those warm, spring days in late March when the air still carried the dampness of an earlier rain and the fresh scent of cedar seemed to linger in the trees like heavy dew. She relished days like these.

When Sylvia came onto the deck by the back door, Charlotte waved her in. She was pouring hot water over espresso coffee grounds into a French press for *café sous pression*. They carried their demitasse cups, the coffee carafe, and sugar on a tray into the living room, where Sylvia heard a tape of Jacques Brel singing unintelligible French in the background. At least to Sylvia it was unintelligible—she had difficulty understanding lyrics even in her own tongue. In French, it was hopeless.

Charlotte told Sylvia her timing was perfect because she had a pretty scary situation of her own to face. Paul was considering trying to get both of his children back. His ex-wife was with her boyfriend much of the time, and Paul didn't have a good feeling about her lack of supervision or even her ability to give of herself to them. While Charlotte supported the idea, she didn't have a clue how to raise children.

"And you're such a natural, Sylvia. I really need to learn from you how to nurture them properly. The poor things already must feel unwanted."

Sylvia told her she'd help her any way she could but also let her in on a little parenting secret. "Nobody knows what they're doing. You try to relax, play it by ear, and let your nurturing instincts take over."

"I don't think I have any instincts. I never even planned on having my own!"

Sylvia hadn't had much time to think about having children either before Alice came along, and she'd felt pretty overwhelmed. But Charlotte's dilemma was unimaginable to her. A mother wanted to give up her children. Who could do that? Sylvia dropped a lump of sugar into her coffee. "But you do have instincts. Look how wonderful you are with your students."

"Well, maybe there's a little hope, but it's much different when you can leave them at the end of the day," Charlotte said. "I'm sorry. Here I go prattling on when you're the one who wanted to talk."

Sylvia explained her concerns about Tom's increasing lack of interest in his kids, how he kept making promises to Alice and Trevor to do things with them and sometimes didn't show up. "He's even cancelled whole weekends."

"I thought he was a pretty devoted father." Charlotte got up and changed the tape.

They were now listening to Pachelbel's Canon, which Sylvia had heard for the first time when she and Anthony had dinner here. The haunting melody moved her deeply, and she struggled to keep from tearing up as she spoke about Alice and Trevor and how much they missed their father. She lit a cigarette.

"He used to be. It's so hard on Alice. After she's been over there, she misses him so much that she has a hard time adjusting to coming back home with me. She can mope around for days. I don't know what to do."

"Like you've said, divorce, moving, and a new school are major changes and take time. You've been in the apartment, what, not even three months! And the divorce was final just six months ago. So maybe it's understandable," Charlotte said. "But if Tom's different than before, something must've changed."

"And now I'm questioning that, too," Sylvia said. "Is he really that different? He always appeared to be attached to his kids, but he never had to take much responsibility in raising them. He was gone all the time."

"And with divorce it takes a consistent effort for him to see the kids," Charlotte said.

"But when he first moved in with Betsy, he wanted to see them every day when he wasn't traveling. I was even worried that they'd want to live with them!" Sylvia said. "A drastic change really occurred after we got back from San Diego."

"Isn't that when he found out about Anthony from the letters?"

"Yes!" Sylvia exclaimed. "Why didn't I think of that? But would he pull away from his kids or try harder to be with them?"

"You said Betsy was the one who reacted most, but maybe he's ashamed about being cuckolded for so many years and can't face you," Charlotte said.

"Or Betsy's anger took over and he didn't want to risk exposing them to that." Sylvia warmed up her coffee with a little more from the carafe.

"Wasn't that also when he found out his business was failing?"

"I didn't learn about it until last month, but that's possible."

"Maybe he's depressed from that. That's more important to men, I think. Success in their work. It's like their identity."

"You have a point. He put our house up for a second mortgage to help finance his new business, then I got my portion from the sale, and now his investment isn't paying off." Sylvia finished her coffee.

"If he has to depend on Betsy, it might make it even worse for him," Charlotte said. "Maybe he's got his hands full trying to keep her happy and there's not much left over for the kids."

"And keeping her happy may be difficult."

"What do you mean?"

"Alice says she yells a lot. Trevor won't call him at all now because he's afraid Betsy will get mad."

"Mad how?"

"Alice told me that Betsy got mad at her for holding the broom wrong and couldn't believe she didn't know how to sweep a floor. She seems to fly off the handle too easily."

"Who knows how to sweep a floor at nine? What is she, Cinderella?"

"That's what I'm afraid of. Alice won't say much more other than Betsy has lots of rules and makes them do chores. I think she's worried that if she tells me more I'll either refuse to let her go over there or make matters worse by arguing with Tom."

"Still, she wants to stay when the weekend is over, so it can't all be bad. It does sound like everyone's walking on eggshells with this woman, though," Charlotte said.

After Sylvia's conversation with Charlotte, she decided she had to try to find out what was going on with Tom. A few days later she called Tom's twin brother, Jim, but he said he hadn't talked to Tom since their birthday in February and Tom had sounded the same as always—upbeat and everything was perfect. Jim said he never did know how to talk to Tom, but he was concerned and said he'd give him a call. If there was anything seriously wrong, he'd let her know.

Sylvia waited. A week went by, and Jim didn't call. Tom was supposed to have the kids the following weekend, so she'd try to talk to him then.

When Tom arrived at their front door, the kids ran and jumped into his arms, almost knocking him over. He seemed almost overcome to see them. His face was slightly flushed and puffy, and he held his children a little longer than usual. He smiled, but the corners of his mouth never completely pointed upward, making it seem halfhearted, as if he was trying to keep his emotions in check. His loose-fitting jeans and oversized red plaid flannel shirt made him look sloppy and overweight.

Sylvia asked the kids to get their duffel bags downstairs then turned to him. "Will you please tell me what's going on?"

"What do you mean?"

"I just know something's up. You're not yourself. Is it the business?"

He let out a big sigh and looked away from her, out the open front door. "I can't talk now. Betsy's waiting in the car."

"Are you sick?"

He moved his hand over his mouth and chin, looking down at his feet. "No, I'm not sick."

"Is it something with Betsy?"

"I'll call you."

"No, you won't. Tell me now." Sylvia heard the kids coming up the stairs. "Before they get here."

Tom held his breath a moment. "Betsy's pregnant. We're getting married next month."

Sylvia closed her eyes in disbelief. Did she hear him right? Married? Another baby? How could he do this to Alice and Trevor?"

"Daddy, Daddy," they called out together. Alice and Trevor hurriedly hugged Sylvia good-bye, and they were gone. The door stood ajar, and Sylvia watched as they pulled away in his dark green pickup truck.

# CHAPTER 29

The initial reactions to Tom's news trickled in like an early spring snowmelt that drips so slowly from the eaves or the boughs of pine trees that one has to stop and listen in order to hear it. Some time passed, and the temperature climbed. And like the droplets that turn into a steady stream and can be heard rushing through downspouts and street drains, the early shock of Tom's news turned into heated outbursts and poured in from all sides.

"For Chrissakes, he can't take care of the kids he's got," Sylvia's dad said. "He should keep his pants zipped!"

And her mom. "I'll bet she's Catholic, too. I remember he didn't want you on birth control."

Tom's twin brother, Jim, told Sylvia his parents were worried about Tom, but Jim just seemed frustrated. "He always flies by the seat of his pants. Why doesn't he ever think before he acts?"

Jim's wife, Cindy, looked to Betsy as the culprit. "She's a thirty-six-year-old woman who *knows* what she's doing. I bet this was the only way she could get Tom to marry her."

Jessica looked at it from a slightly different angle. "Maybe a baby of her own will calm her down, and she'll be less jealous of you and your kids."

Sylvia's primary concern was the reaction of her children. First of all, who should tell them? While it would seem likely to fall under the heading of "Discussions for Tom," she didn't trust how he might present the news to them. With his recent track record of broken promises, what reassurance could he give them that he'd be there for them? Even if he said a new baby would never change how he felt about them, how he included them in the coming months was what really mattered.

As March came to a close, Tom called Sylvia and settled some of her concerns. He asked to have the children spend the week of spring break with him and Betsy, which would include the Easter holiday. "I'm only telling them about the wedding right now. We want Alice to be the flower girl and Trevor the ring bearer. But I don't want them to know about their baby brother yet," he said. "Betsy thinks it's bad luck to talk about it too soon."

"Brother?" Sylvia asked.

"Betsy lost a baby years ago in her first marriage, so she had a procedure called amnio-something and found out it's a boy."

"Congratulations," she said flatly. *Poor Trevor. He'll always be competing for his dad's attention.*

"Thanks," Tom said. He actually sounded happy, like he didn't have a care in the world. "I don't want the kids to feel left out, so I'll let them know later about the baby."

Sylvia wondered which reason mattered the most to him: Betsy's idea of bad luck or his not wanting them to feel left out. "When is it due?"

"*He's* due in July," Tom said.

Sylvia did a calculation in reverse. July to June. June to May. May to April. She got pregnant in October, a month after he moved in. So she's six months along and must be showing. "What's she doing when the kids come over? Hiding under blankets?"

"Sort of," he said. "The doctor told her she had to lie down for her last three months."

"So she'll have to give up her night job."

"Right," he said. There was a pause. "I've been meaning to talk to you about that."

"About what?"

"Money," he said. "The Creative Circle is no more. George isn't paying me after this month, so I'm looking for work." He cleared his throat. "I probably won't be able to pay you for a few months."

"What?" Sylvia sat bolt upright on her bed. "How are we going to survive?"

"You could get by with the money from the house sale."

This was rich. He expected her to dip into her nest egg for child support?

"These are *your kids, too*!" she said, trying to keep her voice down.

"Or I thought maybe you could ask your parents."

"*My* parents? Why not your parents? Ask them to bail you out this time, Tom!"

"You know they don't have the money."

"I don't know that. And neither do you. So *ask* them! If you don't get it from them, you can answer to the court." She slammed down the phone.

Shaking, she dialed Anthony's office and told him about the whole conversation.

"I think you should move on your threat. Call your attorney and find out what to do in case he doesn't pay," he said.

"I can't blow my savings on an attorney."

"Just to write Tom a threatening letter wouldn't cost that much."

Sylvia lit a cigarette. "Can you believe this? But why am I so surprised? He always counted on me to pick up the pieces; why would he expect me to stop now? I thought he'd be different with the kids though."

"I have just the thing to make you forget about him for a while."

"Not possible."

"Think spring break. Just the two of us." He paused.

"I must be dreaming."

"You'll have a whole week, right?"

"Yes."

"I'll get us a condo at Pajaro Dunes," he said. "I'll call you right back."

Sylvia remembered the name Pajaro Dunes because Jane used to talk about it a lot. It was a resort on Monterey Bay and one of Anthony's favorite spots. They used to go there once a year with their kids and another family for vacation. Anthony said it was outside a small town called Watsonville, the artichoke capital of the world, and sat right on the beach with huge sand dunes between the condos and the ocean.

Sylvia always wondered how other families took such vacations, sometimes for two whole weeks. Resorts on exotic beaches, skiing in Colorado or Vermont, cruises or trips to Europe. How did they do it? She wondered if she'd ever be able to travel like that. Growing up, her own family took modest vacations every year: driving trips to Oregon, Florida, and New York City several times, and once they flew to California. While they were nothing fancy, she remembered feeling pretty special because most of her friends went camping for vacation; Sylvia stayed in hotels and ordered room service. At least Anthony accepted vacations as an essential part of living. With him, she could imagine travel as a normal part of her lifestyle.

He called back with good news. He booked flights, reserved a one-bedroom condo on the beach, and rented a car for six days. Sylvia was ecstatic. Right now, even Tom's money woes couldn't deflate her. She even began to think of the new baby as a positive influence over time. Maybe Alice and Trevor would be more included, playing the roles of big brother and sister. It was an encouraging sign anyway that he wanted them for spring break and to be in his wedding.

The next two weeks passed quickly. Sylvia's mood was light, and some of her students remarked that she seemed happier and back to her old self. She still couldn't get used to what she thought of as "being fresh" when her students would get personal with her. *I love your hair that way. Those are great shoes. We thought you were mad at us or something was wrong at home.* They were definitely bolder than the students she had ten years earlier. No homework was assigned over break, and on the last day of school, she wished them all *Bonnes vacances*! Tom picked up the kids as promised, and the following day Anthony picked her up as well.

Standing in the parking lot outside of her apartment, he loaded her bag into his car. "There was almost a glitch this morning. Jane called and wanted me to take the kids for the weekend."

"What did you say to her?"

"I was going out of town on business and otherwise I'd be happy to."

"Was she upset?"

"She had a fit about how selfish and irresponsible I am. That's the first time she actually *wanted* me to take them."

"I know. I'm sorry," Sylvia said. "You must feel bad."

"I'm too excited for us to feel bad." He walked around to the passenger side of his car and opened the door for her. "There was something else she went on and on about though."

Sylvia started to get into the car then stopped. She turned to face him, and their bodies brushed. She could smell his Bay Rum cologne. She noticed the veins in his tanned neck, which seemed to pulsate through her. When she looked into his amber eyes, she saw that he felt her desire, the desire that had suddenly taken hold of her. He cupped her face in his hands. Still staring into her eyes, he pressed her body against the car and kissed her passionately. She felt his erection and wanted him right there. He took her hand and led her back up the steps to her apartment door. He glanced at his watch.

"We only have fifteen minutes or we'll miss our flight," he said.

"Fifteen minutes is all we need."

She unlocked the door, and they fell hungrily into each other's arms. He shoved the door shut with his foot and, leaning against it, pulled her towards him, hoisting her legs around his waist. He undid her bra and buried his face in her breasts. She reached down and undid his pants. After stroking his velvet soft, swollen head, she inched her fingers down then gripped his stiff shaft, rock hard in her hand. She guided him just inside her, and moaning with pleasure, she clutched onto his shoulders, wrapping her legs more tightly around his waist as he pushed deeper inside. Holding her buttocks with both hands, he moved her up and down in rhythm to their heavy, gasping breaths. When he came, he gripped her hard against him, and while still inside her, carried her down the four steps to the living room. Easing her onto the couch, he kissed her gently, brushing his lips over her stomach, and then began licking. He pulled her wet lips apart with his fingers and began sucking her harder and faster until she raised her hips upward and cried out as if in anguish. He stretched out beside her, and they lay in each other's arms for several minutes. She slowly picked up his wrist and looked at his watch.

"Five minutes to spare," she said.

He went downstairs to get a towel and a wet washcloth. They quickly cleaned themselves and, in a rush, left the apartment and headed for his car.

Anthony again opened the door for her to get in. "As I was saying…" He chuckled.

"I promise I won't interrupt you," Sylvia said, laughing.

"Those are the kind of interruptions that make life worthwhile." He leaned over and kissed the top of her head as she slid into the seat.

On the way to the airport, he explained that Jane thought they were having a trial separation to work on their marriage. "Now that she sees I have no interest in trying, she's sure I'm having an affair," he said. "She sees the separation as a setup, a sham, making a fool out of her. She intends to find out *who* I'm involved with."

Sylvia felt uneasy. "Did you tell her you were going to work on your marriage?"

"I let her think so by saying nothing when she assumed it. That was probably a mistake."

"But she's been so angry since you separated she'd hardly speak to you or let you see the kids. It doesn't make sense that she thought you were going to work on the marriage."

"It doesn't make sense to me either. I think she's harbored the idea that I was having an affair for a long time but didn't really want to know. Maybe she thought if she made it difficult to see the kids I'd come crawling back. Since we've only been separated for a few months, and she's seen that I haven't made a move to 'work' on things, she's probably madder than ever that she didn't see it coming." Anthony pulled the car onto the freeway.

"If you told her the marriage was over a long time ago, she probably would've reacted the same way," Sylvia said. "Are you worried?"

"Not really, but the angrier she is, the more money it'll cost. I was hoping to somehow keep her anger in check. I see now how naive I was."

"How do you think she'll try to find out about me?"

"The most likely way would be a P.I."

"What's that?"

"Private investigator?" he said as if she should know.

"You mean somebody could be following us around right now? It gives me the creeps."

"It could be an idle threat."

"We both know her better than that."

By late afternoon they were driving in their rental car from San Jose headed south toward the Pacific Ocean. When a light fog began to drift over the roadway, Anthony said that it was a marine layer that often blanketed the coastline this time of year. Then he squeezed her knee and said with hushed excitement that meant they were almost there. The surrounding land became very flat. On both sides of them were rows and rows of a strange-looking plant. She asked him about it. Anthony suddenly pulled over, got out of the car, and motioned for Sylvia to do likewise. He pointed to the bulbous protrusion on the thistle-like plants, asking if she knew what it was.

She leaned to look at it more closely and smiled back at him. "It's an artichoke. It does look like a flower, but it seems too large for the plant. I would've thought they grew on bushes or trees."

Anthony stopped at a market in Watsonville for basic provisions: bread, wine, and cheese for starters, followed by butter, milk, cereal, bacon, eggs, marshmallows for roasting on the beach, and of course, artichokes, a half dozen. "That should hold us over until tomorrow," he said. Then he wagged his finger at her. "But you're not cooking! Not even the artichokes."

They took several deep breaths of the balmy sea air and jumped back in the car. He pulled her close to him. "I can't wait to spend this time with you here. I've fantasized about you and me on this beach for three years."

The rustic wooden sign, The Shorebirds, signaled the obscured one-lane entrance to the complex. Tall beach grasses grew in clumps in the sandy terrain on either side of the asphalt driveway. Sea-weathered wooden boardwalks with railings ran between the buildings and in the direction of the white-sand beach, which was within fifty yards of the condos. The landscape reminded Sylvia of Cape Cod *sans* wood-shingled houses.

Without unpacking, they ran to the beach. It went on for miles. They kissed and laughed, chased each other, and dug their toes in the sand where the tide could wash over them. Their time was their own. Sylvia had never felt this free: no schedule, no meal preparation, and no to-do list. They ate when they felt like it and went into either Watsonville or Monterey if they wanted more cosmopolitan fare. On the fourth day Anthony said he wanted her to meet his old friend Dick Nyberg for dinner in Santa Cruz.

"But isn't he the one you guys used to vacation with here? With his family?"

"That's the one."

"So he knows about us?"

"He knows, but since his wife and Jane are friends, he hasn't told her about you. He's very excited to meet you."

"I'm not sure I'm comfortable meeting your old 'couples' friends yet," she said. "I don't know."

"It's pretty important to me that you meet him now. I can't tell you why yet. An opportunity came up, and I wanted to take advantage of it."

"Intrigue—now I'm curious."

He kissed her neck. "Please, for me?"

Sylvia put her arms around him. "I think I'd follow you anywhere. Of course, we'll go. I look forward to meeting a close friend of yours."

Anthony dropped on one knee and took her hands in his. "I'm so glad you feel that way."

"I don't understand."

"I know I'm not divorced yet, but I'll remedy that very soon. I promise to devote myself, my life, my everything to making you happy. I want to take care of you. And I never want you to worry ever again about money. Please, Jake, as soon as I'm free, will you marry me?" He kissed the palm of each of her hands and looked up at her.

She was puzzled by his sudden declaration and proposal, but was moved by his emotion and spoke haltingly. "I remember the first time you kissed the palm of my hand—in my family room in front of the fire. I knew then that I would want to spend the rest of my life with you. That's never changed."

That evening as they drove to the restaurant, Sylvia wondered why it was so important to meet his friend now. She wanted Anthony all to herself. She wanted to ask him the reason for all the secrecy but decided not to press him; he'd tell her when he was ready.

The dinner with Dick Nyberg went better than Sylvia had expected. He welcomed her with open arms and said he looked forward to introducing her to his wife, Nancy, which might take a while. He told her Anthony was his closest friend, and he was just happy to see him so happy. He was a burly, wrestler type, but Sylvia found him to be articulate, and he seemed astute in business. He said he was finally doing what he'd wanted to do for years. In three months his own real estate development company would open for business outside of San Francisco, and the only thing left was to find a partner he could trust. Sylvia never put two and two together.

The week went by far too quickly, but Sylvia felt so good about their relationship she didn't even mind when it ended. She could freely admit to herself now, in hindsight, that she'd had doubts about him, especially after he scared her those months ago in the hotel room. That was a side she'd never seen in him before and hadn't seen since. Upon reflection, she decided she'd played a minor part by not speaking her mind, holding back, and harboring questions she'd been afraid to address with him, which helped foster an atmosphere of doubt and suspicion. Since she'd stood up for herself more, drawn boundaries, telling him what she expected from him in regards to his divorce and his role in her home, she sensed a more mutual regard for each other. Like the proverbial onion, another layer of understanding peeled away in their relationship, and she felt sure that they would continue to grow and nurture each other in the years ahead. She had no doubt they were meant for each other.

On the drive home from the airport, she realized how much she missed her children. A week was the longest she'd ever been separated from them. While she'd tried numerous times to reach them by phone, she had only spoken to them once, so she was becoming more and more anxious the closer they got to her apartment. She just hoped they had a good time with their dad. He was to drop them off that evening after dinner.

Before Sylvia and Anthony got out of the car, Isabelle, the mother of Alice's friend, rushed out of her apartment to meet them. "You might want to be forewarned," she said.

Sylvia's insides went to mush. Anthony got out first.

Isabelle put her hand on Sylvia's arm and told her it had nothing to do with her kids. Then she turned to Anthony. "I'm pretty sure your wife was here." She pointed to Sylvia's front door.

They all slowly walked toward Sylvia's apartment. In dripping red paint was a big letter "A." Underneath it was scrawled: GOD WILL GET YOU FOR THIS!

# CHAPTER 30

Late Spring 1981

The phone calls started coming every morning around five. A voice she knew was Jane's would say, "God will get you for this," and then Jane would slam down the phone. Knowing what was coming in the morning, Sylvia took the phone off the hook before she went to bed. When she'd put the receiver back though, it would ring almost instantly. She wondered if Jane just sat there and dialed for two hours until she could get through. After two weeks of this, Sylvia's sleep became fitful.

When she was driving, she found herself checking to see if she was being followed and looking to the right and left whenever she sat at a stoplight. She warily approached her front door at the end of each day afraid of what she might find and scanned her car tires every morning to see if they'd been slashed. Logic told her this was extreme to worry to this degree, but another part of her feared how crazy Jane could get. She remembered long ago when Anthony mentioned she might shoot them. Even Jessica had kiddingly said something to that effect. It was no joke anymore.

Jane called Anthony at the office once to tell him she'd never divorce him. She also said as far as she was concerned her children didn't have a father and he'd never see them again. She wouldn't talk to him after that. Anthony said he wasn't worried about her threats. Legally she couldn't get away with any of it. He was more worried about the effect it was having on his children and on Sylvia and her children.

But Alice and Trevor remained oblivious to what was going on. The evening of their return from vacation, Anthony had rushed out and painted over the message in red before the kids got home. And they never learned about the phone calls. If by chance one of them answered it before Sylvia got it in the morning, Jane would hang up. At least she didn't punish the children for their mother's misdeeds. Alice commented on occasion that Sylvia seemed sad and asked what was wrong, which she answered by saying she was just tired and ready for the school year to be over. Sylvia was confident that Alice didn't know the real reason, since she refused to talk to anyone about the situation on the phone when the kids were home.

Living on the other side of town was a bigger relief than Sylvia could've imagined: different schools, different grocery stores, and different friends. There was always the off chance they'd run into each other, but Sylvia hadn't seen anyone from her old neighborhood since they had moved. And she was more watchful now.

Alice and Trevor were preoccupied with the bunny Tom and Betsy had given them for Easter. Tom had made a large cage on three-foot-high legs and set it up on the small patio behind Alice's bedroom. Sylvia was upset that she hadn't been consulted about taking on a new pet but was glad now for the diversion the bunny created. It also helped the kids cope with the disappointment of more broken promises they were enduring once again with their dad, such as no-shows at school events, phone calls that never came, and cancelled weekends.

Betsy's bedridden condition contributed to her apparent fragile state of mind, which meant she couldn't or wouldn't tolerate the presence of Tom's children. Too much mayhem made her jittery and out of sorts. It also meant their wedding plans changed from a hoedown in a barn setting to a quiet ceremony in their living room, which the children attended. Alice handed Betsy a bouquet, and Trevor handed his dad the rings. They said they'd have the barn "wedding" after the baby was born.

Tom found a job in pharmaceutical sales and hadn't missed any support payments. His territory was restricted to the outlying Portland area. Twice a week after work he made an effort to take the children out for a bite to eat, but their time was sometimes cut short because he had to hurry home to Betsy. Alice said he carried a new gadget called a beeper so he could be reached in case of an emergency.

All of this led to Sylvia rethinking her once-hopeful outlook that the new baby might improve their relationship with their dad. If anything, it could get worse when the baby finally arrived. If Betsy was jittery and out of sorts now, wait until she hadn't slept for weeks on end or became worried about germs around her newborn. The scenarios could be ongoing and hurtful to her kids.

With the school year coming to a close, Sylvia was looking forward to her parents' two-week visit at the end of June. They were allowing Steve to stay home alone in Ohio since he was taking his medication regularly and working three evenings a week for a community-based program called Clean Sweep. Groups of clients, those with mental illnesses or drug abuse problems or both, met at various locations to clean office buildings, stores, or hotels. Vivian said he hated it and was embarrassed to be doing janitor work, but he went anyway because Matt insisted on his doing something productive. Her dad even said, "Hell, I don't know why he should be embarrassed. I worked as a janitor all through college to pay for my room and board."

Sylvia hadn't told her parents about Jane's behavior. Her mom particularly would worry about her safety. The phone calls were becoming intermittent, but Jane was now sending Sylvia hate mail saying she'd get even with her someday for destroying her family and included quotes from the Bible about God's wrath and seeking vengeance. Her biblical zeal began to remind Sylvia of Steve's psychotic behavior when he didn't take his meds. Sylvia didn't believe in literal interpretations of the Bible, but she had an eerie feeling that a person with a strong enough intent could affect harm on someone else just by willing it, like someone putting pins in a voodoo doll. Charlotte told Sylvia to just throw them unopened in the trash.

Anthony was seeing his children even less than before, so he was spending more time at home with Sylvia. They seemed to be settling in and becoming more like a family. Sylvia wondered how he could do this without pining for his own children, thinking this would make his children's absence even more difficult to endure. But he never acted troubled and seemed to genuinely enjoy Alice and Trevor. Maybe he was able to separate the feelings because they weren't his own. Maybe Alice and Trevor were doing the same. They were all getting along so well she found herself envisioning their future together. The only doubt she had was regarding how this would work with everyone living in the same small town. She didn't want to look over her shoulder forever.

One evening Anthony asked Sylvia to arrange a babysitter because he had something important to discuss with her. He asked her to meet him at his place this time. When she arrived, he had the table set, the candles lit, and the wine poured. John Denver was playing, and Anthony was singing along. He took her purse and swooped her up in his arms for a spin on the "dance floor."

She giggled. "You're unusually happy."

"I'm excited and busting with good news," he said. "We had to celebrate tonight."

"Don't keep me in suspense."

He went over to his stereo and turned the music down. "First of all, Jane's attorney is having some effect on her. She's no longer refusing to divorce me."

"That is good news!"

"That's not all." He handed her a glass and held his up for a toast. "Dick Nyberg wants me to be a full partner with him in his real estate company."

She almost choked.

He took her glass from her and drew her toward the couch to sit down. "It means we'd have to move to the San Francisco area."

She jumped up wide-eyed. "Move?" It seemed incredible for him to even suggest it to her.

"I know this must come as a shock since you haven't had the benefit of thinking it through like I have."

Sylvia shook her head. "How could you keep this from me?"

"I wasn't *keeping* it from you. C'mon, Sylvia. Sit down so we can talk about it." He reached for her hand and patted the couch.

*Where had he done that before? In the hotel room.* She felt like he was patronizing her again, coaxing her like he would a child. "I don't want to sit down!" She paced back and forth across the room. "How long have you been *thinking it through*?"

"A few weeks before we went to Pajaro Dunes," he said. "Dick called me and asked me if I was interested.

I didn't say anything because I wanted you to meet him first."

Sylvia stood by the window and bit her thumbnail as she watched the setting sun. The soft, orange glow made everything in its light look better: richer in color, more vibrant, more beautiful. But the warm cast was short-lived and would last only a few minutes. She didn't move. "You said you wanted to take advantage of the opportunity while we were in Pajaro Dunes for me to meet Dick, your old friend, like it had just come up. But you planned it all in advance. That's why we went there, wasn't it?"

"Not really. You needed a vacation, and Dick and I had been talking around the same time. Why are you acting like I was trying to trick you?"

She turned around to face him. "Because the trip feels like a setup. You painted it differently than what it was, and I wasn't included."

"So? I wanted to surprise you."

"I don't think so." Sylvia took a deep breath. "You're doing the same thing now. Cavalierly announcing a new job and a move. Making the decision without me. Coloring it with candlelight and wine, pretending it's a big celebration to avoid the enormity of what it means to me and my children—"

"Of course, I'm thinking of you and your children! How it might be better for all of us to move away from our angry, jealous, unreliable exes. How it might be even better for your kids if they didn't have to contend with Tom and Betsy day after day, week after week, wondering if he'll call or show up. Or if she'll be sweet and embrace them or turn on a dime and be moody and lash out. So an opportunity for us to really start over *is* cause for celebration."

"If you had discussed this with me from the beginning, I might've looked at it that way. Or at least if you'd brought it up on our trip after I met Dick. But this is like dropping a bomb."

"I didn't talk about it then because it wasn't for sure. There were bank loans that had to come through for Dick, which just did. I didn't see the good in burdening you for no reason. You've had enough sleepless nights lately."

Sylvia figured he also didn't want to spoil their time together with weighty discussion. Maybe he had a point. The trip probably would've been ruined for them. Still, to exclude her made her feel invisible like she'd always felt with Tom. "You dismissed me by tiptoeing, by not being open with me. And I don't like the feeling of being played."

Without looking at her, he got up, grabbed his wine, and went into the kitchen. He began eagerly stirring a big pot on the stove.

Just looking at the back of his head, bowed down, as if concentrating on his sauce, his tan, muscular forearms exposed by the rolled-up cuffs of his yellow oxford-cloth shirt, made her realize that what she'd said on their trip was true—that she'd probably follow him anywhere because she couldn't risk the possibility of their growing apart, or not being together. She believed that absence could make the heart grow fonder, or wander. They had come too far and given up too much for her to take that chance.

The lingering silence made Sylvia uncomfortable. Being this direct and open was new to her, and she began questioning whether she'd said too much or exaggerated the way he handled the situation. She wanted to fill the space with more words to better explain what she meant or go up behind him and put her arms around him, but instead she sat back down on the couch and waited. She picked at what was left of her fingernails and waited some more. *And we'd be living together. How can I justify that?*

Finally he turned and walked slowly toward her. The exuberance in his expression was replaced with a tender, rather humble regard. His chin against his chest, he peered at her coyly. A quiet, soothing smile crossed his lips. "Maybe you're right. I can see how you'd think I was trying to hide things from you, but tonight was when I'd planned to discuss everything. I just wanted to present it in the best possible light so that—"

"You'd get the reaction you wanted?"

He sat down beside her. "I guess."

"Manipulator," she teased.

He reached around her shoulder and pulled her against him. "Maybe I've been in creative finance too long."

"I just don't want you to handle me the same way."

"Still, there's something to be said for the right timing, but I'll do my best to keep you informed as we go along."

"So we can discuss it together."

He nodded.

She'd been thinking how much easier their life would be if they weren't living in Lakeside, but she had never considered leaving the state and taking her kids that far from their dad. "But how can you leave your own kids behind?"

"Well, that's the other part." Anthony looked toward the kitchen and jumped up. "I forgot the pasta!"

"You mean there's more you haven't told me? Jesus, Anthony."

"Calm down. You haven't given me a chance to get to it!"

He pulled the saucepan off the stove and poured the steaming pasta into a colander. "I've made my special Bolognese sauce that you love," he called out to her.

"I don't think I can eat yet. So, what's the other part?"

He rushed in and sat back down next to her. He took the red-striped dish towel from around his neck and wiped the sweat off of his forehead, then tossed it across the room toward the hallway. "Jane's moving back with the kids to Long Beach to live with her dad when school lets out. We're putting the house up for sale next week."

Suspicion about his motives came back. "When did you know about her decision to move?"

"About a week ago."

"So now you'd be closer to your kids with this job."

"Yes."

"Is that why you want to take it?"

"No." He sounded like he was struggling to be patient with her. "Remember when her mom got sick, and I thought she might move back there? There was no new job for me then, and I had no intention of leaving here. Starting my own company with Dick is something he and I have talked about for years. I believe this is the moment to jump."

She couldn't see the big picture with all the pieces of the puzzle piled so high in front of her. "This is a lot to digest."

He got up. "Speaking of digestion, let's eat and let all of this simmer."

Sylvia joined him and carried the pasta bowl and the salad to the table. He did make a mean Bolognese sauce, which smelled divine. She was beginning to feel hungry for this comfort food after all. They sat quietly for several minutes, eating their salads, then Anthony served the pasta. Sylvia took several bites and sighed with satisfaction. "How far away would you be from your kids?"

"A good five-hour drive."

"Aren't you upset about being that far away from them?"

"I've been upset for so long about not seeing them regularly that another roadblock almost seems expected somehow. It'll mean that they'll only come during school vacations."

"Which is when my kids, if I decide to do this, would see their dad I suppose." Sylvia felt teary and tried to stifle it by taking another bite of spaghetti.

"Don't worry, Jake. We'll make all of this right for them." He reached across the table and squeezed her right hand, which rested motionless on the table.

Taking children away from a parent could never be made right, she thought. But isn't that what she'd already done? "When does Dick want your answer?"

"Yesterday."

"So he wants you to start right away?"

"No later than August. Maybe we could go down to Los Altos and look—"

"Where is it exactly?"

"Just south of San Francisco, near Palo Alto. Wait 'til you see it. It's quaint, like a village, and the trees lining the streets are covered in white lights all year round. It's quite a charming place."

Sylvia couldn't believe she was having this conversation with him. She never thought that Anthony would end up wanting to change jobs and move away. And to start a brand-new company. She thought of Tom and wondered if the same thing was happening to her all over again. One of the reasons she'd fallen for Anthony was because he was so stable. An accountant. To imagine him in the same circumstances as Tom was completely baffling to her. But were they the same? Anthony had a profession at least and knew how to manage money. She wished she knew the right questions to ask. She wanted a guarantee that she wouldn't end up in the same place again. "I wish it wasn't happening so soon. I need some time to think about this."

"Nothing has to be settled right now. Like I was saying, when you go with me to see it and look at the schools, I know you'll feel better."

"Maybe you could go without me to make sure the job is what you think it is. Then after six months or so, and your divorce is over, we could look at plans to be together."

"That's sensible." Then he laughed. "But do you really think that's realistic, for us? We can barely last two weeks without seeing each other."

"Maybe it's time for us to be sensible."

# CHAPTER 31

Wednesday, September 2, 1981

It was their last night in Oregon, and the children had finally fallen asleep. Sylvia was lying next to Anthony on the living room floor in the dark. In the dim light from the parking lot, Sylvia could make out the disorderly array of cardboard boxes filled with her kitchen, her bathrooms, her bedroom, and her children's belongings. The apartment felt barren, just like her insides, and she was filled with a sense of foreboding. *What am I doing?* She knew by his measured breathing that Anthony was asleep; she wanted to slip out from under his arm and go downstairs to pull her children close to her—one on each side of her to make her feel safe. But she didn't want to awaken him.

Anthony's explosive outburst from earlier that evening resounded in her head. Trevor had been playing around, being silly, and jumping off the four steps to the living room pretending he was jumping into the swimming pool that was waiting for him at their new home in Los Altos, California.

Anthony had asked Trevor to stop, but Trevor hadn't yet learned to detect the thin veil of restraint in Anthony's tone, the one with the slightly higher pitch, a tinny quality, which, along with the tight smile, disguised his mounting anger. Trevor didn't stop. And Anthony blew. "In my house, I'll only tell you once! Get downstairs now and get ready for bed or else!"

The sudden eruption made Sylvia recoil in disbelief that he'd talked to her child that way. It was bad enough that he had shouted at all, which her children weren't used to, but he had no right when he wasn't even their father.

Trevor had the frightened look of a whipped puppy. His mouth turned down, and his bottom lip began to quiver. One foot at a time, he had slowly stepped back toward the stairs then hung his head, turned, and quietly slunk down to his room.

Sylvia had immediately reacted. "What's gotten into you?" When she went to comfort Trevor, Anthony tried to stop her, saying Trevor needed to get used to his way of doing things. Sylvia would have none of it. "He's just a normal five-year-old letting off steam. And he's excited about the move! Why would you want to ruin that for him?" She had rushed downstairs.

Now, lying on the floor in the dark, she began questioning what her insides were telling her. *Does one outburst make the whole move wrong? But maybe this was a sign that I'm supposed to pay attention to—the one thing to show me that I should've stuck to my guns and waited.* How was she supposed to know for sure? Maybe in decisions this big the right thing to do was never clear. You just had to take the chance and stay committed to work through the differences. If she let her doubt and fear take over at every disagreement, they'd never become the family she thought they could be. Still, she wondered if she'd ever get used to his "way of doing things."

The following morning Sylvia was awakened by Alice quietly leaning in close to her face. Alice giggled, and Sylvia pulled her down on top of her. The space on the floor next to her was empty.

"Did you see Anthony?" Sylvia asked.

"He and Trevor went to get donuts for the trip," Alice said.

"Sounds good." Sylvia hoped that Anthony wanted to make up to Trevor for being so hard on him the night before. She needed to see Trevor's face though, before she could feel totally at ease.

"Daddy said he'll probably see me in three weeks because he has a business trip in San Francisco and I can stay overnight with him in the hotel," Alice said.

"That would be wonderful, honey." It saddened Sylvia that in her own small way, Alice had already found some resilience to the heartache she felt about moving away from her dad.

Alice snuggled into Sylvia's side and mumbled, "He cried really hard when we said good-bye. I felt like I should stay with him."

Sylvia held her tight. A small kernel of fear planted itself for the future. "Did you ask him if you could?"

Alice nodded slowly. "He said he'd love that someday, but right now they had their hands full with the new baby. And anyway, he'd come see me as much as he could."

Sylvia ached for her. "I'm sure he will."

She and Tom had mapped out together a loose plan of the children's visits to Oregon over the next six months. As much as Sylvia wanted them with her, the children would be with Tom for the major holidays since, he had argued, she was the one who'd chosen to move so far away. The only issue to hammer out was who would pay for the flights. Tom, of course, didn't think he should have to pay for any of it for the same reason.

She hadn't discussed this yet with Anthony because she didn't know where she stood on the matter. If he refused, she couldn't blame him. Paying for the flights now might set a precedent, and they'd never get Tom to do his share. But she wouldn't let this stand in the way of her children's need to be with their dad. If she had to, she'd pay with her money, twenty thousand dollars, which was staying in Oregon in a money market account earning 16 percent interest. Her safety net.

What she and Anthony had discussed was the month-long trip to Europe the following summer that Anthony's parents had already arranged and paid for. Sylvia's parents agreed to come to Los Altos and stay with the kids. That way, Scott would be back from Saudi Arabia, and they would be able to visit him and Amanda, too. Sylvia pointed out that San Diego and Los Altos weren't that close—sometimes Midwesterners didn't realize the size of California—but her mother scoffed and said they knew very well how far apart they were. "You forget we lived in Los Angeles before you were even born."

Sylvia stood and pulled Alice up from the makeshift bed on the floor. She suggested they get dressed so they'd be ready when Anthony and Trevor got back.

By the time they returned, the two moving men they'd hired had arrived and were loading the boxes onto the truck. Donut box in hand, Trevor grinned as he placed the treasure on the counter. "Anthony let me pick all the donuts for us!"

Sylvia smiled at Anthony, and he winked back at her. "He did?"

"Did you get my favorite?" Alice asked.

Trevor rolled his eyes toward the ceiling. "With chocolate frosting?"

"No. Old-fashioned." She started to open the box.

Trevor tried to stop her. "You can't open them until we're on the trip!"

"Maybe we could have *one* before we leave." Anthony put his hands on Trevor's shoulders. "What do you think, Trevor?"

"Yes! Let's have one now." He looked up at Anthony. "But then, can I have another one in the truck?"

"You sure can. While you're at it, why don't you offer a donut to the men?"

They each grabbed a donut before Trevor scurried outside, the box held high.

"Can we both ride in the truck?" Alice asked.

"But your mom would be all by herself in her car," Anthony said.

Relieved that Anthony was suddenly so popular, Sylvia said she'd do whatever the kids wanted to do. So it was settled. The kids would ride with him, and they'd stop on the way for a decent breakfast.

Sylvia was glad there were no more tearful good-byes to put a damper on the morning's upbeat mood. There'd been enough of that the night before at the neighborhood potluck. Still, it had been exactly what she'd hoped it would be—a festive, heartfelt farewell party. Jessica had showed up even though she'd expressed her grave reservations about Sylvia's moving so soon.

"Why doesn't he go first? To get settled in his new job and be ready for you guys," Jessica had said.

"He's been doing that," Sylvia replied.

"Six weeks isn't long enough. I'm just afraid this is happening too fast."

"We've been waiting for years!"

"But his divorce isn't final yet. You shouldn't go until it's final."

Sylvia couldn't argue with that. She found it very discomforting and hoped that he'd be single by summer at the latest. The thought of being with his parents with him not yet divorced made her cringe. There was still the moral dilemma of them living together, something she thought she'd never do. From the beginning she'd already compromised the values she had more than she ever dreamed herself capable of. For her it boiled down to the simple fact that she felt compelled to follow him after what she'd sacrificed to be with him. She wasn't about to get off a fast-moving train before it arrived at the final stop.

Charlotte had been much more supportive, perhaps since she'd done basically the same thing *sans enfants*; her biggest misgiving seemed to be losing Sylvia and their French connection. She had come to the teacher-student going-away party at the school, where she and several others had made Sylvia promise to stay with teaching. Sylvia planned on substituting at first, and when the children were settled, she'd think about committing to a job. What mattered to her the most was Anthony's reassurance that she didn't have to work.

As the small caravan pulled away from the parking lot, Sylvia took one last long look. There were a lot of things she'd miss: Jessica, of course, and their smoke-filled late-evening talks; preparing her French lessons in the job she'd grown to love; the cedar smell on misty mornings or waking up to an ice-covered wonderland and not being able to drive; walking to Charlotte's for coffee and French conversation. She had taken strength from the sight of the ever-present peak of Mount Hood that could be seen from anywhere in town and just the simple comfort of knowing her way around. And then there was Red. She felt she was leaving her beloved Roo Roo behind, giving up for good any chance of finding her again. She blinked back tears and said a silent prayer that Red was in the loving arms of another family.

*****

Friday, September 4, 1981

Their white-framed ranch-style home was barely recognizable to Sylvia as they pulled into the driveway and under the carport. Maybe it just looked different in the dark. After the whirlwind house-hunting trip she and Anthony had taken in mid-August, she could hardly remember anything but the beautiful backyard with the pool, brick patio, and surrounding lawn with large trees that she couldn't name—trees with thick, low-hanging branches that were perfect for kids to climb.

Since there were few rentals to choose from, availability had been their main concern. They wanted to move in time for the start of school. That and price, of course. Sylvia had been shocked that this three-bedroom bungalow with an outdated eat-in kitchen and two fifties-style bathrooms rented for thirteen hundred a month, more than twice what they would've paid in Oregon. She hoped they could afford it, because she really had no idea what they could afford.

"I told you I'd take care of you," he had said. "Starting with our new life together, I'll handle all the bookkeeping. No more bills to pay or expenses for you to track anymore."

Sylvia told him how relieved she was that she'd no longer have the burden of these responsibilities. "But I still need to know what's coming in and be involved with what's going out."

"Of course," he said. "We're partners, Jake."

Right before the move, Anthony had traded his Porsche for a Chevrolet Camaro, a car he'd wanted since high school. She was disappointed that he didn't have the Porsche anymore—she looked forward to driving a luxury sports car; a Camaro didn't fit her image of the Italian sophisticate she'd fallen in love with either. Then he "surprised" her by buying a speedboat so they could take trips to the Sacramento Delta and water-ski. Once again, he hadn't consulted her about any of this.

While she still didn't have any idea what he earned, what bothered her even more was that she found herself too timid to ask him. *Is he making me feel like I have no right to ask? Maybe because I'm not working? And we're not married? Or is it my old hesitation to stand up for myself that's coming back to haunt me?* She thought she'd be happy to be taken care of, but she didn't want to start their lives together this way. She'd have to bring it up again.

The kids were asleep in the backseat when they arrived. Anthony went inside to turn on the overhead lights in the kitchen, hallways, and bedrooms, then called for them to come check out their new home. When the kids realized where they were, they jumped up and went inside. They slowly took in the kitchen, the living room with the used brick fireplace that took up one wall, and the small family room one step down to the left. Alice whispered something to Trevor, and all of a sudden they stampeded back through the living room and down the hallway toward the bedrooms. Sylvia followed, telling them that the bedroom with the bath at the end of the hall was for her and Anthony. Alice called dibs on the one with the walk-in closet next to the master. Trevor wanted the larger one with the big window overlooking the backyard. As the kids were peering out the window together, they called out in unison, "There's lights in the pool!"

Anthony had snuck outside and turned on the pool lights to surprise them. He walked into the bedroom with their suitcases. Smiling, he asked, "How about a night swim?"

Trevor was wide-eyed. "Can we?"

"But is it heated?" Sylvia asked.

"I called the owner yesterday and asked her to turn it on," Anthony said. "Last one in is a rotten egg."

Sylvia gave him a big hug.

"Let's hurry!" Alice opened up her suitcase, grabbed her suit, and in a flash was changed and ready to go.

"I can't find mine," Trevor whined.

"Just go in your underwear," Anthony said. "It's California. Remember?"

His mouth hanging open, Trevor burst into a big grin. "Okay. I will."

Sylvia and Anthony followed them outside and watched them slowly navigate their way down the pool steps and into the heated water.

"It's so big," Alice said.

The pool was much larger than most backyard pools. It was rectangular and twenty yards in length. To the rear of the yard there was a tool shed. Sylvia knew Alice would soon make it her own, filling it with Barbies, blankets, and art supplies.

Sylvia and Anthony joined the kids in the pool. Anthony took turns tossing Alice and Trevor off of his shoulders until Sylvia suggested they call it a night. They all decided they needed to get rubber rafts, inner tubes, and beach balls right away.

Since they had to wait until the next day for the movers, that night they made camp on the living room floor. Anthony brought in only the boxes filled with bedding, which had been the last to be loaded. Sylvia created a giant bed, but each one had his or her own blanket. Anthony said they should make it like real camp and handed each of the kids a flashlight. Alice and Trevor snickered and giggled, making scary faces by putting the flashlight under their chins. Then finally all went quiet.

The pool lights were still on, casting a soft glow through the sliding glass door. Sylvia slowly turned to face Anthony to see if he was asleep. Anthony leaned toward her and began giving her light, quick kisses on her neck and face. He brushed her nipples gently with his hand until she felt the sudden quickening between her legs. Having to be still and quiet only heightened her desire. She carefully rolled on top of him then over him and onto the carpet. She stood, pulling him up with her. He grabbed a blanket and dragged it down the hallway behind him as they made their way to their bedroom for the first time.

The next morning the kids woke up with only one thing on their minds: pool toys. Anthony said he'd take them later when the stores opened, but right now they needed to get some breakfast before the movers showed up. He said he'd run to McDonald's for Egg McMuffins, hash brown potatoes, juice, and coffee, then left.

Alice wanted to explore the neighborhood on her bike, the new three-speed she'd gotten for her birthday. Sylvia wasn't sure this was a good idea even though the neighboring streets were quiet, flat, and simply laid out.

"You don't know your way around yet, and I can't go with you because somebody has to wait here for the movers."

"I promise I'll just go down our street, around the bend, and back," Alice said. "And anyway I wrote our address on a piece of paper just in case. See?" Alice showed Sylvia where she'd written, "1295 Chestnut Street."

"I want to go, too," Trevor said.

"You haven't ridden enough. You stay with me for now."

"He can come, Mommy. I'll go slow," Alice said.

"Why don't you take a ten-minute ride, and we'll wait here. Then *maybe* Trevor can go, too." They agreed.

Their house was situated on a corner, so Sylvia pointed out the name of the adjacent street, Almond Avenue, and that their school was just a few blocks down.

"So that's why it's called Almond School." Alice smiled.

Sylvia gave her a kiss on the top of her head and said they'd be waiting right there. The moment she was out of sight Sylvia realized Alice wasn't wearing her watch. She sat with Trevor on the split-rail fence that lined their front walkway. After fifteen minutes, Alice zoomed up the sidewalk from the opposite direction and onto the front yard. She was out of breath and said Trevor could come now because the streets were really easy. Sylvia said okay after she ran inside and gave Alice her watch.

"You be back in *ten* minutes! By then your breakfast will be here." They disappeared around the bend, Trevor's little legs pumping hard to keep up. She looked at her watch: 8:15.

Sylvia went inside to check if the phone line was activated as scheduled. Amazingly, it was. She felt like calling her parents then decided against it—there wouldn't be enough time for a proper conversation. The doorbell rang. The movers had arrived. She told them to start unloading the truck and went inside to direct them where to put various pieces of furniture. The one couch would go in the living room with the dining room table at the far end. She was setting the kitchen chairs around the table when Anthony appeared. The smell of deep fat-fried hash browns filled the room. He put the two bags of food on the table and gave her a hug. "Where are the kids?"

"Oh, my God." Sylvia looked at her watch: 8:45. "They took a bike ride and were supposed to be back twenty minutes ago."

Anthony gave her a squinty-eyed look like she must be crazy.

Her insides were draining as she imagined them lost or lying hurt somewhere. She started toward the door to the carport. "We have to go look for them."

Alice practically knocked her down on her way in. She gasped for breath. "I can't find Trevor!"

"What do you mean?" Sylvia demanded. "What happened?"

Alice began to cry. "He was behind me, and then he wasn't. I looked all over."

*Sometimes Alice gets lost in her own world. How could I have put her in charge?*

"C'mon. Let's get in the car, and you show us where you went." Anthony was stern.

Sylvia put her arm around Alice and said it wasn't her fault. "We'll find him, honey. He can't be that far."

Anthony said he'd tell the movers. Sylvia grabbed one of the food bags for the kids. In a few minutes Anthony was behind the wheel with Alice sitting in the passenger's seat solemnly pointing as she tried to reconstruct her path. From the backseat, Sylvia started to explain the circumstances of the kids' bike ride to Anthony, but he just held up his hand to quiet her. For the next twenty minutes they combed the neighboring streets in tense silence, pausing only briefly to ask the occasional neighbor standing outside if he or she had seen him. Sylvia's panic was growing. *Her precious Trevor wandering around frightened in a strange place.* She berated herself over and over for being so thoughtless.

Finally, about half a mile away from their house, they found him huddled on a curb, his head buried in his hands. His bike was lying on the sidewalk next to him. Sylvia practically jumped out of the car while it was still moving. At first she thought he was hurt, but Trevor jumped up and ran to her. His tear-stained face was streaked with dirt, and he clutched her legs, sobbing. "I couldn't follow her. She was too fast."

Alice came running and bent over, nuzzling herself against his back. "I'm sorry I lost you," she whimpered.

"You're okay? You're not hurt?" Sylvia asked.

Trevor nodded.

"Thank God." Sylvia picked him up and pressed his limp body against her. She held him all the way home.

Anthony loaded his bike in the trunk and said nothing to Trevor on the ride back to their house. He pulled in the front and parked along the curb. After he shut off the ignition and they got out of the car, Anthony told Sylvia to put him down.

Trevor slid down the front of her body. He stood there looking at the ground.

"Take your bike to the garage and go to your room," Anthony said. "You can't ride your bike for a week."

A chill ran through Sylvia. After his warmth toward the kids in the pool the night before, she was dumbfounded.

Without so much as a glance in her direction, he turned and disappeared into the house.

*Why is he punishing Trevor? A frightened five-year-old needs comforting, not punishment.* Anthony must be mad at her, but why would he take it out on Trevor? Ignoring his command, she grabbed the bag of food from the front seat and guided Alice and Trevor to the back patio to eat so she could talk to Anthony alone. She said she'd join them in a few minutes.

Anthony was sitting at the kitchen table eating an Egg McMuffin and drinking his coffee. He didn't look at her or offer her the bag of food.

She stood on the opposite side of the table, glaring at him. "What are you so upset about? It makes no sense."

He gave her a smirk and shook his head. "How could you be so irresponsible, Jake?"

What was once an endearing pet name came out sounding like a moniker for a petty thief. She wanted to tell him not to call her that anymore.

"I know I shouldn't have let them go, but Trevor shouldn't be punished for my mistake." She still felt shaky from the incident and wished he'd put his arms around her and apologize, or at least comfort her after such a scare. "Everything turned out fine, for God's sakes."

"Everything's not fine!" He got up and put his hands on his hips. "That kid runs wild, and you don't do anything about it. He needs discipline."

Sylvia bristled. "Not your kind, he doesn't."

"You don't know what the word means. He has you so wrapped around his little finger, even your own daughter can't reach you," he said, pointing his finger at her.

There was a knock on the wall. One of the movers excused himself for interrupting and said he needed some help. Anthony rose quickly and went with him.

Sylvia was furious. Trevor was *not* wild. If anything, he was somewhat timid and cautious and never got into trouble. She was certain that Anthony's reaction was not about Trevor's behavior. There was something else going on with him. She was reaching in the bag for her coffee when it hit her. *He's jealous!* She started thinking about Anthony's relationship with his own son, Ricky, and recalled that Anthony thought Jane babied him, too.

What stood out in her mind, though, was that Anthony's mother sent him away to military school when he was six. When he told Sylvia about it a long time ago, she had felt so sorry for him. She couldn't imagine a mother doing that. And he said he never felt close to his mother. *How could he? She abandoned him.* Was Sylvia going to pay for his "missing mother" with constant battles around her doting affection for her son? She felt sick inside—Anthony had gotten mad at Trevor the night before they left Oregon. This was the second time in three days. Even if she understood the reason behind his overreactions, she'd never allow her Trevor to suffer for his problem.

Then there was his outburst about Alice. It resounded in her mind because Sylvia's mother had said something similar to her when Trevor was a toddler and Alice was seven or eight years old. Trevor had always been a cuddler and often climbed into Sylvia's lap, where he'd sit for long periods content with her hugs and kisses. One of those times, her mother gently suggested that "Alice still needs your attention, too." Sylvia always felt hurt that Alice preferred being with her dad and was perhaps unwittingly holding on to her son too tightly, who seemed to need her affection more than his sister. But she hoped she'd changed since then, particularly since the divorce. She made sure she and Alice had daily alone time together and didn't jump immediately to Trevor's call when it might interrupt her time with her daughter. Still, Anthony's remark had struck a vulnerable place in her, and she couldn't ignore it.

Sylvia joined the kids. Trevor was covered with dirt and still had tear stains running down his dust-covered cheeks. She needed to give him a bath. Alice wanted one, too, so they bathed together. Throughout the day they helped each other set up their rooms. Trevor wanted to know if Anthony was still mad at him. Sylvia explained that sometimes people get angry when they're really worried or scared and that was probably why he acted that way.

Over the course of the afternoon, the growing discomfort of Sylvia and Anthony not talking to each other was palpable, and she felt she had to make a move to restore peace. Maybe she was feeling a little sorry for him after thinking again about the way his mother treated him, but mostly, she didn't want her children to start their new life in a tension-filled, angst-ridden home. Anger and accusations would only make things worse. Besides, she was never good at arguing—she barely knew how. She decided to do the opposite. Soften him up. *Put my arms around him and apologize for causing today's fiasco.*

She heard the sound of cardboard flaps ripping open in the family room and wound her way around the maze of boxes in the living room. His back was to her. She stood six feet away and took a deep breath. In her most docile tone, she called to him. He turned around. He wore a dispirited expression, like someone who's too tired to try anymore. She pursed her lips contritely, raised her eyebrows, and with a pleading look, apologized as she put her arms around his neck. "And I'll try to do better with the kids. I just want us to be happy together."

He held her tightly and mumbled into her neck, "Me, too, Jake."

*****

November 15, 1981

Sylvia found the village atmosphere in Los Altos enchanting. Moss-filled flower baskets and decorative banners hung from the vintage street lamps throughout the town. White lights were strung through the trees on Main Street, giving it a warm, holiday feeling year round. The small-town community seemed to pride itself on traditions and activities for children, especially during the holidays, and Sylvia wanted to take full advantage. For Halloween, the four of them had each picked one pumpkin to carve from the pumpkin patch that sat in an open field on the outskirts of town. Afterwards they went on a hayride in a straw-filled wagon pulled by a team of draft horses. Many of the stores were decorated with cornstalks and scarecrows, and some handed out free candy during Halloween week. A haunted house had been organized by the Heritage League. For Christmas, Sylvia learned there would be a Festival of Lights parade in early December, caroling for anyone who was interested, and breakfast with Santa. Alice and Trevor were completely caught up in the festive surroundings.

Sylvia hoped to become a part of this quaint, upscale community and reach a point where she and her new family felt a sense of belonging. If she jumped right in and became involved in a community group, maybe she could speed up the process. How long would it take? Six months? A year? She'd lived under cover for so long in Lakeside that she longed to live out in the open again, free of secrets. More than anything she wanted this relationship to work; to be a normal wife and mother with a family to raise. She longed for the time when Anthony was no longer married to Jane and, once again, found herself waiting for that to happen.

By Halloween, Tom had seen the children on two different occasions while he was on business trips in the Bay Area. One was just for the day. The other was an overnight, so the children stayed with him in a hotel. Even though she didn't think it was any of his business, Sylvia ran Tom's schedule by Anthony first, to keep the peace. She had a hard time convincing him it was okay for them to miss school, but he had finally relented. He'd been at work when Tom picked up and dropped off the children each time, which was just as well. When they said their good-byes, the children hung on to him so that he practically had to peel them off of his body. Tom was tearful along with them, and when he left, they ran to their rooms sobbing. Sylvia brought them together so the three could sit, holding on to each other, while she listened to their despair, trying to comfort them when there was nothing she could say to take away their pain. She waited until they calmed down enough, then suggested they go out somewhere, maybe for ice cream at the old-fashioned soda fountain in town. And she'd thought about how much worse being this far from their father was than she'd ever thought possible. Wasn't it just like Tom to realize now how much he missed his kids? She quietly hoped he regretted that he didn't see them when he had the chance.

Her home life had become a tricky balancing act to avoid upsetting Anthony. As hard as Sylvia tried, the amount of attention she gave him never seemed to be enough. The tension continued to revolve around Trevor. Anthony just didn't have patience with him, nor with what he still referred to as Sylvia's lack of discipline and structure. Alice posed no problem for him. They seemed to genuinely enjoy each other's company, and many evenings, while Sylvia was putting Trevor to bed, they watched TV or played card games, such as Kings in the Corner, and sometimes worked on puzzles together. He helped her with homework and admired how well she did in school. Sylvia thought of his daughter, Alexia, and the close relationship they'd had.

Alice said she liked this school better than her old one and felt like the teacher's pet. Her teacher was an artist and marveled at Alice's ability. Within the first month she had a best friend, Julie, who lived a few blocks away. Trevor was in kindergarten and was one of the youngest in the class. The teacher was a kindhearted, gentle soul who didn't see the need to push him toward reading or basic arithmetic yet. He just wasn't ready. She said he got along well with the other children and was a sweet, happy spirit in the classroom. At this stage, that's what mattered to Sylvia the most.

Still, the initial months in her new home were like a roller coaster. Sylvia kept telling herself that the first year was supposed to be difficult, and in time, Anthony would adjust to their differences and go back to being the man she fell in love with, the one she could lean on, cool and calm under pressure with a sense of humor. When the opportunity arose to attend a panel on parenting at Almond School, Sylvia asked him if he'd like to attend.

"Sounds like a great idea." Anthony added that maybe he'd finally get some professional backup.

As they sat in the gym listening to the panel, one woman in particular, a middle-aged no-nonsense family therapist from Finland named Irmeli, caught Anthony's attention. Her position, that children needed structure and discipline from their parents, naturally spoke to him. Afterwards he said, "I like her approach. Let's go talk to her."

Sylvia thought if they found someone he believed in, maybe they could find a way to mesh their styles. They made an appointment for the following week.

Irmeli's office was in her home. She ushered them through the living room into a den with a couch and several chairs. "Who wants to begin?" she asked cheerfully.

Anthony sat with his arms crossed over his chest, slumped on the couch. "I'm unhappy because of Sylvia. She doesn't know how to discipline her children."

*Psych 101,* Sylvia thought. *No one was happy or unhappy because of someone else. If he's going to make this all my fault, I might as well go home.*

Irmeli peered over her wire-rimmed glasses first at Anthony then at Sylvia. Her subtle Scandinavian accent with its distinctive lilting quality rolled through her words. "Different parenting styles can cause a great deal of tension, which is detrimental to the children. Oftentimes, parents simply repeat the patterns from their own childhood. Do you think that might be the case here?"

"Probably," Sylvia said. "My parents rarely raised their voices. And they never made a federal case out of our bedtimes or household chores. My parents told us over and over what good children we were. And, according to them, our teachers said they should've had three more."

"So there was little structure, and you were happy as a child." Irmeli tilted her head.

Sylvia nodded. "Very."

"And, Anthony, what about you? Was this very different from your childhood memory?"

"Very."

There was an uncomfortable silence. Sylvia sensed him withdrawing as if he couldn't compete with her *laissez-faire* Pollyanna background. She should've let him go first.

"Not all of us had a *Father Knows Best* experience, which calls into question that it could exist outside of television," he said.

Sylvia flushed with embarrassment at his pointed insult.

Irmeli threw her head back with a laugh as if to toss off his remark. "Unless you believe that perception is nine-tenths reality."

"Fine." He looked at Sylvia, then at Irmeli. "Can we just get down to practical matters, here? I thought you were promoting discipline for children."

"Discipline has many interpretations," she said. "That is why I wanted to understand a little of your backgrounds. From this, we can find where the greatest differences lie and proceed from there to establish a set of guidelines that both of you can live with."

"Fair enough," he said. "I grew up in a military school, so we're as far apart as any two parents could be."

"That's possible, but as long as both of you are willing to compromise for the sake of your relationship and the children, it is quite doable," Irmeli said. "How did you feel about your school experience?"

"I hated military school."

"Anything in particular you hated?"

"Having to spit-polish my shoes when I was six," he said.

"Anything else?"

"I never had any free time to just be a kid. Every minute was regimented."

"So for you there was too much structure," Irmeli said.

"Definitely," he said.

A faint sliver of hope ran through Sylvia.

"Do you think that for some of the other children this amount of structure might've been welcomed?" Irmeli asked.

"I remember a few kids who seemed to eat it up. Marching in precision formation. Saluting. Lights out at eight and up at dawn or else."

"So you'd agree that some children respond to a stricter regimen than others?" she asked.

"Of course. That's not what we're addressing here," he said. "We're talking about a problem of no structure at all."

"Perhaps that is subjective as to what one's experience has been," she said. "Do you think the military school environment taught you any important life lessons?"

Anthony's disdainful look reminded Sylvia of an obstinate child. "To respect authority."

"Are Sylvia's children disrespectful toward either of you or other adults?"

"No," Anthony answered.

"Do they misbehave? Or get into trouble at school?" she asked.

"No. That's not really the point."

"And what is the point?" she asked.

"That they learn at an early age how to be more self-sufficient so they don't have to rely on their parents to do everything for them," he said.

"Would you agree with that, Sylvia?"

"I wonder how self-sufficient a five-year-old can be. What does that really mean?"

"That you shouldn't jump like Edith Bunker whenever he wants something," Anthony said.

"Just when *you* want something?" Sylvia retorted.

"Responding to a husband is different than—" he began.

"Which you're not, are you?" Sylvia smiled tightly. She then turned to address Irmeli. "My biggest concern is the lack of consideration for the huge changes taking place in my children's lives. Moving out of state and leaving their dad. Adjusting to Anthony as a parent. Rather than jumping into rules and structure, what about some leeway for all of these adjustments?"

Irmeli nodded in agreement. "You're both on the right track. All of you are adjusting to tremendous change, which is bound to create tension. Children do need to learn self-care that is age-appropriate. The reason, however, is so they can develop self-reliance, which builds confidence. As they grow and take more and more responsibility for their own needs, they build self-esteem and integrity."

Sylvia listened intently. Maybe she could tweak her parenting style somewhat, but they'd have to come to terms on the key phrase. "If we can determine what might be age-appropriate for Trevor, perhaps it would be a place to start."

Irmeli brightened. "That sounds quite reasonable. What do you say, Anthony?"

"If we can take something home with us, the session will be worth it."

"Wonderful," she said. "I might add that it sounds like Alice and Trevor are adjusting quite beautifully in school and have new friends as well. You must be doing something right, no?"

Under her guidance they established a few new guidelines at home. Anthony added a few of his own, but Sylvia went along, compromising her usual, more relaxed style, thinking he might soften and be less petulant. There were strict bedtimes (eight for Trevor, nine for Alice), baths every night, packing their own lunches, making their beds before school, and homework right after school. None of these duties was bad for them, but the dictatorial way he implemented them, and the reproaches or the rolling of the eyes whenever there was a misstep, caused Sylvia to dread the evenings. Following Anthony's lead, she did her best to train them and herself, like a little family of seals, but most of the time she felt like rescuing them, particularly Trevor.

Anthony showed him how to draw his own bath and clean up afterwards. He taught him to drain the soap dish and how to properly fold and hang his towel. Sylvia stood out of sight at the far end of the hall and watched as Trevor spread the towel out on the floor then took one side at a time, pulling it toward the center. Because he was so small, he had to move back and forth from one end to the other to match the sides to the center. Then he called Anthony to check how he did. Sylvia wanted to rush in and tell him he was perfect the way he was, and it didn't matter how he folded his towel.

She had flashbacks of Jane and Anthony's regimented household that she'd always assumed was under Jane's command—and all the yelling and the deepened furrow between Jane's eyebrows at the age of thirty-two. How long would it be before she had one to match?

*****

Thanksgiving Week 1981

The Baldwins were a saving grace for Anthony and Sylvia and the children. Suzie Baldwin worked for Dick Nyberg, Anthony's partner, and like a mother hen, had taken Anthony under her wing during the summer before Sylvia moved down. An older couple with four grown children, Suzie and David lived in neighboring Palo Alto in a beautifully restored three-story rambling Victorian home.

The moment Sylvia crossed the threshold, she felt at home. They had an easygoing, open-door lifestyle where friends knocked briefly and just walked in. The house had a lived-in quality with stained glass windows, handmade pottery items, needlework projects, and soft, comfy furniture with colorful, hand-knitted throws strewn across the backs. Alice and Trevor loved going there, which fortunately was often. They usually had dinner together once a week. Suzie seemed to innately grasp their need for the comfort of her loving arms and carefree manner. Her home became a refuge.

Anthony and Sylvia were invited for Thanksgiving with the Baldwin clan, twenty-five in all. Alice and Trevor were in Oregon with Tom and Betsy. Tom had said he couldn't pay for the children's flights this year but promised to for spring break. With Irmeli's help, Anthony was less hard-nosed, so he paid for their tickets. At Tom's request Alice and Trevor would be gone for six days, which meant they'd miss two days of school before the holiday. To Sylvia's relief, Anthony went along with that as well.

With the children gone, and this being their first time alone together since the move, they were able to rekindle the love and passion for each other they'd always known. Anthony surprised her with a two-night getaway in Carmel. They didn't talk about the children, the business, or Anthony's divorce, which wasn't progressing because he had to start the whole process over again once he'd moved to California.

The six dreamy days passed quickly for them. On the drive home, with each passing mile, Sylvia could feel the weight of his buoyant mood gradually slip into despondence, until a tense silence draped the air like damp moss, and the familiar dread seeped back into her core.

They'd been seeing Irmeli on a weekly basis and had scheduled an appointment two days after the children returned from Oregon. The subject of Anthony's children finally came up. Every attempt he'd made to see them proved unsuccessful. Jane wouldn't cooperate, and his new lawyer wasn't very helpful.

"Why aren't you pushing for your legal rights?" Irmeli asked.

"My wife's poisoned my kids against me. I think the lawyer is right. I should wait a while until she calms down. She's prone to hysteria."

"When did you see them last?"

"I've talked to them on the phone a few times, but I haven't seen them since we moved into our house."

"Why is that?" Irmeli asked.

"I tried to see them the week before Thanksgiving. I called a day ahead and said I was coming. I knew my daughter was waiting for me, but when I arrived my son, Ricky, ran out and started hitting me. Jane started screaming at me to leave, and Alexia hung by the front door like she was afraid to go against her mother. Then Jane's father came out and threatened me to get off of his property, saying that I was causing a disturbance. So I left."

Irmeli raised her eyebrows, looked at Anthony, and said this was undoubtedly a source of anguish for him that needed to be dealt with. His children needed to know that he would fight for them; otherwise, they'd accept what their mother said as true. The pain of being denied access to his children would also erode his relationship with Sylvia and her children. She couldn't emphasize enough the importance of acting soon. She suggested that he find a new attorney and start demanding his rights.

Something didn't sit right with Sylvia after this session with Irmeli. On their way home in the car she asked him, "Is there something new that's happened to make Jane angry all over again?"

"Other than I haven't sent her a child support payment since September?"

"What?" Sylvia couldn't believe it. Anthony kept a separate checking account to track his child support expenses. Since the checkbook stayed at his office, Sylvia never saw it, and he never shared that information with her. She just assumed he was paying nine hundred a month, the amount he told her was agreed upon through Jane's and Anthony's attorneys in Oregon. The two hundred and fifty she received from Tom went into their joint checking account. All she knew was that he deposited four thousand a month into that account, which was more than enough for them, far more than Sylvia was accustomed to. "Why did you stop paying?"

"Because she refused to arrange visitation," he said.

"I can't imagine your attorney recommending you do that."

"He didn't."

Sylvia shook her head. Then she lit a cigarette. "When did you stop taking his advice?"

"When he told me to lie down and wait for Jane's anger to subside. I'm thinking about switching attorneys."

The puzzle pieces were piling up again, and Sylvia struggled to make sense of what he was telling her. "But why would she have refused you visitation in the first place?"

He pulled his Chevy Camaro into the driveway. "She probably panicked about money when the house in Oregon went into foreclosure."

# CHAPTER 32

January 6, 1982

Sylvia had never seen the skies open up this much, even in Oregon. The rains began several days before and just kept coming. Within forty-eight hours floods and landslides spread over ten counties in the Bay Area. For the second time in its existence, the Golden Gate Bridge was closed on the Marin County side. Twelve-foot walls of mud rushing into neighborhoods were not uncommon; some came so fast that bodies were found in bed with their dogs. Creeks turned to rivers that moved like "aqua rocket launchers" thrusting logs and rocky muck into roads and buildings. The term *El Niño* was introduced to the general population to account for the dramatic storm pattern taking place.

Anthony said an El Niño typically hit every few years in the Western Pacific and Australia due to warm weather currents, but he'd never heard of an El Niño effect on their own West Coast. The strength of this one was apparently unprecedented. Unlike the eruption of Mount Saint Helens, during which

Sylvia felt connected and motivated to action, she felt more like she might be washed away, swallowed by the cross currents that surrounded her.

Within their neighborhood gutters were flowing at curb level, narrowing some streets to only one center lane. Sylvia worried the water would rise onto the sidewalks and flow toward their house since they were on such level ground. And she worried about general flooding even though the local news said otherwise. *If the storm is unprecedented, how would they know?* Alice and Trevor were in rain boots, slickers, and fisherman's hats every time they ventured outdoors—somehow they still got wet.

Once, in the middle of the night, each of them woke up from the pounding rain and ended up huddling under blankets on the living room couch. Anthony built a fire in the fireplace, and Sylvia made cocoa. They played Crazy Eights and stayed home the next day. During Mount Saint Helens, a sense of surviving the elements seemed to bring the family together, if even for a short while. This disaster seemed to bring them closer, too, only this time she hoped it would last.

The drama of the weather momentarily took her mind off Anthony's foreclosure woes, but many doubts lingered. Because she didn't understand enough about banking regulations, she wasn't sure what caused a foreclosure. Was it from not making house payments or property taxes or both? And how long did it take for a bank to foreclose? Surely more than a few months. When she had asked him about the details, he had said something about the loan balance being too high for a bank to refinance during a down market. The loan-to-value wasn't there.

"Why would you refinance though?" She had seemed to recall that he'd done it before.

"To reduce the monthly payments," he had said. "Remember, we bought when interest rates were high."

No, Sylvia didn't remember. His explanation had sounded like he was blaming the economy for getting in over his head. *And didn't he specialize in banking loans?* He had said a lot of people got caught in the downward-spiraling housing market. He also said that she could count on him to rebuild—after all, that was his business. According to him, in a year or two they'd be able to buy a home.

She was troubled that one of the outstanding qualities that made Anthony stand above Tom, his capability in finance, the one thing she'd always counted on, seemed in jeopardy. She wanted to believe him. She wanted to believe that divorce always causes financial havoc, just like it had for her. But she'd also believed Anthony was too financially savvy to "get caught" like everybody else. Maybe Jessica's hunch was right. The lavish spending was the root of the problem: his family trips and overseas travel, new Porsches, their three years of hotel rooms, dinners in chic restaurants, and more recently, expensive gifts for her. During their affair, he had complained that he couldn't buy her things like he wanted to. As soon as Tom was out of the house, he started either giving gifts such as a suede jacket and skirt or paying for things such as her car repairs.

By the end of January the effects of the natural disaster that had hit the Bay Area were still being felt. Cleanup was underway, but it would take years, and for some, rebuilding was impossible; the land had washed away, and there was nothing to build on. While Sylvia felt fortunate that they'd escaped the problems so many others were facing, she saw parallels to the welling disaster at home. Without a financial foundation, she questioned whether rebuilding would be possible for them as well.

One evening after the kids were asleep, Anthony told Sylvia he needed to discuss something with her. He got up to shut off the TV then sat back down beside her on the couch. He took a sip of wine and cleared his throat. "I know what we said before we moved here about you working."

"That it was up to me."

"Right." He tilted his head and pursed his lips. "We may need you to help out sooner rather than later."

"What do you mean? Like substitute teaching?"

"More like a full-time job."

"How could this be?"

"I didn't change attorneys after all, too expensive, but it looks like child support will be higher in California. And I'm trying to pay off all the credit card bills left over from Oregon along with attorney fees, which I haven't paid for a while. So—"

"You keep dropping bombs on me."

"Bombs keep dropping on me."

She sat up straighter and turned to look him in the eye. "Not really. Foreclosure doesn't happen out of the blue. You're still keeping me in the dark."

He lit a cigarette, exhaling as he spoke. "I thought the house would sell, which would've cleared up everything."

"It was hardly on the market long enough to sell." She didn't take her eyes off of him. "What do you mean, 'clear up everything'?"

He didn't look at her. "Car payments, Jane's move, overdue taxes—the bills I just told you about."

"Why didn't you tell me about this before?"

"I didn't want to worry you before the move with something that might not materialize."

"This is a total shock to me. If we had talked about this before the move, I would've been mentally prepared to go to work. It feels like you've been stringing me along."

"I thought I was sparing you. But isn't the end result the same and not knowing gave you a few carefree months?"

*Carefree? He couldn't mean it.* "You're worrying me more by withholding information because now I can't trust what you're telling me. I need to know everything from now on." She thought about suggesting they talk to Irmeli then changed her mind. She'd go alone.

He reached over and put his hands on her shoulders. "Fine. I get it now. This is all pretty new to me. I never talked about finances with Jane. She *never* wanted to know. So when the Oregon house problems began, I debated whether to tell you or not, especially after what you've been through with Tom."

Sylvia had no choice but to give him another chance. The hard reality was he had to take care of his first family before her and couldn't take care of her like he pretended he could.

He took her chin in his hand to look at her directly. "Really, Jake. I'll tell you everything from now on."

She took his hand in hers and held it in her lap. "I haven't had a full-time job since my kids were born. And I'd need day care for Trevor." The thought of setting all this up was making her heartsick. And queasy.

"It wouldn't be for long," he said. "I figure a year at most."

"You can't say that for sure. Let's be honest about this."

"I am. The credit cards would be paid off for one, and most of the attorney fees will be behind me."

"Before I start job hunting, I want to see all your bills and I want to know exactly what you earn."

"I'll bring them home tomorrow with all my income statements."

Sylvia couldn't ask for more than that right now. She closed her eyes as he pulled her against his chest.

"I didn't mean for it to go like this." He kissed the top of her head. "I love you more than ever, Jake. Hang in there with me. I promise I'll make it up to you."

*****

March 9, 1982

Five days a week Sylvia returned home at four o'clock from her unchallenging office job, a boring blend of secretary and office manager duties for a beeper company with six employees. She'd never worked in an office before and felt trapped that she no longer had summers off or school vacations to spend with her kids. The idea of only two weeks a year was stifling and scary.

On the other hand, while she loved teaching itself, the demands of junior high and high school also left her feeling trapped. Sylvia was obligated to remain in the building during school hours and felt monitored just like the students. A student walking down the hall had to produce a hall pass from his teacher—without one, the teacher was reprimanded. If late, the student needed a written excuse from home. The teacher, however, could never be late; an unsupervised classroom was mayhem waiting to happen. Medical or professional appointments had to be scheduled after school. For Sylvia, it meant arranging a babysitter or a friend's house for her children. If one of her children got sick, she had to have lesson plans ready for a sub. Since a French sub was difficult to find, her classes usually fell behind in her absence. Every night she had homework or tests to grade. Sometimes she wondered if she'd have more autonomy and less babysitting teaching college level, but that required at least a master's degree.

The office atmosphere at the Beeper Company was more like a sociology class of laid-back, trustworthy grown-ups, minus the learning curve. There was no daily preparation or work to take home. And her annual salary was fifteen thousand, three more than when she taught. Maybe it was boring, but Sylvia was there for a paycheck and a job without demands beyond her time there. If she had to be late or home with a sick child, it was a simple phone call. She felt lucky that the owner of the company was a devoted father whose children were a top priority in his life. While she'd never take advantage of his good attitude, it was a welcome relief to have the pressures of teaching lifted for now. The office was also close enough to home that she could ride her bike. And she got free use of a beeper. She hadn't found a need for it yet, but Alice and Trevor had fun taking turns beeping each other at home.

Before taking the job she had told the owner about the trip to Europe for the month of July. He had no problem with it as long as she didn't expect to be paid, which she didn't. Spring break was coming up fast. Sylvia didn't have to worry about Alice and Trevor at home all day with a sitter because they were going to Oregon for the week. Tom still couldn't pay for their flights. In fact, he missed the last child support payment. Anthony grudgingly agreed for them to pay since the cost would be about the same if they had a sitter for five days.

What troubled Sylvia was that he was beginning to grumble about her money "just sitting up there in Oregon when we could use it to pay for extras, like your kids' flights." Now that he was no longer excluding her from knowing the extent of his debt, he was treating her more like a business partner who hadn't contributed his percentage. It was a double-edged sword. Since she had demanded to see his bills and his paychecks, the façade he used to hide behind was gone. No longer able to pretend, he stopped sweet-talking her about how he'd take care of her. Rather, he went in the opposite direction—implying that she should contribute more. Sylvia believed working full-time was contribution enough. With his income at roughly sixty thousand, it appeared they could live reasonably well without going into further debt. Still, she worried that it wouldn't be long before he'd really begin to pressure her about her nest egg.

*****

April 8, 1982

Before going to work, Sylvia picked up the phone to call her brother Steve. It was his birthday. Her mom answered and said Steve was still asleep.

"Are you all right, honey?" Vivian asked. "You don't sound like yourself."

Hearing her mom's sympathetic voice of concern caught her off guard, and Sylvia suddenly felt like she could cry. She wanted to tell her that life with Anthony wasn't working out like she'd hoped. That he wasn't financially secure and that's why she had to work so soon, and she still didn't feel at ease with the way he treated Trevor and was beginning to feel stuck in a problem she didn't know how to fix. "I'm just in a hurry to get to work."

"Are the kids okay?" Vivian asked.

"They're fine. They just left for school. By the way, I finally sent you that picture of Trevor that was in the local newspaper a while back."

"When his kindergarten had that Chinese thing?"

"A parade for Chinese New Year—the year of the dog. The only picture was of Trevor in the dog costume! It's adorable."

"Wonderful. I can't wait to see it."

"Do you have your flights for this summer yet?" Sylvia asked.

"We're all set. We're so excited to see the kids and your house. Even Steve is looking forward to it," Vivian said. "And Scott gets back in a few weeks."

Sylvia missed her family terribly. "I almost wish I could stay here with you guys."

"But you must be thrilled about going to Italy and Greece. And being in France again."

Sylvia thought she'd be more excited, especially since his parents were paying for everything. She hadn't been to Europe in fourteen years; right now, July seemed so far away. "I wonder if I'll even understand French spoken by a native—"

"Hold on, honey."

Sylvia heard her calling out to Steve then she came back to the phone. "Steve just got up. Can you wait a minute?"

"Sure. I'll wait."

There were muffled voices, and then the click of another phone picking up and Steve's gravelly, deadpan hello. When she wished him a happy birthday, there was a silence.

"Oh yeah. It's my birthday," he said. "I'm thirty-two, and I still don't have a college degree."

"Lots of people don't," Sylvia said.

"You and Scott do." He coughed hard. "Why did you call?"

"To wish you—"

He started laughing and mumbled something unintelligible—something about birthdays—and then started singing like the Mad Hatter. "A very merry unbirthday to us, to me—"

"Steve?"

"What?"

"Did Mom make your favorite cake today?"

"I don't know. I just got up." He started laughing again. "What is my favorite cake anyway?"

Sylvia thought a minute. "Marble?"

"Yeah! Or yellow with chocolate frosting. I think that's my favorite. You were wrong, Sylvia. I don't want to talk anymore."

"Okay, Steve. I'll see you this summer, right?" she asked.

"Are you coming here?"

"No. Mom said you're coming with them to California. To stay in our house."

"I can't keep up with you, Sylvia."

"I can't keep up with me either."

"Are you really divorced? Tom was a nice guy. I always liked him." Under his breath he mumbled, "I guess I shouldn't say that."

Sylvia couldn't tell if Steve wanted her to answer his questions. He seemed to be talking to himself most of the time.

"It's okay for you to say that. Tom was a nice guy. But Anthony's nice, too."

"Are you really living with him and not married? Aren't you afraid you'll go to hell?"

"I don't believe in hell."

"Isn't he Italian? They're too hot-tempered. Remember the Ventaros? I hated going over there. They were always yelling."

"You might be right."

"Does your house really have a swimming pool?"

"Yes."

"Remember when we were at the Crawfords in L.A.? And got in trouble throwing a ball too close to the picture window?"

"I'll never forget." Sylvia looked at her watch. She was late for work.

"They had a really big pool. Is yours that big? I'm gonna get off now," he said. "I have to pee."

The phone clicked and disconnected. Just as well. Sylvia had to leave.

Anthony stuck his head in the bedroom. "How's Steve?"

Sylvia got up from the side of the brass bed where she'd been sitting. "I thought you left."

"I forgot my briefcase."

She followed him down the hall toward the kitchen. "He sounded pretty good. Once he woke up."

Anthony stopped and turned around. "*And* I need your gas credit card."

"I only have one. What happened to yours?"

"I don't have time to explain right now."

She pulled out her wallet and handed it to him. "Did you lose it?"

"Not exactly. I'll explain later."

That evening the kids were doing their homework at the kitchen table, while Sylvia was fixing one of their favorite dinners, hamburger pie. Anthony came in the door from work and kissed her on the cheek. "Well, this is nice to see. Getting your homework done?"

Alice answered yes. Trevor said he was doing pretend homework, but really he was coloring.

Anthony set down his briefcase and poured two glasses of red wine. "But you'll be ready for the real thing next year, won't you?"

Trevor nodded.

"Can you guys go to your rooms and do that? I need to talk to your mom."

They slowly gathered their books and papers then looked up at Sylvia as Anthony rifled through his briefcase. She nodded to them, and they quietly left the room.

Anthony called out down the hall, "I'll let you guys know when it's time to set the table."

Sylvia put the casserole in the oven and sat down. He set several pages of an official-looking document on the table. He took out his cigarettes, lit one for himself, and offered her one. She took it, and he lit hers. "I got this notice the other day from the IRS for overdue income tax."

"For how much?"

He took a gulp of wine and pointed to the amount. *Twenty thousand!*

Sylvia felt like someone punched her in the stomach. She had never heard of anyone owing that kind of money. His credit cards were bad enough at fifteen thousand. It would take years to pay off everything.

"I called my attorney. He said we could request to pay a monthly amount or I could file for bankruptcy, which is what he thinks I should do."

"Bankruptcy? Don't they take things away? Like cars?" Sylvia asked.

"Only if you own them. Mine's leased."

"What about mine?"

"We're not married. They can't come after you."

For the first time Sylvia felt relieved they weren't.

Anthony looked like a card shark as he held the cigarette between his lips, squinting through the smoke trailing up his face. He took out his wallet and put her Shell card on the table. "Which means I won't have any credit cards for seven years. I'll need to use yours."

She cringed at the thought that now he'd depend on her good credit. "But you haven't filed yet, have you?"

His smile was more like a grimace. "No, but what else am I going to do? Unless—"

"Unless what?"

"Unless you contributed your money."

"I can't believe you'd ask me that."

"If you were serious about us, Jake, you'd consider it without my asking."

It was one thing for him to ask her to use her money to help pay for some expenses but quite another to manipulate her by suggesting she should save him from bankruptcy.

"If you were serious about us, you'd be divorced by now."

*****

May 1, 1982

Trevor's kindergarten class had a May Day celebration with a makeshift maypole in the center of the classroom. The teacher held the pole while each child held a long brightly colored crepe paper streamer trailing from the pole's top. They sang songs for the parents as they walked in a circle, their teacher turning the pole as they walked. Trevor grinned at his mom and Anthony as he sang "Farmer in the Dell" and "Four and Twenty Blackbirds." Sylvia and Anthony chuckled as he passed by them, and Anthony leaned over to tell him he was doing a good job.

As Sylvia stood among the other parents, she covered her left hand with her right, something she'd been doing at school functions since her arrival in Los Altos. She also might put her hands in her pockets or place them in her lap, making sure her bare ring finger was unexposed. She was used to being self-conscious about her bitten-down fingernails, so the same tactics were practically a habit. As she stood there with him, she faced the fact that despite their being together she was still in hiding. And she hated living with the continued worry of being found out.

Anthony had gone ahead and filed for bankruptcy. He still hadn't seen his children. And he wasn't hesitating to ask Sylvia to move her nest egg out of Oregon. Even though his parents were paying for their trip to Europe, he said they still needed to take cash with them—fifteen hundred was what he suggested—and she should use her money. After paying the bills off from her divorce, her entire net worth consisted of the remaining seventeen thousand from the original twenty-three she got from the sale of her house.

She considered calling Jessica about the mess she was in but didn't want to admit that Jessica might've been right about telling her to wait until Anthony was divorced before she moved. She couldn't bear to tell her mother that she'd made another mistake with her life. The list was growing from as far back as her marriage to Tom and her unexpected pregnancy—both had happened sooner than her parents had wanted for her. Their overall message: Before settling down as a stay-at-home wife and mother, their twenty-four-year-old daughter should use her talents to explore and enjoy life through interesting work and travel—an unusual message for its time.

In Sylvia's senior year in college, the unspoken pressure to find a husband had been evident by the number of women getting engaged and setting wedding dates by graduation. Sylvia had known of only three in her sorority who didn't marry, who chose to pursue careers instead. Still, the fact that Sylvia hadn't really established herself solidly in a career had been a disappointment to her parents, but more so to her mother. Maybe she had just wanted Sylvia to take advantage of all the opportunities in front of her, to live the life she never had. Even so, Sylvia felt ashamed to face letting them down once again—especially when they'd been so understanding about the affair, the divorce, and the move. To top it off, they were coming to take care of the kids while Sylvia went to Europe. No, Sylvia couldn't possibly talk to her mother this time. Besides, it would worry her too much. She had enough anxiety living with Steve day in and day out, hoping against hope that he'd recover. Sylvia thought of Scott, but he wouldn't be back from Saudi Arabia for a few weeks.

And then she realized whom she needed to talk to all along. With a tighter schedule and less money, she and Anthony hadn't seen Irmeli in two months. Sylvia made an appointment to see her alone, something she'd intended to do a few months ago.

The following week, Sylvia was sitting in Irmeli's home office explaining their financial difficulties, her working full-time, his request to move her money from Oregon, and now his specific demand to use her money for their trip.

"So you have this money from your former marriage," Irmeli said.

"Yes. I resent that he'd even ask me to dip into it," Sylvia said.

"Legally it is yours. He has no right to it, even if you were married to each other."

"So what do I say to him?"

"Haven't you already made it clear? Just by leaving it in Oregon?"

"Apparently not, or he wouldn't keep asking me."

"Is he usually persistent in what he wants?"

"Always."

"Well then, why would you expect he'd be different about this?"

"I thought he'd respect what's really mine."

"Maybe to him, leaving your money in Oregon represents a lack of commitment on your part," Irmeli said. "Your safety net, just in case."

"It *is* my safety net—and more than I could earn in one year on my former teacher's salary. So what's wrong with playing it safe? He of all people should understand why I need that."

"Perhaps now that he's in financial trouble, he's afraid you won't stand by him."

Sylvia shifted in her seat. It was true that she'd been thinking of her hurried decision to move as a mistake since she found out he was financially unstable. But his duplicity upset her even more. She looked down at her hands, openly resting on each thigh. *At least here I don't have to hide.* "His financial expertise is what attracted me in the first place—that and his worldliness."

"He probably knows that."

Sylvia explained in detail how Anthony had repeatedly deceived her about his outstanding debts, which made it so difficult to trust him.

"A man's ego can be quite fragile when it comes to finances. Did the two of you not discuss finances before you decided to move?"

"Not really. I started to several times but didn't push it. He had a big house, drove a Porsche, and traveled to Europe. He led me to believe that he was a man of means," Sylvia said.

"So you relied on outward appearance rather than actual fact."

"I suppose that's true."

"Is there a reason you didn't 'push it' with him?"

"I had no reason to doubt him. Managing money is his profession. Knowing so little about it, who was I to question him?"

Irmeli took a few notes. "Did you get the impression he'd be offended if you asked?"

"I think that was part of it. That he'd think I didn't trust him." Sylvia asked if she could smoke a cigarette.

Irmeli said okay and got up to open the window. "Perhaps it would've been worth taking the risk to offend him, since now you don't trust him anyway."

Sylvia nodded. "If I knew then what I know now—"

Irmeli peered over her wire rims. "What would you have done differently?"

"I don't think I'd be here."

"So would you say you're less committed to the relationship?"

"I'm not sure how committed I am right now," Sylvia said. "But I've gone through too much and put my kids through too much to give up at this point."

Irmeli gave her a soft, comforting smile. "And how much time do you think you should give it?"

Sylvia pondered this. "About a year feels right to decide if we're going to work out. We moved here last September."

"I think it's good to have a timeline. In the meantime, does Anthony appear to be disclosing the information you want?"

Sylvia said this time she thought so and felt more reassured since she had access to his income and bills.

"Your relationship should improve now that there's more honest dialogue between you, but building trust again will take time."

The idea that in Anthony's eyes Sylvia's perception of him was directly tied to his financial strength brought a different slant to his behavior for her. "I can see why he was so hesitant to tell me what was going on and why the Europe trip would mean a lot to him. He's talked about us going ever since we first met."

"Such an exciting trip might be rejuvenating for both of you," Irmeli said.

"So am I being unreasonable about my money?"

Irmeli's eyes widened a bit. "What if you were?"

"I don't want to be."

"What's wrong with being unreasonable?"

It seemed obvious to Sylvia that no one would want to be unreasonable, would they? She didn't know how to answer that. "He'd be unhappy with me?"

"So what if he's unhappy with you?"

It was so quiet Sylvia could hear Irmeli's pen as it moved across her pad. She looked up at the ceiling and took a drag on her cigarette. "It makes me feel like I've done something wrong."

"So if he's unhappy with a decision you make, perhaps with your children, for example, you feel uncomfortable enough that you should go along with Anthony to make him happy? To keep the peace?"

Sylvia remembered their first visit in her office when Anthony had said he was unhappy because of her. She didn't think she believed it was up to her to make him happy, but maybe she'd deceived herself. Maybe that's exactly what she was trying to do. She was definitely trying to avoid upsetting him, for her children's sake as well as her own. "Pretty much."

"How would you describe the way your mother treated your father?"

"She waited on him hand and foot." Sylvia thought for a moment. "But I never thought she did it because she worried about how he'd react. She just wanted to please him."

"Do you think your mother bowed to his wishes while denying her own?"

"Maybe, but I didn't think that was so unusual for the fifties. Her world was always wrapped around him and us kids; she seemed quite happy."

"So would you say she was a good role model for you?"

"I felt lucky to have such a cheerful, fun-loving mom. And my friends liked to be around her," Sylvia said.

"Does that mean, then, she was a good role model?"

Sylvia stubbed her cigarette out in the glass ashtray on the book stand next to her. "Not really. Around high school age I started to feel differently. I suppose I was losing respect for her."

"Why was that?"

"Well, she seemed shallow and opinionated. She judged people by how they looked, what they had, or where they lived—outward appearances mattered most." Sylvia stopped and thrust her hand to her lips. "Oh, my God. That's what I just did. Does this mean I've become my mother?"

"Would it bother you to resemble your mother?"

"If it means I'm superficial, it does." Sylvia told Irmeli how her mother also seemed so dependent, almost helpless; how she wanted to see herself as the opposite, strong and capable like her father. "Dad was more of an intellectual—he cared little about material things. I didn't think I cared much for material things either, but maybe I do."

"Wanting financial stability and nice things for a comfortable life don't make you a superficial person. Would you say that your father didn't seem to judge others in the same way as your mother, then?"

"No, he didn't. And with him *I* never felt like I was being judged."

"But with her you did?"

Sylvia slumped in the chair. "She praised me a lot, but I usually felt what I did wasn't quite good enough."

Irmeli asked if Sylvia could think of an example.

Sylvia explained how her mother never had thought her best girlfriend measured up to their standards—she was from divorced parents and lived in a poorer side of town. Sylvia's boyfriend hadn't been acceptable either because he dropped out of college after his first year. "This is so petty, but she criticized the crown I wore when I was homecoming queen as cheap-looking and the picture of me in the newspaper as unflattering. It seemed as though she'd always find fault with something or someone, and I'd feel deflated even though it was couched with praise and wanting the best for me." Sylvia also told Irmeli about the disappointment she had sensed around her marriage and pregnancy. "I never felt she was saying things out of meanness, but she managed to take the wind out of my sails."

"So would you say you didn't feel safe sharing your feelings with your mother?"

"Yes. I ended up feeling hurt a lot and never really confided in her."

Irmeli stretched her legs out in front of her and crossed her ankles. "Did you share your feelings with anyone?"

"Not when I was little, but I don't remember ever being asked to talk about them. If I felt like I was going to cry, I'd be embarrassed and go to my room. I thought there was something wrong with me because I was overly sensitive."

"This feeling that something is wrong with you may stem from a fear of being judged. What do you do with your feelings now?"

"I guess I try to control them when they're negative," Sylvia said. "I try to make them go away or steal away somewhere so no one else finds out I'm upset."

"What would happen if somebody, like Anthony, found you?"

"I'd feel silly and wouldn't know what to say."

"What about being honest?"

"Lately, they have to do with him, so I can't say anything."

"Why not?"

"He'd just try to show me why I *shouldn't* feel that way."

"You mean he'd reject your feelings?"

"I suppose that's it." Sylvia realized her behavior was no different now than when she was a child. "So I'm hiding how I feel because I might be judged and don't want to risk feeling rejected."

Irmeli smiled. "You're on the right track. Perhaps that's the same reason you don't probe beyond the surface, for fear of interfering and being unreasonable, which might also lead to rejection."

"That makes sense, but what do I do about it?"

"Well, if you continue to hide, you may lose perspective of who you are or never find out who you are because you're too busy trying to please others, fearful that the real you is unacceptable. And bottled-up feelings usually find ways to come out, often inappropriately. Standing up for yourself is the place to begin. Did you ever stand up to your mother or ever argue with her?"

"Mostly I tried to ignore her remarks and say nothing. I believed it was futile to confront her. Like a dog with a bone, she'd never give it up."

"So, like Anthony, she was persistent, too, and you were more comfortable remaining silent, being the 'good' girl to keep the peace?"

"So, I'm reacting to Anthony like I did with my mother." Sylvia sat up straighter. "I heard somewhere that we usually marry one of our parents."

"Yes, most often it's the parent who was the primary nurturer."

"I know I didn't marry my father. I'd say Tom was even his opposite. And Anthony's personality hardly resembles my father's either. He's spontaneous, not cautious and measured in his words or actions like my dad; neither one is an intellectual, but Anthony is much brighter than Tom. Marrying my mother seems so odd, but in a lot of ways they seem to resemble her more."

Irmeli chuckled. "In what ways do they seem similar to her?"

"She has a fun-loving, even silly side and is affectionate. She also loves a party and is quite flirtatious. She's the one to go to for fun, but not with problems or complaints, just the good times."

"It seems that you've thought about this before."

Sylvia nodded. "A little. I've thought about the obvious fact that I'm attracted to flamboyant men who are nothing like my father, but I never connected that likeness to my mother until now. I also see that by deferring to both men, I've repeated my mother's behavior."

"How did your father react to your mother?"

"I don't remember them arguing, but when I was a teenager before my brother got sick, I noticed he was putting her down a lot."

"How so?"

"He'd tell her to quit yapping, that she didn't know what she was talking about. Or he'd roll his eyes and leave the room when she was in mid-sentence. I can't remember him ever showing any affection for her, unless she initiated it; then he'd stiffly give her a hug back. He treated her almost with disdain."

"So your father withdrew from your mother also. How did his behavior make you feel?"

"I sided with my dad most of the time. My mother would spout off something so maddening I could understand his frustration."

"What was so maddening?"

"Her opinions about current events for instance. She'd always begin her comments with, 'They say.' And I'd usually jump in with, 'Who's they?' She'd just talk over me without answering or say, '*They* are the experts.' Like the time she said that science had proven 'Negroes' were of inferior intelligence to whites. When I challenged her reasoning, she said something like: 'Just listen to the way they talk! You can't understand one word.' Then she'd try to convince me that she wasn't prejudiced. They were nice people and shouldn't be treated badly but wouldn't want them in her neighborhood because 'they don't know how to take care of property, and as soon as they're allowed in, property values go down.' By this point in the conversation my dad would've disappeared. It took me years to realize that I could never engage in such topics with her."

"Fear and ignorance are usually the basis for such thinking. Your solution to not engage is a way of standing up for yourself, which is good."

"At the same time, though, I felt sorry for her because my dad and I, in spirit, were like a team, so she must've felt rejected by both of us."

"Since you felt safer with him, it's understandable that you'd take his side. You also may feel some guilt about these feelings toward your mother. Not being able to identify with her would explain why you have difficulty giving yourself as much as you deserve, or thinking you deserve as much as a man gets."

"I always thought a father's support was the most important for a girl's self-esteem."

"Without it, her life can be filled with self-doubt, that's true. It's important, but aligning with the mother, the same sex, provides a valuable basis for a daughter's place with the opposite sex. Without realizing it, you probably wanted your mother's approval as well."

"I think that's true even if I didn't think I did, but I always seemed to come up short."

"That would explain why you're drawn to what your mother would find acceptable for you. You're still trying to obtain her approval."

"I would think I'd have outgrown that by now."

"I see people in their sixties who're still hoping for their parents' approval."

A wave of self-pity came over Sylvia. The little girl in her, mouth turned down, trying not to cry, was praying not to feel so hurt for not getting it right. "Sixty? So how do I avoid that happening to me?"

"You've already begun by uncovering what's behind your own behavior. Stop to acknowledge what's going on inside. Honor your feelings because they're a precious part of you. Eventually you'll be able to accept them without letting them control you. You're already speaking up more for yourself with Anthony, aren't you?"

"I'm trying, but I have a hard time sticking with my decisions when it comes to him."

"You've agreed he's persistent. And he's a great rationalizer."

Was Irmeli trying to tell her something? Give her a psychological hint? Sylvia struggled to figure out the meaning behind it. *Rationalizer.* The harder she tried, the more elusive it became. A minute passed in silence. "I feel uncomfortable."

"Good. Try to sit with that feeling a little longer. Don't be afraid to live with your uncomfortable feelings until you discover what you want to do with them." Irmeli leaned forward in her chair. "And remember, it's not always up to you to make the peace."

Sylvia nodded, trying to absorb what Irmeli was saying, then risked feeling stupid and even more uncomfortable. "What's a rationalizer?"

"Someone who justifies his actions to make himself right."

"He blamed the economy when his house went into foreclosure," Sylvia said.

"That's a little different, but you have the idea. We call that externalization—blaming outside forces when things go wrong." Irmeli looked at the clock sitting on the table next to her chair. "We're running out of time I'm afraid. Let's go back to your immediate concern for the moment. Perhaps you want to decide if going to Europe is important enough that you'd use some of your own money."

"My parents have bought their tickets to come out here. Anthony's parents have paid for our plane tickets and hotels. It would be so complicated to bail out now. And I want to go. Very much."

"The last part is the most important. You want to go. If you used some of your money, would you still enjoy the trip? Or would you resent that it wasn't what you expected?"

"I don't know. I think I might be too vigilant about how we spend it."

"Would Anthony try to borrow the money from another source if you didn't use yours?"

"Maybe. But I do believe that he'd hold a grudge if he had to borrow it. Or maybe he'd try to charge everything on my bank card."

"That you *can* control."

"But if he did, I'd probably pay it off with my money anyway." By the end of the session, Sylvia was realizing that she wasn't as uncomfortable about the idea of using some of her money for their trip—it was the trip of her dreams. But she'd stand firm after that, and she'd never move the rest of her money out of Oregon. Whether Anthony liked it or not.

Irmeli was right; Sylvia already sensed that she was changing. When she came up so easily with a deadline for the relationship to work out, she realized it must've been on her mind awhile. And it felt good to say it. For the first time it dawned on her that in their relationship his happiness took precedence over hers. Every issue seemed to revolve around making sure he was happy. She wondered when that had changed. Or had it always been that way? It was time for her happiness and that of her children to come first. She didn't have all the specifics of what that might mean yet, but by uncovering what was going on inside she felt confident that she'd know what she'd need to do.

She was learning so much more about herself by looking more closely at her feelings during childhood. Inwardly she'd always been reserved, almost shy, like her father, who didn't seem to know how to share his feelings. Maybe he felt threatened by her mother's judgmental attitude, too. She recalled her mother badgering him to stand up more for himself in his work, because someone else had gotten a promotion instead of him. He was smarter and was the logical choice, but he didn't "speak up." The phrase rang in her ears. She could practically hear her mother saying it to him. She often tried to push him. It was a revelation to Sylvia to see them so differently. Even though it appeared he was treating her mother like she was invisible, maybe he was the one who'd felt criticized and rejected by her. So he dismissed her, acted resentful, and hid away, seeking solace in his trumpet playing, golf, and yard work. Sylvia considered the possibility that she herself might be hiding safely behind her children. Maybe the solace she was seeking she'd found only in them.

# CHAPTER 33

June 30, 1982

Sylvia was finally excited about their trip to Europe and withdrew fifteen hundred dollars from her savings. She emphasized to Anthony that this was the last time she'd dip into her nest egg. If she had to remind him again, so be it.

With the kids in tow, her parents drove them to the San Francisco airport. Steve was still asleep on the hide-a-bed in the living room when they left. As they approached the airport, a typical dense summer fog enveloped the terminal and runways.

"Sure hope it lifts in time for your flight," Matt said.

"They'd better not take off anyway," Vivian added.

Alice looked at her grammy. "They're not gonna do that! They have rules, you know."

Sylvia put her arm around her mom. "She's just concerned for our safety, honey." Since the session with Irmeli, Sylvia felt more compassion for her mother. If she treated her with more tenderness, who knows, with the trickle-down effect maybe her father would do the same. He was less brusque with her than he used to be, which Sylvia figured was due to the heartache they shared over Steve's illness. At least it hadn't driven them apart. Sylvia noticed that her mother had become more grounded and less concerned with superficialities over the intervening years. At any rate, she was more grateful than ever to have them here to look after her kids.

The flight took off on time, and soon they were on their way to New York to change planes for Rome.

Vivian had given her a leather-bound travel diary for her birthday. Sylvia promised herself to keep a detailed account of all the hotels, restaurants, and monuments during their month-long trip and hoped she'd stick with it. She even noted the movies they watched on the TWA flight out of New York, *You Oughta Be in Pictures* and *Absence of Malice*, then thought she was already overdoing it and they hadn't even arrived yet.

> 10:30 a.m.
>
> Arrived in Rome. Hot, cloudy w/patches of sun. In our pensione, St. Elisabetha, our room overlooks the Via Veneto. Anthony's parents came by around one and took us to a plush restaurant for lunch, Giorrosta Toscana. Most fabulous meal I can remember. Really expensive—$100 for four.
>
> We're on cloud nine—his parents are warm and gracious.

Walked to Piazza di Spagna then a five-hour nap. Woke up at 10:30 p.m. and went to the Fontana di Trevi, had pizza at a "bar" and a gelato, just sat and people-watched. Loved how crowded it was so late at night.
It feels like we don't have a care in the world.

July 1
Up at 5:30. Jogged in the Villa Borghese, then breakfast. Took a bus to the Vatican, then Piazza Venezia but got off too soon, which turned out terrific because we walked side streets. Vendors everywhere. Bought lunch provisions and had a picnic. Anthony bought me a beautiful white eyelet sundress. (Or did I really buy it?)

July 3
Took 8:15 a.m. train to Grossetto on the Italian Riviera. Anthony Sr. picked us up. Drove to Hotel Roccamare where Sophia Loren and Ponti have a cottage. Our own huge room and bath w/view of sea. Went to beach.
Franca was topless! She's thin but wrinkled and has big boobs. All the women were topless—didn't know what to do—kept my bikini on.
Elegant buffet on terrace for dinner. His parents are so easy I feel right at home—I'm not even uncomfortable about his not being divorced. Maybe they've adopted a European attitude. Maybe it's way too soon.

July 4

> Four of us drove to Pisa. Got woozy climbing the tower.
>
> So impressive. Leans way more than I expected. Anthony and I are having fun trying to speak Italian with my Berlitz book. His dad is fluent, so he helps us. Can see how much Anthony resembles his dad—charmingly cool, gregarious. Mom more reserved but has nice sense of humor. We have a lot of laughs.

The next morning Sylvia noticed that her new Canon camera was missing, a birthday gift from Anthony for the trip. She'd left it hanging on the back of her chair at dinner in the restaurant of the hotel the night before. When she mentioned it to Anthony Sr. at breakfast, Sylvia shuddered at his sudden reaction. His face blushed deep crimson. With fists clenched he bellowed that he wouldn't stand for such treatment. He threw his napkin down on his plate full of scrambled eggs and jumped out of his seat. "I'll get to the bottom of this." Waiters clambered to his side, but he waved them off as he stormed out.

As they sat in the gentility of this seaside patio surrounded by flowering trees, soft breezes, and sterling coffeepots, Sylvia didn't have the courage to look around for other people's reactions. The clink of silverware on plates and the other diners speaking in hushed tones seemed to heighten the awkward silence at their table.

Anthony shook his head. "You never should've told him."

Franca shot Anthony a glance. "You don't know how it is here. Your father's right. You can't let them get away with stealing, especially in a place like this."

How could Franca so calmly defend her husband's behavior? Was she immune to his outbursts?

Ten minutes passed before Anthony's father came back with the hotel manager, who wanted to know exactly the type of camera and where they'd been sitting to determine who'd been their waiters. He anxiously promised over and over that he'd find the thief. He assured them he'd get in touch with them since they were leaving that morning.

The way the other waiters glanced nervously in their direction made Sylvia nervous, too. She could see that Anthony's father had influence, but that's not what made her uneasy. As they halfheartedly tried to go back to their breakfast, Anthony Sr. easily returned to his gregarious conversation like nothing had happened. No apology, no comment—as Franca had pointed out, in his eyes the theft warranted his reaction. Sylvia thought of the adage about the oak tree and its acorn. No wonder his son took charge, demanded that everyone fall in line, and justified his actions.

The four of them had traveled six days together without a hitch, not counting the camera mishap, from Grossetto to Venice to Ancona, where they boarded a small cruise ship for the two-day trip to Piraeus, Greece. Cruising on the Adriatic Sea, Anthony was demonstrative toward Sylvia, even around his parents. He openly kissed her on the forehead or bare shoulder and held her hand or put his arm around her wherever they walked and when they sat next to each other. Anthony Sr. chuckled to Franca about the two lovebirds and would tease them from time to time. As they basked in the sun on the deck of the ship, he said how happy it made him to see his son so happy and leaned over, took Sylvia's face in his hands, and said, "*Bella facia.*" While she enjoyed his good-natured, open show of affection, she'd seen what was lying underneath. His happy-go-lucky demeanor lasted only until someone crossed him or didn't follow his rules.

And hadn't she seen the same thing in Anthony? Sylvia couldn't deny she was enjoying his attention and responded in kind, but too much had happened between them for her to believe that this meant anything more than what it was—a romantic display. Perhaps it was for his parents' benefit, to show them how good they were together, to prove his life with Sylvia made giving up his children worthwhile. The spectacle was natural to him because that's who he was, good in public as the affectionate, easygoing, convivial guy until they got somewhere alone. Then he'd often let her know how unhappy he was with something she'd done or said.

At home he expected his rules to be followed to the letter. Eight o'clock bedtime meant just that—with a look of disgust he had tossed his watch into her lap one night after she'd finished putting Trevor to bed at eight fifteen. Her insides had frozen. Food on a plate had to be finished—he filled Trevor's plate and made him sit at the table until he ate all of it. When Sylvia tried to object, she saw the flash of anger in his eyes that she'd seen in the hotel room so long ago and didn't want to risk his possibly taking it out on Trevor. When she refused to get an attorney to garner Tom's wages for back child support, Anthony didn't come home for two days. He never explained or apologized, and Sylvia had never told anyone.

She didn't doubt that he wanted to spend his life with her, as long as he could dictate the terms and badger her into compliance. He'd expect her to go along like she always had, but that was no longer possible for her. Here in an exotic climate she could play the docile partner in love. Because she could imagine what was ahead as soon as they went back home to reality, she carried no illusions about this romantic interlude.

They arrived in Athens late the next night where Anthony's parents had a spacious, antique-appointed penthouse. It was breathlessly hot and difficult to sleep, but Franca had big sightseeing plans for them the next day. Sylvia would've almost preferred to stay inside with the extreme heat and dusty, smoggy conditions of the city where it seemed few places were air-conditioned. But Franca was a real trooper and insisted. Anthony Sr. was back at work in downtown Athens, so the three of them spent the next two days touring the city—to Lycabettus, the highest point in the city (fortunately by taxi); the Kolonaki (old town); lunch in the Plaka; the Pantheon; the Parthenon temple on the Acropolis—and the third day at Marathon Bay when Anthony Sr. joined them.

Each day they'd end up at his office, where they basked in the coolness of the air-conditioned rooms. Each night they'd dine no earlier than nine and stay out until two in the morning at a nightclub or outdoor café. Sylvia was amazed at their stamina and at how much they drank—she could barely keep up. But they were having a ball together, and she was enjoying their company. At dinner the night before she and Anthony were leaving for their four-day island cruise, his parents' surprise for them. She was really going on an exotic cruise, an even better one than *The Love Boat*. Then his dad told Sylvia he had another surprise for her.

"My *bella facia*, see what I have for you!" With great fanfare he made her close her eyes.

When she opened them, there was her stolen camera. She gasped.

"It arrived at my office today. And just in time for your cruise."

Sylvia thanked him then got up and kissed him on the cheek. As she sat back down, Anthony mumbled under his breath for her ears only, "I hope no one lost a finger on that one."

After dinner Sylvia said she wanted to call home. She'd talked to her kids twice from Italy and once from Athens. She wanted to be sure to reach them before the cruise, because she wouldn't be able to call for five days. Vivian answered and sounded cheery but out of breath.

"Sylvia! Let me get the kids. They're in the pool. Everything going well?"

"Fantastic," Sylvia said. "How's everything there?"

"We're having such a ball with them. And we're going to see Scott and Amanda tomorrow. We'll take the kids to SeaWorld and the zoo."

"That's so great, Mom. How's Steve doing?"

"He seems to be enjoying himself. Takes his meds and is sleeping less. He walks to town every day for his iced tea."

Sylvia laughed. "He found another hangout, huh?" She heard voices in the background that she couldn't make out. "Is somebody there?"

"Why, yes. Tom's here. With Betsy and their son. She's sure no looker—doesn't hold a candle to you–"

"What?" Sylvia faltered. She couldn't picture them wandering through her home. *With my parents!* "What are they doing there?"

"Tom had a business trip, so they all decided to come. We said 'sure.' The kids are thrilled to see him, of course. Even Steve was happy to see him. Tom was always so wonderful to Steve. They're just here for the day. Tom's going to barbecue some chicken here tonight." Vivian called Alice and Trevor to come to the phone. "It's your mom! Calling from Greece!"

Somehow Sylvia didn't want to talk to her kids anymore and hear all about how much fun they were having with their dad at her house with her parents. Even though it was the best thing for her kids, she felt like Tom and his family were invading her privacy.

"Mommy! I miss you." Trevor's little voice made her want to cry. "What's a 'greese'?"

Trevor always made her laugh. "It's a place, honey. I miss you so much."

"How many days 'til you come home?" he asked.

"About two weeks, but you're having fun with Grammy and Granddad, aren't you?"

"Yes! And we're going to see Shamu the whale tomorrow. And Daddy's here. We've been swimming all afternoon."

"That's a nice surprise, I bet. Is Alice nearby?"

"Alice! It's Mommy!"

Her dad came to the phone and said Alice was still in the pool with Tom. So Sylvia told him to tell her she loved her and missed her and wouldn't be able to call for about five days. He asked her all about the ruins in Athens. When she told him how hot it was, he said he'd never be able to stand it.

"But I'd sure like to see that part of the world someday. I always thought Egypt would be fascinating, too," he said. "Sounds pretty terrific for you."

Sylvia felt so sad all of a sudden. She wanted to be able to travel somewhere exotic with her parents. Take them on a trip. They'd never even been to Europe.

When she hung up, she collected herself but wondered if she should tell Anthony about Tom being there. *No more hiding*, she thought. She went back to the living room, where Anthony and his parents were having after-dinner drinks. Sylvia matter-of-factly told them all what was going on at home.

"Now that's how a divorce should be," Franca said.

"It's civilized," Anthony Sr. chimed in. "Why shouldn't everyone get along? They're his children and their grandchildren!"

"Jane is insane to carry on the way she has," Franca said. "It's terrible what she's doing to those gorgeous children of yours, Nat."

"Nat?" Sylvia asked.

"That's my nickname because I couldn't say my whole name when I was little," Anthony said.

"You should be going after her with your attorney. Not letting you see your own children must be illegal," Franca said.

Anthony seemed tense. "Mom, I'm doing what I can."

"If you need money to fight her, just ask me," his dad said.

"I don't need your money," Anthony said.

Sylvia looked at him directly as if to disagree. If his parents wanted to help him, why not let them?

"Do you know Jane's returned every gift we've sent the children? She's sent them all the way back here!" Franca was beginning to slur her words.

Sylvia was shocked Jane would do such a thing, although her disturbing phone calls after she found out about their affair proved her capable of such bizarre behavior. But why would she punish the grandparents? Anthony said he was sorry they were being hurt by his divorce, too, but to trust that he was doing everything he could. They said their good-nights, and he ushered Sylvia to their sweltering room. Sylvia felt sticky from the thin layer of sweat covering her body and stood directly in front of the fan in the dark.

"I'll be glad to be alone with you again on our cruise." Anthony began slowly undressing her while kissing her neck, shoulders, and back.

Since they'd been alone very little thus far, Sylvia wanted to make love as much as he did. Knowing they'd have the next four days together though, their lovemaking could wait. "I need to talk to you about what was just said in there."

"Let's not ruin this."

Sylvia moved away from him, but he caught her arm, pushed her onto the bed, and fell on top of her. She lay naked from the waist up. He held both of her arms down as he buried his face in her breasts, playfully licking her nipples. She felt his erection and tried to squirm away.

"I mean it," she said. "I don't want to do this right now. We need to talk."

"It can wait," he said breathlessly.

"No, it can't." She twisted her body away from him, managing to get onto her left side.

"What the hell?" he said as he rolled off and lay facing her backside. "I won't talk about my parents when they're in the next room."

*But having sex wouldn't be a problem?* "I don't mean your parents. I mean Jane."

"Christ, Sylvia, what about her?"

She sat up. "Did something else happen with her or your kids that you haven't told me?"

"I've told you everything." He grabbed a pillow and threw it hard across the room.

She flinched.

"What do you want from me?" he demanded.

"The truth! Why would Jane send all those gifts back if she didn't have a reason?"

"You said yourself she was half hysterical. And even Jessica told you she might be crazy enough to shoot you or us or something that nutty. Remember? So why would this sound so out of reach? Mailing back gifts to exile my whole family because I left her fits the profile. At least it's better than shooting us."

What he said made sense for someone with Jane's frame of mind. But had he done something else that drove her to it? Now that she had a clearer picture of Anthony's controlling behavior, she presumed he'd behaved the same way with Jane. After years of trying to please him or keep his moods from spiraling out of control, only to have him leave her for someone else, her boiling point probably hit with a vengeance. Sylvia usually placed fault with the woman, rarely the man; just as she'd always stood by her own father as if he were blameless. Maybe she'd misjudged her mother and was doing the same thing with Jane.

Anthony got undressed in the dark and threw his clothes over a chair. He sighed and sat back down at the edge of the bed. “The point is she wants to hurt anyone connected to me, even at her kids’ expense. And you know how she always hated my mother and never felt accepted by her. Maybe that’s part of it.”

Sylvia got up and took her dress all the way off. “I wonder how long a person can stay this angry.” She was suddenly exhausted and didn’t want to talk anymore.

“Even if she stays mad for the rest of her life, we can’t let it stand between us.” He reached for her. Her fatigue gave way to desire, and naked, she willingly straddled his lap. “And I want you to start trusting me,” he said.

The magic of the Greek islands was introduced to Sylvia at their first stop, Mykonos. She could’ve stayed there for weeks. The quaint whitewashed houses, tiny shops with original handmade items, and the famous windmills enthralled her. They had a drink in an open-air bar-restaurant that sat at the water’s edge. There was a soft breeze, and as the sun was setting, Sylvia couldn’t imagine a more romantic place in the world. And right now, she couldn’t imagine being with anyone else but him.

The islands were sheer enchantment: from Mykonos to Ephesus, Turkey, then Rhodes, Crete, and finally Santorini. They rode donkeys up the six hundred steps to the top of the volcanic island, which turned out to be terrifying for Sylvia. The animal kept bumping against the low stone wall where the steep, rocky precipice dropped to the water. She really thought she was going to fall. By the time they reached the top, she could barely relax enough to enjoy it.

The last ten days of their trip would begin in Nice, France, and continue northward as they drove to Paris. Before they left Greece they had two more days with Anthony's parents. Sylvia almost hated to leave them. With his parents around Anthony was on his best behavior and, of course, they didn't have to think about money; with the trip winding down she feared Anthony would become more moody. During cocktail hour on their last night, Franca brought up the divorce again. "Why is it taking so long?"

Anthony patiently explained the circumstances without telling them about the bankruptcy.

Franca took another big sip of her Manhattan. She repeated as if for the first time how it wasn't right he couldn't see his kids, that Jane was nuts and had returned their gifts.

"She's just angry and wants to get back at him. She'll get over it." Anthony Sr. put his arm around his wife and pulled her to him. Comfortingly he said, "Give her time, Franca."

"Can we stop talking about this?" Anthony asked.

"We're just happy you and Sylvia have found each other. And a word of advice that we practice ourselves, always have: Never go to bed angry. Now how about a toast to your future and off to dinner?" His dad raised his glass, and they did, too.

That night they joined another couple at a taverna commonly referred to as a Bazooki. After the meal, singers came out on stage to perform. Waiters came by the tables asking the guests if they wanted to purchase flowers and plates. If the audience liked the performance they threw flowers—if they *loved* the performance they tossed stacks of dinner plates right on the stage. Anthony Sr. bought a stack of ten for each of them. Sylvia thought it was the craziest thing she'd ever seen and threw plates with abandon. Afterwards there was a pile of broken china lying all over the stage. They left around two in the morning and were off to France by late the next afternoon.

*****

July 18, 1982

As it turned out, the French portion of their trip was not paid for by his parents, other than the flight from Greece. Anthony Sr. made the hotel and rental car arrangements for Nice and Paris, but Sylvia and Anthony would have to pay for it. Sylvia had learned about it on their flight to Nice.

"Why didn't you tell me before we left the States?" she asked. "We could've cancelled."

"To be in Europe and you not go to France? You must be joking," he said. "I couldn't live with myself or you."

By not telling her before they'd left on their trip, though, he was deciding for her again—from his job change and move to the divorce setbacks, his financial debt and bankruptcy. This time, however, it seemed like he had deliberately set her up. "I appreciate your wanting that for me, but when you purposely leave me out of the decision, and it concerns my money, I feel used."

"You're making a mountain out of nothing. Besides, I didn't know before we left home."

But he was contradicting himself. "So when did you find out?" she asked.

"What difference does it make *when* I knew?"

The stewardess interrupted by asking if they wanted something to drink. Anthony ordered two glasses of complimentary Bordeaux.

"You didn't even ask me what I wanted to drink," Sylvia said.

"You just won't quit." He took out his cigarettes, and with eyebrows raised, he dramatically offered the pack cradled in the palms of both hands.

"Thank you for asking." She took one, and he lit hers first. "Anyway, I think you knew all along. That's why you insisted I use my money."

"Think what you like," he said dismissively.

"Was it that you didn't want to admit to your dad that you'd have to check with me first?" It would always be like this with him. "It looks like you lied to me again."

"Cut the drama, Sylvia. Since we couldn't change the date of our flights out of Paris, there was nothing to be done.

We can't do anything about it now, so let's just try to enjoy ourselves."

He was always talking in circles around her. All she could hear was Irmeli saying he was a great rationalizer. As she sat quietly fuming, she also heard Irmeli saying that she owed it to herself to have a good time. After all, she was paying for it! And spending fifteen hundred dollars to be back in France wouldn't put her in the poorhouse. She had to try to make the trip worth every penny. By the time they landed, she was almost enthusiastic again.

During the first few days on French soil Sylvia struggled to make herself understood or to understand what the natives in their rapid-fire execution were trying to explain to her. She'd expected to have problems initially. What she hadn't anticipated was Anthony's irritation with her efforts.

The first morning she tried to get directions to the Chagall Museum from their hotel concierge. Anthony stood off to one side pouting like a child who wasn't chosen to play on the team. When she asked what was wrong, he replied, "I thought this was your second language. At this rate it'll take all morning to find out what we need to know."

"So, without your parents to take care of us you're going to take it out on me?"

The concierge stared at them, shrugging with his whole upper body.

"If you just spoke English, we'd be on our way by now," Anthony said.

Having the opportunity to speak French again with natives while in their country was something she'd waited years to do. And it was all on her dime. She'd have a good time with or without him. "If this is how you're going to act, I'll go by myself." Sylvia turned on her heels and left him standing in the lobby.

When they tried sunbathing, Sylvia found the stony pebbled sand beaches disappointing after the pristine velvety ones in Greece. Not only was the beach uncomfortable, it was too crowded.

It was more than her struggle with the language that was bothering Anthony. He was also unhappy adjusting to the accommodations. He wasn't used to a one-star hotel like L'Oasis, where the bathroom was down the hall, and after two days of living on a budget, his spirits hadn't lifted much. It was as if he was personally insulted that they had to pay attention to price, while Sylvia thought it could be romantic or even fun to 'live on the cheap' with picnic lunches and drives through the countryside. At least that was the atmosphere she tried to create.

With the excellence of French cuisine, the most modest café was never disappointing. For lunch they could have *salade niçoise* or *omelette provençale* for only sixty francs—at 6.67 francs to the dollar, it cost nine dollars for both of them. They stuck to the *prix fixe* menu for dinner. Simple, regional fare in bistros or brasseries situated on the cobblestone side streets in historic old town provided dishes like bouillabaisse and coq au vin at bargain prices. With Italy practically next door, pizza or pasta such as ravioli *aux artichauts* was plentiful. After weeks of lamb souvlaki in Greece, French food was welcome relief.

Along with Sylvia's French, Anthony's mood began to improve, although she didn't directly link the two. She liked to think that her upbeat attitude about how happy she was to be back in France was infectious. But the great food and frequent sex were probably the real reasons.

He playfully took a croissant at breakfast one morning and teasingly tore it apart, slowly feeding it to her piece by piece. "One for you. One for me." She closed her eyes and groaned with satisfaction as the last buttery, flaky morsel melted in her mouth; he said this called for more than food and led her back up to their room. At last they were making love again with abandon, sometimes outdoors in quiet seclusion, sometimes in their room twice a day. Sylvia was aware that sex always played a large part, if not the most important part, in their relationship; from the beginning it was the cement that held them together. Since she'd never experienced such passion before, she didn't want to admit the power their sex life might still hold on her at this stage in their relationship; nor did she want it to override the importance for her need to have a mutually respectful partnership, which was paramount. But passion by its very nature wasn't reasonable or sensible or rational, and in a weak moment, their renewed intimacy led her to hope their bond was restored to what she thought they once had. Simply put, she wanted to believe in him again, if even for a little while. Being in France only accentuated her fantasy.

Their last afternoon they drove their Renault 5 east along the Riviera with a lunch of bread, wine, and cheese and perched themselves on a *corniche* overlooking the Mediterranean near the resort town of Cap Ferrat. Winding their way through other resort towns such as Villefranche-sur-mer and Beaulieu, Anthony saw how close they were to Monaco. “Let’s dress up and come back tonight to play blackjack,” he said.

Warning flags went up for her. First of all, what the hell was he thinking when they were practically counting *centimes*? And secondly, he might have to rely on her French, and she knew nothing about gambling terminology—a lethal combination with his mercurial moods. “Maybe we should hold off. We don’t need to gamble to have fun tonight.”

“If we promise to play with, say, forty dollars, we won’t go broke,” he said laughingly. “C’mon, Syl, remember how much fun we had in Tahoe?”

She did remember. He had taught her how to play blackjack. She’d sat for four hours nursing twenty dollars and always came out ahead. It *was* their last night in Nice. She was tired of analyzing his every word and her every action. And he’d been so loving. She didn’t want him to hold it against her if she said no. What was wrong with just having a little fun? So she agreed.

The atmosphere in the main casino was like something out of a James Bond movie. Just approaching the tables made her nervous, but Anthony moved right in like he'd been doing this for years. She liked watching him—his cosmopolitan demeanor exuded confidence, and he moved through the surroundings as if in his element. It reminded Sylvia of the man she fell in love with, and she was excited to be there with him. The minimum bet was a whopping five dollars—enough for two bottles of table wine. She'd never played a hand for anything above two dollars. As it turned out, the game of blackjack needed no translation, and after three hours they came back one hundred and fifty dollars richer. He called her his "lady luck." And she desperately wanted to believe him, to believe that their own luck was changing.

They pulled out of Nice early the next morning and headed north toward Grenoble, where Sylvia had lived as a student, and the town of Annecy, whose lake that nestled in a glaciated valley, was referred to as the "Pearl of the Alps." During her student days this was the region she recalled with the most fondness, and in particular, the village of Talloires, where she'd stayed with a group of students on one of their designated weekend excursions. Ironically, the *San Francisco Chronicle* had written an article in the travel section a month before their trip highlighting Talloires and L'Auberge du Père Bise, a hotel and three-star restaurant located on the lake of Annecy. That was where she wanted to stay but hadn't imagined they could afford it, until now.

En route they stopped at a PTT and telephoned the L'Auberge. They reserved the only room left, a fortune at five hundred francs, seventy-five dollars a night. With their winnings at the blackjack table they decided to live it up. Anthony was happy again, singing expansively, even when, due to a forest fire, they had to detour one hundred kilometers out of their way through a treacherous one-lane alpine road. After her experience in Santorini, she couldn't bear to look down as they climbed higher and higher through tighter and tighter hairpin turns. She prayed they wouldn't come upon a vehicle approaching from the opposite direction. Two nerve-racking hours later they were back on flat terrain and ready for lakeside comfort.

They passed quickly through Grenoble. With all the new *autoroutes* Sylvia didn't recognize a thing and didn't care to stop in the intense summer heat. When they reached Annecy by late afternoon, it was overrun with camera-toting tourists and adolescents congregating on side streets with portable radios that blasted competing loud music. She had a hard time absorbing the changes she saw. The charm of the ancient pedestrian bridges that spanned its numerous canals was lost in the pandemonium. All she wanted to do was get to Talloires, six miles away. The critique she'd read in the *Chronicle* assured her that nothing had changed there.

The L'Auberge, situated on Lac d'Annecy, with its grassy lawn stretching to the water's edge, was a paradise to behold. One night was surely not going to be long enough.

They wanted to spend a few days here and cut Paris shorter. The following morning their concierge found a room next door at the seventeenth-century L'Abbaye for forty-five dollars a night, which seemed like a bargain. They stayed two more nights, and Sylvia was in heaven. Frolicking here by the lake in luxurious style suited them well, and Anthony was the happiest she'd seen him since their arrival in France.

Her French was vastly improving, though complicated menus still gave her trouble. And when she mistakenly led Anthony to believe he was ordering veal one night when he was ordering kidneys, she realized underneath how worried she still was that he'd be angry with her when he found out, *if* he found out. She was trying to concentrate on her own happiness, but with such a moody, easily annoyed partner, she saw how difficult it could be. When he behaved unreasonably, she always reacted as if she was responsible, or she tried to control his testiness by avoiding a situation that might upset him, censoring her own feelings. But it took situations like this to come to grips with what she was feeling and to "sit with the uncomfortable feelings and then decide what to do about them."

The last leg of their trip was their drive to Paris, where they'd stay in another one-star hotel. It was only for two nights. She figured she could handle just about anything for two nights, even his downward-spiraling mood, which she'd come to expect as a foregone conclusion.

Indeed Paris was a disaster, but in so many unexpected ways. With no place to park their rental car, Anthony straddled it on the sidewalk and street, like so many other cars, by their hotel in Montmartre, a three-floor walkup with no air-conditioning and the bathroom down the hall. The next morning they found all the car windows smashed and a ticket on the windshield. According to Anthony, she should've been able to read the parking signs, so he wasn't speaking to her. She was feeling as damaged as the little car. To make matters worse, it was up to her to settle matters at the police station. They took buses and metros to reach the station, which took most of a morning. They sat for an hour in a crowded waiting area until Sylvia begged to be heard by fabricating their case, saying that they might miss a flight if the *commissaire* couldn't speak to them right away. To her relief it worked. He took pity on them and tore up the four-hundred-franc parking ticket; he also provided a police report for insurance on the car damage, which would have to be settled through the car rental agency. Since Anthony's dad had made the arrangements, he told them not to worry. He'd handle it from his end.

For their last breakfast in Paris, Sylvia and Anthony sat at a sidewalk café and ordered café au lait and two chocolate croissants. When Anthony took it for granted that she should order his coffee the way he liked it, watered down, she refused. Throughout most of their trip in France she'd tried to make everything all right for him: whether it was finding restaurants they could afford, ordering his food, asking for directions, calculating their francs, or settling with the *commissaire*. But nothing would ever be all right for him. "Order your own coffee. I'm not taking the blame anymore for something that has nothing to do with me." He wasn't happy. And she didn't care.

# CHAPTER 34

October 15, 1982

The September deadline had come and gone. For the past two months Sylvia had been playing a charade, acting as if her feelings for Anthony hadn't changed, that all would go on as before, when the whole time she'd been trying to mentally formulate a plan to leave him. So many things had bothered her about him for so many months she had expected to come to the realization on her own that the relationship was really over. When it did come, the suddenness made her realize that she'd been avoiding the inevitable. What made her sad was it took her son's unhappiness to make her wake up.

*****

In mid-August Trevor sat at the kitchen table after he'd come home from playing at a friend's house, while Sylvia fixed him an afternoon snack of apple juice and "cinnamon" toast. The "cinnamon" was equal amounts of sugar and cinnamon dusted on buttered toast. His calves dangled from the chair seat, the toes of his tennis shoes barely brushing the floor. She set the juice in front of him. With his elbow on the table, his head was tilted, resting in his hand. A wisp of wavy blond hair fell across his knitted brow as he glanced up at her. With a defeated expression, he asked, "Why doesn't Anthony like me?"

No particular incident had prompted his question, and Sylvia felt heartsick in its honesty, which begged for an answer. She had to face what Trevor put into words so simply. There was no point in asking him why he thought that or what was said to make him feel that way—that would seem like he had to defend his question with proof. And why should he when all along she'd seen enough examples of Anthony's slights and criticisms herself?

The straightforward innocence of his question pushed Sylvia right off the fence. No more straddling both sides, trusting that more time or more therapy could make their family unit work. It never mattered whether he liked Trevor or not. What mattered was how Trevor felt around Anthony. A situation where her son's self-worth was at risk was no longer acceptable. She had to make a plan and soon. At that moment, though, her son needed an answer.

She knelt beside him and put her hands on his shoulders, looking at him earnestly. "Honey, believe me when I tell you there's nothing about *you* that makes Anthony behave the way he does sometimes." But she wanted more convincing ammunition. "He didn't get along with Ricky, his own son, either."

Trevor nodded solemnly, and since Sylvia couldn't give him more of an answer than that, she relied on diversion, and took him to town for an ice cream.

There was some relief in finally deciding on a direction, but she had a lot of questions to answer before she'd let Anthony know that she saw no future for them anymore. Foremost, she wondered how long it might take living in these circumstances for Trevor to incur any possible long-term emotional scars. She didn't want to make any rash moves—she'd made enough of those already—so at the end of August she sought Irmeli's guidance.

"The two of you should come in together to discuss how you want to proceed. In order to handle the split in a mature fashion, that is, without any extreme emotional reactions, there should be a specific plan."

Sylvia flinched inside at the image of the two of them sitting there when she told him. "I suppose you're right. I don't know how he'll react."

Irmeli added, "Of course, the children's welfare must come first." She went on to say that Trevor shouldn't be left with any deep-seated problems if Sylvia moved on by the end of the year, but she wouldn't recommend letting it get beyond that. She also helped Sylvia address the various options to consider. Would she stay in Los Altos to keep the kids in the same school? If so, she'd need a better paying job unless Anthony helped out, which Sylvia assumed wouldn't happen. Or would she return to Oregon so the kids could be near their dad? It was too late to get a teaching job for the current school year. And no matter where she went she needed to find a place to live.

By the time the kids started school, the dizzying array of options made Sylvia feel like she was in quicksand up to her knees and sinking fast.

Alice, now in sixth grade, seemed happier in school than Sylvia could ever recall. It pained her to think of pulling her out and moving her again. The teachers loved her; she had many friends, was involved with activities after school, and was still getting along well with Anthony. She might want to go back to Oregon to be near her dad, but she was fairly confident that Alice wouldn't look forward to going back to school in Lakeside. Thinking of Alice, Sylvia seriously considered trying to stay in Los Altos. For Trevor, the school situation was a different matter.

In June, at the end of the school year, Anthony had argued with Sylvia about the kindergarten teacher's recommendation that Trevor be held back. He had insisted that Trevor needed to learn basic skills, like reading and arithmetic, that he wouldn't get spending another year in this kindergarten. They played and sang and didn't attempt to teach reading or even how to write their names. Sylvia didn't think Trevor was ready to move on, but thought Anthony had a point. His teacher was more playtime-oriented. They talked with the first-grade teachers and then went to Irmeli to help sort it all out. The final decision was made. Trevor moved up to first grade, which made him pretty happy, and, of course, had made Anthony happy, too. Sylvia still had reservations since Trevor was the youngest in his class.

Now in first grade, Trevor was lost in the crowd, literally; there were almost thirty children in his class. He was behind from the outset; all the other children knew how to read and do basic arithmetic. Not only was his self-esteem in jeopardy at home, he had only his social skills at school to rely on to help fill in any gaps. He was well-liked and that counted for a lot, but he was beginning his school experience feeling "dumb," in the lowest reading group, the lowest math, and would need remedial help. Evenings at home were becoming more tense and tearful because Trevor didn't know how to tackle his homework. Sylvia sat with him to explain it, but his frustration often ended with an exasperated, "I'm never going to get this!" and his abrupt departure.

*****

Sylvia woke up most mornings with a feeling of dread. It was already October, and she didn't seem to have enough energy to get through a day, much less make a life plan for herself and her children. She wondered what had happened to her conviction and courage, but mostly she wondered what it would take for her to finally get on with it. She hadn't even made an appointment with Irmeli to tell Anthony what she'd decided about their future, or rather the lack of one. As the days dragged on she continued to hide her turmoil, counting the number of days she had until the end of the year.

When Alice asked if she could have her first boy-girl party, Anthony was enthusiastic for her and suggested that she have a Halloween party where everyone dressed in costumes. The two of them planned most of the activities for the party: contests for costumes, bobbing for apples, pass the orange, guess the number of candy corns in a jar, a few word games, and maybe dancing. Alice wasn't sure anyone would want to dance. She and her mom would decide what food and decorations to have.

About four days before the party, Anthony suggested that Trevor go to a friend's house during the party, and then return home afterwards. Sylvia was shocked at the idea.

"Why should he have to leave home?"

"Little brothers are just annoying to have around at Alice's age," he said. "It's not fair to her."

"Where would you ever get that idea? Alice wouldn't care at all." Sylvia was emptying bags from the grocery store. She was getting upset and put the fresh green beans in the pantry.

Anthony reached in and took them out. "Don't these go in the frig?" He chuckled and asked her what was bothering her so much.

"I think it makes Trevor feel like you don't want him around. He's having a hard time right now, and being excluded from the fun here isn't fair to him."

"Well, I think you're making this a little bigger than it needs to be. He'd be home by nine. He'd have more fun at Jarrod's house anyway. What does he want with a bunch of preteens giggling and running around whispering secrets to each other?"

"Families should participate in all occasions together. He shouldn't be left out," Sylvia said.

"And Alice *does* mind if he's there."

Sylvia turned around with a Campbell's Tomato Soup can in each hand. "You asked her?"

"Yes, and she said she'd like it better if he wasn't 'spying' on her and her friends."

Sylvia didn't think it sounded like Alice to say that. Anthony may have talked her into it, although she couldn't imagine why he would. She said she'd think about it and talk to Alice.

Anthony took the soup cans out of her hands and put them away. "Let Alice have her night. I don't think we should wait to talk to Alice and ask Trevor—there won't be enough time. That seems only fair to Trevor."

Trevor walked into the kitchen. "Ask me what?"

Playing the loving father, Anthony picked him up with a big grin and asked Trevor right then which friend he'd want to spend the evening with Friday.

"I thought you needed me to be here," he said. "To help with Alice's party."

Sylvia was livid. Anthony was going to make this happen no matter what she thought. "We could use your help, sweetie. Let's go talk to Alice about this." She didn't look at

Anthony's face as she led Trevor down the hall to Alice's room. He followed them.

She knocked briefly on Alice's door and opened it. They all walked in. "Trevor wants to know if you need him to help with your party, honey," Sylvia said.

Alice, seated at her desk, looked up from her homework. She looked at Anthony and back at her mom. "Let me talk to Trevor alone."

Sylvia pulled the door shut and turned to Anthony saying they needed to talk. He followed her into their bedroom, and she closed the door behind him. "You didn't even wait for my answer. You do this over and over again, and I can't live this way anymore. We need to see Irmeli as soon as possible."

"Christ, here we go with the drama. One evening at a friend's and your precious Trevor is damaged for life. He's a momma's boy, and you're not helping him."

"I don't care what you think, and I'm sick of you judging me," she said.

There was a knock at their door. Sylvia opened it. Alice had her arm around her brother, and they were smiling. "Trevor wants to go to Jarrod's, and I promised him a big piece of cake when he gets home. *And* a swim in the pool with me and Julie afterwards, when it's dark!" Alice's friend Julie was staying overnight after the party. With that she tickled Trevor, and the two of them scuttled down the hall toward the kitchen with a screech and a holler.

Sylvia stood there with a blank expression. "I guess they worked it out themselves."

"Alice knows how to handle him better than his own mother."

The night of the party Anthony dropped Trevor off at Jarrod's after the majority of Alice's friends had arrived because he wanted to wait to see their costumes. Jarrod's parents would bring him back around nine thirty or ten. Alice looked fabulous dressed as a skeleton; she drew the bones with white glow paint on black tights and a long-sleeved black T-shirt. About fifteen kids came, and as much as Sylvia and Anthony tried to maintain some order, the house turned into mayhem. The kids played a few games, but mostly they hung out around the pool, talking the night away, while Anthony grilled hamburgers and hot dogs for their dinner. Only once did Sylvia need to break up a boy and girl standing off in the corner of the backyard kissing.

By nine thirty, most of the kids were finishing cake and ice cream, but by ten most of them had been picked up by their parents. A few stragglers waited with Alice outside on the front stoop. The party was over. Sylvia was about to call Jarrod's house when Trevor walked into the living room with Jarrod's mom. They chatted briefly and said their good-nights.

"Do I get my piece of cake?" Trevor asked eagerly.

Before Sylvia could answer "You bet," Anthony appeared, telling him that it was too late now. In his phony singsong tone, he said, "Wow. It's ten thirty already! Let's get you upstairs to bed."

"We promised him. That's not fair." Sylvia guided Trevor to the kitchen.

Anthony trailed behind them. "We said he could have cake if he was home at nine thirty, not ten thirty."

Sylvia put her arm around Trevor and steered him to a chair to sit down. She cut a piece of cake, put it on a plate, placed it in front of him, and handed him a fork.

Anthony stepped closer to her, his hands on his hips. "What the hell do you think you're doing?"

"He's getting what was promised whether you like it or not!" She glanced in the direction of the living room, worried that Alice or her friends might be within earshot.

Anthony was trembling with rage. His fists clenched and unclenched, and for a split second, Sylvia thought he was going to hit her. She picked Trevor up and sat down with him in her lap, quietly protecting him. He stared down at his cake, tears slowly rolling down his cheeks. Behind her she heard the familiar grinding and tap water running, as Anthony was angrily shoving the rest of the cake down the disposal. A hollow fear gripped her insides. Trevor couldn't eat, so she took his hand and they walked to his room, where she stayed with him the rest of the night.

# CHAPTER 35

The Next Morning

Sylvia carefully eased out of Trevor's bed so she wouldn't wake him. One subtle movement at a time: a leg, an arm, then her upper body, slowly lifting herself up. She shifted the covers off of her and tucked them gently around him, kissing him lightly on the forehead before sitting upright. With both feet planted on the hardwood floor, she had a start when Trevor rolled abruptly on his side, flopping his left arm where her body had been. She sat motionless for what felt like a full minute then moved toward the door. He was still sound asleep when she quietly shut his bedroom door behind her. Feeling a little shaky from the cake fiasco, she stood barefoot in the hallway fully dressed from the night before, wondering which way to go.

She wanted to change her clothes but wasn't going to go to her own bedroom, where Anthony was probably sleeping. So she headed toward the kitchen, the one room where there was always something to do, something to keep her moving while she thought about what had happened and what she was going to do or say when Anthony woke up. *Should I just tell him right away that I'm leaving? Or do as Irmeli suggested and wait until we have an appointment? Should I take the kids somewhere for the day?* She checked the time on the kitchen clock. It was only six thirty. Since it was Saturday, at least the kids wouldn't be up for a few more hours.

She thought of something her mother told her years ago. When a crisis comes and you don't know what to do next, think of what you'd normally do, and do that. In other words, one thing at a time; keep it simple to clear your head. So Sylvia made coffee. While it dripped into the carafe, she decided she'd check the living room and start cleaning up from the party. If she kept busy, maybe she could wipe away the cobwebs cluttering the corners of her mind.

She was about to pour a cup when she felt him right behind her. Before she could turn around, Anthony's hands crawled around her waist and over her belly. Repulsed by his touch, she sucked in a breath. The attack of butterflies that brought with it the hollow emptiness she'd come to know so well took on an ominous quality, foreboding now—it seemed to spread from the depth of her, creeping up, up toward her heart, and finally arriving, shrouding it with dread. "Stop it." *Too much of a gasp, not enough firmness,* she thought.

He pressed harder and worked his way to her breasts, clutching them hard. "What's the matter, Jake?" He nuzzled his scratchy, unshaven chin into her neck. "Don't I turn you on anymore?"

She wrenched away and moved across the room, backing up against the pantry. "That's right—you *don't* turn me on anymore." She thought of all the times in the past few months that she'd avoided his gaze, his touch, his advances, or made sure he didn't see her in her underwear, hoping to avoid having sex with him. But it didn't always work. When it didn't, she did what she'd learned to do from all of her years with Tom, what she had never thought she'd end up doing with Anthony—she faked orgasms to get it over with.

He reached for her and clutched the hair at the back of her head. "You didn't come to bed last night." His eyes had a glint like he'd caught her in a lie that he'd punish her for. He pulled her so close she could smell his breath, stale from cigarettes and wine. "We never go to bed angry, remember?"

"I'm never going to bed with you again." Seething with anger, she pronounced each word evenly. "You're hurting me. Now let me go."

"I'll never let you go," he said through clenched teeth.

"You don't have a choice," she said emphatically.

Then suddenly he did let her go. He ambled across the kitchen and stopped in front of the carafe. He took several deep breaths and poured two cups of coffee. In a flat tone, he asked, "One sugar, right?" Not waiting for a response, he dropped a lump of sugar in a mug. Not looking up, he held it out to her.

Sylvia stood fixed in place cautiously watching him go through the motions, acting like nothing had just happened, like this was a usual outburst on a Saturday morning. She made several steps toward him and quickly took the mug with both hands to stop the shaking. She wondered what he'd do next, and more important, what she should do next. The last thing she wanted was to provoke him further.

He turned, sat down at the table, and patted the chair next to him. With a half grimace, half smile, he looked at her. "Sit, Sylvia; we need to talk."

She took a sip of coffee. On top of his condescending, unapologetic tone and patronizing gesture, her scalp was sore, and she couldn't contain herself. "I'm not sitting down or talking to you! Get your things and be out of this house in an hour." Wanting only to get away from him, she said she was going to start cleaning the living room and headed there. Her breathing was ragged, and she needed to do something to steady herself. On the floor behind the armchairs she spotted candy corn. She set her mug on the floor, then got on her hands and knees to pick it up. The more she looked, the more she found, and she considered shoving it all under the area rug. She listened for his footsteps down the hall toward the bedroom, but all was quiet. Moments passed. Her hands filled with the candy, she sat back on her heels to empty them into a ceramic bowl on the side table, when he snuck up from behind and hit her hard on the back of the head. The blow knocked her forward onto her chin, sending candy corn flying in all directions, clattering to the floor.

"Don't you ever tell me what to do!" He seethed. "Now, get up; you need to fix breakfast. The kids can clean up this mess." He stormed out of the room.

She heard herself moan and was suddenly terrified for her safety. She had to get out of the house with her children. She couldn't imagine they were still asleep but hoped they were still in their bedrooms. She needed all of her cunning now. Feeling light-headed she struggled to her feet and followed him to the kitchen.

Anthony took out a frying pan and started cooking link sausage. "I guess I'll get breakfast going. How about setting the table, Jake?" He sounded almost carefree.

Her whole body trembled. *He's really crazy.* Trying to calm herself and think more clearly, Sylvia took plates from the cupboard shelf. The two-toned forest green dinner plates had speckles that made them look handmade and were her favorites, the ones from a pottery outlet in Oregon where she'd shopped with her mother and they each bought four place settings. *He's a walking time bomb. We need to get out of here right away.* She set the plates on the table. He started singing a Billy Joel song. *I need a place to stay. Who can I call?* Scott was home, but he lived too far away to come over in a hurry. Anthony was singing loudly now. "I need to know that you will always be, the same old someone that I knew." She took out the silverware. *Get to the bedroom phone.* "What will it take till you believe in me, the way that I believe in you? I said I love you, and that's forever—"

"My head hurts." She asked him politely, "Will you please stop singing?"

He looked up from the stove. "I'm just trying to make us both feel better."

"The only way I'll feel better is if I lie down for a while. Besides, I have to go to the bathroom." Sylvia started down the hall toward the bedroom. *Who can I call?* In the year that she'd been in Los Altos she hadn't made any friends of her own. Trying to keep all the plates in the air at home with Anthony left no room for her to ever get involved with girlfriends. And she'd been embarrassed to admit they weren't married. *Thank God, we're not married.* Then she thought of the one person she could turn to—their refuge in Palo Alto, Suzie Baldwin. Alice and Trevor had even stayed at their home on several weekends so Sylvia and Anthony could spend time away together. Although she'd been Anthony's good friend before the move, Sylvia had come to know her quite well and had confided in her about some of their problems, which didn't come as a surprise to Suzie. She'd said, "For one thing, I hope therapy gets him out of denial about abandoning his kids." Sylvia had often wondered what the "other thing" might be, but failed to ask her.

Sylvia shut the bedroom door, hesitated, then locked it. She sat on the edge of their bed, her brass bed, and picked up the phone. She jumped as she heard the doorknob turn. *What's her number?* She knew the number but couldn't think of it. She fumbled with the address book in the nightstand, then remembered. "Sylvia! Let me in." She dialed. She heard metal clicking in the doorknob. *Please answer. Trevor and Alice must be awake.* The phone rang and rang. Suddenly he was in and lunged for it. The phone crashed to the floor.

"You're not calling anybody!" He hit her on the shoulder with his fist, knocking her onto the bed. She reached up and hit him back—in a flurry of arms and legs he struck her many times, then slapped her across the face. She tried to roll up into a ball, but he was quickly on top of her, trying to hold her arms down, when she kneed him in the stomach. He let go of her, and she managed to stand up, stumbling for the doorway. He caught her by the leg, tripping her, and she slammed facedown on the floor, her hands barely bracing her fall. Pain shot up both arms. He kicked her repeatedly in the thighs, buttocks, and sides. She rolled onto her back and began kicking her legs furiously to keep him away, when she heard crying coming from the hallway.

Sylvia pushed him hard in the groin with both feet and heard him swear as he fell down. She scrambled to get up and ran to find her kids. Alice's door was open, but she didn't see them. She thrust Trevor's door open. They were sitting huddled on his bed and ran to her when she appeared. Gathered close on either side of her, they were crying as she moved them all forward down the hall. She nudged them on ahead. "Quick, get in the car. I'm right behind you." They ran ahead, through the kitchen and outside to the carport. They got into the backseat as she ran to the driver's side. Not looking up, she grabbed the keys from under the mat and started the car. She gunned the engine and backed out of the driveway. Glancing over her shoulder she saw Anthony running out the front door toward the front of the car as if to prevent her from going forward. She stepped on the accelerator and swerved around him. In her rearview mirror his image became smaller and smaller until she turned the corner and he was completely out of sight.

On their way to Palo Alto, Sylvia kept checking the rearview mirror. *What if he tries to follow us? He must know where we're going.* Meanwhile, she tried to reassure her children that they were never going to have to live with Anthony again. Not that she thought they'd believe her at first. She'd need to reassure them every day for a long time to come, but until they moved out of the house and were living without him, they most likely would have doubts—and fears and nightmares. And she figured, so would she.

Her mind wouldn't stop replaying, visualizing his crazed expression, hearing his snide remarks, taunting her, running his hands all over her, and she tried to shut out the images of the physical attack that continually resurfaced, to push them somewhere else, to no avail. She shuddered. What if the Baldwins weren't home? Would they go to a motel? *I don't have my purse!* Her fingers were sore from gripping the steering wheel too tightly, and she opened and closed her hands to bring the circulation back.

Alice and Trevor had climbed to the passenger seat as soon as they were safely out of the driveway. Alice held Trevor in her lap. They were no longer crying but sat dazed, staring straight ahead, not saying anything.

Sylvia noticed they were both dressed. “When did you put your clothes on?”

Alice looked solemnly at her mother. “When I woke up from all the noise in your room, I got scared and was going to get away on my bicycle. But I didn’t want to leave Trevor, so I woke him up and told him to get dressed, too.”

Sylvia stroked her hair. “That’s my girl. Even when you’re afraid, you do the right thing.” She mentioned what a good thing it was that Julie hadn’t stayed overnight after all.

Alice smiled a little. “Mommy, where *are* we going to live?”

Sylvia didn’t think she was ready to answer this question, but it came out of her mouth like she’d been planning it for weeks. “We’re going back home to Oregon.” Just saying it out loud brought relief.

“Really? Are you sure?” Alice sounded hesitant like she was afraid to be hopeful, which made Sylvia wonder how happy she’d actually been in Los Altos. Sylvia was learning that her Alice was a survivor, someone who could accommodate herself in adverse situations and come out on the other side. She knew how to save herself.

“Will we live near Daddy?” Trevor asked.

"Yes. We'll live in the apartments where we were before." She tried to sound confident, hoping an apartment was available.

Trevor leaned out of Alice's arms and thrust both of his around Sylvia's neck. He spoke into her shoulder. "That's the best news I've ever had."

Sylvia reached around his body, squeezing him, then rested her cheek on the top of his head. "For me, too."

"Can I call Daddy to tell him?" Alice asked.

Sylvia said it would be better if she spoke to Tom first, but after that they could talk to him. She didn't want to call him at home and risk Betsy answering, but she couldn't wait until Monday when he'd be in his office. Checking with the apartment complex in Lakeside was the first call she needed to make. *How can I pack everything with Anthony around? Somebody needs to be with me.* Maybe Tom would come down and help them pack or move or just take the kids home. She wanted to talk to her parents and needed to call the schools here, and in Oregon, and she had to quit her job. Her head began throbbing. Before she did anything, she needed to rest.

Sylvia turned onto the street where Suzie and David lived. They passed a child on a bicycle, a teenager walking his golden retriever without a leash, and a man and woman puttering in the garden. She envied them doing mundane weekend things at home and wondered if she'd ever get back to a life without drama. She told herself right then to never forget this moment. To promise herself that if she'd ever again have the good fortune to see her life as commonplace, dull, uninteresting, or boring, she'd make herself sit back, smile, and consider it a privilege.

About half a block away she saw a middle-aged couple, apparently out for a morning stroll, dressed in sweats and tennis shoes walking toward them.

"It's them!" Alice cried. She rolled the window down. "Suzie!"

Sylvia pulled up beside them.

Suzie beamed in surprise. But as she peered into the car, a look of concern came over her face. "What's the matter? Are you guys all right?"

Alice burst into tears. "Anthony was hitting Mommy."

Suzie opened the car door, and they both rushed into her open arms. Sylvia wanted to do the same. After Suzie made sure Sylvia didn't need medical attention, they decided that the kids could walk the rest of the way with Suzie and David, while Sylvia drove on to their house. She told her the house wasn't locked, "so go right in, take a bubble bath, and soak for as long as you like. I'll whip up some breakfast. These two must be starving."

When Sylvia arrived, such a wave of fatigue came over her that she just sat in the driveway not wanting to move. *I need a cigarette.* She reached in her glove box and found two left in an old pack—she lit up and leaned back against the headrest. She glanced up at the wraparound porch and noticed the old-fashioned wooden swing hanging by the front window—just like the one her grandmother had in Ohio. When they were little, she and Steve used to sit facing each other, their legs stretched out in front of them, feet touching, while their dad pushed them. She started to get out of the car to go sit on the swing and groaned. It seemed like her whole body ached, and she was cold—she looked down and saw that she was still barefoot. Cigarette in hand, she walked haltingly toward the front porch. Smoking wasn't allowed in the house, so she stubbed out the butt in the dirt and buried it before climbing the four front steps. She made her way to the swing, where she plopped down with a thud. The swing rocked back and forth with little effort on her part, and she gazed out at the huge elms at the edge of the street, their golden brown leaves falling in swirls to the ground. There was a cool, fall breeze, and the gray clouds moving in made it look as if it might rain. In a few weeks it would be Thanksgiving. They were really going back, back home to Oregon. The thought brought a contentedness she hadn't felt in a long time. That's where they belonged. The rest would fall into place.

She heard voices and sat up to see them coming down the sidewalk but stayed put. As they climbed the steps, Alice and Trevor ran over to join their mom on the swing, one on each side. Right now, this was all she wanted: the freedom to hold her children for as long as she needed without being watched and judged or told she was smothering them and that it was wrong.

Suzie brought a couple of blankets and a thick pair of socks for Sylvia. She left them alone for some time until the smell of bacon frying brought on hunger pangs, and the kids bolted inside, with Sylvia a ways behind.

"I set out some sweats for you to wear." Suzie gently put her arms around Sylvia and held her. "Why don't you take that bath now? You'll feel better." With the comfort of Suzie's loving arms, Sylvia broke down. They moved toward the downstairs rear bedroom and went inside. When Sylvia tried to talk, Suzie told her there'd be plenty of time later for talking. "Just let it all out, honey." She examined the left side of Sylvia's face. "Looks like you could use some ice on that. I'll be right back."

"What would I do without you?" Sylvia stammered.

"Well, you don't even need to think about that, because I'm here."

*****

Three Days Later

Going back to the house alone to start packing boxes was a frightening prospect, but she had no choice. She arranged for a moving company to drop off boxes and packing materials on Tuesday, so she had to be there to meet them and take advantage of the hours the kids were in school. The last time she was at the house was Sunday afternoon. Suzie and David had orchestrated with Anthony a sort of truce on her behalf, escorting her back to the house to get enough belongings to last about two weeks. Sylvia didn't know what was said to him, but he hadn't been there when they arrived. This time Suzie reassured Sylvia that Anthony would stay at the office all day and not bother her. Still, she wondered if he knew she was there alone and was nervous waiting.

Over the weekend she had spoken to Tom, who immediately offered to help, even to drive a U-Haul truck down for the move. Fifteen minutes later he called back and told her he couldn't. Sylvia heard Betsy's rant in the background and figured she was the reason he had changed his mind. She was glad she hadn't told the kids—she'd learned that much about dealing with their dad. She had called the one person they could count on. Her brother Scott. She had explained to him that a three-bedroom apartment was available; since she had to pay rent for the whole month of November, she had hoped to move in no later than two weeks from now.

"Don't worry, Syl. I'll fly up next Friday and get you guys out of Dodge way before that."

She had gotten all choked up. "I don't know how to tell you how much this means to me." She glanced down at her arms and legs, blotchy with purplish-blue bruises, and hoped they'd be healed by the time Scott arrived.

"Hey, you're the only sister I've got. Just stay away from that son of a bitch."

"I will."

"Maybe you should get a restraining order."

She had considered his idea, but later, after speaking to Irmeli, decided it wasn't worth the trouble for the little time she'd be in town. By the time Sylvia had reached Irmeli, she learned that Anthony already had. He asked Irmeli to talk to Sylvia to set up an appointment for the two of them. When Sylvia refused, Irmeli suggested that after such a trauma it was also important to show the children they could still talk to each other, behave like mature adults, and separate, if not amicably, at least in a civilized manner. Sylvia said she was still afraid of him and didn't want to be in the same room with him. But she had definitely wanted to see Irmeli before she left town.

The doorbell rang, and Sylvia peeked through the kitchen window for the delivery truck. It was there, and she let them in. They assessed the number of boxes she'd need and began stacking the flattened cardboard sections in the different rooms of the house.

She got to work setting up each box, taping the cardboard flaps. The job was monumental. *First the kids' rooms, then mine. No, mine first, then the kitchen. But the kitchen takes the longest,* she thought as she constructed box after box. When the delivery men left, it was too quiet. After a while, working helped her feel less nervous, and she considered turning on some music. She went into the family room, where her Sony stereo system was situated on bookshelves. She entered the room and stopped abruptly, staring in disbelief. The shelves were empty. The whole system was gone, speakers and all. *He couldn't be this crazy.* But nothing about him would surprise her now.

She went from room to room checking for any other missing items. A creepy feeling came over her as she went through the house, not fear exactly, although she did have a solid case of butterflies, but the feeling of being trampled on and disregarded. When she got to her bedroom, she was feeling slightly panicky. She opened the walk-in closet and gasped out loud. All of her clothes and shoes were gone.

# CHAPTER 36

Two days later Sylvia learned through Suzie that Anthony was driving around with her missing belongings in his car. He wouldn't bring them back until she agreed to meet him at Irmeli's for an appointment. The shock of what he'd done was only outweighed by his justification to Suzie that he had "no other recourse to get Sylvia to see me or talk to me." No way was he going to let her just fade away into the sunset. Even if he stole her things in a fit of rage, his maneuver was well thought out. She'd have to meet with him. *At least he didn't dump it all in the trash,* she thought. As much as she wanted to get her stereo, clothes, and shoes back immediately, she wasn't going to the appointment by herself. She told Irmeli she'd agree to meet him once her brother came to town and could accompany her, which wasn't until Friday afternoon.

She spent the next four days alone in the house packing boxes and was relieved when Friday had finally arrived without incident. The appointment was set for six o'clock. It didn't give Sylvia much time with her brother before the session, but knowing he'd be by her side for the duration of the move gave her enormous comfort. If all went as planned, by that evening she'd have everything back, and by the following Wednesday, they'd be on the road to Oregon.

Since most of her bruises hadn't healed yet, she debated whether to wear long pants and long sleeves to cover them, mostly for her brother's sake but also for hers—it might help hide her shame. The side of her face was healing more quickly and had only slight discoloration. She changed her clothes three times and settled for a pair of wool Bermuda shorts, a sleeveless blouse, and sweater-vest, deciding that overall, she wanted to expose as much as possible for Anthony to see. Even if he wasn't capable of genuine remorse, the array of color from yellow to violet to dark gray-blue that speckled her limbs would be difficult to ignore. The physical signs of what he'd put her through were only part of it, but at least that much she could put on display.

Scott's flight was late, so no sooner did he arrive than they had to leave for Irmeli's. As soon as he saw his sister, his face scrunched up in a painful wince. "Does it hurt to hug you?"

She reached for him. "I need you to hug me, even if it does." She told him how she had thought about hiding the bruises from him at first and why she had changed her mind.

"Seeing what he did has a lot more impact than hearing about it on the phone. But now that I have, I don't know if I can look him in the eye without letting him have it," Scott said. "I can only imagine how you must feel."

Sylvia sat up straighter. "I don't think I could face him if you weren't here. Right now I feel pretty strong. There's nothing for me to tiptoe around or try to word exactly right or defend anymore. God, what a relief."

They turned the corner onto Irmeli's street. As they pulled up to the curb in front of her house, Sylvia saw Anthony's Camaro already in the driveway. Her stomach flopped. "He's here." His car was packed to the roof with clothes.

"And there's your stuff. Why don't I break the windows, and we could just make a run for it?"

Sylvia managed a sly smile. "Don't tempt me." As they got out of the car she couldn't help but notice her youngest brother's imposing presence. She hadn't seen him since his trip to Saudi Arabia. Not only did he tower over her, which meant Anthony would have to look up at him, but he seemed broader, more muscular, through the chest and shoulders. His twenty-six-year-old face had a more mature quality than she remembered—more like a man than a boy. His stride showed a strength of purpose, like a man in charge, a man who knew what his role was here, and his presence made her feel secure.

He took her elbow as they walked up the twenty or so steps to the front door. He looked so worried for her. The depth of his feeling was written all over his face; his big sister, who since childhood had always watched over him, now needed him to watch over her. "I'll sit with you if you want me to."

She stopped briefly to reach up and kiss him on the cheek. "You don't have to sit with me, but I'd like you to wait in a room nearby."

Just then the front door opened, and Irmeli came out to greet them. Her face softened when she looked at Sylvia, and she rested her hands on her shoulders for a moment, reassuring her that she'd keep the session as brief as possible. She showed Scott where he could wait in the living room. Then, for the last time, she escorted Sylvia to the room she'd come to know so well.

Anthony was sitting in the same spot he'd always taken—the far end of the worn, overstuffed couch, closest to Irmeli's chair—leaving enough room for Sylvia to sit beside him. She didn't acknowledge him as she took the wingback chair facing Irmeli on Anthony's right. That way she could avoid looking in his direction.

In a cavalier manner, Anthony said, "Glad you came, Jake." From her peripheral vision she saw him look at his watch. "I thought you might not show up."

Sylvia stayed focused on Irmeli, thinking how his checking the time used to make her practically quiver inside. It didn't affect her now, which empowered her in that split second.

Irmeli opened the session by asking if either of them had something in particular to say.

A full awkward minute passed. To Sylvia's surprise, Anthony sat there like a sphinx. *He's the one who asked for this session.*

"Perhaps I can suggest a way to begin," Irmeli said. "The main reason we're here is to reduce the acrimony that exists between the two of you enough so you can separate from each other with civility. It's also important that the children see you both rise above your hostility toward each other."

Sylvia wondered why it mattered when the children wouldn't see them together again anyway. And what did Anthony care about her children?

Anthony raised his eyebrows. "What hostility? I still want to spend my life with Sylvia."

"That chapter is closed, Anthony. But surely you can't deny that you're angry with her, can you?" Irmeli asked.

"Anger is normal in any relationship, but that doesn't change the way I feel about her."

"However, physical abuse is not normal," Irmeli said. "Didn't you tell me there was something you wanted to say to her today?"

He looked at Sylvia directly, but she wouldn't meet his gaze. "Right. I know how awful you must feel, and I want to apologize for what I did. Believe me, it'll never happen again."

Sylvia thought of Jane and was convinced that he must've smacked her around, too. Had he told her the same thing? Did she take him back because of the children or because she wanted to believe his reassurances? No wonder she refused to let the children see him. It all made sense now.

He waited.

Irmeli was silent.

"Jesus, aren't you going to say anything?" he asked.

"Maybe we should redirect the conversation," Irmeli suggested. "Is there anything left for you in this relationship, Sylvia?"

"No."

"So you're prepared to leave and start your life over with your children. Is that right?"

Sylvia made eye contact with her. "Yes, it's all set. Scott's helping me move back to Oregon next week. I just want what belongs to me."

Anthony slid to the end of the sofa toward Sylvia, within arm's reach. She almost flinched. Instead, she held herself in check and didn't move a muscle.

"I can't believe you'd run away. We've come too far to give up now," he said, his voice rising. "We're better than this, Syl."

She wanted to say, "No, *I'm* better than this." But she stared straight ahead, not focusing on anything in particular. She wanted to put her hands over her ears to muffle the voice that made her insides roil. *Don't let him get to you,* she told herself.

"Anthony, please move back to your original place," Irmeli said. Slowly he slid back. "You physically abused the woman you profess to love, the woman you say you want to spend your life with. Look at her and what you've done."

He seemed startled. He cleared his throat and turned to Sylvia again. "I can only ask for your forgiveness for how I behaved."

She finally looked at him and wondered what in the world ever attracted her to him.

The rust-colored leather jacket he wore made him look sleazy, and his worn black leather loafers were unpolished. He hadn't shaved. Or was he growing a beard? Either way he appeared scruffy and unkempt. His thick wiry hair was kinky and sprouting from his head like a mad professor's. The cool Italian sophisticate she'd fallen in love with looked more like an unrefined, shiftless vagabond. She said flatly, "No one treats me like that. There are no second chances for you." She could've said more, but he wouldn't hear her, and she had no interest in making the effort. He wasn't worth it. Her power was her indifference.

"I suggest we get back to the business at hand here and arrange for the return of her belongings," Irmeli said.

"I agreed to give back her things, and I will. I'm a man of my word. What would I want with them anyway?" He turned to Sylvia once more. "We've had more pressures on us than most couples have in a lifetime. You must believe me when I tell you I'll never do that to you again."

"The harm you've brought on me and my children is unforgivable," Sylvia said.

Anthony finally was speechless. Pursing his lips, he looked back at Irmeli with a helpless, futile expression as if he'd tried, but what good was it going to do?

Irmeli took charge of establishing that after their session Anthony would meet them at their old house, where Scott and Anthony could unload the belongings and deposit them inside. When Irmeli suggested that Anthony be given permission to say good-bye to the children, Sylvia initially refused.

"Why should they have to be on their best behavior with someone they're afraid of?"

"Because their last memory of you two was frightening, they should leave with a positive impression to help them move forward and get past that experience," Irmeli said.

"I see what you mean, but I need to think about this. Five minutes of his acting cordial and shaking their hands good-bye won't erase an entire year of never knowing what to expect from his increasingly unpredictable moods."

Anthony stood and, with nicotine-stained fingers, lit a cigarette as if ready to leave. As an afterthought, he held the pack out to Sylvia. She shook her head and decided right then she would quit.

Irmeli spoke directly to Sylvia. "More importantly, they need to see *you* stand tall, setting the example of the strong, mature woman that you are. That will help them move on more quickly."

Sylvia finally agreed that he could come by Suzie and David Baldwin's to say good-bye to them, but he couldn't hang around. She joined Scott in the living room, and they went down the steps and to her car. As Sylvia was getting in the passenger seat, Anthony called out.

"Scott, hold up a second." He walked over and held out his hand. Mechanically, Scott started to reach out his hand, then pulling himself up taller, crossed his arms over his chest. Anthony shuffled his feet, inhaling the last puff of his cigarette before tossing it at the curb. He tried to engage Scott in idle chitchat about his flight and his trip to Saudi Arabia, but Scott, steely-eyed, stared down at him, curtly telling him he had nothing to say to him. As Anthony headed for his car, he called back, "See you back at the house."

"What's with that guy?" Scott asked as he put the key into the ignition. His face was flushed and his hand unsteady, barely able to contain his anger.

"Let's just get this over with," she said.

When they reached the house, Sylvia waited in the car while Scott and Anthony unloaded her things. After half an hour she was reconsidering her decision to quit smoking. She took the pack out of her purse, staring at the pretty filters with paisley designs. The cigarette named Eve, marketed as the female symbol of beauty and erotic allure, was nothing more than a commercial device to make the woman who smoked it feel more feminine, sexy, and liberated—a cigarette made especially for her. Sylvia had bought into the whole message, but she could no longer afford to be deceived by pretty words and packaging. No more could she ignore her gut instincts. What folly that a man with a Porsche, phony sophistication, and the allure of what money could buy would bring her happiness and freedom. Her freedom could come only from living without pretense and loving honestly without having to hide her feelings. Only then could she recover her true self and the key to her happiness. It was time to listen to what was going on inside, trust what her instincts told her, and act on that. She saw this as another chance to do things differently and was ready to find out what she was capable of doing on her own.

The day before Sylvia left town, Irmeli agreed to meet her for a "good-bye" coffee at a local café. Sylvia thanked her for her guidance in helping her to remove the blinders and face what was in front of her. "The question is why I wouldn't make a move until it turned into a crisis."

"Perhaps a crisis was unavoidable no matter what you did. You mustn't blame yourself."

Sylvia fidgeted with her napkin. "I guess I do blame myself. I should've seen it coming. I'm so ashamed for putting my children through this."

"But you should be proud of yourself."

"What on earth for?"

"You didn't put up with it. You left. Many women don't do that. They have a wish to believe. Physical abuse, or even verbal abuse, is incapacitating over time. Eventually, a woman may no longer think she has a choice and becomes paralyzed—too terrified to leave. As difficult as the circumstances were, you got out and quickly. That's what your children will remember most."

"I wish I could put you in my pocket and take you with me."

Irmeli chuckled warmly. "You can call me whenever you like. May I give you some advice?"

"Please."

"Pay more attention to what a man *does* rather than what he says. It'll help you to trust your instincts."

"I can't imagine having any interest in a man again."

"You will. Just take your time." Irmeli leaned forward, patted Sylvia's hand, and in her distinctive accent, said, "And when you are ready, find yourself a *good* man."

# CHAPTER 37

True to form and despite her protests, Scott wouldn't let Sylvia pay for anything on their road trip. While he went ahead and paid for the rental truck, gas, all meals, and the motel stays, Sylvia decided she'd pay back all of it from her nest egg when they got to Oregon. She jotted down the expenses as they made their way north.

At a coffee shop for their last meal on the road, the four of them sat at a table by a window overlooking the parking lot. Alice and Trevor were sitting on opposite sides kicking each other under the table and giggling while they all waited for their food. Scott said he had a surprise, and this was as good a time as any to give Sylvia a little something. He took out his wallet. Alice and Trevor sat up in silent attention.

"When my flight was late coming into San Francisco, it wasn't because of the usual airline delays." He opened his wallet and handed her three fifty-dollar bills. "Here. The flight was overbooked, and they paid volunteers to take the next flight out. I figured I had enough time to get there for your appointment even if we were a little late."

"Oh, Scott." Sylvia burst into tears. "You're the kindest person—who would ever think of doing—" She marveled at his generosity. It would cover at least two weeks' worth of groceries.

"Now, now," and in his perfect imitation of their dad, "Quit your blubberin'. You're getting the money all wet." He handed her a napkin to wipe her nose.

They all started laughing.

"Wow. Can I see?" Trevor said, staring at the money.

Sylvia handed the bills over, and the kids studied them for a minute. "Who's that?" Trevor asked, pointing to the portrait on the bill.

"It says underneath," Alice said. "Grant. But what did he do?"

"He was a Civil War general and president." Scott took out a $1, $5, $10, and $20, displaying them on the table.

Sylvia listened as he gave her children a mini-lesson in U.S. currency. *Our father to a tee,* she thought. She missed her parents. They, too, had been true to form worrying about her and their grandchildren "getting out from under the thumb of that psycho" as her mother so aptly put it. And that was uttered without knowing all the details; Sylvia had underplayed the escape to the Baldwins rather than drag her parents through the blow-by-blow of the physical fight that dreadful morning. They both tried to talk her into moving back to Ohio, and for a moment, she seriously considered the option. Taking her children away from their father again, however, was not in their best interests.

She wondered when she'd see them again. She'd probably be working full-time soon and wouldn't be able to spend her usual month in the summer with them. Unless she went back to teaching. At this time of year, she wouldn't be able to do that. She'd have to start job hunting as soon as she got back because she didn't want to live on what was left of her nest egg.

It took two days to move in and basically set up house. Their apartment was identical to the last one—kitchen and dining area above ground, living room down half a flight of stairs, and three bedrooms a full flight downstairs at ground level. It was situated just a few doors from the last one, on the same side of the complex with the lush wooded area in back. Scott was amazed at the amount of space, saying it was bigger than his condo for half the price. Alice and Trevor told him he should move to Oregon so they could see each other all the time.

"But where would I surf?" he asked.

"You could ski on Mount Hood instead!" Alice said.

"You've got it all figured out," he said, playfully tackling her with Trevor piling on top.

He stayed through the weekend to help them as much as possible, then had to get back to work in San Diego. He'd taken ten days off already. Sylvia stuffed five hundred dollars in cash in his backpack with a short note: "Just know I need to do this for me." The three of them drove him to the airport. When it was time to say good-bye, they all cried and an empty feeling took hold of her. Being with her brother for so many days made her see how much more enjoyable life could be for her family if they lived closer to each other. Holidays. Birthdays. No one to celebrate with, no one who really cared and loved them the way her family did. And Thanksgiving was just around the corner. But thinking this way was only making her miserable. She chastised herself for wallowing in self-pity. Besides, she was used to spending holidays without them. Maybe missing her family was a good thing, something to be thankful for. How lucky she was to have a loving family to miss!

On the way back from the airport Sylvia stopped for gas. When she got her gas credit card out, she realized she'd forgotten to ask Anthony for the second card she gave him to use. It made her slightly queasy to think he still had something that belonged to her. First thing Monday morning, she'd cancel the card and take him off as an authorized user.

It was getting dark when they got back to the apartment, so Sylvia didn't notice the note on their front door at first. "Come on over. Dinner's waiting!" Brittany's family, Alice's close friend, had invited several other families in their complex for a welcome-back party. The kids were ecstatic and took off in a rush. At least their first night without Scott would end on a happier note.

Within ten days her apartment was completely organized. She'd spent many late nights unpacking because she couldn't stand to live out of boxes. During the day she looked for a job, but it was more difficult than she thought it'd be to find something. With the holidays upon them, jobs seemed to be scarcer. Her friend Charlotte recommended she apply for unemployment, which she did. In the meantime, she tried to sell monthly service door-to-door for a brand-new business franchise, cable television, but few were interested. She was strictly on commission, and since she had to sell in the evenings, she didn't make enough to offset babysitting costs, so she gave it up.

Jessica was trying to help, too. She knew a lot of people in town and was putting the word out for any job possibilities. Unfortunately, she, too, was now going through a divorce and was having problems trying to keep her own life from unraveling. Jessica's situation sounded like déjà vu. The only difference was Jessica wasn't poor. She was in a hot love affair, and the two were planning on marriage as soon as their divorces were final. Her wealthy lover had promised they'd be together in six months, but ten months had already passed. Jessica's divorce was almost final. Apparently, she wasn't able to heed her own advice.

Tom had been reliable in paying the child support. He was doing well in pharmaceutical sales, and it looked like she could count on that. Sylvia wondered whether to try to get more than two hundred fifty dollars a month for both children. As it was, he wanted her to sign an agreement outlining the visitation schedule and health insurance coverage for the children. When he handed her the contract he and Betsy had drawn up themselves, Sylvia read it shaking her head. He only wanted his children one weekend a month and one weeknight for dinner only. And he wanted her to pay the health insurance premium and half of what wasn't covered! She threw it back in his face and said it was outrageous. When she began to blame Betsy, she stopped. *Why am I always blaming the woman?* Betsy might not have liked it that they moved back to town and made her life messy again, but he was their father. He was the one who wasn't standing up for himself and them. Sylvia told him she'd seek legal counsel unless he recognized her terms as well.

Anthony somehow got her number and called her once, telling her he missed her and that he thought they still had a chance. He said it was good for her to take her time, but then he cautioned her. If she waited too long, he might not be there for her. "I can't wait forever, you know. I'm a guy who wants a woman in his life." It was so preposterous, it could've been funny, but not enough time had passed for her to be able to laugh. She doubted there'd ever be that much time.

Sylvia didn't think hanging up on him would resolve anything. If she exhibited any emotion, he might think she still had feelings for him. She just waited patiently, not responding, hoping that indifference would ultimately convince him. When he was done, she said she had to go. And that was that. Her stomach didn't go hollow, no flopping, and no butterflies—finally, her insides had no reaction at all. Since then, she'd had several hang-up calls but wasn't alarmed. Maybe a month was too long for him to wait for her. She hoped.

Despite financial setbacks, life without Anthony was full of joy and laughter. When the kids came home from school or inside from playing, Sylvia let them drop their coats, hats, shoes, or books wherever they wanted. They turned it into a game of sorts.

"Whose shoes are these in the living room?" Alice would ask.

"Mine!" Trevor would holler back. "And I'm leaving them there!"

Sometimes Sylvia would stand in the dining room, hiding, and toss maybe her jacket, or shoes one at a time, or purse over the waist-high wall that looked onto the living room below. "Bombs away!" she'd call.

Bedtime was barely structured; sometimes they made popcorn on a school night and watched television until nine or ten o'clock together. Trevor took pleasure in occasionally heaping his plate with food, leaving half of it uneaten, then tossing it down the disposal. Alice brought friends over on weeknights, sometimes for dinner, which Anthony had never permitted. Maybe Sylvia was overcompensating with her *laissez-faire* reaction, but they all needed it. Sylvia most of all. She was basking in the freedom to be herself with her children.

About two weeks before Christmas Sylvia retrieved her mail and nonchalantly tore open her Shell credit card bill. To her shock, the balance was over eight hundred dollars. She had to sit down. Old feelings came rushing back, as if he was in the same room with her again, ready to punish her for something. But that wasn't quite what she felt either—it was more like the creepy feeling she had when she discovered her clothes were missing. She'd been violated all over again. She checked the dates of the transactions. They were mostly during the week of her move, but some were after she'd cancelled the old card. But how could that be? And why wouldn't the company have alerted her to the high amount when she took his name off the account? Was this his twisted way of trying to get her to contact him? Well, she wouldn't. And she wouldn't pay it either. She had a frightening thought and checked the bill again. Most of the charges were in Sacramento or Bakersfield, but the last two were in southern Oregon. She didn't know where he was living. She'd call Suzie Baldwin in Palo Alto to find out where he lived, just for reassurance. Still, it was over a month ago. Except for the amount of money due, maybe she had no need to worry.

Suzie said she'd seen Anthony several times since their split and knew that he'd relocated in the Sacramento area. "He seemed more accepting that it's over between you two. In fact, he was very interested in another woman the last I saw him."

Then Sylvia called Irmeli. She needed a reassuring session even if it was over the phone. Irmeli was disheartened for Sylvia for having to deal with the outstanding bill but thought it best to let it go rather than try to make him pay. "Eight hundred dollars isn't much to pay for your peace of mind, is it?" To Sylvia it was a fortune. She saw Irmeli's point and wanted to let it go, but was too mad and didn't think he should be let off the hook so easily.

By January, she was on the fast track to get a job. She'd made up a résumé and had a few leads through Jessica's boyfriend, who was well connected in town. Her only office experience had been in Los Altos, and no one seemed to want to hire a former teacher. A sales job was not an option—she wouldn't travel.

Finally in the local newspaper she spotted an ad for a French bilingual executive secretary for a lumber exporter right in Lakeside. She couldn't believe her luck. There was only a post office box listed for mailing a résumé, but Sylvia needed to act. She began calling all the lumber exporters in town inquiring. Since lumber was the state's largest commodity, there were a fair number of businesses listed. But she found the company.

At eight o'clock the next morning she was dressed in her navy blue wool suit and on her way to the location. The 1960s-style two-story building was situated on the lake and was ten minutes from her apartment. She crossed her fingers and said a little prayer. When she walked in, saying she was only there to drop off her résumé, the office manager was dumbfounded that she'd found them. Since she was here, he checked with the owner to see if he could interview her right away, which was exactly what she was hoping would happen. Before meeting with him, the manager explained the job to her.

"It's very important to the owner, who's French, that his secretary speaks the language," he said. "He's been in the lumber export business thirty years and travels extensively. He needs to know that his gal Friday can speak to his French customers who are primarily in Tahiti."

Sylvia was surprised to hear that such a business existed in the small town of Lakeside. He went on to explain that the job was full-time, eight to five, and paid eleven hundred a month, which included health insurance and two weeks' paid vacation. After three months, if all went well, her salary would go up to twelve hundred. Sylvia had aspirations of eventually earning a good living, and this probably wouldn't suit her long-term plan. Right now though, she needed the job. A buzzer on his desk sounded. The owner was ready to meet her.

Sylvia followed the manager to a thirty-foot-long office overlooking the lake. He introduced her to Monsieur George DuBois, handed him her résumé, and left the room. George was an imposing figure, completely bald, perhaps in his early sixties, who, when he stood to shake her hand, towered above her at such a height she had to crane her neck to look at him. He had a Roman nose and was so lean he was gangly. All she could think of was Ichabod Crane.

Although nervous, she took the initiative to begin the conversation in French by commenting with amusement how fitting his name, which meant "wood," was for the business he was in. He laughed, and they chattered on for several minutes. He complimented her French accent, then to her relief reverted to English to discuss the specifics of the job. He was a classic, old-world Frenchman with dignity, grace, and intelligence. Sylvia could type well enough, but she fudged about her proficiency at dictation and avoided mentioning the ages of her children. Within fifteen minutes she was hired. She had one week to make arrangements for Trevor after school.

The thrill of finally landing a job and one where she'd get to use her French put her on a cloud. It was unbelievable, and she had no commute. Through Brittany's mother, Isabelle, she learned about a quality day care center less than a mile from the apartment that picked up the children from school. Trevor and her son, Michael, were buddies from before—Michael would be going to the day care center as well. They could go together!

The only damper on her newfound streak of luck was the continual worry about the Shell credit card debt, which wasn't going away. After numerous conversations and their "looking into the matter," the company claimed no responsibility for any overlap of use during the process of canceling. After all, she'd given the user permission to use the card. Her credit was in jeopardy. She either had to pay or call Anthony. Maybe he was in love with someone else now and would be reasonable.

When she reached him in the early evening, he was drunk and slurring his words. She immediately regretted calling. When she attempted to discuss what he owed her, he scoffed and started talking dirty to her, detailing what he was going to do to her when he drove up there to ravage her one more time. Her whole body started shivering, and she hung up.

But she still couldn't leave it alone. The next day she wrote to Anthony's parents apologizing for her request but documenting her need. Several weeks passed. Then at work one day Sylvia had an international call. She thought it was her boss, but when she went to the phone, she found it was Franca calling from Athens. She said she sent an American check to take care of the matter as soon as they got her letter. They were very upset over Anthony's irresponsibility and wished her well. They mentioned that they still had no contact with their grandchildren and were worried about their only son. Sylvia thanked her profusely. A check for one thousand dollars arrived a week later with a long letter. She felt vindicated.

On a Saturday morning in February, Tom picked up the kids for Trevor's soccer match. Betsy was visiting a sick relative for the day, so he said he'd bring them home after dinner. Sylvia had made plans with a new friend, Patricia, in the complex. Her growing circle of girlfriends was a renewed source of satisfaction that she'd not had for some time. They were going to play tennis at the indoor club where Patricia was a member, then have a quick bite together. The phone rang around three o'clock. Sylvia assumed it was her, but when she answered, there was no one there. She'd almost become used to these sporadic hang-ups. Patricia was to pick Sylvia up around four. Sylvia was getting dressed when she heard the doorbell. It was only three thirty. She threw on a robe and ran up the flight of stairs. When she looked through her peephole, all she saw was a hand holding a single red rose. She sucked in a breath and instinctively flattened against the wall.

"C'mon, Jake, I know you're in there." That singsong voice. "I can feel you on the other side of the door. Let me in, or I'll huff and I'll puff and I'll blow your house in!" The big bad wolf laughed. "C'mon, don't play games."

She slowly moved away from the door and ran downstairs to check Alice's bedroom door, which opened to the outside. She pushed the doorknob button to lock it but couldn't attach the chain because the slot was missing. She'd forgotten to remind the manager again to fix it. The sliding windows were shut tight. She had to call someone. Patricia. Maybe Tom. The police? She heard banging on the front door.

She went to her bedroom and threw on jeans and a turtleneck. Her bedroom window was at ground level at the front of the apartment, so he could see in if he tried. She closed the curtains in a panic. The last time she locked him out, she had never made it to the phone. Not this time. She dialed the police. They said they'd be there in about ten minutes. It seemed too quiet, and she suddenly didn't want to be downstairs. She bolted back upstairs and from the kitchen called Patricia, Charlotte, and Jessica, who said they'd come right over. She felt calmer knowing she wouldn't be alone much longer. She looked out the peephole again. No one.

His voice came from behind her. "You shouldn't treat me like this." He tsked.

She cried out as she turned around, falling against the door.

He was ten feet from her holding the rose by his side. "You had no right to tattle to my parents. You owe me one." He held the rose out to her. "Do you know how you can repay me?"

She was more afraid than she'd ever been. In what seemed like slow motion, her hand reached forward, and she took the rose.

"I'll give you a clue," he said. "Our favorite hotel, for old times' sake."

She cleared her throat and stammered, not sure how to buy time. "I'm sorry. You're right; I shouldn't have told your—"

"Poor Sylvia, so nervous." He reached to stroke her cheek, and she pulled away. "I know how to calm you down. I'm getting so hard, I think I'll just fuck your brains out right here."

She tried to sound interested. "I'd rather go to our hotel, like you said."

"That's more like it. That's my Jake."

"Do you have a reservation?"

"Don't need one." He stepped toward her. "I really can't wait that long."

She stepped to the side and backed into the kitchen. "Not here. I don't want any interruptions." She tried to sound sweet. "We want it to be like old times."

He studied her for a minute. His eyes flickered with suspicion. "Fine. Let's just go." He took her firmly by the arm.

She pulled the chain back from the bolt and opened the front door. Her girlfriends were coming up the steps, like a small posse. Two policemen were bringing up the rear. "Is everything all right here?"

Jessica was exasperated. "A psycho's holding her hostage! What do *you* think?" She put her arm around Sylvia then led her back inside with Charlotte and Patricia.

Anthony, dumfounded, started to protest that Sylvia was grossly exaggerating. When he saw it was no use, he shook his head in disgust and went quietly with the policemen. They said they'd come back later to file a formal report. Her friends stayed with her until the kids got home. Sylvia filed a restraining order. That was the last time she saw Anthony. And he never called her again.

*****

It took a full year before Sylvia stopped hesitating to answer her phone at night, stopped noticing strange cars driving through the complex, or could fall asleep without wondering for a moment whether Anthony might be lurking somewhere in the shadows. But it took even longer than that for her to truly believe she was free of him. She was learning how to live a different way, to lead a life without inviting drama, a life that was no longer pulling her in all directions. She was thriving without a man in her life even under the pressure from Jessica to jump back into the fray.

Her job at the lumber export company was turning into an interesting opportunity. With the lumber market in recession, George's sales staff was cut. She was taking on more responsibility and now handling most of the sales and lumber purchases for the French clients in Tahiti, a niche market, but the company's largest. She requested an increase in salary, and George doubled it. She had no debt and was saving to buy a house.

It took several months, but Alice and Trevor seemed happy with school, although Sylvia knew with children there'd always be bumps in the road. Trevor was repeating first grade, and with the help of tutors provided by the school, he leaped a full grade in reading. According to his teachers, he had a winning sense of humor and was loved by all. He was also playing the clarinet in the school band. Alice got straight As and won first place in the school art fair. Her friends were sweet, innocent girls who were more interested in riding bikes and playing board games than boys and clothes. Sylvia hoped it would last. The kids went to their dad's every other weekend and one night a week for dinner. Sometimes Tom showed up after school to spend some extra time with them alone. He asked them not to mention it to Betsy, however. Since Sylvia was working, the kids stayed a month in the summer in Ohio, dividing their time between each set of grandparents, with the balance of the summer spent at their dad's.

In September, Trevor was going to celebrate his ninth birthday with seven of his friends at home. That morning, Sylvia needed to run to the grocery store before the party to pick up the cake she had ordered. It was a gray, dismal Saturday and was pouring rain, but Trevor wanted to go with her. Alice stayed home to finish hanging crepe paper streamers in the dining room.

With the bad weather, visibility was low and the parking lot entrance was jammed as cars slowly maneuvered their way around each other. They parked at the far end and made a run for it. When they got inside, there was a line at the bakery. Trevor didn't mind. He was too excited about his day. The woman behind the counter presented the chocolate cake with white icing for his approval. There it was. The soccer theme decoration he chose and his name and age printed across the top. He nodded with enthusiasm. "It's perfect."

Sylvia asked him to hold the cake and wait for her to pull around to the front of the store. "It's a good thing you came with me so I didn't have to carry it back to the car in the rain. We don't want your cake to get wet!"

He stood in his yellow slicker with the hood pulled over his head, securely holding the pink cardboard box with his treasure. She helped him set it on the floor of the backseat. He climbed in beside it. "I'd better make sure it doesn't slide around."

They crawled their way through the maze of cars and turned left onto the street to head home. Sylvia looked in her rearview mirror and slowed down.

"What's the matter?" Trevor asked.

"I see a red dog standing in the gas station across the street. I have to turn around."

Trevor jumped around to look. "There's no way, Mom."

While she waited to cross the busy intersection, she stared at the dog standing under cover between the gas pumps and cars as if it didn't know which way to turn. Her heart seemed to beat more rapidly. *Could it be?* There was an opening in the traffic, and she sped across the street. She pulled her car up to the left side of the building in a parking area away from the cars at the pumps. Attendants were running back and forth filling cars with gas. The dog hadn't moved. She told Trevor to stay in the car.

As she walked slowly toward the Irish setter, she could see that the dog had no collar. She began softly calling her name in her baby-talk voice. "Red? Hi, Red." The dog stared back at her. The ears went up. "Roo Roo, is that you?" Then the tail started to wag. The dog didn't take its eyes off of her. Sylvia could see the distinctive bony knob on the top of her head, the tuft of fur standing straight up. Tears rolled down her cheeks, and she was too choked up to utter her name. She knew that face so well, those eyes staring back at her in recognition. Red was wagging her tail hard as they moved more quickly toward each other. Sylvia threw her arms around her and sobbed into her neck.

After a minute or so, the gas station attendant came over and told Sylvia that the dog had been hanging around for several days. They'd asked around, but no one claimed her. "But she looks kinda well fed, I'd say."

It was true. She didn't look hungry, and she wasn't filthy. The gas station wasn't that far from the house where they lived at the time of the divorce. Maybe she'd made her way back and tried to find them. Somebody must've taken her in.

Sylvia and Red headed to the car. Trevor had opened the door and jumped out to meet them. He ran to Red, who licked his face. "Oh, Mommy, she's back, she's back!"

"And on your birthday! What a beautiful present! Let's get her home."

Red climbed right in, and Trevor followed her. Sylvia started the car and suddenly thought of Trevor's precious cake. She was almost afraid to turn around, when she noticed the pink box sitting on the seat beside her. "You even thought to move your cake, didn't you?" Trevor grinned, his arm across Red's back. And if she wasn't mistaken, Red was smiling, too.

The birthday party took a back seat to the excitement over Red's return. The kids wouldn't leave her alone for five minutes. When Tom came by and saw Red, he didn't seem that surprised. Sylvia asked him why.

"I thought I told you," he said.

"Told me what?"

"About two years ago, I was driving through Lakeside and thought I saw Red in the backseat of a woman's car. We exchanged phone numbers, and she told me Red wandered into her backyard with no collar and all skin and bones. So she took her in."

"You didn't try to take her back?"

"I didn't see any reason at that point. You weren't here. We had a new baby. She had a good home."

Sylvia didn't need to hear any more of his justifications. She just held her hand up. "Jesus, Tom. She's a part of our family."

Red became the center of their household. They took her for walks in the woods twice a day. The neighbor children thronged around her whenever she was outside. At night she took turns sleeping with each of them. She settled during the day on the couch or the enormous floor cushion in the living room. The glaring problem that they could no longer ignore was that only small dogs were allowed in the apartments. Sylvia didn't have enough money to buy a house yet, but if they had to move for Red's sake, they would. They had all wandered too far from home for too long to risk being apart from each other for even a short time.

Patricia and a few other families in the apartment complex who had come to know Red's story pleaded with the manager to let her stay. When he refused, they started a petition requesting that Red be able to live her final years as the mascot of the complex. It was unanimous. The manager threw up his hands.

Sylvia sat home many Saturday nights, and this one was no different. The phone rang, and Alice jumped up to answer it. "For you, Mommy. It's Jessica." She handed Sylvia the phone.

Jessica asked Sylvia what she was doing.

"Hemming a pair of pants."

"On a Saturday night?"

"You know I don't mind staying home."

"Well, you shouldn't be home every weekend. We've got to find someone to get you out," she insisted.

"No, we don't."

"But you need to get back into circulation. This isn't healthy."

"Healthy is being home with my family," Sylvia said.

Sylvia petted Red, who was curled up next to her on the couch. She looked at her kids wrapped in blankets, sprawled on the living room floor watching TV. She looked at the scene around her and thought back to the time, not so long ago, when she longed for just such an evening. For a life without chaos, a life that was commonplace, uninteresting or lonely to some. She hadn't forgotten her promise to herself in Palo Alto to consider it a privilege if she ever had the good fortune to have such a life again.

"But aren't you bored out of your mind?" Jessica asked.

Sylvia sat back and smiled. "I'm happy to tell you that I am."

New

C¹/₁

NC

NNS

Made in the USA